ARMAGEDDON

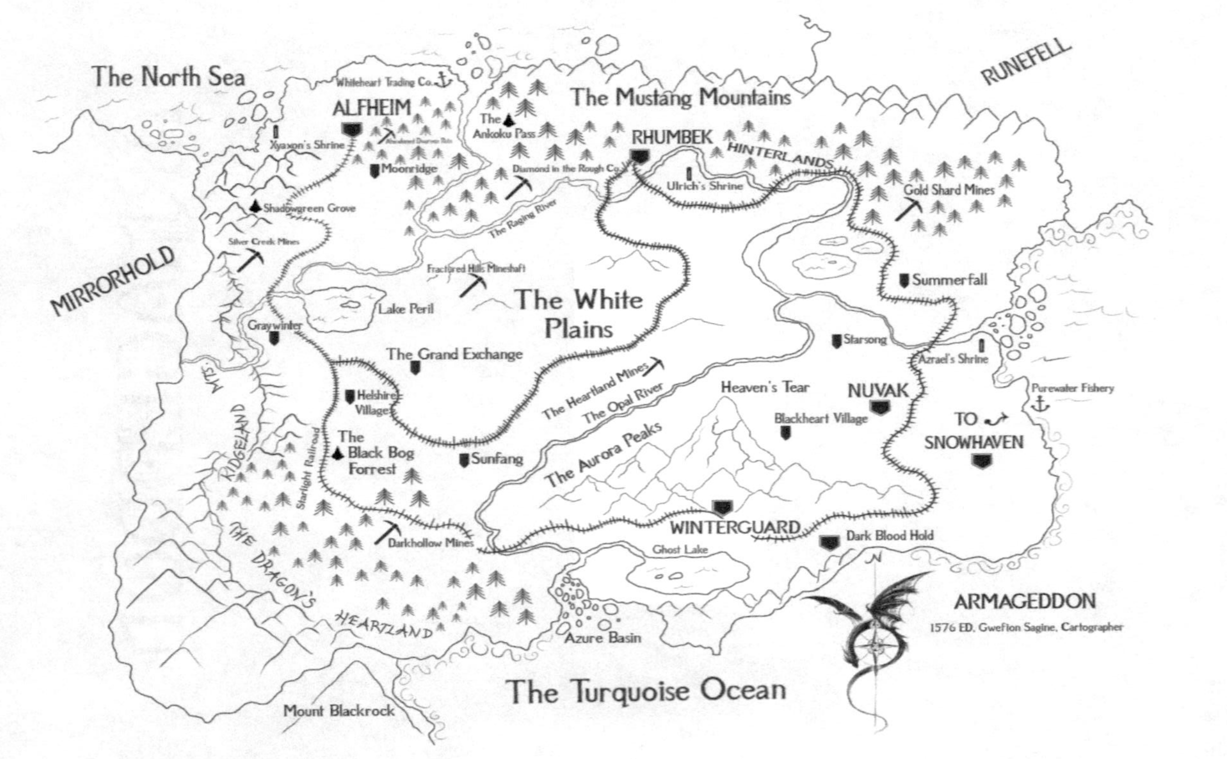

The North Sea
RUNEFELL
The Mustang Mountains
Whiteheart Trading Co.
ALFHEIM
The Ankoku Pass
RHUMBEK
HINTERLANDS
Xyaxon's Shrine
Abandoned Dwarven Ruin
Moonridge
Diamond in the Rough Co.
Ulrich's Shrine
Gold Shard Mines
MIRRORHOLD
Shadowgreen Grove
The Raging River
Silver Creek Mines
Summerfall
Fractured Hills Mineshaft
The White Plains
Lake Peril
Starsong
Graywinter
Azrael's Shrine
The Grand Exchange
The Heartland Mines
Heaven's Tear
NUVAK
Purewater Fishery
The Opal River
Helshire Village
Blackheart Village
TO SNOWHAVEN
MTS.
RIDGELAND
The Black Bog Forrest
Sunfang
The Aurora Peaks
Starlight Railroad
Darkhollow Mines
WINTERGUARD
Dark Blood Hold
THE DRAGON'S
Ghost Lake
N
ARMAGEDDON
HEARTLAND
1576 ED, Gwefion Sagine, Cartographer
Mount Blackrock
Azure Basin
The Turquoise Ocean

ARMAGEDDON

Book 3 in the Armageddon Trilogy

C.D. MULLER

Lunar Wolf Press

To Richard,

You couldn't wake up.

CONTENTS

CHAPTER 1: THE AWAKENING

Selena Liongod opened her eyes and squinted at the sunshine streaming through her window like sparkling gemstones. Her heart soared when she saw that she was back in her room at the barracks in Alfheim. Well rested and rejuvenated, she stretched and was more relaxed, not feeling this way since—

She shot up in bed, head whipping around, remembering what had happened to her and her friends in Snowhaven. Flipping over her covers and inspecting her body, she gasped when noticing her wounds and scars: they were all gone. Even her left hand—no, Medusa sliced it off, but it was back. Selena lifted her left hand to check it, and sure enough, it was real. Exhaling in relief, she thought someone was playing a cruel trick on her with the tormenting nightmare from the Water Kingdom capital.

Thor, everything is fine, and we're back in the city. Selena zipped out of bed and snatched her robes. Thor, the Divinity Dragon, was her companion, half-brother, and best friend; the two shared a telepathic link, allowing direct and intimate communication between only a dragon and their handler, no matter how far apart they were.

However, he didn't respond, and she thought he was resting in solitude by the dragons' quarters. *I'll go and visit him; he must be worried sick about me.*

Selena rushed to get dressed and laced up her boots as her heart raced with excitement; she wanted to see her friends and family, her dragon, and her husband-to-be, Admiral Genesis Silver Altessa. But when she ran out the door, the barracks vanished, and she now stood within a castle courtyard.

Mossy flagstone paths separated the emerald sea into two, with a great oak tree standing tall and proud in the middle with dawn's light lancing through its greensward. Its enchantment beckoned her forward—the verdant lawns steeped in plushness and opulence.

A golden twinkle brushed against her ears when she heard Silver's voice. "There's my new apprentice." She twirled around on her toes, and there he was, wearing the same long white buckled jacket strewn with roped blue feathers, and his gleaming smile and ice-blue eyes hiding behind a pair of spectacles with his snow-white waist-length hair reflecting in the sunlight. Although Selena was a petite lady, his height gave him the privilege of towering over most people, aside from her father. He clapped his hands together after taking a step forward. "How do you like your new hand?"

She curled her fingers and tightened her knuckle, wondering how Silver could accomplish such a feat— especially since it looked identical to her old limb. She realized the replacement only when she turned her palm upward and noticed that her mark—a perfect circle with a crescent shape set within—was gone. A sudden loss of identity made her body feel limp and numb, her heart throbbing in her throat. "How did you do this?"

Silver's smile faded, and he squinted at her in disbelief. "Don't you remember? After you and Thor came back to Alfheim, I went straight to work on your new hand. You kept asking me many questions about how I was to accomplish this, and you were afraid of being put under for the operation. I can't count how often you said you wouldn't wake up."

More confused and addled than before, Selena neither remembered sharing this conversation with him nor recalling his plan to make her a new hand; she quickly realized she had no recollection of how she and her friends escaped Snowhaven and arrived in Alfheim. "None of this makes any sense." Silver's face immediately turned blank but didn't offer a reply to her suspicions. "Besides, I'm awake now." Selena's cheeks burned when he still ignored her words, and she suddenly felt the urge to scream.

Her ears tinkled with the sound of a child's laughter; a little girl appeared from behind the old oak and ran towards Silver. Selena couldn't help but notice how the child shared the same copper skin tone, chocolate-brown hair, and sparkling emerald eyes. "That's me when I was little."

Still ignoring her older self, Silver smiled and swooped the little giggling girl in his arms, and she leaned in and kissed him on the cheek; Selena could hide her blushing. "Teacher, I learned how to make fire."

"That's wonderful, my dear—you'll make a great apprentice yet." His grin grew. "Now, please, don't be afraid. You will wake up. Please, wake up."

Baffled and undone, Selena felt out of touch with reality as she continued to wonder what he meant. A flash of light blinded her vision, and she now stood on the cliff overlooking the North Sea, this time with Thor. As thrilled as she was to see her dragon again, Selena couldn't help but think, *None of this makes any sense. How did I get from Rune Citadel to here?*

Her head swiveled, body quivering from not remembering how she moved from one place to the other, but she was relieved to see Thor was the same as always: he was already the size of a large ship, and she guessed he weighed close to twenty tons by now. His magnificent bone mask decorated with sharp horns gave him the image of wearing a crown, fitting for the King of Dragons. Her eyes caught the glimmer from his tear-drop-shaped ruby scales, sparkling from the gentle evening light, and she couldn't help but adore Thor's rainbow glitter refracting across the ground and his golden chest plate. Regardless of his intimidating and almost regal-like appearance, he was undoubtedly one of the most beautiful dragons she had ever seen.

Selena reached out to pat his thick tree-trunk-sized neck, half expecting him to be an illusion, but her face lit up when she touched his shiny gemstone hide. *Is it truly you?*

Snaking his head down to hers, Thor's massive honey amber eyes, like two gold ore moons, locked with her brilliant emeralds. **My dear.**

She was so happy to hear his voice again and couldn't control her eyes stinging with tears as she opened her arms to embrace him. *I was so afraid that I wasn't going to see you again. What happened? Are you all right?*

I-I don't know, but I was so afraid I had lost you.

She buried her face into his shoulder, not caring that his sharp armored scales poked and scraped against her face. *I was too, but it was so strange. Just a moment ago, I was in Rune Citadel with Silver as he talked about my new hand. He kept expressing his fear that I wouldn't wake up.* She paused when she came to the horrible conclusion that it was only a hallucination. *My mind is playing tricks on me.*

Thor took a while to acknowledge her distress, his eyes unblinking. **That is strange.**

Are you not going to argue with me?

Why should I? If you think you're hallucinating Silver, I believe you may be right.

Why aren't you asking me more about this? You always argue and question me if it doesn't make sense. Her eyes filled with tears when he didn't reply; she imagined him too.

Thor reared his head back and swept his tail across the ground, creating a small surge of dust and rock, and unfurled his massive wings with orange and red membranes dabbed in more glorified oval specs of purple and yellow dotting the edges. The evening sunlight lanced through his wings like stained glass windows in a cathedral.

Please, will you wake up? As her face shimmered in tears, Thor immediately jolted up from his spot and reared up, putting all his weight on his haunches while his head thrashed around to search for her. **Where did you go?**

I'm right here. Please, you can't be a hallucination, too. Can't you see me?

He ignored her. **Where are you? Come back and wake up.**

Thor reared his head and roared before unleashing a deadly torrent of flame and lightning towards the sky, the earth quaking beneath her feet and rippling like a water's surface. As his rage and fury grew to that of a brewing storm, Selena attempted to escape his violent attack, but the vengeful depths pulled her in.

Her vision faded to black before her eyes brightened to a new scene: she was back in Snowhaven, lying in the snow and ice in a crimson puddle. Hovering over her were her friends: Azrael, Doragon, and Rahim, all huddling under Doragon's protective silver-tainted wings within a magical barrier; even the dark maelstrom threatening her allies couldn't dull the Sunbeam Shieldtail's sleek, golden hide.

Selena wanted to yell when she saw her blood splattered over the ice, but her lips were stone cold, and she was completely limp. She was utterly helpless and couldn't move or make any noise to get their attention; it felt like a hand covered her face to prevent her from making a sound. The sudden absence of all noise made her heart race in fear, as the deep ringing within her ears echoed louder with each passing second; all she could do was watch Rahim, in tears, deck Azrael hard in the jaw.

Suddenly, Azrael grabbed her, and the two and Doragon vanished in the melting darkness. However, a new vision flashed before her, and Silver held her within his arms under the charcoal grey sky; the rains and wind echoed for an eternity before she realized they were flying.

Silver leaned in to whisper in her ear. "Please, wake up." Her lips sewn shut; she couldn't tell him she was awake, stuck as an immobile corpse. Rahim's hand reached across to touch her shoulder, and she was ecstatic to see him there too, but now she wondered what happened to Azrael and Doragon. Silver immediately retaliated and swatted Rahim's hand away. "Don't touch her. Don't you dare touch her, do you understand me? Keep your damn hands off of my woman." Only when Rahim withdrew his hand did Silver continue. "Please, come back. I love you—wake up."

As she fought through the forced silence, Silver's and Rahim's faces melted away with the rain, and her surroundings faded to black—she was finally able to move again. Her chest was about to burst as her breathing turned ragged and fast; digging her nails into her palms, Selena curled into a ball. She was about to slip into the darkness any moment, with the cold consuming every part of her body; she couldn't draw a single breath as she swirled in the void, trapped in her pandemonium of madness.

Yet, a small dot of light appeared in front of her, and at first, Selena thought she had finally fallen victim to insanity. However, more specs flashed around her, and her sight grew blurry. When the flecks vanished, and she could see again, Selena was trapped in Niflheim. Finally recognizing her scenery with freedom of control, a massive wave of relief washed over her as she crossed her arms over her chest and shivered, her breaths turning to fog. "It's cold here. What's happening to me?"

Unsure of what to do, she looked up to a burning aurora painted in the sky while the iridescent clouds writhed around the colors like milky smoke, aesthetic and illusory. Sieves of mist caressed the sapphire blue stone pillars towering beside her as the realm's spectral gas gilded with eerie intent around two silver ore moons hiding behind the northern lights. Selena's eyes drew to a whirring waterfall ahead, its teal tear tracking the rugged face of the distant broken tower and plunging into the abyss below.

"You must wake up." Like the sun itself, if it could speak, that voice sounded like Xyaxon; her heart wavered in delight that the Divine reached out to her, and she hoped he would pull her from the darkness threatening to drag her away.

And yet, he repeated what her friends and loved ones asked of her; Selena couldn't understand it. "Wake up? B-but I thought I was already awake."

"You're trapped in the realm between being awake and asleep, a prisoner within your mind."

"That doesn't make any sense."

"It doesn't?" Xyaxon sounded surprised. "The mind will often use small details or scenarios to help you realize that you're asleep and wake up."

Selena's lower lip quivered, with her heart caught in her throat. "I-I don't understand."

Xyaxon continued. "Sometimes, it may take days, or even years, for you to finally wake up." Without warning, his voice roared like thunder. "Wake up!"

Her hands immediately shot up to cover her ears, and she heaved over, the air in her lungs sharp with every breath she took. Soon Niflheim, along with Xyaxon's voice, faded, and she was trapped in darkness.

Am I dead?

Then, Thor's voice again twinkled and sparkled like the stars singing within her clouded thoughts. **Please, wake up.**

I-I don't know how. She could hear him again—how she longed to be with him once more, but Selena feared she would never escape her eternal prison.

Yes, you do.

I can't.

"Yes, you can." It was Silver's voice this time.

Selena trembled as she wrapped her body around in coils, eyes closed as she continued cupping her ears. "I'm so scared. I don't know what to do."

"Yes, you do. Please, wake up. Wake up...."

*****

CHAPTER 2: THE LIBRARY

$\mathcal{S}$elena's eyes fluttered open. With her head feeling light and dizzy, she found herself cradled by two colossal, scaly arms, and her eyes stung with tears when she saw Thor's large snout lying next to her side. From her vision, the beautiful crimson and golden dragon looked the same, and she began doubting if she was indeed back or if her mind was playing another trick on her.

When she reached to touch his gemstone hide, his beautiful voice returned to her. **Please, wake up.**

Afraid he was another hallucination, Selena's fingers trembled across his shiny scales, and her face gleamed like the morning sun. *I'm here.*

Thor's breaths quickened as he whipped his head around and pressed his nose into her abdomen. Then, without warning, he licked her—his tongue slippery and slimy, like a snake's. She pushed him away, but Thor, being much stronger, remained where he was, the forked ends tickling her cheek.

Stop that.

You have no idea how happy I am that you finally woke up. Now, you have to deal with me. Instead of arguing, Selena laughed. **What's so funny?**

I'm finally awake. I'm not hallucinating you.

What do you mean? As she explained her dreams, Selena felt relieved to see him act as he should, reassuring her she was no longer feverish. When she finished, Thor's lips curled over his fangs, and he growled. **I can assure you that I'm as real as the sunrise. I've waited two weeks to see you as so much as stir.**

I heard you and Silver; you two wouldn't stop telling me to wake up, but two weeks? Not believing it to be possible, her legs suddenly turned to rubber, and her stomach sank the more she considered the nightmares and dreams that plagued her during her unconscious stupor.

We hoped you would pull through if you heard our voices—I worried you would never wake.

After sharing affections, she pleaded for Thor to remove his paw so she could sit. When he did, Selena saw they were in a pavilion fit for a dragon—sitting on golden wood tiles emitting a comfortable heat within the confines, though it had no walls, catching dawn's bright ways. Two massive columns with her boots and Dragonheart leaning against the structure streaked with gold across the white marble stood post to the entrance, sparkling and burning under the morning sun.

After her eyes fully adjusted, Selena seized the chance to admire the decoration upon the ceiling, painted and enameled in brilliant rainbow colors and dazzling gilt. The roof soared high enough overhead to touch the heavens: Thor would have neither issues nor difficulties coming underneath. A flickering blood-red shimmer sparkled across his diamond scales as flecks of crimson and purple light reflected from his brilliant hide glimmered about the pavilion; together, they were like heaped mounds of treasure.

Where are we?

We're near Heaven's Tear by Silver's library.

Her head buzzed in inquiry as she wondered how it fared to Dragonstone Estate—Silver's massive property in Alfheim. She wanted to see what treasured tomes and secrets hid within; only the Divines knew the glory of what awaited. When she strained her neck to look beyond the marble columns, she only caught a glimmer of stone before collapsing again.

Sighing and resolving that she would visit his library in a short while, she found herself still wearing the same clothes from when she and her friends were in Snowhaven but was shocked to see the freshly mended clean fabric of spider silk and Royal Tidalwalker dragon scales. The sleeveless blue dress clad in gold trimmings, charcoal grey scarf, and blue elbow-length gloves were a gift from Silver, made to withstand melee and magical attacks.

Around her neck was her wolf-carved totem strewn by a strip of leather, gifted to her from the Aynu wolf pack to commemorate their alliance. The onyx stone pendant was around the size of her thumb, symbolizing her undying loyalty and protectiveness for her friends and family. Her friends each received a unique carved necklace: Thor and Doragon had dragons, Azrael had the raven, and Rahim had the fox.

Realizing she hadn't bathed in some time, Selena sniffed her arm only to find her skin smelling like soap; Thor explained Silver took it upon himself to keep her cleaned, to which her face immediately burned in embarrassment. **You smelled of something awful. You couldn't afford to be ashamed, and you needed it after being imprisoned.** Thor crinkled his snout and stuck out his tongue in disgust.

Selena chuckled, the humiliation still burning her cheeks. Yet, she couldn't shake off a burning itch in her mind, and her heart stopped when she saw her left hand—

no, there was no hand but a bandaged stump. The urge to scream crept upon her, but a memory flashed through her mind like a lightning bolt.

Thor closed his eyes and turned away when he noticed her reaction. At first, Selena refused to accept the encounter with Medusa; it happened so fast—quicker than falling asleep—that that would have been the end of it, and she would have been none the wiser; there was no pain as she slipped into the void. There was nothing.

I wasn't just unconscious, was I? I was gone. She paused upon stumbling through this grim realization. *What happened to the others? Rahim? Azrael? Doragon?*

Thor still avoided her gaze, but he swished his tail across the smooth tile. **Rahim is fine. I believe he's with Silver.**

But what happened?

I don't want to talk about it. Though still stiff, Selena re-positioned and sat up a little, begging and pleading to hear his tale. Eventually, after enough prodding on her part, Thor added: **I don't remember what happened, but all I know is that Azrael and Doragon brought you back before vanishing.**

Selena felt eternally grateful for what Azrael and Doragon had done for her, but she was more worried about the consequences of their actions. It wasn't like they used the Well of Souls this time; no, they had to venture inside the Soul Gate to bring her back, whatever that was. Yet, this wasn't the first time the Shepherd of Souls saved her; when she and Thor were on trial after the Council discovered her identity, Azrael, through extreme measures, convinced Vidar to keep the pair in the Force and saved her a trip to the gallows.

She couldn't help but look back to what remained of her arm after Medusa had sliced her hand clean off and shuddered; her mind refused to shake away the memory of her final moments before slipping into Oblivion. Seeking vengeance against Medusa made her hiss through her teeth, and her fury billowed, waiting to erupt like a volcano; it never mattered that she was Selena's clone. Their adventures in Snowhaven were a nightmare.

Thor gnashed his teeth and whipped his tail around his sides when asked about Medusa's whereabouts. Selena flinched from his sudden hostility; he flexed out his ivory claws and began pawing at the ground, taking clumps of dirt with each pass he made. **Her soul now rots in Oblivion.**

When he made no further comment on how the treacherous snake met her end, Selena made the painful assumption that he was somehow involved with her demise but didn't wish to distress him with questions and accusations. After calming down, he snaked his head around and nudged his nose against her head. **Your hair has grown.**

Without realizing it, her only hand immediately shot up to feel the silky strands of her chocolate-brown hair draping over her shoulders. It grew fast, especially during their journey to the Water Kingdom capital; she wasn't sure if she should cut it or leave it be.

I think it looks best to keep it long. Thor's sudden chuckle rumbled deep within his throat before adding, **I suppose we don't have to call you Andric anymore.**

Maybe. Selena's stomach sank at how she had to hide behind the facade, as it was the only way she could protect Thor from the Council until they unmasked her disguise to the world. Since the botched mission, she supposed Thor was right and could finally retire the alias. *How did Silver find us?*

Thor yawned and flexed his claws over the pavilion's edge, tail twitching like a playful cat. **He tracked**

us down in Starsong while we recovered and urged us to take shelter here where it was safer.

Growing restless from laying down for so long, Selena worked on sitting up, but a sharp pain shot through her back and chest, keeping her paralyzed for a moment before collapsing on Thor's arm. *What in Oblivion?*

You're supposed to be resting, not moving so much at once.

I'm done resting. Why can't I move? Instantly, the memory of her fallen hour jolted through her mind, replaying how a massive spike made from her blood tore her back and chest open; the pain tormented her as it surged through her back like lightning. It went away as quickly as it came, but she suffered through the agony that ultimately led to her death in that brief span.

When Selena recovered and caught her breath, a plume of smoke followed by ember shards erupted from Thor's nostrils. **Blood magic. It radiates with the same dark energy that follows the Lich and the Order.**

After failing to push away his snout as he, once again, nudged it into her abdomen, Selena's fears took hold of her. Suddenly, her mouth and throat turned dry when she wondered about the possibility of her permanent handicap or if her back and chest would worsen over time. Per Thor, she was trapped in a coma for two weeks— already mid-Astar—she had assumed Silver took charge as her healer, but her wounds showed no signs of recovery.

I-I must go and see Silver. He'll know what to do. Before she could sit up again, Thor lifted his paw and pushed her down into his basket arms. *What are you doing?*

You're too weak. I'm not letting you out of my sight.

I need to get up.
No, you don't.

Please, I must see Silver and Rahim.

No! Thor's voice roared like thunder within her subconscious, making her recoil. He opened his massive maw, which, to Selena's fear and dismay, could swallow her whole with ease. **I chased those two out of here earlier. You will stay where I can keep an eye on you.**

Selena was surprised to hear that he could shoo Silver away, as he couldn't be easily deterred. *You said we're in Heaven's Tear at his library, yes? I'll be fine. You know Silver won't let anything happen to me.*

I'm worried about Ulrich. He lives at the summit, remember?

Yes, I do, but I'm sure Ulrich is entirely sane again. He only becomes a mad god once every era. Still skeptical, Thor snorted and added more pressure to the weight of his paw. She may understand why he was apprehensive, but Selena was annoyed that he wouldn't even let her see the others. *Please, let me get up.*

I said no.

Silver and Rahim deserve to know that I'm finally awake. What if I promise to return after I check in with everyone? Thor's lips twisted into a snarl, and he snapped his head around. *Please?*

The mighty dragon gnashed his teeth, but he lifted his paw with extreme caution before swiveling back around and making direct eye contact with her, the fire burning within his irises. **I want you back soon. If not, I'm going to hunt you down myself.**

I promise I will return, my dear one. I'll keep talking to you if that will make you feel any better.

Maybe. With great care, Selena did her best to tough out the pain and sit up, but her back and chest stung like she was thrown into a pile of jagged rocks, and she collapsed again. **Are you all right? Do you need to lay back down again?**

Selena ignored his mothering comments and worked on making herself stand. She muttered under her breath repeatedly, "Stand up." After convincing herself enough, she found the strength to stand. Her legs wobbled beneath her, but she focused on keeping her stance and stepped forward. Her muscles trembled, but her body adjusted after a few struts.

Slowly, Selena turned around to hold Thor's head with her intact hand and gave him a quick kiss on the cheek. *I'm all right, mother hen. It will take some time to walk properly again, but it's nothing that a little exercise won't fix.*

Thor's snort followed with ember shards that dispersed before hitting the floor of his pavilion; he remained unconvinced. **You should go before I change my mind.**

You're something else. Heeding Thor's caution, she planted her steps warily towards her shined and clean boots and sword. However, after lacing up her shoes, her eyes caught the glimmer of Thor's golden bracelets and ruby chain lying next to his saddle propped up against the pavilion's archway. She was glad to see he rested without the harness chaffing his scales but noticed it was now too small compared to his new and sudden growth since Snowhaven. She would have to ask Silver for assistance to augment it, but the bracelets had clasps that allowed for an effortless adjustment, accommodating a dragon's ever-increasing development. However, Thor not donning his gold and ruby chain added more to her confusion.

Why aren't you wearing your jewelry?
I didn't care for them.
That isn't like you. You loved your trinkets. When Thor didn't answer, Selena whipped her head around,

shocked, but she couldn't stop grinning. *You don't have to wear them if you don't want to—I was only confused.*

You were more important to me than any fancy jewelry or gold. Feeling touched by the deep sentiments, she stumbled back, wrapping her arms around his thick neck, and ran her fingertips along the jagged edges of his gem-like scales. He lowered his head and laid his face against her back. **You mean more to me than all the gold in the world. My necklace and bracelets could never replace you.**

Aww, you did care about me.

Thor snapped his head back and turned away, as was his way to hide his embarrassment. **Just go before I change my mind.**

Selena couldn't stop snickering, but her thoughts raced to what awaited her in Silver's library and immediately wondered if it looked like Alfheim's. She stepped out into the sun for the first time in almost two months, only to be blinded by the sudden burst of light. The bright rays warmed her skin—how Selena missed it. She could stand there for hours, and it still wouldn't be enough.

Although tepid and sunlit, a deep white fleece covered their plateau near the highest point of the Aurora Peaks. An emerald sea of pines lined the cliffs, the verdant trees standing as guardians to a single tower beyond the pavilion stretching towards the heavens, with rocks of ice and stone decorating the mountainside. A single path with stairs of stone curved around the spire and mountain, slithering up to where Selena assumed was Ulrich's lair. Dismayed, she couldn't see beyond the ring of clouds that circled the peak, blotching all from the world below.

Water trickling somewhere along the side of Heaven's Tear, Selena trekked down the broad stairway from Thor's pavilion and tracked the winding path paved with grey stones full of queerly shaped rocks leading to the three steps of Silver's tower. Her heart and thoughts racing, Selena brushed her hand against the oak door, and before she could reach down to turn the knob, she felt it give way and walked inside to a breathtaking view.

She stood within an enormous, circular room where rows of books graced the walls, finding not a speck of dust or a single text out of place. Her eyes drew to a massive sandglass with small blue glass-like gravel sitting perfectly within the enclave of the black, rune floor, the almost empty top barely brushing the gilt-painted ceiling. A spiral stone staircase writhed around the sandglass like smoke, gleaming from the massive wide window lined with velvet seats, shutters inlaid with mother-of-pearl.

Ecstatic, Selena darted to one of the books and began browsing through the antique set. "All of Armageddon's history, everything about magic—it looks like it's all here. This collection is incredible." She stopped when a tinkling sound played in her ears; someone played the piano.

Intrigued, Selena followed the decadent tunes up the spiral staircase. Each floor she passed was different; the second level was adorned with decorative mounted antlers, leather couches, and chairs lined with the finest silks as a fire roared within the stone hearth. An empty cooking pot rested in its metal rack over the licking embers next to a pile of freshly cut firewood ready to feed the restless inferno. The smell from the nearby kitchen tickled her nostrils, and immediately her stomach rumbled when she realized how hungry she was as she saw wooden shelves of foods—cured and smoked meats and cheeses wrapped in oilskin—and spices stacked across the walls. Nearby stood barrels with fermented vegetables and sacks of potatoes and flour.

The sound twinkled from the third floor, beckoning Selena to follow the stairs to a long, carpeted corridor. There were three apartments, but the sound was coming from the first to her left. She listened to the beautiful sound and then cracked open the door.

She admired the august taste of the room as gas lamps, and a gigantic ivory clock stood amid the profusion of golden ornaments. In the middle was a couch covered with embroidered cushions, and behind the furniture was a young woman playing a grand piano, mesmerizing Selena with the gentle music. The young lady, whose hair was long and white as snow, performed without interruption, her fingers dancing across the keys. Selena didn't think much of it until she saw Silver appear through the crack.

He took his place next to the woman to watch her play, and a new feeling erupted within Selena: jealousy burned within her like a fiery passion. She wasn't sure what was happening, but she didn't like what she saw. No, maybe she was overreacting, but still, she wanted to know who this young lady was.

When the stranger stopped playing, she stood up from her seat and gave Silver a quick hug. "It's great to see you again."

"Likewise." Silver smiled and offered her a place to sit on the couch. "How have you been after all these years?"

How did he know her? Selena's stomach tightened into a knot as her mind raced to a possible companionship the two had shared in the past. If that were true, why would he reunite with her? Selena and Silver were engaged. Unless—

She put her hand to her mouth as tears started to trickle, rushing to the assumption that Silver perhaps believed she would never wake up and would find another companion without a second thought. It couldn't be right; it was all just a misunderstanding, and he would never do that.

The woman crossed her legs as she sat down. "I've been doing well, thank you. After all this time, I never thought I would see you again." Her fingers wrapped around an offered cheddar biscuit when Silver brought over a porcelain platter and took a small bite. "Everything hasn't been quite to my liking."

"Nor mine. I've been working on a plan to help win this war, but I fear that we may be too late to make a difference." Silver reached over to his tea set sitting on the table next to him and offered the lady a cup. He sighed, and the two gingerly sipped from their dishes. "The eclipse is nigh, and lately, my focus has been on the wedding. I pray we will have one."

Selena felt like her heart tore out of her chest; he had given up on her. Upon hearing enough, she backed away, too distracted by her thoughts to avoid bumping against a potted plant sitting on a desk behind her. It slid off the table, and she couldn't prevent the ear-shattering crash of glass against the floor.

Both Silver and the woman turned towards the source of the noise, and when he and Selena locked eyes through the door's crack, she panicked and darted down the stairs. Her heart thumped louder than the sound of him calling her name.

Thor's voice boomed within her panicked subconscious. **What happened?**

Leave me alone.

Please, talk to me. She ignored him, even as she bolted out the front door and ran to the cliff's edge, and Silver appeared behind her seconds later. It wasn't too long before Thor emerged from his pavilion, and as his eyes landed on Silver, he growled and bared his fangs with his wings unfurled, but Silver ignored him. **What did he do to you?**

Leave me be.

"You're finally awake." Silver's voice sounded fragile. Selena's hand shook at her side, but she reached up and wiped her tears away to keep herself from breaking any second. "Look at me. Please." Silver took a step forward and reached for her, but she snatched her arm away and recoiled to her pent-up grief. "Everyone was expecting you back at Alfheim last month, but I went after you when you never returned. There is so much to discuss. Please, turn around and look at me."

She still couldn't bear to meet his eyes, and her lips trembled with what she was about to say. "I-I didn't mean to interrupt."

He squinted at her through his perched glasses. "Interrupt what?"

All she could muster was, "You and your lady friend." Her words tasted vile.

"Lady friend?" A few seconds later, she heard Silver laugh, and her cheeks burned, insulted that he found humor in all she said.

What in Oblivion did he think was funny?

He cleared his throat and readjusted his spectacles. "You mean my sister."

CHAPTER 3: EBONY

His sister? Time froze as Selena slowly swiveled her head over her shoulder to look at Silver. "Oh." That was all she could say. He grinned and made haste to reach where she stood. Meanwhile, Thor stood back on his haunches and kept his guard up as if he was about to attack Silver in that instant, like a snake ready to strike.

Still ignoring the threatening dragon, he lifted her chin to meet her gaze and brushed away a tear with a sweep of his thumb. "I'm sorry I never mentioned her before, but I haven't seen her in years. Honestly, I thought she was dead until she showed up earlier today." Silver laughed, but she still failed to find the humor in his explanation; she was no longer mad at him but now angry herself for jumping to such harsh conclusions when there was an apparent reason. Only when Silver extended his arms did she accept his affectionate hold.

She found the right way to apologize for her harsh reaction when Silver didn't deserve it through fuddled speech. "I-I'm sorry. I overheard parts of your conversation with her, and when you brought up the wedding, I thought—"

Silver raised an eyebrow, genuinely confused by how she perceived his last conversation with his sister. "Yes? I meant our wedding, as in yours and mine. Did you believe I would leave you?" Before looking up, Selena wiped the rest of her tears away, pushing back the stinging pain of guilt for thinking he would abandon her; he gently kissed her crown. "You know me better than that, my dear. Come with me. I want you to meet her."

Thor growled through his fangs when she and Silver walked past, but the demigod strode forward without a second glance. **What did he do to you?**

I was being foolish.

It took him a moment to realize what she meant. **I still find it strange that you humans only take one mate.**

We humans get emotionally attached easily.

I may not fully understand it, but I would tear his limbs apart if he ever hurt you. As Silver and Selena re-entered the tower, satisfied, Thor finally tucked in his wings before returning to his pavilion.

Along the trip back to the apartment, Silver talked a little about his sister insisting on playing the piano to break from their conversation regarding current events while keeping his arm wrapped around her shoulder. During his briefing over his sister's history, occasionally, his eyes darted to her bandaged stump, and he would cringe. When they strolled past where Selena knocked over the potted plant, it shocked her to see it stand as if she had never touched it; she assumed Silver had fixed the incident.

Their visitor waited near the doorway, hands clasped behind her back, standing about as tall as her brother. Her snow-white hair flowed to her waist with an identical pair of glasses sitting on the bridge of her nose, like glass cases protecting her amethyst eyes. Her pale skin glowed from the sun's touch, her ebony suit magnifying the glint kissing her cheeks. Strapped over her back was a sword with a curved blade; Selena imagined the mastery of her honed skills.

Silver stretched out his free hand towards her. "Allow me to introduce the Divine Crown Princess herself: Selena Liongod. My dear, this is my sister, Angel."

"Please, call me Ebony. Like you, Silver, I prefer not to use my real name."

Selena gave Ebony a proper bow, but Ebony dropped to one knee. Silver gave a firm nod through tightly pursed lips, but Selena, unsure of how to accept the sudden regal formalities, reached out to shake Ebony's hand when she stood. "It's a pleasure to meet you, Ebony."

Bemused, Ebony met her gesture, ignoring her brother's rude gaze. "The pleasure is all mine, Your Imperial Highness. My brother told me so much about you before you finally awoke. I feel like we could be friends already."

"I heard you playing earlier. It was lovely."

"Thank you," her purple eyes sparkled, "Silver has told me of your accomplishments, especially with your swordsmanship. Quite frankly, I'm impressed, and perhaps you can show me your skills one of these days."

Selena was thrilled to hear Ebony's compliments, but Silver interrupted their gloating moment and cleared his throat. "Miss Liongod is very tired. When she is fully rested, you two may indulge in conversation. For the time being, I request to spend the remainder of this day with her alone."

Not taking any offense to the sudden disruption, Ebony bowed her head. "Of course. I will take my leave, but I must ask your permission to meet with your dragon. I saw him on my way up here, and I was very intrigued when Silver told me of his rare nature."

Selena grinned. "I don't see why not, and I'm sure he will be more than willing to accept an adoring visitor."

There was a faint twinkle in her violet eyes; Ebony shared her enthusiasm, pleased by her willingness to make the accommodation.

As she relayed Ebony's request, Thor chittered in the delight of receiving company. **She may, but I want to hunt first. I will return within an hour or so.**

Selena reiterated his reply without fail, and Ebony seemed gratified with his approval of the meeting. "Thank you for arranging that on my behalf, Your Imperial Highness. You two are the light in this dark world. Farewell." She dismissed herself from their company and strolled out of the room.

Before Silver could suggest their well-earned privacy, Selena immediately demanded to meet Rahim, to which he smiled and gestured towards the door. "Of course. Since Thor chased us out, Rahim has been keeping to himself, rarely coming out even to eat."

That was surprising, as food easily satisfied his foulest of moods. Selena's heart sank, and her steps felt heavy as she approached his room further down the corridor. She heard Rahim shuffle around when she knocked on his door. "What is it, Silver? I told you, I'm not coming out anymore until Selena wakes up."

"It's me."

In that instant, she heard shattering glass, and the door swung open. Rahim Branwen's sandy brown hair was messier than usual, covering his pale, freckled face but unable to conceal the dark circles around his chocolate eyes. Yet, when he looked up, the sun lancing through the nearby window brightened his eyes like pools of amber; without warning, Rahim grabbed and held her tight. "You're awake. You're finally awake! Thank the Divines."

As happy as Selena was to see him again, she felt her body crush within his embrace, his Aynu fox necklace clanking against hers, and she struggled to push him away, but he tightened his grip. "I'm fine—really. Please, release me before I can't breathe."

After reassuring himself it wasn't a dream, Rahim finally released his deathly hold. After returning to the previous apartment, the two made themselves comfortable, greeted by Silver serving fresh tea and biscuits. "For once, I couldn't agree with you more. I'm starving; I feel like my stomach is eating itself."

Joy erupted from within her breast as Rahim returned to his old self again. It felt like a lifetime since she had the chance to sit and relax with her friends, and seeing Silver and Rahim laugh and chat with her made her feel like the shadow of Snowhaven was lifted, even just barely.

"My dear, how do you like Thor's pavilion?" Silver asked, "I put it together myself shortly after you three arrived."

"It's lovely, and I'm sure he appreciates it very much. Whenever he's curled up, he looks like a pile of jewels basking in the sun." Her complimenting his gift to Thor made Silver's eyes sparkle like the stars. After inquiring how the floors radiated with so much heat, Silver described, with great enthusiasm, that he channeled steam from heated pools hidden underneath the mountain, and the pavilion was built directly upon the vent. "Since the pool is deep underground," he continued, "the heat isn't as intense and more controlled."

While Selena was still trapped in Silver's fascinating explanation, Rahim swallowed another bite and wiped away the crumbs sticking to his mouth. "Tell her about that new project of yours."

Selena's eyes brightened. "What kind of project?"

Silver stood up and began fishing through his pockets, muttering where he could have placed his diagram drawing of the infernal contraption. At last, he flung the paper down on a cleared-off table and unrolled it for the two; Selena's eyes immediately widened when it looked like a schematic for building a new hand. "I've been working on this since you three arrived, and I was hoping to complete it before you awoke, my dear: I call it a prosthetic hand. Though it will be mechanical, it will still work as though it were of flesh and blood. I'll show it to you later—it's still in early development."

She faintly recalled her dreams and wondered how she knew about his plan if he only ever spoke of it to Rahim; perhaps she overheard their discussion without being consciously aware. Selena smiled and took another sip from her cup, intrigued with Silver's idea, and she was willing to try any of his suggestions. After all, he was the first to resurrect the dead, and she was his first and only success. This man—no, demigod—was a genius.

However, their pleasant conversation took a drastic turn when Rahim briefly mentioned Alfheim's terrible fate, and when he couldn't finish, Silver managed to fill in the rest of the grim details. "There is nothing left of the elven city once those creatures were through issuing their destruction."

Selena's heart froze, and she thought she was struck with a deadly blow to the face. Her mind raced to their encounter with Medusa and recalled when she announced that Niamh was leading the masked dragons— the Nidhoggr—back to Alfheim; her veins turned to ice when the horrible revelation crumbled upon her Niamh, although brainwashed, was responsible.

Silver's words sounded faint, but his voice returned to her ears as she snapped back to reality. "Your father and General Araneus suspected that the Council planned the dragon egg delivery mission as a setup, but we discovered it too late. Now, Alfheim—" He abruptly stopped, and Selena knew he couldn't bring himself to repeat it.

She looked down at her trembling hand while Rahim poured himself a cup of coffee after finishing his tea. "We found out when the Dark Master's subordinate, Medusa, ambushed us," she said. A slight noise escaped from Rahim's throat at the sound of her name; he curled his fingers and dug his nails into his palms but offered no other response to the horrors Medusa made them endure in the Water Kingdom. Judging from the smoldering glare in Silver's eyes, Selena knew Rahim went to great lengths in detailing the events while trapped within her mind. She shared his resentment, as did Silver.

Tight-lipped, Silver nodded, and the three briefly went over their shared knowledge of what they discovered while serving on opposite ends of Armageddon. Rahim, however, remained silent most of all, possibly still reminiscing over their imprisonment and Niamh's dark fate. Selena cursed her luck when she and her group found her too late in Snowhaven; she was already brainwashed and corrupted. She knew how much it killed Rahim to watch Niamh descend to madness; he liked her enormously. He probably even loved her, for all Selena knew, but Rahim never admitted it.

Per Silver, while Medusa and the Lich's forces kept her group detained, and before the Nidhoggr returned and attacked the city, the Council stormed through Rune Citadel to dethrone and kill her mother. Much to her relief, he assured her that her parents were still alive. Her Former Imperial Majesty, Selena learned, currently waited in Dark Blood Hold: the Shadow Templars' fortress near Winterguard led by Lord Vincent Godfrey.

Rahim's eyes lit up, and his face grew pale at their mention. Confused and bemused, Selena had to explain, on multiple occasions, that he already knew about their existence, but he continued denying his knowledge. "Do you remember Kain?"

Rahim raised a brow. "Kain?"

"The man who saved your life when we found Ragnarok."

His face drained of all color when he finally realized who Selena referred to; his hands immediately shot up and over his head. "And he said he was a captain of the Shadow Templars. Why did I not remember that?"

Silver and Selena exchanged puzzled glances, and she sighed as she told Rahim how they served the imperial family. "I would be grateful one Templar saved your life."

He bit his lip but nodded all the same. "I can't believe I didn't remember. I've been acting like a mental lunatic prattling about the Shadow Templars like I never knew they existed."

"You were out of it for a while after Kain rescued you. You may have forgotten while you were under."

"It felt like a dream, honestly."

Silver snorted. "You'll be re-acquainted with Kain soon enough, Rahim." Rahim's only response was to make a rude gesture, but Silver only laughed it away before Selena could scold him for his inappropriate behavior. Their silly banter was interrupted by her further inquiry of her father's whereabouts, and she immediately regretted asking when Silver promised the grim news. "Your father returned to Alfheim and confronted Vidar. I fear for his safety, and only the Divines know what they're doing to him if he's not dead already."

"My father is still alive. Vidar wouldn't kill him, at least not yet, so he must be in prison somewhere."

Selena noticed the furrow in Silver's brow as he shifted uncomfortably in his chair, and her eyes sparkled like a blazing ember when she got the confirmation she needed. "If he is in prison, he would be in Mortemholdt —the only penitentiary in Armageddon, but large enough to hold all its citizens ten-fold. Mortemholdt isn't exactly the most pleasant place to go, my dear."

"How can we rescue him? Isn't Mortemholdt in the opposite direction?" Rahim asked.

Silver nodded, but he couldn't tear his pleading gaze away from Selena, possibly as a small effort to dissuade her decision. He sighed when he realized that she had already made up her mind and wouldn't change her answer. "It's suspended high above Lake Peril, between Alfheim and the Grand Exchange. We've flown past it when you and Thor first reported for duty."

"We must rescue him. I bet you anything my father had his reasons for allowing the Council to capture him. You know he does, Silver."

His expression lit up the whole room. "You're right. That would be just like your father."

Rahim still appeared to be reluctant. "I'm not sure that I like the sound of breaking into one of the world's deadliest prisons. Mortemholdt holds the most deranged and dangerous prisoners; some famous murderers and psychopaths from Runefell and Black Star are there."

Giving the two a harsh, cold glare, Selena made her intentions clear that saving her father would be their top priority, but she only backed down when Silver acknowledged her wishes. "And we will. But first," he pointed to Selena's left arm, "let's wait until I finish your prosthetic. You can't expect to save your father if you're missing a hand." Expressing her impatience, he continued to be reassuring. "Your father will be fine for a while. I promise we will save him, but you must get well first, and we will work on a plan in the meantime."

Selena was almost too afraid to ask about the others. However, her face brightened up the apartment when Silver confirmed some good news: General Araneus and Aracania survived and escorted her mother to Dark

Blood Hold—and the Oracles. Loki and Neith sought refuge in Nuvak with Chaliss until it was safe to rendezvous with the former Empress. Selena thanked the Divines under her breath, offering a quick prayer for all those who the Dark Master and Council murdered. Rahim also allowed a sigh of relief to escape his lips when hearing his mother, Chaliss, was still safe in Nuvak.

Still, Selena couldn't believe that her father allowed this treachery to slip under his nose; after meeting him in Starsong, he assured her that Snowhaven was well with no suspicion that the Lich had control of the capital. Yet, His Majesty, King Boreas Tristan, was murdered by Medusa and the disguised Justiciar William Holland immediately after the group delivered the Mythic Flight dragon eggs—the offspring from the mighty elemental guardians next to Divinity Dragons in power.

While Silver and Rahim shared their thoughts on how they could break into Mortemholdt, Selena's lip curled into a snarl. *We could have taken the eggs someplace safe. Now, because of me—oh, I gave the eggs to the Lich.*

Thor overheard her harsh thoughts and immediately interjected. **My dear, you did nothing wrong.**

Darkness came when I gave the Dark Master all that remained of the Mythic Flight. I was the one who brought down the Empire, and I didn't even know it.

She shuddered at his sudden booming voice. **How could you have known? How could any of us have known?** When Selena didn't answer, Thor lowered his tone to a gentle whisper as much as a dragon could. **You only did the best you could. No one knew of the Council's betrayal until it was too late. If you blame yourself, I'm also at fault. But we're not here to pass** judgment, for the longer we dwell on past mistakes, the farther away victory will be.

But I did this.

Then, I did this too. I was following blindly, as you were. He paused, allowing his words to sink in but pressed on. **The Lich and the Council will face our wrath, and we will rain fire upon them. We will fight back with the strength of a thousand dragons.**

You're always so confident, and I wish I could be more like you.

Believe me when I say you're more than you think you are. Soon, you will burn brighter than all the stars in the sky.

Selena was interrupted by Silver's raised voice and hissing through his teeth at Rahim; the two wondered how to deal with the Council's new creations possibly guarding Mortemholdt, or, as Silver preferred calling them, "those damned abominations." She flinched upon hearing how he regarded the masked dragons. Of course, she was angry about their role in Alfheim's destruction but upheld a different view after meeting the hatchling, Tiamat, and how she protected her against an attack from one of her own; she felt unsure how to tell Silver what she had learned about the creatures.

"They're not abominations." Before he could fire another response to her objection, Selena added: "They're Nidhoggr. While we were in Nuvak, we came across one of their whelplings." While she recounted how Tiamat sacrificed herself to save her life, Silver kept whipping his head around to gain validation from Rahim, who only shrugged before gulping down another cheddar biscuit. Silver sucked in his cheeks when she finished her story, and he turned away and began pacing.

Rahim chimed in to break the uncomfortable silence that followed. "I thought she was mental too, but she was right." He hung his head in shame. "I felt bad after all the things I said, and I was the first one who wanted to kill it. But, those things took Niamh, and I'm still angry."

"The Nidhoggr were brainwashed just like Niamh was. They're not responsible for their actions." Selena offered Silver a pleading gaze, but he focused on the floor as his steps quickened. She and Rahim exchanged glances before she came up with an idea. "Maybe the Nidhoggr can help us fight against the Lich. I found out what works for them: food was a good training tool."

Silver paused with his back turned to them. The only sound Selena heard was her heartbeat growing louder in anticipation of what he would do or say next. She half expected him to burst with anger at considering the possibility of trusting the Nidhoggr or even questioning Selena's judgment. However, he whispered, "I trust you, my dear, but they're under Vidar's control. How could we get them to side with us?"

"I-I don't know, but we can figure out something." Giving up her case, she sighed, silently admitting that Silver's argument made sense. Any hope of acquiring a legion of Nidhoggr shattered, and Selena was again at a loss. They couldn't march down to Alfheim and demand control over the Nidhoggr army. Even if the masked dragons agreed to fight for her, Selena would have to confront Vidar and the Lich, and she was nowhere near ready to face them in battle. She hadn't mastered her dragon state yet, let alone confidently use Aether magic.

Rahim interrupted and voiced what she feared, growing weary of running into every dead-end plan. "Let's put aside the plan regarding Mortemholdt for now. What else can we do? The Empire has fallen, and the Day of Eternal Darkness is only a month away. If you have any ideas, Silver, now is the time."

Silver smirked; Rahim acknowledged his brilliance, which surprised Selena. "Indeed, I do. I found a way for you to control your dragon state, Selena." His voice sang like bells from a church.

Her eyes widened, and her heart fluttered as her hope returned. "You have? How?"

"Do you two remember Ulrich?"

Rahim cringed at the sound of the Divine's name, and Selena knew he had not forgotten his near-death experience at the dwarven capital. "Do you mean that giant green dragon that almost killed us in Rhumbek?"

Silver had no regard for Rahim's resentment of the Divine, as his smug expression did not change. "That's him. He lives here at the summit." He pointed at the ceiling, his gleaming grin stretching across his face.

Rahim's face turned pale, and a shiver ran up his spine. "That dragon lives here? Why in Oblivion would you take us here?"

"Ulrich is completely sane now. Even when he goes on his rampage, his only goal in mind is to destroy Rhumbek and nothing more." While Rahim was busy muttering profanities under his breath, Selena asked how Silver knew about the curse, to which he only shrugged. "I don't exactly follow the god's rules." He laughed, but when he saw that the two weren't satisfied with his answer, he added, "I'm an exception to that rule. Mortals aren't supposed to remember the details of the curse or Rhumbek during their destruction. I'm a demigod, so I don't count."

Rahim jumped from his chair and pointed the finger at himself. "But why do I still remember? That dragon tosser almost killed us."

Silver shrugged. "I dunno. You'll have to ask Ulrich about that, as I don't know all the details of the curse."

Selena became distracted by Thor's humming. **Interesting that Rahim didn't bring up you or me when he asked why only he remembers.**

Being Divinity Dragons, we are gods in our own right. She wasn't sure if she liked the sound of that, but she could tell that Thor was satisfied.

After Rahim finished calling Ulrich many inappropriate names, Silver further explained that, aside from being a god of war, destruction, and technology, he and Xyaxon were both responsible for the existence of Divinity Dragons. Since both she and Thor were such, the Divine would know how to help unlock their true power. "Before you awoke, I paid Ulrich a visit, and after much discussion, he agreed and is currently waiting for you two whenever you're ready."

Rahim hung his head. "Great, you want us to get help from a god that's already tried to kill us, only to stop and possibly save those goop dragons who have already *tried* to kill us. You know what? I'm ready—let's do this." Silver and Selena shared a hearty laugh; she felt an enormous sense of relief wash over her to see her friends smile, even for a small moment. She had no idea how she would accomplish mastering her dragon state, but her only hope was getting help from Ulrich.

After reiterating Silver's discovery to Thor, he grew agitated, and although he wished to depart immediately, he knew Selena needed to take care of other matters first. **Besides, it will probably be best to wait until Silver finishes your hand.**

And to save my father.

The laughter died, and Silver declared he would take them to meet with Lord Godfrey at Dark Blood Hold once they finished all they needed to accomplish.

Selena nodded, her heart fluttering within her chest. Knowing they still had allies to help fight back gave her hope; there was a chance to save their world. Not all was entirely lost. "Be that as it may," she began, "Lord Godfrey shouldn't mind our delay if we arrive with the Shadow Emperor."

*****

CHAPTER 4: KISSED BY AN ANGEL

I am life and death. My Divine fire will reign. Thor, the master of the sky, soared upon the breath of the Divines as he prepared himself for the evening hunt. The sun inched closer to the line where the land met the sky.

Although he understood Selena busied herself in spending time with Silver and Rahim, Thor snorted, for she wouldn't spend the remainder of the evening with him; if she was cold, his pavilion was nice and toasty. However, he would soon expect his new guest—at least he wouldn't be alone—and although Ebony wished to meet him, Thor wanted to eat first. Still, the idea of Selena with Silver sometimes made him feel ill, and as much as he was willing to accept the demigod in their lives, Thor was still not wholly ready.

His wings shook the heavens as the world bowed down to his might. Thor was colossal compared to any dragon he had ever seen, yet his growth knew no bounds. During their time in Heaven's Tear, while waiting for Selena to wake up, Thor's size amassed to that of a twenty-gun first-rate frigate. The length of his wings could wrap around Silver's vast tower and still overlap. Thor would have no issues carrying a small battalion of about three hundred fully grown men, or even more if his harness could allow it.

The Divines themselves should fear me.

The setting sun made his scales glisten and shine like diamonds. He was a jewel in the sky, and Thor was proud of his might and beauty.

His eyes turned red when they caught a massive stag drinking from a pond. However, when Thor's shadow drifted across the ground, the animal swiveled its head and immediately ran off. Thor looked forward to the chase; he purposefully roused his prey into running, as Thor maintained his speedy advantage. The mighty dragon swooped down and tackled his game from the sky when he was upon the stag. He felt the animal's spine break from the force and the crunch of flesh and bone from his claws. Satisfied, Thor steered himself back to Heaven's Tear with his kill. As big as the stag was, the animal only served as a snack.

He needed to eat constantly every four to six hours when only a hatchling. Now, he could go for days or weeks without the need to hunt and sustain himself through sporadic small kills and still be satiated; Thor wondered if he would reach the point where he no longer needed sustenance.

Silver's tower stood boldly below him; Thor was as graceful as a swan, landing near his pavilion fit for a king or a god. He dropped his latest catch near his roost, but before he could lay down and enjoy tearing through flesh and bone, a figure of a woman caught his attention.

Thor's heart was about to burst from his chest.

My dear one, is that you? Have you returned to me?

She didn't reply immediately. *I'm still here with Silver and Rahim.*

He snarled at how short she kept her answer; it was as if she didn't want to join him.

As the woman approached, Thor was disappointed to see someone else. He hissed through his clamped fangs and flickered his tail, smashing it against the ground until he realized the woman was most likely Ebony; she had the same glasses and snow-white hair as Silver that glistened with iridescent radiance from the setting sun. Her sudden appearance didn't matter, for Thor wished it were his beloved companion coming out to join him instead. She belonged to him and no one else, so why couldn't Silver understand? His head drooped while he sulked in somber silence.

The black-suited woman sauntered with poise and elegance through every light step she made, and her hand rested upon her sword's pommel belted to her waist. She stopped when Thor gave her a warning growl. To Thor's surprise, Ebony didn't remark his sudden hostility, but she grinned and bowed. "It's such an honor to meet the King of Dragons himself," she began, "it's a pleasure, Thor. I waited outside until you returned from the hunt. I understand it's unwise to interfere during a mighty dragon's meal." Thor held his head high from the formalities and bowed, too but kept their introductions short; Thor whirled around and gobbled up his latest catch within seconds, bones and all. Ebony watched him with deep fascination, but Thor paid no mind.

Ebony took a step forward while he picked and cleaned his ivory talons. "My brother, Silver, told me so much about you and Selena. You two are the Divine's gift to this world." Having fed his ego, chittering, Thor snaked his head down to properly greet Ebony. She inched forward and stretched out her hand, only for Thor's nose to meet her open palm, and for a brief moment, the two locked in silent communion.

After they backed away, Ebony took a seat beside him with Thor's permission. She clasped her arms around her knees and told Thor stories of her past adventures, speaking for hours until the sun nestled between the mountains and the moon blared in the burning sky.

Ebony's words enchanted him; Thor didn't know what was happening, but he fell under her spell. It reminded him of whenever he and Selena used to sit and read together before the pair joined the Force, and suddenly his heart ached for Selena to be by his side again. And yet, Thor found himself longing for more of Ebony's attention, listening to stories he only dreamed about from the books Selena read. She spoke of discovering great treasure, battling ancient creatures of legend, riding the rare unicorn as a child, learning different sword techniques, conquering distant lands; her fables were endless.

Thor inched closer with each new tale until his head draped over Ebony's shoulder. She stopped and smiled, reaching over and stroking his snout and neck. Without saying another word, she stood up, and her appearance began to change. To Thor's shock and amazement, she transformed into a black dragon—similar characteristics to an Imperial Pearlscale save for the coloration—beautiful enough to make the Divines weep. Her smooth, onyx hide was as radiant as the moonlight glistening upon her slender body. Oval specs of orange and amethyst glowed against her midnight, leather-bound wing membranes. Two body-length tendrils flowed from near her nostrils and danced in the air long her sides. Thor noticed the trembling frill along her jawline, and a strange feeling washed over him. Ebony stood to his shoulders, a decadent beauty.

She must be a shapeshifting demigod, like Silver.

Ebony bowed her head. *Indeed, I am. I'm a demigod as old as my brother.* She stepped closer, and before

Thor could brace himself, she rubbed her snout against his. Thor couldn't understand what was happening, but he felt such a burning desire erupt, like his heart would eventually explode. *I identify as a dragon,* Ebony continued, *because being a mortal is boring. Taking a human form is my way to blend in if I must.*

Thor didn't care what she preferred, but all he knew was that he wanted to remain by her side. He craved her. Thor couldn't explain his sudden desire, but it grew so much that he was afraid he would be unable to contain it.

Suddenly, Ebony's trilling fins along her face twitched as she yowled. Her call beckoned Thor forward until she leapt up with a sweep of her wings and began climbing towards the stars. With a flicker of his tail, Thor gave chase. At first, Ebony put a great distance between them, but Thor picked up more speed, and soon, the world spun around the two as Thor finally caught her.

His desire grew as he wrapped his tail and wings around her, and the two dragons became intertwined. Exhilarating passion burst between them as Thor dug his claws into her gleaming hide, and Ebony followed his movements as they swirled into a downward spiral. Before they hit the ground, Thor and Ebony finally broke free and circled back to the pavilion.

Although the ritual only lasted seconds, Thor knew he wanted no other future mate. He only desired her.

*****

CHAPTER 5: REVELATION

Rahim plotted their course as he and Silver heavily discussed the plans to break into Mortemholdt; meanwhile, Selena looked over the prison's blueprints Silver found from his library, showing her and Rahim all the blind spots that he knew existed. It wouldn't be safe for Thor to linger around, nor would there be any room, so once he dropped them off, the group would be on their own until they were ready to meet up again.

"According to Silver's prints," Rahim pointed at the schematics, "their armory would be nearby. We can disguise ourselves as guards until we find your dad, Selena. Then, we can gather back at the exit, and we'll be home free."

Selena felt uneasy with how he made their plan sound. "I feel like it's not going to be as simple as that."

Silver sang, "If all else fails, we'll blow the damn thing up."

Selena shook her head. "No, we don't need the Council on our tails. If Vidar Helios and the others can easily overtake Alfheim, imagine what they could do to us —not to mention if their Nidhoggr battalion are there." Silver and Rahim shivered from hearing their name. "We know Vidar is much more cunning than we give him credit for."

Mortemholdt was about a week's flight from Heaven's Tear; the trio agreed to go over their allotted provisions the day before to ensure they would have enough for about two weeks' worth, including their soon-to-be fourth passenger.

Falling deep into their planning, Silver and Rahim slowly—perhaps not purposefully—omitted Selena from the conversation. Only when she tapped on their shoulders did they realize their mistake and, in reconciliation, attempted to include and ask for her opinions. However, she noticed the two began isolating her once more. She ultimately decided to sit down, biting down on her nails in anticipation, waiting for them to finish their discussion.

Thankfully, Thor's upbeat attitude served as a nice distraction from her friends' rude dispositions; yet, she couldn't help but notice that he had been in high spirits since his meeting with Ebony. *I take it that you're enjoying her company?*

I am. Ebony is a shapeshifter like Silver, and she prefers to be a dragon. She sat with me for hours, sharing stories of great treasure and battles.

That sounds lovely. Selena couldn't help but feel that he was more than happy with his time with her.

It's not what you think.

Do you like her?

She's fascinating.

You didn't answer my question. Do you like Ebony?

Thor snorted and seemed almost embarrassed to answer. **I do but as an acquaintance.**

Highly suspecting his lies, Selena bit her bottom lip as she kept her snickering to a minimum not to interrupt Silver's and Rahim's conversation—Thor wouldn't admit it. *You can't lie to me. I understand something happened between you two, and I believe you admire her.*

I never said I didn't, nor did I deny that something happened. Leave it.

Selena's cheeks burned when she realized what he meant, and her wide grin brightened her entire face. *You'll hear it from me for a long time after this.*

Oh, don't be rash. Does it matter?

No, it doesn't. Does it bother you that Ebony is a shapeshifter?

No, but does it disturb you that Silver is too? Thor had a point, as the versatility of Silver's nature never occurred to her. Although he could be anyone or anything, Selena still loved him for who he was, not what he was. **Besides, she and I only talked.**

I know you're lying to me. Before, you said you didn't deny something happened, and now you're saying the two of you only talked.

Would you please leave me alone?

You're a lousy liar. I can't help but notice how happy you are.

Thor paused to collect his thoughts and fight through his shame. **Is that a bad thing?**

No, it's not. I only want you to be happy.

I want to see you happy, too.

Selena began to understand how Thor felt when Silver asked her to marry him. She was ecstatic for him and wanted their relationship to evolve, but she began to fall victim to her swirling emotions. It wasn't because of Ebony's nature; Ebony could be whatever creature she chose. It mattered not to say the least—no, Selena slowly succumbed to the burning jealousy that plagued her when seeing Ebony for the first time. However, she kept her thoughts to herself, unwilling to invite Thor's harassment for going through the same wild emotional wave he did; she worked on convincing herself her feelings were unwarranted.

When Silver and Rahim were satisfied with their plans, Rahim stood at the table in silence while Silver, expressing the need to check on Selena's new hand, briefly left the room through a hidden door beside the ivory grandfather clock. However, Rahim's demeanor changed as he hung his head while holding on to the edges for support; his muscles tightened, and he deeply inhaled when Selena asked about his welfare. "I dunno. I'll be fine."

"I know you better than that. Please, tell me what's wrong."

Rahim clenched his jaw. "I detest talking about how I feel."

"I will pester you until you tell me."

"Stop. I don't want to talk about it. All right?" Selena recoiled from his sudden built-up anger, but she withdrew from their quarrel. Before she had a chance to say another word, Rahim bade her good night before heading back to his room as soon as Silver returned; Selena could only give a silent answer by shaking her head when Silver mouthed quietly, "What's wrong with him?"

After peeking down the corridor and assuring Rahim settled in for the night, Silver closed their door before returning to his chair. "We shouldn't be disturbed for the rest of the evening." He offered her more green tea brewed explicitly for her with a side of honey. "Interesting fact, my dear. This drink was also your father's favorite."

She took slight satisfaction that she shared minor similarities; the sweet nectar laded the air after stirring in a spoonful and quenched her throat. "How is your experiment coming along?"

"Quite nicely, although it's taking a while to finish fine-tuning it. I'm currently charging it with Aether energy through a focus crystal." After requesting permission to hold her bandaged arm, Silver pointed to various spots at the severed end. "I plan on attaching it to your different nerve points. Much like how blood flows through your veins, the new hand will be powered by channeling your Aether, which will allow you to touch, but it also needs its own to keep it fully energized."

"If I understand correctly, it will be like its own battery source."

"Exactly. In the meantime, after I attach it to your arm, it will occasionally need to be recharged through the focus crystal because the energy cannot sustain the device indefinitely, but you'll have two hands again."

Silver's explanation reminded her of dwarven technology. Although the dwarves weren't magically adept, they still figured out how to utilize Aether as an energy source for their inventions; the starlight reading device left behind in the ruin outside of Alfheim, to Selena's realization, used Aether channeled through crystals to operate their machine. It almost made magic a little primitive if the dwarves could harness spirit energy efficiently. "That's still incredible—I can't wait to use it."

However, Silver's disgruntled face made her regret her enthusiasm for the future procedure; he scratched the top of his head. "Uh, as a word of caution: it will be painful. I have to connect it directly to your nerves." He made an uncomfortable noise, and Selena clicked her tongue against her teeth, reluctant at the excruciating idea. "I do have a suggestion, however. If you trust me enough to do this, I can always put you under anesthesia, so you don't feel a thing while I attach it."

Selena had heard of the practice, but most of the medical professionals in the Empire weren't too familiar with it. The idea initially came from Runefell, but the other regions have yet to adapt to their more advanced methods, and she asked if Silver possibly learned from the doctors over the border. "Oh, I've been around, as you know—I happen to be a doctor and a surgeon. After being alive for over sixteen thousand years, you tend to learn everything."

"Your abilities never surprise me as I've come to expect the height of your capabilities. Is there anything you haven't done?"

Silver's laughter boomed throughout their apartment before taking another sip from his cup. "Nothing I can think of, my dear."

She fingered the edge of her cup. "Have you ever done surgery before?"

Silver's eyes gleamed as he smiled. "Of course. Not counting helping you in that dwarven ruin, I've performed countless others." Mystified and intrigued, Selena pointed out his assistance didn't count as surgery, but Silver explained that healing was more complicated than she realized; ensuring every muscle was repaired and tying every blood vessel was challenging enough. Azrael taught her the art before when helping Tiamat's wounds, and she instinctively grasped the concept as she always did in magic: Silver, however, had to learn and perfect his profession.

However, Silver's tone changed. His face turned grey when he disclosed his medical involvement on the night she was born: assisting her difficult birth and surgically removing her from her mother because of her stillbirth. After her mother recovered, her parents grew desperate to save her and attempted the illegal arts of human transmutation. "They tried for so long to conceive a child that they didn't want to lose you," he continued, "but as a consequence, in dabbling in the dark arts, your mother can never carry another child." He paused before carefully adding, "I've also wondered if the disease that torments her connects to her infertile affliction."

"What disease?"

"There's no name for it, but I've caught her vomiting blood several times. I've tried to find a cure, but nothing has worked for her. The illness isn't killing her, but she suffers eternal torment. Divine punishment, I suppose." Silver shifted in his spot and cleared his throat. "My point is that yes, I know what I'm doing."

Selena couldn't fathom what her mother had to endure, and she wished she knew more about her and Phantom Dust. Instead, her parents hid behind secrets and would only tell her if they deemed it necessary; otherwise, she heavily relied on Silver for information. For the former Empress to remain calm throughout the entire ordeal was astounding. "I have no doubt that you do, and I trust you with my life, but do you have all you need for this procedure?"

Silver's attitude immediately lit up from the previous dreary conversation. "Of course I do. I have everything for anything."

Selena's throat swelled shut as she imagined every worst-case scenario, including the possibility of the inevitable occurring. "What will anesthesia feel like?"

Silver scratched his chin as he gandered at the lights; his behavior made Selena believe he had complete confidence in using this practice, which helped ease her nerves. "It will be like taking a nap. You'll go to sleep, and the next thing you know, you'll wake up, and everything will already be over."

Forcibly being put to sleep made her more apprehensive and increased her anxiety. Her pandemonium of madness awaited to trap her within her mind, and she wondered if she would ever wake up again.

Upon seeing her reaction, Silver repeated his reassurances of a smooth procedure and that he would never allow the worst to happen; she was in good hands. "Besides, I will do anything to bring you back. Why, if it weren't for Azrael's promise—"

"What?" When Selena shot up from her chair, the teacup with its small plate fell from her lap and crashed against the floor; Silver's mouth twisted over his unfinished words when he realized his mistake and gave her a dainty smile. "Did you make Azrael promise?" A stone dropped in her stomach when he opened his hands, palms upward as if he had nothing else to hide. "You knew what would happen in Snowhaven. It was either you or my parents."

"No, we didn't know." Tight-lipped, Silver stood up and crossed his arms over his chest while tapping his foot, and, while glaring at him, Selena waited for his plausible explanation. "We didn't know. I wasn't involved, but your mother made Azrael promise that he would protect you, no matter what that meant. Your mother...." Silver trailed off and bit his lip, and it was Selena's turn to cross her arms. "Before the mission, your mother met with Azrael personally and made him and Doragon swear to protect you, no matter the cost. That also meant if the worst were to happen."

"And they swore it," Selena finished for him, still keeping her smoldering glare locked on the fidgeting demigod. It never occurred to her what frightened Silver the most, but she assumed Thor and her were perhaps on the top of his list.

"You know Death always keeps his promises."

Because he's the promise everyone has to keep. "Is there anything else I should know about, oh great and powerful Silver?"

She squinted her eyes at him as his lips twisted, but he clicked his tongue against his teeth as he flinched, mouthing inaudible words that Selena asked him to repeat. Eventually, his speech threw out a "you weren't supposed to have a lifespan."

Death didn't frighten her as much as knowing that her existence defied the natural order. All that Selena could muster to say was, "Pardon me?" Her lungs nearly failed her as it felt like Silver decked her in the gut; she wasn't sure how to take the news of sharing immortality.

Her shock did not surprise Silver, but rather, a hidden smile crept from the corner of his mouth as he gathered himself. "The Divinity Dragon's blood and magic from the Well of Souls were supposed to sustain your life indefinitely," he sighed and turned away, "Azrael and Doragon paid the ultimate price to bring you back."

We must save them from the Lich, no matter what. Protecting Death will help restore balance to our world. Her thoughts vanished, and without warning, Selena hissed through her teeth; an enormous amount of pain erupted across her back—the pain struck her like a lightning bolt, and she convulsed as her body relived her painful last moments before slipping into Oblivion. She leaned forward while flinging her only functional hand behind her back to massage her tearing muscles, and she seized upon the floor. Silver dashed across to join her side, and instead of restraining her, he ensured the area was clear, positioned her on her side, and waited.

When her seizure stopped, Selena still couldn't find the strength to move, her back burning as if Thor had just incinerated her. Silver carefully reached over and pulled down the collar of her dress just enough to see the horrible black scar spiderwebbing across her back and chest with shadow wisps dancing off her skin. The pain disappeared as he fixed her dress, and Selena could sit upright once more, head throbbing as she winced.

No matter how much Silver tried, his shaking hands and pursed lips betrayed his position after listening to her concerns; Selena sensed he had much more to say, but he watched his tongue. "Has your back bothered you like that before?"

Sodden, Selena attempted to catch every breath that escaped her; she and Silver exchanged terrified gazes. "Do you believe Ulrich can help me?"

Silver placed a hand on her shoulder and gave her a comforting smile, but he didn't offer a definite answer. Selena immediately grew cold when he expressed silent doubt in the Divine's ability. "Do you need more to drink? Water? Tea?" Declining his offer for further refreshment, she stumbled to her feet when strong enough to do so, ignoring the occasional strikes of pain continuing to plague her muscles.

"I believe I'm all right now, thank you. Please, do not make such a fuss." Silver heeded her wishes and backed away, but her legs felt like rubber as she made her way to her chair. Regardless of her previous statement, he offered her another glass of tea, which she finally accepted and gulped down. Much to her relief, the feeling returned to her limbs, and the pain finally subsided. "Thank you."

Giving her a firm jerk of his head, Silver dusted off his snow-white long frock jacket, and after waiting for a few extra minutes to ensure her comfort, he gestured to the hidden door beside the giant ivory clock. "Are you feeling up to taking a small tour? Now that we have some time alone, I can show you more of the library."

Selena's eyes lit up like the stars. "I would love to."

"Very good. You saw the first three floors already, but I want to give you the grand tour of my observatory." The subject change lifted the gloomy atmosphere that plagued the two almost instantly; Silver was as excited as a child receiving candy.

He made haste beside the grandfather clock as soon as she stood, holding a tiny ember flame smoldering over his palm. He pressed down on a sequence of points locked in a hidden square grid lighting beneath his fingertips, and a section of the wall opened up, leading to a secret room with another spiraling stone staircase.

The twisting set of steps circled upward in darkness, and as the two walked by, the lamps hanging from the walls sparked a tiny flame. Silver beckoned her to follow him, and he explained what awaited, though he maintained as much secrecy as possible not to ruin Selena's surprise. She did her best not to be overwhelmed with the sheer bliss of seeing Silver's magnificent tower but still allowed her imagination to run wild about what mysteries he would keep in a place that he had built and maintained for so long.

"You will find this so delightful. It will be amazing for you to see. It's not often that I get visitors—wait, I never do. I've spent most of my time here, recording most of our world's historical events and whatnot, but after a few thousand years, I got bored and decided to travel. My research and projects remain here, as this place is safe and not accessible to anyone. Maybe the Council back in the day, but I've denied them access."

"I cannot wait to read what you've witnessed. I bet not a single librarian nor scholar could hope to attain such a treasure." Silver shared in her delight from receiving a massive compliment on his rare collection. "Perhaps, after the war, I would love to travel the world and catch a glimpse of what you've seen, but I assume denying the Council an audience didn't go over too well."

Silver's triumphant smile radiated throughout the spire. "Not at all. Vidar didn't take my sudden privacy lightly, so I enchanted my laboratory. Whenever Vidar and his associates would step foot inside, it looked like an old attic with nothing interesting. After a while, Vidar got annoyed, and the Council stopped coming altogether."

His mood was contagious, and Selena couldn't help but share his victorious grin. "Was the Well of Souls completed here like your other projects and experiments?"

Silver gritted his teeth. "No, I didn't create that here. I had another laboratory specifically for the Well near Alfheim. Still, it was hard to conceal, as the Council was already suspicious of me while working on the project. It radiated with so much magic, and with the Divinity Dragon in my study, the Lich was able to find my workshop and destroy it. If I had the project here, I would have lost everything." Selena nodded, recalling that demons and other magical beings could sense intense energy elsewhere, whether objects or creatures. Shuddering at the thought, she knew Venexus would have found out sooner or later. "The plan was to bring you and Thor's egg here when we deemed it safe to do so, but we were too late, and the Lich had already struck his blow."

Selena rubbed her chin. "Would it have helped, at least with your case against the Council, to have your journal encrypted in a made-up or dead language? Or was it too late at that point?"

"It was already too late, but I've been more careful since. It was a stupid mistake not to do that with the book I gave you and one I hope never to make again."

"We all make mistakes. It happens to the best of us."

"Yes, I suppose." Silver let out a sigh in defeat. "I try to keep some of my projects top secret as much as I can, but there are other things that I don't mind opening to the public. I've shared general research on magic with other scholars across the land and beyond the Empire, notes that proved beneficial, such as finding remedies to once incurable diseases." Silver could not contain his excitement, and he wrapped one arm around Selena to pull her close as the two walked up the stairs. She understood his unfortunate habit of sharing too many secrets whenever excited, and she feared he would have eventually told the wrong person about the Well.

As they finally reached the top, Silver held out both of his hands, the flame snuffing itself out. "Behold." Her knees almost buckled when her eyes drifted down; the thick glass floor showcased the nether sky. Pitch-black at first, but the chamber lit up as the divine cosmos donning diamond stars peered through the see-through dome. Two distant planets floated across the cosmic sea adorned with a blue-green nebula cracking and cleaving the infinite heavens in two.

Desks stacked with scrolls and journals lined the edge of the observatory, each with an oak chair lined with comfortable furs. Surrounding the circular room were more bookcases filled with ancient tomes, vials with different colored liquids, scrolls, alien devices, and much more. Centered at the chamber was a familiar machine Selena recognized from the abandoned dwarven ruin; appropriately aligned focus crystals hung above through metal arches—reflecting beams of energy feeding a crystal fixture dangling above a work table resting in the corner like a chandelier.

Upon the workbench scattered with tools and diagrams, a small glass dome safely guarded a hand made entirely of metal attached to wires hanging from the ceiling; the new prosthetic fed from the Aether lines like a hungry dragon. Underneath its gold and metal-plating were small tubes and valves that would allow the fingers to bend and curve like an actual hand. Blue Aether energy pulsated from the focus crystal and danced around the wires—the magic moving with purpose to rendezvous with the machine.

Silver cupped his hands with his vast grin bright enough to chase away the darkness. "So, what do you think?"

It was her turn to express delight and bliss, and she found herself bouncing in place. "What do I think? Your study is spectacular and outstanding. How is this possible?"

"This is my observatory, as well as my laboratory." She couldn't hold herself back as she ambled over to the mechanical hand but kept her steps light out of fear of breaking through the glass floor. Finding humor in her cautiousness, Silver assured there was no need, and the tempered glass was strong enough to withstand a fully grown dragon's weight. She stood up on her toes with her hand pressed against the smooth dome protecting her new device and inquired about the stage of its development and when Silver hoped to finish it. "Very soon, I can assure you. I'd say within a week."

Selena inched her hand to position it over the prosthetic for size comparison and was pleased to see that Silver had taken her size into account; she knew there was no reason to doubt the thoroughness of his work. He confirmed her suspicions: "I took measurements of your right hand while you were asleep to ensure it would be close to your left." When Selena asked how the observatory could overlook the ether beyond the earth's boundary, Silver called her attention towards another mechanism next to a bookcase: a spherical piece of clear glass freely suspended over a bronzed pedestal.

Selena squinted at it. "What is that?"

"I enchanted this dome to keep track of the cosmos, anytime and anywhere. I can do this if I wish to look at a specific quadrant." Silver touched the sphere.

The sky spun clockwise, the stars turning to white streaks, and when he pulled his hand away from the globe, the heavens halted. Three moons floated above them in the eternal abyss among violet nebula clouds wafting through the Divine's vast pool. "I can look through outer space anywhere I wish, just from using that."

Selena was mesmerized by his enchanted device and suddenly had the deep desire to fly through the swirling colored spires of space one day. "I keep saying all you have is amazing, but I don't know how to describe this. Your observatory is…." Her words failed.

Silver's eyes sparkled when he saw how impressed she was. "I can see it in your face, and that's enough for me to know what you think. Of course, when we're married, all of this will be yours. Imagine all that we could accomplish here together."

Selena couldn't hide her grin. "I would love that very much." She nodded to the glass sphere. "May I ask what you use it for?"

"I use it to read the position of the stars and planets to learn about the past and possible future." Silver scratched his head. "However, I've tried looking into the future of our world before, but it broke the machine. It was such a pain to fix." The concept of time made her recall the giant sandglass occupying the main study; she asked about it, but he was at a loss. "That old thing? Azrael gave it to me shortly after his banishment from Oblivion, but he couldn't explain what it was for."

Noting the nearly empty glass, she wondered if it kept track of the coming winter solstice and the eclipse, but Silver shook his head, as it never emptied from the last event. A stone dropped in her stomach from a sudden revelation. "Maybe it's keeping track of when our world will end, and we're running out of time." Her words tasted putrid. Judging from the look on Silver's face, she could tell he knew or at least assumed that much; Like Xyaxon, Azrael had been secretly warning them in hopes of preventing it.

The world's weight rapidly descended upon her shoulders as she had no idea how to stop the Lich from issuing his destruction. Selena began pacing while muttering under her breath as her anxiety grew overwhelming.

"My dear." Silver took a step towards her, but she ignored him as she hastened her pace, tormented by this constant, impending doom ready to snatch her at a moment's notice; the sandglass made her feel the need to run and fight, but she didn't know where or how. "Selena." Silver inched closer, but once more, she didn't listen.

Eventually, she stopped pacing and shouted, "This is maddening!" Her sudden booming voice didn't stop Silver as he reached up and spun her around. Before she could ask what they could do or if he had any ideas himself, he pulled her close and kissed her with such passion.

Her addled mind untangled itself from the web of madness, and her anxiety washed away. Part of her wanted to push him back, but at the same time, she didn't want him to stop. Feeling him, the smell of him, just being close to him made her skin crawl.

When he pulled away, his face leveled with hers; she couldn't explain how she always fell under Silver's enchantment, and it didn't help her resist when he smiled. "You need to learn to sit back and enjoy life, as you only live once. I wish you wouldn't stress finding the answers. Although I admire your curiosity and intelligence, I wish you wouldn't drive yourself mad by constantly seeking what you want to find. I know that feeling." She lowered her head through hunched shoulders, but while reminiscing upon her silence and before falling victim to her previous dilemma, Silver chuckled and tilted his head. "Do you want me to do it again?"

She couldn't stop her face from burning red as she butchered her words into an intelligible stutter; instead, Selena hastened to a nearby bookcase and began flipping through pages from a random book. Yes, the two would be married, but she couldn't control how something so strong could make her feel weak.

She ignored his smug and pompous face, but his snickering loomed over her head. "Hmm. I may have an idea on how you can stop the Lich. I don't know if it will work or if you can use it, but—"

The random tome within her hands snapped shut like a dragon clamping its maw around its prey. "What's your idea?"

Silver cocked his head and nodded to the bookshelf next to him. "Do you remember reading a little snippet about Revelation back in Alfheim?"

It took her a moment to realize what Silver was talking about, but then she recalled an old journal left behind by Varathka Gundisalvus with the words 'Revelation shall be the only hope of man' ringing through her mind like church bells. "I remember. Death's weapon?"

"Yes, that's it."

Revelation was a soul-eater; the weapon could imprison an enemy's soul, but Azrael never mentioned it to her or the others before. She assumed that for a good cause, he couldn't tell mortals in fear of it falling into the wrong hands—much like Ragnarok. Though Ragnarok was real, Revelation was hardly ever mentioned in previous texts, and Selena had doubted if Azrael's reaper scythe existed. "I thought it was just a legend?"

Silver began humming and placed his hand under his chin as he slowly stepped around her in circles. "Hmm. How very interesting? Oh yes, it's completely fake and utter nonsense. However, if it doesn't exist, where do the stories come from, I wonder?"

"Based on your odd behavior, you either know where it is or have it."

"Oh good heavens, I never said that. No, no, no —by the three Divines, I never said anything about that. I also never said I'm not allowed to say its location aloud."

Amused and intrigued, Selena couldn't help but crack a small laugh. Silver joined her; she grew used to him talking in circles and began figuring out how to pry more information while circumventing any curse her father laid upon him. Silver always seemed to answer her questions without directly violating the spell's rules. "Would it be enough to capture a soul like the Lich's and stop him once and for all?"

"Other than Ragnarok, it's supposed to be the most powerful weapon ever created. It can imprison *any* soul." He looked back at her and gave her another huge smile. "So yes, I believe so."

Her lips tightened as she tried not to grin. "Then you don't know where it is, or you don't have it." He silently declined and attempted to open his mouth, but like before, his lips sealed shut, and his mumbles silenced in the back of his throat. Silver patted down his jacket pocket; she bit her bottom lip and immediately knew he had it in his possession. Thinking that perhaps he had a scrap of paper with instructions or a phrase leading to its location, Selena fished through the pocket he gestured to but was disappointed when she pulled out a small, golden watch on a chain instead.

Twirling the trinket through her fingers, it didn't look any different than any other pocket watch, and yet, the timepiece was beautiful, its golden gleam sparkling in her eyes. Before she could ask about its purpose, Silver, still tight-lipped, held out his hand, and after Selena placed the jewelry in his outstretched palm, he brought it up to his lips and whispered the phrase, "Vor'noctes," and it began changing shape.

Blue Aether encased it within an orb of energy as the gold stripped away, and the timepiece morphed into a battle-ready reaper scythe with a long, ebony handle as the light faded. A carefully carved black skull sat faceted outwards at the top where the blade, made out of pure Aether, sparked to life; three spectral spikes protruded from the mouth while Aether pulsated around the handle and snaked towards the bottom, feeding its energized blue diamond pommel.

Upon closer inspection, Selena noticed a word carved into the snath written in the Elven Language, but she recognized its meaning: Revelation.

*****

High-pitched squeals echoed over the horizon.

The Grand Exchange was only a former shadow of what it used to be as a mysterious fog shrouded the now desolate string of shops. Dark figures marched through the mist with flesh rotting from their bones, stringy, greasy hair glued to their decaying faces. They were once among the living, but now they heed the Lich's calling.

A Nidhoggr flew over them, an undead rider sitting upon its back with purple eyes glaring through the hazy veil. The man wasn't as physically appalling as the undead army parading below, but his pale face couldn't hide the faint, tiny freckles dotting his nose; his dark, amber-colored hair remained neatly combed back, and his purple eyes gave away his true nature.

The man shrieked and ordered his undead followers forward, and the endless scores obeyed the rider's command.

*****

CHAPTER 6: THE DRAGON AND THE ROSE

At first, Selena feared Revelation would be another treasure hunt like it was for Ragnarok but was grateful to see the answer lay before her. Her eyes coveted the weapon, and without thinking, she touched it. When Silver offered to let her hold it, she felt its heartbeat thump within her palm. The handle, icy to the touch, vibrated as if alive. *To think that Revelation was hiding as a pocket watch the entire time.*

Silver first pulled out the timepiece while traveling to Alfheim, and Selena now understood why he never opened it to check the time; she went as far as to assume he wanted to show her without telling. "Are you able to talk about this now?"

Silver held up his hand, and his mouth twisted around for a moment while he issued his test. As Selena figured the curse was still upon him, his mouth opened wide, and he pulled out a handkerchief to catch his series of coughs. Recovering and breathing deep, his words tumbled out, "Yes—after his banishment and losing the ability to wield his weapon, Azrael asked me to protect this for him." He stretched out his arms and popped his back. "It feels so good to say it now."

She propped Revelation up against its diamond pommel, and a small streak of lightning struck against the glass floor but caused no damage. "Would Azrael have any issues with me using it?"

Silver only shrugged as his eyes wandered skyward. "I dunno. Only a god can use Revelation, so Azrael never feared it falling into mortal hands." He drew his hands to his hips. "However, he still wanted its location kept secret, but he never did say why. But you are of Divine birth—I believe you don't count as a mortal, but I wouldn't use Revelation for anything else."

Selena couldn't argue with Silver's logic; using Revelation was their first real plan at fighting back. As for if she could use it, she held on to her doubts and remained unsure if a Divinity Dragon counted as a god, let alone use a god's weapon. Yet, Selena remembered Ragnarok and how she was able to wield it. Perhaps Silver was correct in his assumption. "If you believe Revelation is the best way, I do too. I couldn't even fathom using it for anything else."

"I'm so glad that blasted curse is gone. I still don't appreciate how my old apprentice kept mocking you for never being able to find it. Why I ought to—"

Selena almost dropped Revelation out of shock but tightened her grip when she felt the metal beginning to slip from her fingers. "The Lich was your apprentice?"

Silver bit his cheeks, realizing another slip of the tongue, as was his habit. "I suppose now is a good time for you to learn how it all began to end his reign of terror. But first," he nodded to the scythe. After taking a few extra moments to admire the magnificent weapon, Silver took it back and whispered the exact phrase again; blue Aether imbued the reaper scythe, and Revelation regained its hidden nature as a pocket watch before handing it back. "I can't emphasize the importance of keeping this safe until the time comes when you need it. To summon Revelation, all you have to do is say, 'Vor'noctes.' It means, 'remember you will die,' in the Elven Language."

The phrase rang through her ears like the Pyre's chimes as she wrapped her fingers around the timepiece, the golden glow gleaming in her eyes before slipping into her pocket. "It will be safe with me until Venexus meets his end."

"We will all look forward to that moment, though I wished a better fate for my old apprentice. Now, where did I put that book?" Humming, he rushed to the nearest bookcase, and Selena was intrigued, but she raised a brow when Silver pulled tomes from the shelves and tossed them on the floor behind him. "Where is it? Where is it? Ah, there you are." He dusted off a journal bound in leather and spun around to hand it to her.

Selena reached up and took it with care. "What is this?"

"You'll get a chance to read it soon, but we're going to visit the past for now. Stand close to me." Silver pulled out a second timepiece from another pocket, a beautiful onyx trinket attached to a delicate jeweled chain. He popped open its cover and began winding down the dials, and much to Selena's surprise, the arrows on the watch's face slowly spun counter-clockwise.

She whipped around as time's tapestry began unweaving itself; the events she experienced just then replayed backwards. The arrows on the timepiece spun faster, and their entire existence followed suit until the scenery became a blur. A bright light absorbed the pair when reality faded into Oblivion until the watch stopped counting down, and the world resumed turning once more: the two stood before a young man and woman in the castle courtyard Rune Citadel, its ivory towers stretching high above Alfheim's gilt-painted glory. "What just happened? What did you do?"

Silver smiled and closed the watch. "We've gone back in time to witness a memory."

Selena's breaths quickened, and she looked over at the couple in fear that she and Silver were seen. However, the man and woman ignored their presence. "They can't see us, can they?"

"We can only see history, not alter it."

The man and woman looked close to Selena's age, maybe slightly older. The young maiden shared her resemblance and skin color, but her platinum blonde hair burned like a white flame. "That's my mother. And that man is—?" Selena noted him as an exceptionally handsome young gentleman, tall with soft brown hair.

The two stood side-by-side with each other, training in different stances. In sync, the man and woman summoned blasts of fire through various punches and kicks. Over and over again, the pair exercised together for a while before they stopped and bowed before one another. "You're amazing," the woman said, "I think you've already surpassed me."

"That's impossible. You were always better than me." The two friends laughed but stopped when the man stared at the woman and blushed. He raised his hand to talk to her again, but the woman darted past without offering another word; the man's dark eyes filled with gloom, and he was left defeated and undone.

Silver answered, "Aydin Jormungand." He was the original leader of the Council, but he vanished without a trace around the time Vidar took over; otherwise, Selena hadn't heard his name mentioned since the Lich, disguised as Myrrdin, told the brief tale at Norrington Hall. "But why is Aydin important?"

"You'll see."

A moment after the woman vanished, she saw another version of Silver round the corner and approached the young man. He looked almost the same; the only difference was his short-cropped blinding white hair tickling below his ears, magnifying the hue of his icy blue eyes. "For a shapeshifter, you don't change much."

Silver ran his fingers through his now waist-length snowy hair. "Why mess with a perfect look?"

"Aydin," his younger self began, "you missed your lessons again today."

Aydin bowed his head. "I'm sorry, master. I was training."

"You're supposed to be training with me."

"It won't happen again."

"Good." Aydin ignored his master's snarl as Silver swiveled his head to see the young woman hastening her steps. "I've told you before to leave the Crown Princess alone." Silver's tone softened when he added: "It's not wise to seek out the Emperor's daughter."

Aydin's voice exploded, shattering the soft air. "But I wasn't."

"Enough. Come with me. We have much to catch up on that you missed this morning." Young Silver and the undone Aydin left the courtyard.

Present Silver continued his tale: "Aydin and your mother have known each other since they were children, but Aydin came from nothing; he grew up with no family, but your mother was the first to show him any kindness and help. They were close, and your mother considered him her best friend."

"It seemed like Aydin wanted more than that."

Silver sighed and traced his fingers across the timepiece. "He began developing feelings for your mother, but she never returned them. Unfortunately, that's where his troubles began."

Their vision into the memory transitioned to Aydin working in a blacksmith shop set within a stone atrium with another young man around his age. The two worked together by the clang of their hammers against newly forged swords. The unknown young man's stoic expression on his pale and slender face reminded her of her father. The similar raven black hair swept behind his pointed ears, and his sapphire eyes gave away his identity. "That's my father, isn't it?"

Silver nodded. "Vulduin and Aydin became friends over time, and the two helped in the blacksmith's shop after settling down in Alfheim. At this time, the Emperor arranged the marriage of your mother and father."

Selena wasn't surprised by her father's talents as he helped her forge Dragonheart, a perfect sword of dragon bone and steel that no other artist could replicate. He was a master blacksmith whose work shined from his perfectly honed skills. She relished the new information regarding her parents and muttered her father's name; Vulduin rolled off the tongue much better than Phantom Dust, or D as Silver and Kain called him.

"Did my father come from a wealthy family outside of Alfheim?" Selena was surprised to see Silver shake his head. "How was it arranged for him to marry into the imperial family with no connections?"

Silver chose his following words carefully. "I've known your parents since Alfheim was built. Your father had connections, but I will allow your parents to explain themselves the next time we're all together. I may have a big mouth, but it's not my place to discuss their history." She was still not satisfied, and she continued pestering him for more information, but when Silver was unwilling to budge, she gave up and watched the memory play.

The young Vulduin dipped a new cherry-red sword into a water trough, steam sizzling and wafting into clouds pluming skyward. "I hope your teacher didn't punish you too badly."

Aydin scoffed. "He's talking about wanting to send me elsewhere."

"Why?"

"To move me away from distractions."

Vulduin wiped the sweat off his brow with his sleeve. "Is this so that you can learn how to shapeshift too?"

Aydin sighed and turned away from his partner, focusing on bringing his partially-shaped ingot to the proper heat. "I'm supposed to follow everything he says if I want that kind of power." He scoffed. "I don't want to continue training with him anymore."

Current-day Silver clicked his tongue against his teeth and disappointingly crossed his arms. "I took Aydin on as an apprentice; he was a very gifted student, just like you."

"Why did you need an apprentice?"

"I was looking for someone to continue my work if I'm ever unable to, or maybe I was looking for friendship. I agreed to show Aydin how to become a shapeshifter as long as he did what I said. He needed to work for it, but I was sad to hear that he no longer wished to continue with his studies."

The memory continued. "Why not?" Vulduin asked.

"You know why."

"I hope you realize our families have already arranged our marriage." Vulduin's answer was harsh; Aydin's face burned like fire as he flared his nostrils and slammed down his tongs before strutting off in response to Vulduin's cold reply. He fumbled, taking his apron off before disappearing into the crowd.

The memory shifted through a wash of white light, and Selena and Silver stood in the throne room of white marble within Rune Citadel. Now an older man, Aydin knelt before the two thrones seating the new Emperor and Empress, and her heart swelled when she saw her parents together. They looked so young and full of hope, but she cringed when Aydin's voice rang throughout the keep, addressing the Empress directly. "Your Imperial Majesty, it gives me great pleasure to serve you as head of your new Council."

Her mother's expression remained calm and unchanging, but the furrow in her brow gave away her distressed disposition. "Pray do not disappoint us in establishing this change. Armageddon never needed a Council before, but I trust your judgment above all else, Aydin."

"It's my gift to you, Your Imperial Majesty, and we're here to serve and maintain order. We wish to keep the power balanced for the sake of your people." Aydin tilted his head upward and straightened up as a sinister gleam flashed across his eyes. "Your Majesty, may I speak with you in private?" He glared at Selena's father.

Her Imperial Majesty looked to her husband with a pleading gaze to not leave her side; he nodded for her to continue, watching Aydin's every move. "What you have to say to me can also be said to your Emperor."

"Not this, Your Imperial Majesty."

Before Aryl could object, Vulduin stepped forward and addressed Aydin sharply, "I shall grant you a private audience but make your meeting quick." The Shadow Emperor met Aydin's heated gaze before leaving the keep.

When Vulduin was out of earshot, Aydin slowly approached the Empress. There was a sway to every step he took, and his dark brown eyes filled with smoldering darkness that Selena noticed wasn't there before. "I was overjoyed from the moment you took the throne. You are the ruler of a great Empire. Ever since I first met you—"

"If this is regarding what you've already asked of me, my answer is no. As I've said thousands of times before, my hand was sworn to someone else. I'm now bound to my husband, in both heart and spirit."

Aydin laughed, but he backed up from Her Imperial Majesty's harsh tone. Yet, he continued persisting. "Since I first met you as a little boy, I've always known that you were the woman I wanted to marry. So, here I am."

Her voice roared like thunder as she shot up from her throne. "I won't hear any more of this. I've declined your proposal before, and I am doing it again."

"Think of all the great things we can do together. Armageddon is flourishing and happy, and your Empire is enjoying its golden age. We can share and spread Armageddon's prosperity with the other regions, and with you and me ruling side by side, we can expand our territory."

"I said no. I don't want to hear any more of this."

When Aydin attempted to approach her again, Vulduin emerged from the shadows, chains shooting forth from the crimson sleeves of his imperial attire. They sought after Aydin like angry snakes, but he made no effort to dodge; instead, he laughed as the shackles bound him in place. "I've warned you Vulduin was a threat."

The Empress sat back down with glistening tears stinging her eyes. "This isn't you. What happened to you?" Aydin only laughed. Even as the imperial guards came over to escort him from the castle, Aydin's laughter echoed throughout the keep.

Not offering another explanation to Aydin's sudden madness, silent and pale-faced, Silver twirled the dials from his timepiece; the arrows spun clockwise, returning the pair to the present day. Selena sighed when the memory faded to darkness. "Aydin became the Lich, didn't he?"

Silver wasn't quick to respond, and Selena took that as a yes. "He began seeking power elsewhere after ending his apprenticeship with me. Unfortunately, after escaping Oblivion and wandering our realm for thousands of years as a spirit until finding the right host, Venexus continued planning for the next eclipse until discovering Aydin, using him as his perfect vessel while feeding off his greed, lust, and wrath."

"I saw the darkness in his eyes, and he wasn't even himself anymore."

The void melted like spilt oil, and the two returned to the laboratory. Selena focused on the journal and exercised great caution in opening its secrets, as the pages were old and delicate, dated around 1261 ED, before the One Hundred Years' War. "Is… was this journal his?"

"Yes."

Selena set the book down on the desk with her prosthetic display and flipped it open, hunting through the pages as much as she could do with one hand. The earlier entries spoke of lessons with Silver, but she noticed that each passage grew darker than the last. She only stopped after stumbling upon the first note leading to Aydin's madness and began reading:

"Twenty-first of Varinth, 1261 ED: Such a lovely creature. Pure and sublime. I saw her again today. After all this time, I still haven't found the courage to tell her how I feel. She rushed past me like she knew and would reject what I wanted to say. My master found me in the courtyard after I missed my lessons again.

"Twenty-third of Varinth: Damn having to slave behind a blacksmith's hammer and working with him!

Vulduin, the man sworn to my beloved. I thought he was my friend once. But if the word were to get out that I've fallen in love with the Emperor's daughter, I could be ruined. Castaway and exiled, and I would never get to see her again.

"Nineteenth of Azniine, 1263 ED: I finally told my master I no longer wished to learn magic. He threatened to send me far away from Alfheim, and I couldn't leave. I want to be with her. I finally found the courage to tell her how I felt, but she didn't tell me she loved me back. I proposed, but she rejected me. I will find a way to woo her.

"Seventh of Arelion, 1267 ED: Today, I confessed my love to her again. It was a horrible mistake. I don't know what prompted me to do it, but I wasn't entirely in my right mind. All I wanted was her. Despite their arranged marriage, she was already in love with Vulduin. I proposed, and she still refused. I came to her with ideas on expanding the Empire, but she didn't want to hear them. Instead, she and her new husband had me dragged out of Rune Citadel in chains. In chains!

"Thirteenth of Goldfire, 1269 ED: I need to focus my duties to the Council. I feel as though everyone here wishes for me to be gone and that they may rise against me. I have locked myself in my studies for weeks in depression. For some unexplained reason, I found myself wanting to grow stronger. I know he is better than I. That was why she chose him over me. She doesn't love me because I am not strong enough. She's always had to look out after me since we were little. Why can I not show her that I am powerful?

"First of Mortas, 1270 ED: At the turn of the new year, Vidar Helios stepped up and talked to the Council about getting rid of me. They cannot exile me, for I created the Council! I gave them power, and now they want to take it away from me—no. I will show them all. I will show her and the rest of the Empire that I will not back down.

"Eleventh of Turnadas, 1270 ED: I approached her again. I wanted to apologize. Lately, I've had visions and dreams. They come and go, and I can't make them go away. All I wanted to do was apologize to Her Imperial Majesty for how I've acted out towards her. The things that I've said—I don't remember any of them, but I will never forget the look on her face. She even dared to call me a demon. I'm not the demon! He's been giving me visions and nightmares—he calls to me, tempting me with promises of power. What have I done to my poor princess? I didn't see her again after that.

"Tenth of Korvas, 1271 ED: I don't know when this will end. I've already lost my position in the Council: Vidar successfully had me exiled. All I see are these weird visions, and I hear a voice in the back of my head mocking me and telling me to give up. What have I done?

"Twenty-second of Astar, 1272 ED: I'm already too far gone to know what to do. My mind is changing. Please, help me regain my sanity—i-it's not me doing this. If I do terrible things, it's not me. Forgive me, Your Majesty. I will always love you.

"(date scribbled out) Red... death... blood... die, die, die... all of them must die."

The word 'die' only filled out the pages following the last entry until the end of the book, and Selena shut the journal with her trembling hand. Perfectly aware of the chilling entries, Silver took it away and hid it from her view within his bookshelf. "Your mother found his journal after his decline and entrusted me to hold onto it. I can't tell you how painful it was to watch him succumb to madness."

She didn't dare to remove her gaze from the shelf that hid the journal, now believing it wouldn't be so simple a task in defeating the Lich. If she used Revelation against Venexus, she assumed Aydin would be destroyed in the process—a prospect that made her hesitant against completing the quest she was so sure would be the right decision. However, Selena was no longer confident after sharing her new thoughts with Silver. "Aydin didn't deserve any of this, and he wasn't given a choice."

"I'm afraid there is nothing left of the man who used to be Aydin Jormungand, my dear. His mind has been gone for so long."

"I don't believe that. He's still there somewhere."

Silver gazed upon her in wonder. "My dear, I love that you always see the good in others." He crossed his arms and tapped his foot while deep in thought. "If Aydin is still there, we will try to help him." Selena wasn't sure if he only gave her that answer in humor or if he was giving her his word to try, even if there was no hope of bringing Aydin back. However, he typically did his best to help whenever aid was needed and never intended to keep the truth from her, as the real culprit, her father, always prevented him from doing so; Selena trusted Silver as much as Thor.

He checked the time on his shiny onyx timepiece before slipping it back into his pocket. "Oh my, it's getting late. I'll be checking on your new hand again in the morning, but you should rest for now. The sooner you get your strength back, the better you'll be." Agreeing, she yawned between goodnights while strutting off to join Thor at his pavilion, but Silver stopped her. "Where are you going?"

"I'm returning outside." Genuinely confused, she squinted at him for the rhetorical question—or so she thought—when Silver looked like a tea kettle about to whistle.

"What kind of a host do you think I am? Do you believe I would let you sleep outside? The only reason why you were even out there, to begin with, was because Thor wouldn't allow me to move you inside."

"But from your design, the pavilion is supposed to keep me warm because of the steam vents." She put her hand on her hip, studying the oddity that he was while he attempted to find a better answer to persuade her to his secret hope; her face burned crimson the more she analyzed his hidden motives.

As if she were expecting the gesture, he reached for her hand and held it. "My dear, please, stay with me instead as it's too cold to camp outside. If you stay with me, at least you'll be warm." He withdrew when realizing his request sounded desperate. "That is, of course, if you wish."

All the blood rushed to her cheeks as she decided to give in to his request. "Well, it would beat sleeping outside."

"Yes, definitely better."

"I wouldn't be imposing on you, would I?"

"No, no, no—you're not imposing at all, especially since I was the one who offered. Now you must accept." He smiled and winked before beckoning her to follow him back down the stairs. Endeavoring to convince herself the assumed hidden meaning behind his invitation wasn't what she thought, her embarrassment radiated upon her face when realizing he intended for her to share his bed.

Together, they trekked back through the august apartment and to the end of the corridor where Silver opened the third and final room door. Not able to brace herself from the sudden rush of steam brushing against her face from a waterfall pouring into a pool on the room's right, she was careful to walk over the fur rugs draped over the polished, stone floors. The wide-open, rectangular window led to a small balcony, bringing in the northern lights burning across the heavens—pillows and thick comforters piled within a much smaller gilt-painted pavilion built similarly to Thor's replaced a traditional style bed. The frigid air didn't bother her; she felt wholly toasty from her dragonscale dress and the waterfall's stream.

"I bet not even Rune Citadel had a view like this." Selena rushed over to the balcony to better look at the sky —a stunning tableau of purple and blue lights dancing together in perfect harmony among the diamond-adorned cosmic nether—a scene she could only capture when she and Thor flew together.

Silver came up behind her and put a hand on her back. "It's quite amazing, isn't it?"

"It's breathtaking. You're so lucky to have all this room to yourself, to enjoy a beautiful view like this."

Silver's grin stretched across his face. "May I get you anything? Perhaps something to drink or eat? You haven't had much since I made you tea."

"I am a little hungry, but not to worry. I can get it myself."

Before she could so much as turn around, Silver stopped her. "Nonsense—allow me."

"But you've already done enough for me. I don't want to become a burden."

"Please, don't fret; it's my pleasure. I implore you to make yourself at home. I'll be back momentarily." Silver dashed out before she could argue and closed the door for her privacy.

Feeling a little odd at first being alone in his apartment, eventually, she overcame her awkwardness. Not knowing how long ago Silver assisted with her hygiene care, she decided to wash before he returned: it would take him some time to cook up a meal. She removed her charcoal grey scarf of unicorn hair and enchanted spider silk and folded it over the stacked stone ledge leading to the bath—a bowl of different scented soaps on top of folded towels waited for the next bather.

She began to undress while still keeping an eye on the door, as, unfortunately, there was no lock, so she would have to stay on alert to cover herself if he happened to walk in on her. Thinking it strange that he would have no locks, Selena realized there was no need; Silver's tower remained perfectly safe in seclusion on top of Heaven's Tear. Along with a giant dragon living above, the location and added security would be more than enough to deter murderers and bandits.

Once she folded her dress, gloves, and necklace near her scarf, when it was time to remove her bandages, Selena was reluctant, fearing what awaited her underneath the tourniquet. Her right hand shook as she unwrapped her arm in anticipation of the unexpected. It didn't hurt anymore, but she suffered from a phantom limb—she could still feel her hand and fingers and instinctively try to flex or move, only to be reminded of the nightmare.

Her eyes froze as the bandages fell to reveal a rounded point where her wrist used to be. The wound healed, but the area was scarred to Oblivion and back. The fight with Medusa continued replaying in the back of her mind; her back throbbed and ached just from memory alone, and she convulsed as the sudden pain surged up her spine and down her chest. Snatching and using a towel to muffle her screams, she leaned against the edge of the bath to keep herself steady as her body jerked and twitched, muscles contracting and trembling; it was as if someone placed a heated sword flat against her skin and melted through flesh.

The pain faded as quickly as it came, and her body went limp against the stone cistern. Selena licked her lips when she felt relief and tucked her arm to her side, steadying herself while gaining the feeling back in her rubber legs. After reaffirming her ability to stand, she stuck her foot in the pool, ensuring it wasn't too hot. When satisfied after treading through knee-deep water, she submerged herself underneath the warm and refreshing falls pouring from the trickling source hidden within the mountainside—while a drain at the pool's end recycled the waste. She poured a soap bottle through her hair and lathered on her skin, relaxed by the intoxicating and enticing scent.

Before she could thoroughly rinse off, her heart stopped when she heard footsteps, and the door swung open. Silver came in with a platter of different foods, but he hadn't looked up yet; she snatched her towel. "I made roasted rabbit. I hope you like it with bread and cheese—" He finally looked up to see her completely unclothed, frozen, and both of their faces burned in embarrassment. "Oh my. Is this a bad time?" As he whistled to himself, he turned around to face the door while she rushed to gather her clothes and began dressing with wet skin as fast as she could. "I am terribly sorry. I should have knocked first to make sure you were decent." However, through his shame and gleaming red face, she noticed how he couldn't stop smiling.

After confirming she was now garbed, Silver— with one hand—brought the platter topped with cooked rabbit served over roasted potatoes and mushrooms with bread and cheese and a bottle of red wine with clear crystal cups to a low bedside table near his pavilion bed.

The air settled, and, after he assisted in re-bandaging her severed arm, the two lightheartedly ate and indulged in conversation. Silver spent hours telling her stories of his adventures across the world and accomplishments throughout the years; she laughed at his bragging about being the first to introduce magic to

Armageddon after learning from the dragons but knew his words embellished the truth. He listed the names of his more famous works that cataloged the different dragon species he discovered and recipes for common concoctions to treat and cure most known diseases.

When Selena thought about Marceline, Gundisalvus' daughter, she inquired about her illness, to which Silver confirmed she died from consumption, or as he recently named it, tuberculosis: an infectious disease affecting the lungs. Unfortunately, his remedy developed too late to save her, as it usually was for his occupation, but often the sacrifices contributed to the betterment of all. "Out of all the forms of magic currently in existence, I fancy the art of alchemy."

She smiled at his infectious enthusiasm, and after setting down her wineglass, she leaned against his arms, and the two fell back into the pillows, looking at the colorful ceiling in silence. "You're much more accomplished than I could ever imagine."

"Then imagine instead what we could achieve together." Silver sat up and held her close to his chest with his right arm, taking her only hand to kiss her knuckle. She smiled through her burning cheeks, but her skin shivered when her fingertips and palm brushed against his lips. "I believe you've bewitched me, in both body and soul, my dear, as my love for you grows so strong that I can't stand it any longer. These last few months have been nothing but torment since our engagement." He paused and met her single-teared gaze as it rolled off her cheek and plucked a single white rose from a plume of smoke to give her. She took his offer, its lovely fragrance captivating. A smile creased her lips as she recalled her past birthday: he gave her the same gift. "I burn for you, brighter than the sun blazing in the sky. I love you, and I never wish to be parted from you again."

She looked at him but couldn't say a word; Silver anxiously waited for her reply, and he flinched when she set the rose down and leaned in to kiss him, her hand gracing his cheek. "Then we'll go up in flames together. I love you, too, and I will never part from you again. I'm bound to you in both body and soul; I am yours, and you are mine, now and forever."

Silver's gentle hand brushed against her face, and the two leaned in for another kiss as she closed her eyes and deepened it; she guided his hand to her chest and melted within his touch as he wrapped both arms around her. Her hand found its way behind his neck and pulled him on top as the two collapsed into the sea of pillows.

Her heart was about to burst as he kissed her repeatedly, each deep and passionate before his hands dropped to her waist and slipped off her dress; she shivered as his fingertips brushed against her bare skin and explored her body. She had never experienced such enchanting and riveting passion as the two were caught in the mass of pillows and blankets, their bodies pressed close, the touch of his skin and warm breath upon her neck making her quiver. Whispering how much he loved her, the two wrapped themselves in a passionate and intimate embrace.

CHAPTER 7: UNBENT AND UNBROKEN

Her eyes fluttered open, and she awoke before the sun did, feeling well-rested and exhilarated. When she looked around the pillow mound stacked within a small pavilion similar to Thor's, at first, she neither recognized her whereabouts nor had any memory of the evening prior—it seemed like a dream. Yet when she looked down, she shuffled through the blankets to cover her naked body.

"Good morning, my dear." Amused by her bewilderment, Silver sat cross-legged in a chair near the archway with an open book in his lap that he snapped closed and set aside. "Did you sleep well?" Selena bit her bottom lip and tightened her grip on her safety blanket as he came over to sit beside her and laughed. "You don't need to hide from me."

"Have you been watching me the entire evening?"

"What? Oh, no." Silver reached over and grabbed the tome he was reading. "I left after you fell asleep to work on your new hand. I returned from the laboratory a few minutes ago." He squinted at her with a curious brow. "Do you believe me to be a creep?"

"Of course not. I just—" Before Selena could brace herself, Silver tickled her back and arms. Her laughs echoed in the bedroom as she pushed him away, but Silver stopped and rushed in to kiss her when he saw an opening. Instead of fighting it, she pulled him down into the pile as the two locked in a tight full-body embrace. She broke away but held her hand to his lips to stop him from kissing her again. "If we continue, you know what will happen."

He laughed. "And you still wish to stop?"

"But you still have work to do on your project, remember?"

Silver wrapped his arms around her and rested his head on hers. "Must I? I would rather stay here in bed with you and make love to you all day." He laughed and kissed the top of her nose when he noticed the furrow in her brow. "I know. I was teasing."

"No, you're not."

"You're right. I'm not, but I'm not the one who's naked right now." Her face turned red as she pushed him back before he could rip the blanket away and scurried to her feet with her clothes ready. Even as she was getting dressed, she could still hear Silver laugh at her.

After finally donning her full attire, the two shared morning tea and breakfast of fried eggs with tomatoes and mushrooms served on top, sizzling bacon and buttered toast on the side when Selena voiced her concern regarding Thor outgrowing his harness. Silver agreed to help her resize the leather, but she couldn't help but blush every time she met his gaze between tea sips, even in the middle of casual conversation.

It didn't help whenever Thor kept snickering at her silliness and tugging at their mental link. **I know what happened last night.**

Seriously?

Yes, seriously.

I need you to leave that be. That's between Silver and me.

I will do as I please.

Selena was about to argue with him but noticed that his behavior seemed slightly off; his odd mannerisms made her face burn when she realized why. *You have no right to judge me after the times you and Ebony were intimate.*

Oh? I never said I was judging you.

Good. The pair settled their differences on spending their evening as she took another bite of her bacon. Still, Selena couldn't help but be happy that Thor found a mate, but she never imagined it to be Silver's sister, of all people, or dragons in this case.

"Are you all right?"

It took Silver's voice for her to realize that she stared into space, and she forced herself to snap out of her trance. "Yes, I'm fine."

Silver set his tea down and gave her an inquiring eye. "Was Thor giving you a hard time? I can usually tell whenever you two are talking." Twisting her fork into the yolk of her eggs, she went over Thor's behavior since he and Ebony grew close throughout the previous night. The news didn't surprise Silver, as he shrugged and took another bite of his toast. "Honestly, that's her business. If Thor's happy, I'd say good for them."

While waiting for his project to finish over the following week, Silver assisted Selena in resizing Thor's harness after taking his new measurements. In a much-improved mood, Rahim agreed to help and moved the provisions tied to the saddle, such as blankets and nonperishables, away from their workspace. The leatherworking task took most of the day only because they waited for Thor to return from his flight with Ebony so he could try it on and ensure it fitted properly. Ebony kept a reasonable distance away from the tower, looking like a black sliver in the sky.

The new harness was equipped to carry a large crew of about a hundred and fifty, though Selena knew Thor could ferry more if he wanted. After they finished tying the last straps, Thor stood up and shook his body like a wet dog after a bath, and to both Selena's and Silver's satisfaction, the improved saddle held, and Thor assured them he was more than comfortable. As a small added detail and at Thor's request, Silver used his skills in alchemy to change the gem shining from his front leather buckle, imbuing the stone in a flicker of yellow energy. In seconds, the dazzling ruby transformed into a brilliant sapphire casting azure specs from the sparkling setting sun.

Selena smiled when Thor inspected his new gear. *It's beautiful, but why did you want a sapphire instead of a ruby?*

It's for you. I wanted my new gem to always remind me of you. Selena was confused, but Thor explained, **When you're a dragon, your scales are blue, and I want to carry this shimmering testament.**

His beautiful words made her think of the massive ruby emblazoned upon her chest in her dragon form, and Selena realized it was the same color as Thor's scales. Much like the ruby pommel from Dragonheart, she always carried a reminder of him wherever she went.

After propping the improved harness against the pavilion's marble column, Silver rushed back to check on the new hand, followed by Selena and Rahim. Thor rejoined Ebony in the sky, and the two vanished through the pink and purple clouds wafting through the twilight sky.

Since he was much more talkative in the days following, Selena had plenty of time to speak with Rahim and Thor about the plan to defeat the Lich. However,

Thor was absent-minded for most of it. He would join in on small bits of their conversation but would go silent for long periods; she assumed he was spending time with Ebony, so she left him alone.

As tempted as she was to ask Rahim why he lashed out, she didn't want to dampen his good spirits and ultimately decided it was best to wait until he felt ready to bring up the subject himself. Instead, the two sat together in the confines of Silver's laboratory, waiting for him to finish tweaking his project. His jaw almost dropped to the floor when Selena mentioned her plan to use Revelation and defeat the Dark Master. "Do you believe that Revelation will work?"

"It's a soul eater that can trap any soul, so yes. I believe so."

"Wicked. I still can't believe that your beloved had this weapon the whole time."

Selena rolled her eyes. "You can't tell everyone, 'I have Death's weapon.' That's not how it works."

Rahim waved his hand in her face as if to shoo her away. "Oh, rubbish. We'll swing this thing at the Lich, and ta-da! No more bad guy and no more war." His smile disappeared. "Maybe we can rescue Niamh if we can stop the necromancer."

"I hope so too, and save Azrael and Doragon."

"Aye, and the Mythic Flight eggs."

And Aydin.

Her stomach tightened into knots when she recalled Aydin's journal, and she wondered if she could save him. Selena twirled the pocket watch in her fingers, yet to show Rahim its true nature, but she figured it was best to wait on that for the time being. He knew Revelation was within her possession, but she didn't specify where it was. Rahim, of course, asked her if he could see it, but he understood when she explained it was best to leave Death's weapon be. The Divines always hid their artifacts from mortals—even if only a god could wield them—for a reason, including Ragnarok. Selena knew that it was for the best that she destroyed the ebony blade; she could only speculate that the sword returned to Xyaxon upon its physical destruction, as he never clarified what happened to it.

"It's finished." Selena hopped to her feet and rushed past Rahim to the hand display that Silver had already unhooked from the dangling wires. The device pulsated and hummed with Aether energy like it was alive.

"Whoa." Rahim pressed his face close, but Silver pushed him back and held it out for Selena to get a good look. She glared at her still bandaged arm before reaching out to touch the metal hand, and much to her surprise, it was as warm as her body temperature. Silver already had a chair pulled up by his work desk and asked her to sit; Selena gulped, but she sat down, fearing that Silver was about to start surgery. He explained that, shortly, he would unwind her tourniquet and mark specific points on her skin before the procedure.

During his briefing, Selena reiterated the plan to Thor, but he remained absent-minded. *Are you listening to me?*

I'm still here, and I'm paying attention.

Then what did I just say? When Thor didn't answer, Selena felt her chest swell in pain. *Forget it.*

What's the matter with you?

I'm upset because you seem not to care.

That's not true.

Her eyes shimmered. *I thought it was lovely when you told me about the new sapphire, but your behavior flipped. You've been ignoring me ever since you and Ebony have been together. I truly understand, but don't shut me out when I need you.*

Bullocks. No, I haven't. Selena turned a deaf ear to Thor when he explained his reasoning; she didn't want to hear his excuses.

"Do you understand, Selena?" She huffed when Silver called for her attention and nodded, but he remained unconvinced that she was listening.

"How long do you reckon she'll be in surgery?" Rahim interrupted.

Silver didn't tear his gaze away as she hung her head and sulked. "Maybe six hours, perhaps more. I will have to put her under anesthesia while I work, and then she will need to rest for at least a few days once it's all over." Selena sunk even further into her chair and drew her legs up to her chest.

Rahim squinted at him. "Since when did you become a doctor?"

Silver waved a hand at him as if he were shooing away a pest. "I'm a demigod; I can do anything." When Rahim groaned at his smugness, Silver rolled his eyes. "Seriously, I *can* do anything. I've learned different trades over the years, including being a doctor. I may not be licensed, but I've performed many different medical procedures." The look on Rahim's face was priceless to Silver. "Oh, take care—I am licensed."

Selena didn't pay attention and was trapped in a daze when he showed Rahim all of his certifications in one of his desk drawers, nor did she look up when Silver finally escorted Rahim out of the room. He wished her luck as he walked away, but she withdrew to her somber silence, and Silver closed and locked the door. "Did you want to talk about anything?"

Selena rested her chin on top of her knees. "I'm fine."

"No, you're not. You've been looking down since I said the hand is finished. Is it because of Thor?" She hated that Silver knew what she was feeling and why but was grateful and relieved he could read her actions without her needing to convey them directly. Her tears betrayed her, and she wiped them away before Silver could see, but it was too late. He set the mechanical hand down on the table and knelt beside her. "I don't think Thor meant anything by his absence. He's probably learning how to make time for you and Ebony." He touched her forehead and brushed her hair back. "Remember when I first asked you to marry me? That must have been awful for him, and he most likely didn't know how to handle it."

Selena turned her head away. "You're right, but I am happy for him. I just don't want him to ignore me when I need him. This surgery is mortifying." She nodded to her bandaged arm as more tears trickled down her face. "I don't think he understands what I must go through, and I'm scared."

"What are you afraid of?"

Her face grew glossy, and soon she wouldn't be able to hold herself back from bursting anymore. "That it's not going to work. I'm scared that I won't wake up when I go under for surgery. I'm afraid of dealing with the pain and won't know what to do. I...." Selena's voice trailed off.

Silver stood up and cradled her into his chest while whispering, "Shhh...." As much as she trusted him, she was still frightened and didn't know if she would ever wake up again.

When she finished venting, and while he took his time to get her operating table ready, she finally opened her thoughts to Thor, only to receive a flood of questions and emotions built up during their brief separation. Thor sounded ashamed, as his voice was all but a low rumble Selena often heard him make from the back of his throat.

As much as she didn't want to hurt him, he had to understand the gravity of his mistake.

I overheard you two.

And? Selena still felt sour.

I'm sorry. I didn't realize how terrifying this is for you, and I should have listened.

Yes, you should have.

Don't make this any more difficult than it already is. I'm usually too proud to admit when I'm wrong.

Selena wrapped her arms around her legs and buried her face into her thighs. *You're usually never wrong.*

Be that as it may, Silver is right. I must figure out how to balance my time with you and Ebony.

I needed you to be there for me while I was going through this. You didn't seem interested in what was happening at all.

Again, I am sorry. What more can I do?

Please don't do that again. I need you here.

My dearest one, I'm here now.

Selena swallowed hard. *I soon won't be.*

You will wake up again. Silver and I helped you before, and we will do it again if we must. Selena didn't answer, but Thor followed up with, **Come outside and fly with me like we used to.**

Selena knew it was reckless to ignore a dragon's demands, even if it meant flying, though she was grateful that Thor wanted to spend time with her. She kept eyeballing Silver while he worked, but after enduring Thor's never-ending proposition, she finally agreed to meet him by the pavilion, only after receiving clearance from Silver. "Please, return soon."

Trudging outside with a sour stomach, she didn't intend to admit she wished to be with Thor. As soon as she stepped foot outside the tower, she was greeted by Thor's sun-blazing eye peering over her. His blood-red diamond-encrusted snout nudged her intact arm, and Thor began chittering in glee. **You've kept me waiting long enough.**

Selena reached up and hung her good arm over his tree-trunk neck. *I'm surprised you're not with Ebony.*

Who says I wasn't? Thor snaked his head around her body and pointed his snout skyward.

A black dragon as dark and mysterious as the void blasted through the plume of pink and orange clouds radiating from the sunset. True to her name, her silky smooth onyx scales glistened with iridescent radiance. It looked like a coat of oil was applied to her hide; fins flared from the side of her regal-looking face, brushing against the rushing wind. Two long, tentacle whiskers flowed from the edge of her snout and danced wildly about her. Her wings unfurled like a lady's fan, only for the glowing sun to glitter through the obsidian membranes dabbed in specs of amethyst and amber. Each beat made the air scream from her incredible velocity; Ebony flew away as quickly as she came, vanishing through the fluffy sky pillows.

Selena felt the thorn of envy piercing her side, but Thor swung his body around her. **There is no reason to be jealous, my dear.** When he noticed the look on her face, he inched his head closer, and his forked tongue danced through his clamped serrated fangs, brushing against her cheek.

I'm not jealous. Selena wasn't a good liar; even her inflamed cheeks betrayed her defensive stance.

Thor tapped his ivory claws against the stone pathway, waiting for a confession. Selena bit her lip before spinning around on her toes, ignoring the growing anticipation echoing from every click he made. **I know you.**

Fine. I admit it. Are you happy now? When he didn't reply, Selena continued: *I'm glad for you two, honestly. But—*

But you still feel the same way I did about you and Silver, Thor finished for her.

The lingering silence grew more uncomfortable with each second Selena wasted in not answering. Eventually, she muttered, *Yes.*

My dear, I will never leave you, nor will you ever leave me. We are a part of each other, always. Thor pointed his snout towards the harness still propped against the marble column, and Selena smiled when she caught the gleam from the new sapphire. She fetched the newly mended saddle as he lowered his body to the ground.

It was complicated strapping his harness with one hand, but Thor helped by pinning down the buckles with his claws to keep the leather from shifting. After tugging at the straps to ensure they would hold and were comfortable enough, Thor lowered his gem-scaled-adorned arm, and Selena clambered aboard his saddle. When Ebony made another pass over Heaven's Tear, Thor raised his wings and climbed towards the throat of the world.

Thor and Ebony soared higher and swirled through squall spires as the cold mist kissed Selena's cheek. She held on as best as she could with one hand; the arctic winds attempted to cut through her skin, but she was warm from the dress and Thor's radiating body heat. As the dragons flew above the clouds, Selena enjoyed watching the line where the earth met the divine cosmos. The golden sun made its descent, and the moon and stars weaved in the nether tapestry. Different shades of blue and green trailed across in a burning display like oil paints spilling across a canvas; the northern lights looked close enough to be within her reach.

I want to stay up here forever.

I know your envy in wanting your wings. This burning desire runs deep in your veins, as it does mine. We will fly across the heavens when you master your powers, and you and I will conquer the sky. Our Divine fire will reign.

Thor's maw opened wide to unleash a mighty roar, making the world tremble beneath them. Together, the dragons drifted with the wind in heavenly solace. It wasn't until the moon vanished from the world that Thor and Ebony decided to return.

Silver waited patiently near the pavilion while the dragons landed beside the mountain's edge, but Selena noticed his slight indifference to Ebony; he ignored her entirely and didn't attempt to greet her. Likewise, Ebony kept her back turned to her brother as she nuzzled Thor before leaping a whole body's length upward with one sweep and disappearing over the yielding trees.

When Silver assisted Selena in dismounting and unbuckling the harness, she asked him about the sudden hostility towards one another. "I don't know what you mean." Judging from his harsh reply, she didn't think it appropriate to press the subject further; instead, she followed Silver inside after returning the saddle to its usual spot.

Thor lowered his head to the ground and maintained eye contact until he was all but a crimson slice through the door's opening, and it fully closed. Even as Silver and Selena made their way back to the surgery-prepped laboratory, he continued reassuring, **I won't leave you.**

Rahim immediately dashed over to the two, but Silver shook his head and pointed for him to leave before returning to the sterilized study.

"There we are." Silver re-sanitized all his equipment and washed his hands while Selena undressed to cover herself with a thin sheet. Her hand shook as she tried to tie her hair up in a loose bun while convincing herself she was only going to sleep and would wake up with a new hand. She hoped this would work but carried no doubts against her surgeon; Silver was a genius.

Even as she got ready, Thor's words continued to warm her cold thoughts. **You're in good hands.**

I know.

You're unbent and unbroken. You are unstoppable.

Even as she lay on the operating table and donned the mask—attached to a tube connected to a strange apparatus—Silver gave her, she felt her heart trapped in her throat; her beats sounded like a ticking clock. Air pumped through into her nostrils from the device, and as she inhaled the gas, Thor kept talking to her until she ultimately passed out. It was almost like an induced death, faster than falling asleep.

Her eyes flickered open before realizing it, and Silver had already finished. Her arm was sore; it burned like fire as if her limb had been sliced off by Medusa again. She felt dazed and confused, and her blood ran ice-cold. Silver stood over her and held his hand to her forehead after disposing of his operating gown covered in blood and his plastic gloves. Her eyelids felt heavy. "I-is the surgery over?"

Silver smiled and offered her a blanket. She flinched at the touch of metal on skin, and only when she looked down did she see her newly attached hand. After receiving his nod of confirmation, Selena focused on moving her index finger; a burst of energy surged through her arm towards the device. Heart racing, she then worked on moving the rest of her fingers, and much to her delight, it functioned as well as flesh and bone. It worked.

Silver was satisfied with his work after inspecting the hand to ensure all was in order. "Everything went very well, but you will need to rest for a few days. I told Rahim of the news, and he will be able to see you tomorrow."

Selena wanted to sit up, but her muscles melted into the bed. It seemed unreal that the entire day had passed while trapped in a dreamless sleep. Despite Silver insisting on a good meal, she couldn't and slept for the remainder of the late day and evening, her foggy dreams echoing Thor's words as he kept talking to her during recovery.

Over the next few days, she moved her arm around and extended her fingers to grow used to the strange cold sensation flowing through her arm—oh, how great it was to have two hands again. With the new appendage tapping into her Aether energy, as Silver promised would happen, she could also feel what she touched. It would still take some time for her to adjust to the constant feeling of metal-infused flesh, but she was thankful for what Silver did.

He had Selena practice reaching out and grabbing small objects to get more familiar; all was working correctly, and he was pleased to see there were no issues and that she had grown accustomed to how it felt. "I don't know if I've already told you this, but you are amazing, Genesis Altessa. Is there anything that you can't do?"

Silver grinned. "You can stand to mention it more and not that I'm aware of."

With Silver's clearance, Rahim was finally able to visit and see how Selena was doing. He was in complete awe when he watched her operate it. "I'll even admit, Silver, you've outdone yourself." His smug expression glowed from Rahim's compliment.

Later that evening, Silver graciously prepared roasted pork with seasoned boiled potatoes and vegetables drizzled in brown gravy made from the pork's leftover juices for dinner. She welcomed their pleasant company and the delicious dishes. Among their many topics of conversation, Silver believed that she should be well enough to resume her usual routine but advised waiting for at least one more day before making their trip to Mortemholdt.

"It's not like I'm going to be doing anything strenuous." She was itching to leave. The longer they sat and waited, the worse off her father would be. "Besides, I can always rest on the flight there."

Though Silver still disagreed, Rahim wiped his mouth with his napkin and interjected. "Selena is right. I think she'll be fine, and besides, I can always help her. It's not like we're going to be fighting anybody."

"Let's hope we don't have to, but I don't want her pushing herself." Silver hissed at Rahim and nodded at Selena's new hand.

Selena dropped her knife and fork against her plate with their bickering, and the clank caught their attention. "It's insulting to talk about someone in front of them. I'm right here, and you two can speak to me directly." Ignoring their ashamed faces, she rubbed her new hand, the metal pressed and sewn into skin still alien to the touch. "I don't need either of you two helping me. If I need to rest, I will have plenty of time to do so on the way to Mortemholdt."

"You should rest here."

"I want to go, and you can't stop me."

Silver closed his eyes as he dropped his utensils, metal clattering against the porcelain plates, and his chest swelled. She could tell he was getting angry, but she didn't care and was ready to go, either with or without Silver's help. "You're right, my dear. I can't stop you. I...." Silver held his tongue and sighed as his lower lip quivered but eventually gave her a firm, jerky nod.

This confirmation was as much acknowledgment as she would receive from him, and to Selena, it was enough; she nodded and declared, "We'll leave in the morning."

After she squashed all future arguments about their hasty plans, Rahim took his leave after supper and tea to prepare for the evening. On the other hand, Selena marched towards Thor's pavilion despite Silver's objections to fetch her sword still propped against the marble columns. Thor and Ebony were gone, probably out hunting; she wished to see him soon, hoping to show him her new prosthetic but settled on the idea that it could wait until morning. Eventually, Silver followed to ensure that she wouldn't overexert herself or the device but kept his distance so she could have her space.

Regardless of how simple their plan was, she needed to be ready, and through practicing swinging her blade at a tree with her new limb, she was pleased to see her untarnished skills; touching the cold metal made her hand feel sensitive, like an icy treat touching the bottom of her teeth.

Can you hear me, or are you two too busy?

It took Thor a moment, but he responded. **I am here. I'm not too busy to talk to you.**

I'm able to use my sword again.

That's great. Ebony told me earlier how she wanted to practice with you after you felt well enough.

That's fine, but it will have to wait until we get back from Mortemholdt.

She is agreeable to waiting.

Silver watched as she made her last few swings and beckoned her to return inside. While making their way back up the stairs, he bombarded her with questions about how the new hand felt, and other than the minor sensitive inconveniences, she assured him that all was well. Yet, the only detail that she didn't like was that her mark was gone. Like how she felt in the dream, it was strange not having it anymore, as the symbol defined her, and she felt Medusa had stripped it away.

CHAPTER 8: WHISPERS IN THE DARK

Armageddon slept under the burning blue sky. Selena awoke to the northern lights, but she saw that Silver had already packed the supplies needed for the trip. After the two spent the evening together, she fell into sleep's deep torpor. Slightly unnerving that he never slept, Silver dedicated his free time to working on unfinished laboratory projects or reading—she supposed that being an immortal shapeshifter, he didn't need to rest.

Once Silver and Selena gathered the blueprints and supplies to Thor's pavilion, Rahim joined with his luggage slung over his shoulder as the two finished strapping down Thor's harness. Thor ignored the couple as they locked gazes and blushed; instead, he snaked his head down to get another good look at his new sapphire pendant, admiring its gleam. Rahim snickered at Selena when he noticed her odd behavior, but he kept his opinions to himself.

Selena helped Rahim tie down his baggage to the saddle before spinning her head around. *Where's Ebony?*

She left for now, but Ebony will return after our mission. Thor fixed his gaze heavenward and let out a long moan, followed by a plume of smoke fuming from his nostrils.

You miss her already.

Enough with the teasing. Thor snaked his head around to sniff her new hand. **It's about time I got to see it. Your hand reminds me of the old dwarven contraptions.**

Silver did say their technology inspired it.

Incredible. Am I assuming it's working well?

Well enough.

What do you mean?

It still feels strange.

You'll grow used to it, and you finally have two hands again.

Thor stepped down the marble steps from his royal pavilion when everyone was aboard, ready for flight. The sky was still dark, but the faint sun crept over the horizon; the forming black clouds rumbled and swirled in place as they swallowed the rays of sunlight in the distance. Thor spread out his massive wings, tightened his leg muscles, and launched himself in one enormous leap. The sky howled as his wings swept through the fading stars. Selena belonged up here—if only she could freely turn into a dragon and join him in flight; she was envious of Thor. Although it had been a few days since their last flight together, it felt like an eternity.

I know of your envy. What is a dragon that cannot fly? Thor released a steady jet of flame, and Selena only grinned as she embraced the freedom of being so close to the heavens.

Rahim pulled out his spyglass from his pockets and looked at the black clouds brewing. Flashes of lightning cracked the sky in two, and the thunder roared like a flight of dragons. It wasn't raining yet, but Selena knew they would have to take shelter soon, her mood keeping surprisingly calm. Silver, meanwhile, sat cross-legged against the side, and although he looked perfectly relaxed, he would occasionally cast a worried glance. Yet, to his surprise, she wasn't affected by the coming storm.

Rahim dismissed the charcoal sky and breathed in deep. "I can't believe I'm saying this, but I miss flying. I miss the adventures."

Selena shook her head. "I don't know about the adventures. Let's not give the Council a reason to hunt us down."

Silver raised a hand, warranting an interruption. "No, they won't. The best part is that they think you're dead. Now, we don't have to worry about them tracking us down."

That struck a nasty blow for her. "They think I'm dead?"

Rahim and Silver exchanged glances. "Isn't that a good thing? That means we don't have to worry about hiding too much." Rahim punched into his palm. "We can sneak around the Empire and plan a counter-attack. Those tossers won't know what hit them."

Thor chittered in agreement. **Rahim is right; we'll be safe for now.**

I-I dunno.

We'll be able to save your father undetected. Once we return to Heaven's Tear, we'll have plenty of time to train with Ulrich.

She sighed, unable to ignore this advantageous approach. *That's true.*

Selena reiterated Thor's thoughts audibly, and Silver grinned. "Yes, indeed. Soon, you'll be able to crumble mountains with the snap of your fingers." He demonstrated the gesture. Feeling defeated and undone, she tightened her grip around the leather reins, her knuckle turning white. Unsure if she approved of hiding behind her dead alias, the more she thought about it, the more gratifying the idea of a future counter-attack.

The lightning and thunder didn't let up, but she remained at peace. Silver, on the other hand, kept studying her behavior. "I'm surprised at you. Are you sure you're feeling all right?"

"What do you mean?"

"You're not afraid. I'm delighted to see that, but the storm isn't bothering you."

"Oh. Azrael helped me." Selena wasn't sure what to say; it wasn't until she and her friends made it to Nuvak on their mission from the Council that Azrael helped her cope. Since he placed the spell on her, it seemed as though the soothing enchantment rewired her mind to block out the surrounding storm.

"I see." Silver closed his eyes, but he smiled. "I'm glad that you're doing well." If Selena didn't know any better, she could have sworn that Silver was jealous. She wasn't sure how to approach the subject without triggering his emotions. After a few moments, however, she didn't have to worry about bringing it up. "How did Azrael help you overcome your fear of thunder and lightning?" When she recounted the tale, all Silver could say was, "Oh."

"It was so that I could continue with our mission. Nothing more."

Silver raised a brow in confusion. "Do you think I'm mad at you?"

"You sounded as if you were."

"Nonsense. My dear, I promise I'm not. That would be ridiculous of me to be." Silver scooted closer and wrapped his arm around her. "I'm glad to see that the storm no longer bothers you."

"But I assume you're a little jealous of Azrael. Am I right?"

Silver bit his cheeks. "I won't lie. I am a little."

"Even though you have no reason to be?"

"Even then." Silver leaned in and gave her a peck on the cheek, giving Rahim an excuse to poke fun at him behind his back while smiling disgustingly and sticking out his tongue. Selena kept mouthing for him to stop, but Rahim laughed.

A few days had passed without disruption from the brewing storm, but the clouds continued swirling above. While Selena maintained their course, Silver and Rahim discussed the blueprints and their strategy again. She looked over her shoulder to better hear what was said as they kept their conversation private, and she wasn't involved; instead, she found an opportunity to jest. "What are you two muttering on about over there?"

Silver shoved the blueprints behind a bag. "Only the usual, my dear."

"The usual? Care to explain?"

"He means the usual of him being a horse's arse." Rahim flinched when Silver slugged his shoulder.

Selena's eyes bounced between the two before facing forward again. *Why won't they let me be part of their plans? I can still fight.*

I believe they're cautious after what happened to you in Snowhaven.

Do they see me as being incapable of protecting myself? Am I that helpless?

Of course not. He's undoubtedly only going along with Silver's nonsense. You understand how Silver is, and now he has Rahim doing the same thing.

What about you? Are you feeling the same way?

Thor snorted and bristled. **I'm trying not to be.**

Selena caught Silver and Rahim hunched over the outlines, but she withheld further questions, for they wouldn't answer her. Instead, she rested, resolving that, eventually, she would force the truth out of them, or at least Silver—he always had a hard time keeping a secret. Selena looked up at the sky, her eyes fixating on how the clouds moved with haste and purpose, with the sunlight cracking through the monochromatic clouds to distract herself. While she dozed off, she was kissed by a drizzle, and within moments, the drops turned to frozen daggers.

Silver joined her side and helped direct Thor to take refuge near a small set of mountains around the edge of the White Plains. "We'll rest here before pressing forward."

Thor's smoldering pupiled-slits fixated on a cavern overlooking a cliff, and with extreme care and caution, he landed beside the entrance. He unfurled his wings and shook the water droplets off his hide before tucking them back to his sides. The trio dismounted, and Rahim took it upon himself to make a small campfire while Thor circled Silver and Selena, wrapping his body around the two in a protective embrace.

"Here, you may wear my jacket if you wish." Silver helped her dress in his white frock coat lined with dragon scales from an Imperial Pearlscale, but his hands withdrew. She was surprised by him apologizing profusely for accidentally touching her chest, not realizing what had happened.

Selena's face burned, but she flashed him a smile. "It's okay. D-don't worry about it."

Rahim, however, exploded as he threw in the last of the sticks to feed the licking flames. "What in Oblivion do you think you're doing? Keep your bloody hands off her."

An evil sneer played on Silver's lips as he reached behind her and grabbed her chest on purpose. "Do you mean like this?"

Selena, face fuming, froze in her spot while Rahim rushed over and backhanded him away. The force of the blow knocked Silver to the ground, and his nose started bleeding. "I-I deserved that."

"Don't touch her like that, you pervert."

On the other hand, Selena snapped the jacket closed to hide her chest. "Rahim, that's enough."

"Don't tell me that you're fine with that *deviant* touching you like that."

"Well, er, yes, I am." Rahim's mouth opened wide, and his eye twitched. "If I weren't, I would have said something myself. I know he respects that."

"But—"

"That's enough. It's my call, not yours."

After wiping away the last bit of blood, Silver took his place beside her and wrapped one arm over her shoulder, reaching around and squeezing her left breast. "Like what she said: if she isn't fine with it, she'll be the one to tell me."

Before Rahim could deck him again, Selena elbowed him hard in the side. "No more of that in the open. I think that's quite enough." Her voice was stern and direct, but her face was still flustered with embarrassment.

Silver held his side and heaved over. "Fair enough, my dear."

Meanwhile, Thor watched the scene unfold while swishing his tail around in amusement. When Selena met his gaze, Thor's scaly lips folded into a sneer, and her face burned when she realized he was laughing at her. **I don't believe those two will ever stop once you and Silver are married.**

I have a feeling you're right.

The four spent the evening hiding in the cave until the morning when the rain stopped, and the howling winds ceased. Yet the clouds continued billowing overhead, thunder rumbling and echoing across

Armageddon. Thor made up lost time by flying non-stop throughout the following three days. Selena encouraged him to feed, not doubting his endurance, but he assured her he was satiated.

My last hunt was more than enough to sustain me for a week. However, to ease her concerns, Thor maintained a steady pace through slow and steady wing beats that wouldn't tire him.

For entertainment, Selena watched Silver and Rahim argue with each other like they did when they first met, only this time to see who was more protective. Selena wasn't sure if she should feel annoyed or amused. Rahim slammed his pack down and doubled his arms over his chest. "I still didn't think that was appropriate."

"It is none of your business what my wife and I do."

"She's not your wife."

"She will be soon."

"That doesn't mean you should act a creepy little perv." When Rahim saw that this made Silver angry, he began chanting. "You're a dirty old perv; you're a dirty old perv."

"Stop that. I am not—I care about her."

Rahim scoffed. "Honestly, if I were you, I wouldn't want to see her coming on this mission."

Silver pulled out a white glove from his pocket and slapped Rahim's face, initiating a gentleman's duel. "How dare you? Did you think I wanted her to come?" Rahim snarled while rubbing his face, but Silver's face boiled. "Why did you change your mind? You agreed with her while I was the one who originally wanted her to stay."

Rahim grumbled and turned away. "I didn't want to sound like an arse."

Selena was done. "You both are." Both Silver and Rahim's heads refused to turn, but their eyes moved downward. "I can hear you two. Do both of you believe I can't handle this? The next time I hear you two arguing over whether I'm capable in battle, I will throw you both overboard with one hand behind my back. Thor won't need to buck you two off." Rahim's face turned paler than a ghost as he squeaked like a mouse. Silver opened his mouth to object but recoiled when Thor snaked his head around and snarled through braced serrated fangs; even Silver was wise enough not to argue with a Divinity Dragon.

Ignoring their horrified faces, Selena snatched their plans away; Silver and Rahim recoiled from her tenacity, for her intentions were clear, and she would be a part of this. According to the blueprints, the storage closet where the guards kept extra uniforms was near their drop off location; then, it was a matter of finding her father's prison cell.

By the following midday, Selena and her group flew over the Grand Exchange, and she was expecting it to be as lively as during her first visit. Much to their added disappointment, the once blissfully busy string of shops grew dark and damp with boarded up and shattered windows, permanently closed for business. A thick veiled mist shrouded the Exchange, and the trio held their breaths when they saw a row of shadows slowly trekking down the alley. Their steps were heavy and fell like stones dropping, and even from their height, Selena could hear moans and groans. Yet, she couldn't quite put her finger on it, but the residents seemed odd; they marched as a herd from the Black Bog Forest but slowly.

Rahim squinted his eyes and leaned over. "I've never seen anyone act like that before. What do you reckon is going on with them, Silver?"

Silver grabbed his chin and looked at them quizzically, studying their unusual behavior. "Nor have I, and I have no idea. How unusual."

As Thor flew closer without attracting unwarranted attention, Selena was disheartened to see the Black Pub's shattered windows, and the flame that took on different shapes was snuffed out, just like the life of the Grand Exchange. Selena tightened her grip on the saddle's edge as Rahim swiveled around and asked, "Should we go and help them?"

Silver immediately declined. "We continue to Mortemholdt. We'll figure out what's happening here later."

Selena spun in her seat. "They may be in danger. We should help them."

"I promise, in due time."

"But we can't leave them."

Silver lowered his voice. "We can't abandon your father either, and that's our mission right now. Besides, we will need Vulduin's help if these residents are in danger. We will return for them, I swear it."

Selena couldn't tear her eyes away from the ghost town nor from the growing image of what appeared to be a dragon emerging from over the horizon; it launched itself straight for them, and suddenly a shrill like Death's calling boomed in the air. *What is that?*

Thor growled between his clenched fangs, and he picked up the pace. **Darkness and black magic—the demonic abominations are nearby.**

An eerie ring shattered her ears, the chilling whispers in the dark making her skin prickle; it was the same call she heard whenever an evil presence was nearby. When the dragon and its rider drew close, Thor roared; a colossal Nidhoggr around his size carrying a rider with glowing purple eyes flew at them with alarming speed.

Smoke plumed from its oily drenched black hide as glowing crimson eyes pierced from the sockets of its ivory bone mask. The metal-hued clouds couldn't dull the sheen from its razor-like wings slicing through the air, whispering like unsheathing a sword.

Silver and Rahim scooted close and urged her and Thor to keep flying forward while all three prepared their weapons for battle, as the rider would soon be upon them. Thor roared and gained speed towards Lake Peril, but the massive Nidhoggr was faster than he was and nipped at his tail. However, Rahim looked over his shoulder, and his eyes widened when he saw the rider. "Dad?"

Both Silver and Selena wheeled around, but they didn't have time to consider his implications. Thor made a steep dive, and he moved out the way just as the Nidhoggr swept overhead with outstretched sword-like talons, but it missed by a mere breadth. The deadly creature screeched once more before steering itself around and launching towards the group for a second assault. Just as the beast was upon him, Thor reared his head back and spewed forth a torrent of fire as a desperate act to hold the undead dragon back. It only bought them a few extra seconds, but it was enough for him to dodge. Yet, the creature's mask was slightly damaged, but it thrashed wildly, whipping its head back and biting and clawing at Thor's neck in retaliation.

While Rahim stumbled in loading his revolver, Silver jumped out of the harness, shapeshifting into his wing-less dragon form. His sheen-white scales and azure mane greatly contrasted the entanglement of black and red scales as he slithered in between the writhing behemoths, using all his strength to pry the Nidhoggr away from Thor. Fearful that he would be torn to shreds, Selena noted that Silver's snake-like hide was unscathed among the melee of claws and fangs. Yet the Nidhoggr ignored the white serpent dragon; it opened its maw and clamped its fangs into the side of Thor's neck. In between snarls and roars, Thor attacked with a flurry of blows and deep scratches and furrows as he swung his massive tail, thick and heavy like a solid steel rod, towards the entangled beast.

Meanwhile, Selena drew and swung Dragonheart at the creature, focusing every strike of her blade at its exposed jawline, but the Nidhoggr maintained its grip and sank its fangs deeper. The two dragons began spiraling downward; Thor locked within its fangs and talons as he continued clawing at the beast in between cries and roars of anguish. Tormented by his pain, Selena thrust her rose-tinted ivory blade into the side of the creature's neck. Eventually, their conjoined attacks forced the Nidhoggr to release after finally succumbing to her strike.

However, the unrelenting and emotionless rider, whose skin nearly frayed from his neck and hands, drew his weapon. Rahim aimed his gun at the man's hand and fired his first shot, but the rider gave no response to having it blown to bits. Instead, he looked at Rahim and smirked. Tears filled Rahim's eyes as his hands struggled to keep his firearm in place, but Selena whipped out her Force-issued dwarven-made Winclock revolver and fired twice. The two shots launched through the rider's face and shoulder, blasting off rotten flesh, but he still didn't react.

Instead, the stranger ordered his Nidhoggr to leave, and the creature pushed itself away from Thor. The sudden disentanglement forced him to spread out his wings to catch his fall before hitting the earth. He strained at first, but he managed to level himself parallel with the ground before the velocity proved too great. The Nidhoggr and its rider left as quickly as they came, the dark whispers echoing through Thor's and Selena's minds following this mysterious handler; he and his undead companion led the massive horde away from the Grand Exchange.

CHAPTER 9: MORTEMHOLDT

Rahim held his revolver close to his chest, ignoring and turning away as Silver returned to his human guise and inquired about his welfare. When neither Selena nor Silver could make eye contact with the distraught Rahim, they hastened to Thor's neck injury, and through the dragon's swaying, unsteady flight, the two worked together and mended his wounds. However, Rahim's quivering hands couldn't hold the gun anymore, but he made no effort to pick it up as it fell to his feet.

"What's the matter with you?" Selena asked him when she and Silver finished their healing session. Rahim wrinkled his nose and shook his head, but he didn't reply.

Thor stretched out his neck and moved his newly healed muscles. Delighted with their work, he picked up his pace and maintained course towards Mortemholdt. Before the group knew it, Lake Peril was soon well within aerial view. **Thank you. My neck feels much better, but is Rahim okay?**

I dunno. He won't say anything.

Silver actually came over and put a comforting hand on Rahim's shoulder, but he shrugged it off and hurried away. "I heard you say 'dad' earlier. Was he—?" He met Selena's horrified gaze when Rahim didn't move and hung his head. "I'm so sorry. Truly, I am."

"That wasn't him." Rahim's voice was hoarse and hard for the others to hear, shattering like glass. "He couldn't have been my father."

Selena approached Rahim from the side, but he moved further down the saddle and rummaged through his bags, pulling out a scrap of paper before she could inquire further. Only when she inched closer did she realize that it was a photograph of Chaliss with a man by her side; much to her dismay, it was the same stranger they had just fought. Rahim sniffled and turned his back to her before stuffing the picture away. "Before, when you asked me what was wrong, I didn't want to admit that planning to rescue your father made me think of my dad. There, happy?"

Selena's face turned pale. "I'm never happy when you're upset. You've never mentioned a word about your father."

The grim atmosphere made the trio shift uncomfortably in their seats, and Rahim bit his cheeks. "He left my mother right after I was born, so I never knew him. The only thing I have to remember him by are just old pictures. I managed to grab one before we left Helshire to remind myself that I did have a family. Sometimes, he crosses my mind, but it never bothered me—not before now." He couldn't help but shift his gaze towards the fleeting image of the mysterious rider, and his shadow vanished over the horizon. "I didn't want to mention it because it's never been about me."

It was like Rahim had struck her across the face. "You shouldn't think like that. If something ever upsets you, you have every right to bring it up. Please, tell me everything you know about your father."

"There isn't much to say. I barely remember Arawn—my dad. He left my mother, and that was the end of it. Still, I always wished I knew what happened to him, but I never thought he joined the Order."

"Maybe he didn't have a choice."

The two were interrupted when Silver suggested asking Ulrich if there was a way to save Arawn, but Rahim doubted that the Divine would be willing; Selena, however, suspected he didn't want to face the hard truth. Eventually, he sighed and said, "I hope you're right." He finally picked up his gun and holstered it to his belt.

Only when he refused to indulge her curiosity did Selena return to her seat; Rahim kept silent even when Thor gained speed towards Lake Peril. Instead of invoking him any further, she began pestering Thor and rubbed the base of his neck where his wounds were. *How are you feeling?*

He snorted. **I've already told you I'm okay since you and Silver healed me.**

I'm just making sure.

Don't start bugging me because you can't get Rahim to talk.

Selena leaned up against one of his horns. *But you would tell me if something is troubling you, right?*

Of course, I would. When Thor knew his answer didn't satisfy her, he added, **But Rahim isn't like me. I've always confided in you. I can't hide anything from you.**

No, you can't, and nor can I.

Meanwhile, Silver pulled out the blueprints to go over the plans with Rahim once more as a diversion. It seemed to help some, and the distraction lifted his spirits; Selena grinned to see his improved mood.

Thor coasted for another day and a half, allowing the updraft to carry his weary wings. When his throat ached from thirst, Selena summoned water from the clouds and air, creating a massive bubble that Thor chomped through, taking huge gulps from each globule.

Silver offered him his familiar brew: a stamina restoration elixir, but Thor declined. **I am well enough to fly to Mortemholdt.**

Will you be well while waiting for us? I don't believe the prison has quarters to accommodate a dragon your size, my dear.

Thor snorted but only agreed once the floating jail was well within their aerial view; Silver administered his tonic, and Thor licked his chops, pupils dilated to slits, and his wing muscles eased. **I'm ready, my dear.**

The island prison was suspended high over Lake Peril, where the water looked like a black mirror, but, as the name suggested, dangers lurked beneath the dark surface. Nobody knew how deep the lake was, its glossy and eerily calm surface like the void. Writhing in rings around the floating skull-shaped prison was an unnatural mist, hiding Mortemholdt from any passerby; its height made it easy to miss.

Silver explained as they drew close, "No one has ever escaped Mortemholdt, except for Vulduin. Prisoners have tried in the past, but…." Upon reaching the lake's edge, Selena watched as rotting corpses bobbed up and down along the water's surface; the smell of rotting flesh laded the air and made her want to vomit. "The last person released from here was Gundisalvus before his death. Otherwise, you're here for life."

Thor tucked in his wings and shot straight up towards the skull ruins like a freshly fired bullet. His steep climb almost rendered his passengers defenseless against the piercing wind; the three and their bags would have fallen overboard if they weren't buckled and strapped down with belts and carabiners. Selena's eyes watered as the air screamed into her ears, but Thor slowed down and extended his massive wings to slow his flight, and the trio wallowed in relief and finally relaxed.

He brought his three riders to a hidden enclave with a single metal door, the platform hosting two metal docks that Selena assumed were made for ships to make port, but she had never heard of a vessel flying through the sky before—save for those carried by dragons. Rahim's eyes circled the map of Mortemholdt while Silver and Selena dismounted and pointed at their current location, clarifying this was a docking station. "I've heard rumors of sky pirates whose ships fly instead of sail. This area could be where they drop off deliveries and other goods, but I don't know when the next one will be."

Selena's heated glare almost melted the door off its hinges. "Then we must make this quick."

Thor opened his maw and spewed strands of fire and lightning towards the sky. **I'll destroy them myself.**

You're certainly as large as a heavy frigate, but I still wouldn't dare.

Thor warned, **If anything happens, let me know. The Council can't do anything to me if I decide to destroy Mortemholdt.**

No, but they can ambush us, or worse: the Nidhoggr.

No, they won't, and I don't give a damn about the Nidhoggr. I will get to Vidar before he even knows what happened.

As confident as Selena was in Thor's abilities and powers, she knew that Vidar was always prepared. A concealed revolver was belted to her waist, as Dragonheart would be a dead giveaway to their ruse; Rahim matched her caution, as their plans were never guaranteed.

Stay close. I'll let you know when we're ready.

Of course.

As Thor, their only means of escaping this floating isle of death, flew away, Selena's anticipation arose as she wrapped her metallic hand around the door's handle.

As expected, the door was locked. Silver and Rahim stood back from her single smoldering glare, not daring to oppose her involvement. She held out her index finger—a needle of fire erupting from the tip—and carved a large circle around the handle, holding the flame like a curved talon. The metal melted like a hot knife slicing through warm butter; the piece shifted when she finished, and Selena grabbed and pulled it out before swinging the door open, tossing the hunk of metal over the edge, and the three ran inside.

From the schematics, the supply closet wasn't far. After Selena, Silver, and Rahim found their way to the room, they made haste to dress in their disguises before they were seen. As dark as it was, a gas lamp was left behind by one of the guards. Silver lit it, and Selena and Rahim hunted through the shelves containing the helmets and uniforms they needed until finding what was appropriate to their size. Selena's hands fumbled through adjusting her silver buckles and breeches and clasped the center buttons before smoothing out the wrinkles upon the black uniform. Last but not least, to complete the ensemble, she donned a black helm with a flippable visor. "I hope your plan works, Rahim."

Rahim finished his costume, and, aside from his slight advantage of height, the two looked identical within their disguises. "Remember, we just need to lie low until we find your father." The two paused and looked at Silver, who refused to remove his jacket, and Rahim smacked his forehead in frustration. "We're supposed to be undercover."

Through his arrogance and smugness, Silver adjusted his collar. "I like this jacket."

Rahim growled, his eyes blazing from under his helmet. "Argh, we don't have time for this—"

Selena pressed her fingers to her lips when she heard footsteps approaching the door. "Shh." The three pressed their backs against the shelves, praying the guards didn't detect them; the footsteps continued past the closet and faded down the corridor.

After sharing a sigh in relief and when it was safe to do so, Rahim gritted his teeth and pointed a finger in Silver's face. "Okay, fine. Why don't you shapeshift into something useful if you won't wear a disguise?"

Silver shrugged, and, as if to humor Rahim's suggestion, his appearance transformed into a correctional officer; however, his formal captain's jacket remained unchanged, save for the colors to match the proper uniforms. Rahim closed his eyes and mumbled what Selena could interpret as inappropriate under his breath. "This tosser, I swear by the Divines…."

After making final adjustments to their masquerades, the three left the closet one by one in single file. The metal interior trapped the heat and the smell of festering sewage; Mortemholdt was as bright as the gathering gloom of dusk. Selena flinched from the piercing screams of the tormented inmates echoing through the corridors. They eventually reached an open area; the metal corridor with railings circled the prison's interior, with cells lining the walls. The rooms were solid concrete cubes with only one way in and no windows, utterly disorientating by design. Based on her harrowing experiences from Snowhaven, Selena assumed the prisoners had no concept of time, and the confinement alone would make a person forget their name.

She leaned over the railing and saw that they were on the second floor, whereas above them were many more; it was as if Mortemholdt never ended. Rahim walked up to one of the cells and tapped lightly on the door but flinched when a shrilling scream answered his knock. "How will we find your father?"

An idea brightened Selena's thoughts when she heard multiple voices speaking to one another from down the hall. "I can ask one of the guards. Follow me." She gestured for Silver and Rahim to follow as she chased down the voices.

As the three turned a corner, they paused before colliding with a correctional officer amidst the vilest creature whom Selena swore she would kill with her bare hands if she ever saw him again: Ashur Bel. His sleek, crimson hair pulled back over his pointed ears, showcasing the arrogant sneer upon his narrow face. After ditching the usual attire worn by those sworn to protect Armageddon, he donned the comparable uniform the trio wore: the differences were the gold trimmings, buttons, and buckles, and both arm sleeves bearing an unfamiliar insignia of a serpent slithering in a circle with its mouth around its tail.

"The Lich's mark," Silver hissed under his breath, and Selena and Rahim shuddered upon seeing it for the first time.

The similarly dressed Vidar Helios himself was following them, a putrid plump half-elf who was as loathsome as rotten cheese. His shoulder-length white hair and matching eyes made him look like a ghost, contrasting his slightly tan skin tone, not nearly as dark as Selena's or her mother's. As short as she was, Vidar stood to her shoulders; given Ashur's height—matching Silver's—if he wanted to, he could easily overpower the Council leader like an adult to a child. Seeing the two made her stomach curdle.

Silver grabbed her shoulder to keep her from acting out of impulse. Selena swallowed hard, but the three remained calm through the guidance of Silver's unworded gestures; Vidar and Ashur took no notice of their group as they passed each other.

The guard following Vidar and Ashur lifted the visor of his helmet. "Can I ask you a question about the prison?"

"No, you can't sneak off to the wine room and get drunk," Vidar lazily said, "I can't tell you how many times you new people get caught."

Ashur sneered when the security officer recoiled and cleared his throat. "Must you be too hard on the boy? Listen, if you decide to go in there, don't let the Warden catch you."

"Oh, come off it. Captain Dante Battleraven of the *Blood Diamond* delivered that wine. I'm not about to waste it on the guards."

"I still don't trust those sky pirates—"

The guard interrupted their bickering. "No, that's not it. I heard about a dangerous prisoner brought here not too long ago." Selena's ears perked up as she came to a halt. Rahim and Silver kept motioning forward and urged her to turn at the next corner so they could eavesdrop.

Vidar's beady-eyed expression fixed upon the recruit with great curiosity as he rubbed his chin. "Dangerous prisoner? I think you mean Vulduin."

Ashur's bellowed laugh drowned out the prisoners' tormented screams. "I believe the new guy is scared. I wouldn't bother about Vulduin. The Warden keeps him in a special cell far away from the other prisoners below the first floor: you won't have to worry about setting eyes on him."

Still unsure of his safety, the guard followed his two superiors down the corridor and up the stairs leading to the next level; Selena restrained her shaking fists but couldn't contain her blood from boiling. Rahim caught her attention, interrupting her poisoned attitude; he scratched his head in utter confusion about their search being more straightforward than they thought. Silver, however, watched their enemies vanish above them like a hawk and snarled in a warning. "I feel like that was a set-up. Perhaps Vidar and Ashur know we're here."

Still sour, Selena spun her head around. "How, if we're in disguises?"

Rahim pulled out their map and unrolled it. "Regardless of whether it's a trap, there is something down there. I think it's still worth looking at."

While the trio deeply discussed their next course of action, they were wholly interrupted when the halls were filled with running guards. Through the alarm and sudden panic, Rahim rolled up his map and stuffed it away before the three were caught, but the security officers paid no attention to their awkward idleness.

However, one guard stopped and confronted them, pointing to the three with shaking fingers that matched his trembling voice: "We need your help. One of our guards was attacked by our prisoner downstairs." The officer hissed through clenched teeth when the trio didn't follow his immediate command. "Come on, and move your arses."

Upon exchanging glances, Selena, Rahim, and Silver finally followed the beckoning officer and rushed below past the different identical and disturbing levels; Mortemholdt grew darker, and the air turned thick as they made their descent.

"The prisoner snuck up from behind," the guard explained through their haste, "I always warn our recruits to be wary of that Vulduin. There's a reason why the Warden put him down here."

The stairs led the group to a single cubed room with a metal door when they finally reached the bottom of Mortemholdt's nearly endless abyss. Selena and her friends met with a pell-mell mass of uniformed soldiers forming a circle around the door, and her group pushed their way through the human barricade only to see a tangle of chains thrashing wildly like a rampaging beast in the air. Two unconscious guards lay sprawled on the ground, but the others couldn't remove them from harm's way without Vulduin striking them down.

The Shadow Emperor stepped forward with his hand extended, ready to attack at any moment. Stripped away of the usual attire of his formal crimson jacket, breeches, and boots, to the trio's dismay, the barefooted Vulduin now donned tattered clothes; his dirty and tangled raven feathered hair hung plastered to his chiseled and broken face. "Come any closer, and I will rip you all to shreds. I hadn't done anything before that one provoked me." He pointed at the first soldier he brought down.

Dad, it's me. Selena wished to speak up, but she couldn't without jeopardizing their rescue operation. Her heart sank to witness his psyche break, as Vulduin always remained calm and collective; she believed him incapable of losing his temper before now.

The guard who led the group down to Vulduin's cell stepped forward but recoiled when Vulduin whipped a chain, lashing it near his legs. "Take one step closer; I dare you." The circle of guards squeezed in, and Selena was involuntarily pushed forward only to fall victim to his merciless attack, and one of Vulduin's chains wrapped itself around her. "I will rip you apart."

Rahim and Silver were about to intervene, but Selena yelled at them to stand by; she tightened her muscles as the chains constricted her body like a massive boa squeezing the life out of its prey as the desperation to fight back crept forward. Yet, she did her absolute best to keep calm while working up the strength to say, in a cracked and shattered voice, "Dad...."

It was all she could muster. None of the guards heard her, but Vulduin's eyes widened, and his jaw dropped; he immediately released his chains, and Selena collapsed to the ground, heaving and gasping while holding her almost crushed sides.

Among the frenzy of guards rushing over to subdue the frozen Vulduin, Silver dashed through and assisted Selena to her feet after ensuring no physical damage other than severe soreness. His inspection was wholly interrupted when one officer pointed at him and ordered, "You, help me take him in."

Hesitant in leaving Selena and Rahim behind, Silver, through choking on his saliva, obediently marched forward and grabbed Vulduin's stunned arm while his officer comrade snatched the other. As if to play his part, Silver spoke in Vulduin's ear. "The Warden will deal with you, *Phantom Dust*." He whipped his head around to face Silver, instantly seeing through his disguise. "Don't worry. We will figure out a better plan."

Rahim tugged on Selena's arm and beckoned her to follow him with the others as they dispersed, but she watched a small smile crease Vulduin's scruffy and greasy face as he was taken away.

CHAPTER 10: THE PRINCE OF SHADOWS

Vulduin was escorted up several flights of stairs, the trembling sentry focusing on not losing grip on his wrists while Silver leaned in to hear what his friend had to say. "None of you should have come." Silver's eyes darted to the other guard to ensure he didn't hear; to his relief, the man was too distracted not to give in to his fear.

"We came here to save you. Why did you attack them?"

"They provoked me."

"I've never seen that side of you before." Vulduin only grunted at Silver's remark, making his second escort quiver in his boots.

The three reached the control room and brought Vulduin inside an empty, closed-off area across the corridor. Their prisoner took his seat in the only chair available within; when Silver saw the chair's restraints, he was reluctant when his fellow guard began with the first set. Vulduin nodded, and Silver assisted with the remaining straps to tie his wrists down on the armrests. Once they finished, the guard made haste to leave the room, but Silver remained behind. "What are you doing? The Warden will be here soon."

"I just need a few moments alone with our prisoner."

With the uncomfortable atmosphere looming over them, the guard shivered but tucked his fear away, hands clasping behind his back. "Only the Warden can be alone with Vulduin. His orders."

"If you have an issue with it, you can tell the Warden yourself." Before the officer could object further about his safety, Silver pushed him away from the door and locked himself inside, and soon, panicked pounding knocks rumbled across the metal walls.

Ignoring the guard's alarming fist slams attempting to break in, Silver was close to sharing his new escape idea, but Vulduin's dark face brightened with a sneaky-looking sneer. "I can't believe I'm saying this, but it's wonderful to see you again, Genesis."

"I told you, don't call me Genesis—it's Silver."

Vulduin leaned in as much as he could and whispered, "You can't blow your cover."

The pounding stopped, and Silver's head snapped upwards as the two heard footsteps echo down the hall. "Listen, we'll have to work out a new escape plan. I think I know what to do, but it will require a huge distraction. I'll talk to Selena and Rahim after we finish here."

Vulduin's heated gaze burned into the back of Silver's neck. "You were supposed to take her and Thor to Dark Blood Hold. That was the plan."

"Plans have changed. I...." Silver's voice trailed off when the footsteps grew close; he immediately unlocked the door, anticipating the Warden's swift arrival. "I'll tell you more later."

The metal gate swung open, and a highly dressed official in battle attire stepped forth. A half-elf nearly towering Silver, the Warden donned his sleek black and gold uniform, closely resembling Silver's disguise; bereft of wearing a protective headpiece, his stark and rounded pale but flustered face beamed at the two as if he would explode within seconds. "What are you doing? I've given orders that this prisoner is off-limits."

"Sir, I apologize. I was stepping out of line, but I wanted to tell this twat what I thought of him."

The Warden was not amused; he hissed through his teeth. "Get out." Silver scrambled out of the interrogation room before exchanging a glance with Vulduin, and the Warden grimaced. "I will deal with you later."

Dismissing the scowling looks from his partner, Silver mimicked his stance, and the two took their post outside just as the Warden closed the door. "Well, well, well. Here you are again."

Vulduin grunted and turned away to avoid the curator's hazel eyes. "Your guards provoked me."

"That's not what I heard. My guards informed me you tried to use magic to escape."

"I wasn't trying to escape."

The Warden spun around and kicked the back of the chair. It fell forward, and Vulduin's head kissed the floor; he snarled between his teeth when his eyes caught the Warden's boots. "I thought I'd made myself clear the last time we had our little chat. Nobody has ever escaped from Mortemholdt."

Vulduin chuckled. "I thought I broke that record the last time I was captured." The Warden reached down and pulled the chair back on its legs, Vulduin's head swinging upward from the sudden thrust. "Your soul to Oblivion. If we have this conversation again, you will pay the price."

The Shadow Emperor snarled as the foul cockroach of a man provokingly shoved his face close, daring Vulduin to strike. However, their interaction was interrupted as the door swung open, light peering over their dark encounter; Silver and the guard accompanying him rushed inside, and the two asked, "Sir, are you okay?"

The Warden pushed past them both and marched down the corridor. "Get this prisoner out of my sight."

When Vulduin was escorted back to his cell, the mass of guards had vanished and returned to their posts, leaving his lonely prison cell shrouded in a black velvet curtain of shadow. Before the guard assisted Silver with detaining the Shadow Emperor, Vulduin called him out, "Did Lord Godfrey send his regards?"

Head spinning, Silver attempted to ask for clarification, but the assisting sentry paused right before clamping Vulduin's chains shut. "Nothing can fool you, Your Imperial Majesty." Dropping the links, he fell to his knees after pulling off his helmet. Merely a young man, his skin was as beautiful as obsidian, and his jet-black hair tickled his ears. His crimson eyes pierced the darkness when he looked up, and the disguised guard grinned to show his pointy teeth, revealing his vampiric nature. "Damien. Damien Godfrey, at your service."

"The Prince of Shadows," Silver began and bowed, "it's been a long time. You've certainly played your part well, Your Highness."

Damien rose to his feet and held his helmet over his chest. "It has, Silver. After the Empress and General Araneus arrived at the keep, they told us what had happened. My father sent me to find you," he then addressed Silver, "but it appears that you beat me to it."

The prince was interrupted when two other sentries arrived at their scene. Both Silver and Damien stood in front of Vulduin as flesh shields, preparing for a possible fight, but they relaxed when one guard lifted their visor, and their eyes darted between the three, forcing out a "how goes it, fellow guard?" through a nervous, high-pitched tone.

Before Silver could say a word to them, Vulduin immediately looked up to the second soldier, and his eyes filled with tears. "Selena, you're all right."

She lifted her visor, shaking her head while pointing to the unknown man, but Damien immediately stepped forward with his hands up in surrender, clarifying his allied stance. Rahim grunted as he surveyed their post, ensuring their conversation remained private. "So are we." Yet, he recoiled upon seeing Damien's fangs, and he couldn't help but squeak like a mouse. "You're a vampire."

Hesitant at first, Selena removed her helmet and dropped it on the floor, still at a loss to Rahim's disposition against their race. "What is it with you and vampires?"

"They're scary—vampires drink and suck your blood."

Damien rolled his eyes and brought his hands up to his face to make them look like claws, followed by a hiss. Rahim yelped and jumped back but collected himself and faced the humiliation of the group laughing at his reaction. "Please, don't let my nature alarm you, as I am in complete control. The needs of Armageddon come before my own needs as a vampire."

Turning a deaf ear to their conversation, Selena and her father met for an embrace, and Vulduin kissed the top of her head. "You should be more careful. I could have killed you back there." He gestured to the Shadow Prince and began introductions. "Selena, Rahim, this is Prince Damien, the son of Lord Godfrey. Your Highness, this is my daughter—"

Damien's jaw dropped upon hearing her name and imperial affiliation, and he fell to his knees. "It's such an honor to welcome you, Selena Liongod, Queen of Dragons."

"Queen of Dragons? No, you're mistaken, Your Highness."

"The Shadow Templars have served your family for generations. There isn't a soul alive who hasn't heard of your exploits and power: you have the blood and soul of a Divinity Dragon, and it's only proper to call you the Queen of Dragons. You give people hope, Your Grace." Intimidated by the sudden formalities, she turned her pleading gaze over to Vulduin, but he only nodded.

Rahim's eyes widened, and he snickered. "Oh, hail the Queen of Dragons, the greatest of us all, blessed by the Divines." While Silver chuckled, unamused and her face burning, Selena reached over and slugged Rahim hard in the shoulder. "What did you do that for?"

"Stop it. Why am I already assumed to have taken the throne when that right belongs to my mother and father?" When Vulduin didn't answer her, Selena's chest tightened.

Her lips curved into a snarl when Thor chimed in.

I believe it suits you.

Please, not you, too.

You're the Crown Princess. It only fits for you to be the queen or empress.

But I don't want to be either.

Selena's look of apprehension betrayed her; Vulduin kept shaking his head when she attempted to gain reassurance that she wouldn't take the throne. Her chest swelled with each second that he refused to acknowledge her trepidation. Instead, he dismissed the subject entirely. "We will talk about this later. What are you doing here?" Vulduin's smoldering glare burned with growing fury as he met Silver's avoidant gaze. "I expected Silver to take you and your friends to meet with the lords at Dark Blood Hold."

Selena interrupted before Silver could answer. "We came here to save you before it was too late."

"I would have been fine. None of you should have put yourselves in danger on my account. Lord Vincent Godfrey was expecting you all weeks ago." Vulduin's eyes continued burning like a deadly inferno, and everyone but Selena stepped back.

"Don't fault Silver for this," she sternly began, "I was the one who wanted to rescue you first while he and Rahim tried to dissuade me." Believing she made her point clear, Selena's face suddenly turned white when Vulduin looked down to see her mechanical hand.

"What in Oblivion happened to you?" She didn't answer, and Vulduin's expression shattered, his face becoming like porcelain. "What happened in Snowhaven?"

Selena withdrew her arm from view and veered away. "I'll explain on our way to Heaven's Tear if you allow us to help you escape." When Silver and Rahim wouldn't budge from Vulduin's interrogation, he paused amidst the dreary atmosphere silencing the group; even Prince Damien held his tongue in fear of triggering an explosion.

Vulduin finally and reluctantly agreed; after he was free to do so, Silver changed the subject and shared his plans to modify their prison break, as Vidar and Ashur were within Mortemholdt—and the Warden would be watching Vulduin like a hawk. "We'll need a huge distraction to make our escape," he explained.

Catching on to Silver's idea, Rahim held his chin, and his eyes brightened. "Why don't we let the prisoners out all at once? The Warden, Vidar, Ashur, and the guards will be busy dealing with them, and we could sneak out."

Silver bit his nails, squinting at the stairs until a revelation presented itself. He offered to set Rahim's plan in motion: "Prince Damien and I passed by the control room earlier while escorting Vulduin to the Warden's room. I'll sneak up there and find the levers to release the prisoners." The three agreed to wait at Vulduin's cell while Silver—morphing into a fly—made his way back to the main floors to look for the control room. He zipped past the guards completely undetected and, after searching through several flights of stairs, finally found the main switches that powered all the cell doors.

A lonely guard stood post in front of the various levers within a small, enclosed room protected by thick, tempered glass walls. Before the security officer could react, Silver had resumed his disguise behind him, wrapping one arm around his neck with one swift movement and grabbing his other. His victim fought and struggled, but Silver brought his restrained arm to an angle and placed his palm on the back of the sentry's head, incapacitating the officer within seconds.

Ensuring the conflict hadn't attracted unwanted attention, Silver set the guard's unconscious body down and pulled the various levers within the control box. Soon, Mortemholdt shrieked as the bells and alarms rang, the doors to the cells opening up floor by floor. Howls and screams flooded the prisoner housing area, and in moments, the convicts ran from their chambers and began clawing and tearing at one another. The grotesque institution immediately turned to chaos and bloodshed.

Various guards arrived to help take control of the scene, but by the time they came to the control room, Silver had already changed into a flying bug and was on his way back to Selena and her group. He sneered as the officers attempted to close the cells, but the prisoners were already rampaging through the bloody halls, their murderous war cries ringing like the tolling of Death's bell.

The Warden rushed past the guards towards the control room and nearly threw himself over the railing to see the graphic scene of freshly torn limbs and crimson puddles. "Who let the prisoners out?! They're always to remain in lockdown!" He turned to the panicked officers swarming behind him. "Take control of the situation, now."

"Yes, sir."

The Warden's knuckles turned white as he firmly grasped the railing as his sentries prepared their weapons, gritting and hissing through his teeth. "I know you had something to do with this, *Vulduin.*"

Meanwhile, Selena, Rahim, Vulduin, and Damien were already making their way up the stairs just as Silver re-joined them in his recognizable form. Before he could fully explain the screams, the group shuddered when a stream of blood poured down the steps. Silver said, "We should be able to sneak through the commotion."

Luckily, both sides were too busy to notice as Selena's group made their escape, dodging the security officers and inmates as they rushed through the bloodied corridors. While Rahim guided them towards the entrance, Selena tugged at Thor's mental strings, alerting him they were close, and he said, **I will meet you there.**

Also, would it be all right to carry one more?

What do you mean?

We picked up a new friend.

I have no issues carrying a hundred more if my harness would allow it.

Rahim ran ahead towards the metal door they had initially entered when it was in plain sight. "My Queen, this way." Selena did her best to ignore him while he laughed through his teeth, but she elbowed him in the side.

Vulduin came to an immediate halt and held up his arms, preventing the others from dashing past him. It didn't take the group to wonder why for long when a formidable figure approached from the shadows near their exit, and the Warden of Mortemholdt stepped forward. Soon, as if appearing from a thick veil of fog, his militia of guards lined up beside him. Selena stepped back until she felt a gun's barrel pressed into her back; another wave of officers appeared behind and trapped the group.

"I knew you did this, Vulduin," the Warden began, "but I've already told you that no one escapes Mortemholdt."

"And I've told you that I've already broken your record."

Before the Warden could make another move and bark his orders, Vulduin stepped forward with a summoned tangled mess of chains whipping at his feet. The Warden dashed to the side and called waves of fire mixed with lightning bolts thrashing like the tentacles from the Kraken, and their attacks clashed like two swords in a duel.

The circle of guards pulled out blades and guns, but Rahim was faster; within a blink of an eye, he aimed and shot his revolver with such precision that he fired down a row of guards before they could launch a single bullet. Silver was impressed, keeping his back to Rahim's as he slammed his fist against the metal wall: parts of the prison's structure broke off and landed upon the guards swarming the group.

Amidst the heat of combat, Selena raised her hands, crafting a shield to protect herself from the oncoming wave, but her barrier transformed from a sphere to dancing flames of energy pluming from her body.

Ignoring the imminent danger, the guards lunged for her, but those approaching caught on fire. Flames as intense as a dragon's, her pursuers couldn't withstand the heat; they dropped and rolled, but their wasted efforts couldn't extinguish the eternal blaze consuming them into piles of ash.

Yet, when the sentries switched targets to go after Rahim and Silver, she stepped forward with her hands dangled with fingers curled—like a puppeteer's—and the guards stopped dead in their tracks. Selena slowly brought her hands down through clenched teeth, and the guards unwillingly obeyed her movements. She had them under her control, much like what Silver did to Rahim when he first taught her magic.

She wasn't sure how she did it, but she began understanding and feeling their Aether strands; Selena was manipulating their spiritual essence coursing through their veins, giving her absolute control over their movements. She ignored the horrified expression on Rahim's face as she jerked her hands to her right, and the guards flew and slammed into the wall. Silver, however, watched her skill with admiration as he believed in her vast talent.

While Selena and the others subdued their pursuers, Prince Damien sunk into a pool of shadows amalgamating and billowing beneath his feet before more of the Warden's men overpowered him. The darkness carried him across the floor, and suddenly, he surged back to the surface, and the phantom magic caught the officers near him, leaving them frozen and suspended in the air.

While keeping her eyes fixed on the guards to watch for any sudden movements, Selena heard Thor growl. **Where in Oblivion are you?**

We're a little held up at the moment.

Allow me to guess: you got caught. After Thor had his share of laughs, his tone lowered to a snarl. **I'm going to get you out.**

No, we're taking care of this.

Thor ignored her completely. Before anyone had a chance to move to safety, the metal door leading to their rendezvous point blew off its hinges from a torrential inferno blast throwing it across the hall. The Warden and his guards cowered down but quickly regained composure to investigate the source of the explosive conflagration; as they drew close, Thor spewed forth another, incinerating those approaching. The Warden ducked to the ground with his hands over his head to avoid the dragon's attack. The remaining guards defied orders, rushing instead towards dealing with their escaped prisoners to avoid facing Thor's fiery wrath.

When the Warden didn't move, Vulduin beckoned the others to follow him outside, but he spat on the ground near where the overseer huddled. "Looks like this is now the second time I've broken your record."

The Warden peered up through his hands covering his face, only to be greeted by Thor's opening maw. He scurried to his feet and moved out the way just in time before Thor released another fire blast, the embers from the attack searing parts of his uniform.

Selena waited near Thor's massive head as he finished his torrent, her arms crossed over her chest as she tapped her foot. *I think you over-did it.*

Thor's maw snapped shut, extinguishing his stream. **As I recall, you were the ones who got caught. I just saved you.**

Yes, I suppose.

And I suppose a thank you is in order.

Thank you.

Satisfied, Thor lifted his heavy neck resting upon the platform and leveled himself with the edge. Rahim and Silver boarded first and assisted Vulduin and Selena; however, Thor growled and bared his fangs when Damien approached, and the vampire prince took a step back until Selena came to his defense. *He's with us.*

Who is this?

The extra passenger I mentioned: Prince Damien Godfrey, Lord Godfrey's son.

On the other hand, Damien was more interested in Thor's magnificence. "It's not very often that I get to see a dragon but to think a *Divinity Dragon*. It's an honor to meet the King of Dragons."

Selena swore Thor had this glow about him every time he received a compliment; he lowered his defenses, allowing Damien to climb aboard when fulfilled. Chittering as he arched his neck away, he shoved himself away from the island after everyone was safe and buckled on his back, Mortemholdt slightly swaying from Thor's colossal weight pushing against it upon take-off.

With the wind of the Divines urging them forward, Thor flew as fast as his wings could carry them away from Mortemholdt, but a pit dropped in Selena's stomach when a dragon's silhouette emerged from over the prison—a Nidhoggr. The group looked at the undead dragon in dismay, but it didn't give chase. Instead, it circled the island, roaring as if it had chased them off. As the Nidhoggr hovered near the loading docks, astride the creature's back were two riders: Vidar and—

"Niamh," Rahim said quietly, and he sunk into his seat in despair.

Meanwhile, Vidar and Niamh watched Thor disappear over the horizon with satisfied smirks.

*****

CHAPTER 11: BORN OF BLOOD AND FIRE

The Hinterlands echoed with the howls from the Aynu pack as the crescent moon hung over the endless green sea of trees. Winter was coming soon, and they must be ready. The snow-white She-Wolf, Kiba, and her mate, the black wolf Alpha Male, Maru, organized several hunting groups to help stockpile supplies; the Aynu felt a great evil was coming, and they knew that the day the sun turned black would be the world's requiem.

The wolves weaved in and out through the lush green sward as they focused on the hunt. Kiba's blazing yellow eyes glowed in the darkness, and she disappeared ahead of her group while her warriors dove through the guardian trees, following in a circular line and wrapping the group around a large, fleeing elk. However, the prey was never able to outrun Kiba's hunters. Just as the pack trapped their next meal, Kiba emerged from the darkness and thrust herself upon the monolithic ungulate, and one by one, her wolves launched themselves into the pile. The elk tired and gave up, and the She-Wolf aimed straight for the throat with claws sharp as a sword.

They enjoyed the spoils of their kill as a family, and when they finished, they hauled their remaining prize back to the Ankoku Pass. The hunting party threw the giant elk into their food cave, but Kiba noticed that only her team had returned; it was nearly dawn, and Maru and his group were missing. After ordering some of her wolves to take shifts in guarding their territory, she sniffed around until catching her mate's faint scent.

She rushed back to the trees, tail wagging like a puppy. Yet, she paused when Maru emerged, blood dripping down his black fur. Part of his ear was bitten and torn off; he limped and held up his right front leg. Kiba growled and barked as she circled him and licked some of his wounds. *My love, what happened?* she asked him through their shared mental link as the Alpha Male stumbled through the brush of leaves.

Maru's different-colored eyes shimmered—his right ice-blue and left chocolate-brown—and he held up his broken wrist for Kiba to see when he changed back into a human; his wolf mask blotted with blood, the crimson stains reflecting dawn's rays. "We were ambushed."

Snarling through clamped fangs, Kiba morphed into her human form, her messy white hair matching her gleaming wolf mask painted with red claw marks, her thoughts caught in a frenzied mess. "What did this to you? I will kill them."

Before Maru could answer, a loud shriek thundered over their heads, and the two alphas cowered. A shadow loomed overhead, and to their dismay, they saw the same creature they had encountered before when Selena and her friends received Artio's blessing; the undead dragon flew above the canopy with a saddled rider. The remaining Aynu who stayed behind from the hunts paused and watched the shadow dragon in absolute silence and horror.

Following this creature was a thick, darkening mist that consumed the Hinterlands, and the ground began to quake. Kiba took to Maru's side to protect him when a stampeding horde of deer rushed through their site. As much as the wolf pack usually welcomed the abundance of prey, the Aynu understood the warning signs and ran away with the herd. "They're coming." Maru coughed up a little blood, struggling to keep up with Kiba.

"Who's coming?"

"The undead ones that killed my unit."

The Nidhoggr continued flying ahead of the wolf pack, unleashing its thundering shrill, and, as if heeding its call, scores of the undead flooded through the Hinterlands, arising from the fog and marching towards Alfheim.

When Kiba saw the wave upon wave of rotting corpses, she changed into a wolf and barked her orders for her pack to follow her and Maru. Likewise, the Aynu transformed and followed the She-Wolf and the limping Maru out of the infested forest. For now, the undead soldiers paid no attention and kept following the Nidhoggr until some broke from the herd and tracked the wolves down. Kiba turned to a couple of her warriors who ran with her. *Help me.*

Breaking from Maru's side, she and her two hunters joined together to take down their pursuers. Kiba flew at one and decapitated it with her claws, the flesh and bone tearing easily without much effort. However, the head was still alive and kept trying to attack by chomping its teeth at her face; the She-Wolf yipped and dashed away with her warriors.

Yet, the rest of the undead noted the call of their fallen comrade, and when Kiba saw the swarm rushing at her pack, she ordered her fighters to stand down. She swooped and helped Maru onto her back and ran as fast as she could while he grimaced from the pain. The undead suddenly hastened their pursuit, moving too quickly, easily closing the distance between the wolves, and the Aynu grew weary.

Maru soon toppled over after losing too much blood, and Kiba dove down and stood over him with her fangs bared, ready to fight. The rest of the pack joined her, and the Aynu huddled against the massive wave rushing towards them at full speed. The two alphas prepared for what they expected to be their final stance; Kiba wanted to remain by Maru's side until the end. The two wolves nuzzled their noses together and closed their eyes, preparing to enter Oblivion.

Suddenly, before the undead reached and swarmed the pack, a controlled green cloud of toxic venom plumed from the sky, consuming and disintegrating the undead creatures within seconds. Luckily, the wolves remained a safe enough distance from the lethal mist. When Kiba opened her eyes, she saw a black dragon with purple fins slithering down its spine sweeping overhead, spewing out an additional venomous blast, strafing one group after another. Aboard the dragon was a heavily armored rider wielding a revolver—a 'fire stick' per Kiba. The two killed the undead with ease.

"Lower, Aracania. Fire!" The dragon obeyed and steered herself over another horde with an exhaled cloud of acid and poison as her handler head-shot down a row of rotting corpses with quick and deadly precision. Meanwhile, the Aynu moved away from the dragon's attacks as the haze drifted closer. The wolves watched in both awe and fear as their new saviors swept through the abominations; concurrently, the Nidhoggr and its rider observed from a distance.

The new handler astride the venomous dragon eyed the remaining undead horde standing in horrifying silence as they waited for their ringleader. When the dragon, deemed Aracania, finished her onslaught, the Nidhoggr shrieked, ordering the rest of its herd to make haste towards the ruined elven city. Aracania snarled and almost gave chase but maintained her position aloft, hovering as she flapped forward and backward simultaneously. Kiba morphed into a human as Aracania landed among the pile of corpses; the She-Wolf stood before her injured mate to keep the strangers away.

Aracania was a rare species with venomous abilities, called the Aracania Venomtooth—hence the name. Her daintier and slender frame compared to dragons like Thor and Doragon made her more agile and acrobatic while airborne and was still strong enough to carry the weight of about fifteen fully grown men. Her sleek black hide gleamed against the sunlight, speckled with green and light purple flecks down her spine, dabbing the edges of her deep amethyst four-spined wings. Purple fins strung along her sharp spines down her back and tail, while her lean and narrow face was devoid of decorative spikes, save for two on her head and another set on her jaw corners. Each foot had three ivory claws, sharp enough to rip a man clean in half.

Her handler, a young gentleman in his twenties, belted his revolver. The dragon hissed, but the rider spoke in soft and gentle tones. "Easy, Aracania. Please, forgive us. I'm General Araneus Morleth, rider and handler of Aracania. We saw that you were in trouble while transporting supplies." Resembling more of an elf than his grandfather, Vidar Helios, his mother of pure blood and father with a watered-down bloodline, Araneus Morleth was considered the youngest war general in history. He wasn't as fair in complexion as most elves, but the alikeness was evident upon his narrow face; his maroon hair christened with silver streaks couldn't hide his pointed ears, nor his deep purple eyes.

Kiba growled and spat on the ground. Aracania roared through serrated teeth, but the general dismounted and stroked her neck, helping ease the tension. Being their saviors was the only reason Kiba withheld her attack; instead of wasting time talking to these strangers, the She-Wolf longed to see them leave so the pack could hide and lick their wounds.

"Leave us. Now." She scowled for allowing herself to communicate with the dragon rider. She had already made an exception once before, but she was not so willing to grant another; this courtesy was more than enough. Maru, however, whimpered as he limped over to her, then to the general with his paw held to his chest. Kiba snarled and rushed over, scolding and steering him away.

Araneus cleared his throat, hesitant in continuing to address the Alpha Female, but Aracania slipped a protective arm around her handler, preparing to whisk him away at a moment's notice. However, she reluctantly pulled back upon his request. "A call went out that your pack needed aid, and it looks like we got here just in time. Please allow us to grant you a safe passage."

Kiba spun around and stood on her toes to bring her face close to Araneus', her voice shriller than a grave's beckoning. "What call?!"

General Araneus didn't flinch from her sudden hostility, despite Aracania lowering her head and giving Kiba a warning snarl to back away. "From a former member of your pack."

Ignoring Aracania's intimidating stare, Kiba's eyes lit up, and she immediately assumed Selena and her friends were perhaps the ones who sent help. The blood-stained faces of her survivors betrayed their grim disposition: they lost their home a second time.

Whines and whimpers shattered the tense atmosphere while the wolves inched forward, casting pleading gazes. Kiba looked down at her mate, and Maru nudged her with his nose, edging her to make the right decision. Knowing the pack's wishes, she nodded and backed away, allowing Maru to get the assistance he needed; the general aided him in mounting Aracania, and with Kiba's permission, the dragon carried him while maintaining a single eye fixed upon the She-Wolf.

After almost an hour of walking with their new allies in utter silence, General Araneus and Aracania led the surviving members of the Aynu towards a huge caravan line snaking southeast across the White Plains.

"Before finding your pack, we've been shipping supplies from Runefell, but we had to use the secret tunnels through the Mustang Mountains to remain undetected. We will give you all safe passage to Dark Blood Hold, and there, we will reunite you with the survivor from your pack." Kiba didn't pay much attention to the general's words; she was thrilled to possibly see her old friends again. The Aynu would be together once more.

*****

Armageddon's crisp, cold air cut through their skin like daggers as Thor continued his steady course leisurely. Dawn's shimmering rays intensified the glow from Damien's crimson eyes, making Selena quiver. However, the prince's appearance didn't stop Rahim from badgering him with questions about when the young prince first turned, what it was like to be a vampire, and, with reluctance, inquired about their diet.

Much to Selena's relief, Prince Damien didn't offend Rahim's curiosity and was more than happy to oblige. "We among the Shadow Templars have evolved over the years, and we've grown more powerful than normal vampires; even the sun no longer hurts us, but it's still quite a nuisance." Silver's explanation for Kain's tolerance reminded her that the only way to kill a Templar was to chop their head off and hoist it on a wooden stake during the sunrise; otherwise, the sun alone couldn't deter them.

Grunting and groaning in discomfort, Damien pulled his hood over his head for protection. "We gain sustenance through animal blood, as mortals no longer allure us." He explained how the Templars raised fodder to ensure a constant supply. Much to Rahim's surprise and amazement, Lord Godfrey's vampires only needed to feed every fortnight. "When you think about it, it's not much different than your farms raising cattle for slaughter." When Rahim prodded further about his youth, Prince Damien facetiously added, "I may look young, but I used to be your age about two hundred years ago. Vampirism will do that to you." Selena and Rahim laughed, and the uneasiness faded.

Silver crossed his arms, however, for he was not amused. "When you're a sixteen-thousand-year-old demigod, then maybe—"

Vulduin reached over and pinched his ear like a mother would discipline a misbehaved child. "That's enough. You will be respectful to the Prince of Shadows."

Upon further inquiry, Damien explained his arrival to Mortemholdt in a hot air balloon, which he disposed of in the lake after his arrival, avoiding leaving a trace. Selena was so used to flying with dragons that a hot air balloon sounded foreign to her; she remembered her father traveling by zeppelin when he met them at Starsong, forgetting that luxury.

Rahim's smile faded when he looked back at Mortemholdt. Seeing Niamh again shattered his spirits, and Selena knew he was formulating a plan to save her upon their next meeting. She scooted close to him and rested her hand on his shoulder, joining in his silent communion. When he acknowledged her presence and touch, Selena made the reassurance of "we will save her."

Rahim thought hard for a moment, with a pucker in his brow. "I know." Silver, meanwhile, kept his distance while Selena did her best to comfort him. As much as he and Rahim teased and bantered with one another, Silver knew this was not the best time for his remarks, and Selena was grateful for his silence when Rahim needed it most.

Vulduin leaned forward with a sharp gleam striking through his deep sapphire eyes, noting his grim behavior. "I see you two were very close. Was she—?"

Rahim's head snapped around, and his face turned red. "No, we're only friends—nothing more."

Unfazed by his hasty reply, Vulduin shrugged, returning to the calm demeanor that Selena often recognized. "My condolences for Niamh. That thing she was riding has been calling itself Fafnir." He met the group's confused gazes as he locked his hands together, knuckles turning white. "It was the first time I've heard one of those undead *things* speak, like a series of shrieks. None of the others could mimic Fafnir's speech, and I'm astounded this one learned our tongue."

Selena recalled Fafnir taunting and goading them at the Ankoku Pass; Rahim scowled and hissed through the grinding of his teeth, "Fafnir will pay for taking Niamh."

After sharing Rahim's resentments, Selena shot her father a quizzical glare. "How do you know?"

"I've learned many things during my imprisonment." Vulduin couldn't remain still as he continued casting a rueful glance at Prince Damien. "How long ago did my wife arrive?"

Damien's dazzling, bloody glare was like that of a poisoned rose; lovely to look at but deadly upon touch. "Her Imperial Majesty, General Araneus, and his dragon, Aracania, arrived at Dark Blood Hold a few weeks ago, Your Majesty. After ensuring Her Majesty's safety, the general left to Runefell shortly after arriving to help us deliver supplies and reinforcements for the war."

Selena looked down at her feet and twiddled her thumbs, unable to share her father's enthusiasm for her mother's safety. Thor swiveled his head to fix his giant, amber eye on her but slightly recoiled when she waved her hands, dismissing his concerns. It was Prince Damien who broke the awkward interaction. "My Queen, what's wrong?"

Her head jerked up at the unfamiliar regal address, and suddenly, her throat felt scratchy and dry. "Err… nothing. Please, there is no need for titles and formalities when addressing me."

"Do you mean 'My Queen?'"

"Yes. You may call me Liongod, as I'm not a queen."

Vulduin interrupted this time before Selena could oppose any further. "That wouldn't be proper for someone of your status and birthright." Her vexed expression became adamantly clear, and he only continued after struggling with hesitation. "When we defeat the Lich, your mother and I don't want the throne."

Selena's eyes darted to her friends as her stomach sank to her feet; her fear had been realized. "No."

Vulduin turned a blind eye to the horrified, pale expression on his daughter's face. "That will mean someone else will have to take the throne, someone with the rightful claim—"

"No."

"Who is pure of heart with a solid mind, someone always willing to do the right thing to protect her people —"

"Please, no...."

Vulduin raised his hand, preventing her from speaking further. "We will discuss this in due time. Your mother and I had already decided this before Vidar took me as a prisoner."

Selena spun from her seat, hair whipping from her sudden movements. "I don't want to be a ruler."

Silver's eyes brightened, and he raised a hand for a chance to speak before Vulduin could address Selena's objections. "Ah, you see. The best kind of monarch is the one who doesn't want to rule at all."

Selena's eye twitched. "Please, don't encourage this."

"But it is your birthright. Queen or Empress, you could call yourself whatever you wish, as you'll still rule over an empire—"

The sheen from Vulduin's deadly expression made the others cower down, but Selena, not intimidated, kept her position; he inhaled deeply, refraining from raising his voice. "Enough. We will discuss this later." His eyes shot down to her new hand. "Now, you and Silver owe me an explanation of what happened to you."

Although Silver was unwilling, still heated, Selena immediately told her father what happened in Snowhaven, if a little short and direct. Rahim chimed in to fulfill the rest of it after she fell in battle, and Silver followed by describing his latest invention and how he attached the new hand. During their tale, Selena noticed how Thor's body language changed. He lowered his head, and the flap of his wings turned sluggish; a few low growls and snarls escaped from his clamped maw, increasing in frequency as their story continued.

Her father's already pale face became like milky white; Vulduin closed his eyes for a moment, squeezing a single tear dripping to the edge of his lean jawline. "I-I am so sorry."

Selena wasn't sure if she wanted to hear an apology, as it wasn't good enough to account for all she and her friends endured. Instead, she asked, "Did you not think anything was amiss when you returned from Snowhaven?" She had to keep her tongue in place in fear of losing her temper when now was not the time.

"I met with King Boreas Tristan personally to guarantee your safe arrival with the Mythic Flight clutch, and he assured me that you and your allies would be treated like royalty."

Tears rolled down her cheeks. "I had expected more of an answer upon hearing of my death."

If Vulduin detected any vehemence, he did not show it. However, he held his head in shame and defeat. "I'm so sorry, and we have done our best to heed Azrael's warning and prevent it, but believe me when I say your mother and I are grateful for his promise. To answer your question, no, I did not think anything was amiss in Snowhaven." Selena kept her smoldering eyes focused on the reins as she tightened her grip; even the Aether pulsing through her mechanical hand hastened. Silver, Damien, and Rahim inched a little way down the saddle, but Vulduin remained steady to face her building fury. "Vidar assured us that you were safe and even gave us forged letters delivered from Snowhaven he swore were in your handwriting, and we were fools to trust him. It was too late by the time we discovered the truth." He rubbed his temples, mortified for being so easily deceived. "Your mother and I believed we were doing the right thing, but instead, we lured you right into their trap. I don't know how we can ever make this right by you and Thor."

There was so much that Selena wanted to say, but she didn't. Instead, she turned away. "It's fine."

"No, that can't be it—"

"I said it's fine. Leave it alone." Her sharp tone made everyone jump; even Damien shuffled his feet and moved over a seat. Silver looked to Rahim to see if he knew why she snapped so suddenly, but he only shrugged.

Vulduin held his gaze a little longer before averting his eyes down. "Very well then. I will leave it alone, but to imagine you meeting that wretched snake makes me want to vomit. In the beginning, I thought that Vidar made up Medusa's story. I overheard so much."

"You allowed Vidar to imprison you so that you could spy on him. There is a better way to do that." Selena crossed her arms and grunted at realizing her father's true intentions behind his capture.

"What's better than completely submitting to your enemy and making them think they've won? When they have that advantage, they will tell you everything as a way to boast that they've always had the upper hand," Vulduin's tongue clicked against his teeth, "Unfortunately, we're still in quite a predicament. The Empire has fallen, and we still don't have a plan to stop the Lich."

Selena remained unconvinced that her father had made the right choice. "What else did you learn?"

"The dead are coming back to life. Vidar and Ashur are calling them 'Dreygur.'"

The strange and unusual behavior of the former Grand Exchange residents suddenly made sense. As the tension grew from the silence, Silver broke it. "We saw the Dreygur on our way to Mortemholdt. Is there anything we can do?"

"Alas, there's no cure for death." Vulduin paused and shared a dishearted gaze with all his passengers. "There is more. Those abominations that attacked

Alfheim and kidnapped your friend were made from Thor's essence."

Silver had more reaction than Selena or Thor; he leapt from his spot and threw his hands. "That's not possible."

"I overheard Vidar telling Ashur. I promise you, it's true. The Lich worked on his stratagem right before Flying Officers Gromm and Beck rescued Selena and Thor. Dragons were rounded up and killed, only to be brought back through the new Well, more powerful than ever. Before his hatching, the Lich used Thor's essence and magic to twist and distort the undead dragons, thus making them stronger."

Selena finished his explanation with, "And the eclipse will make them unstoppable."

"Precisely. And Medusa—"

Selena hastily interrupted, snarling upon hearing Medusa's name again. "Was cloned and made from my blood. That's what she told us when we were captured in Snowhaven."

Her father flinched but nodded. "It was disturbing to hear her tale, to say the least."

"What do you mean?"

Vulduin closed his eyes and recalled Vidar and Ashur's harrowing scene during his imprisonment: the two presented him before the new Well of Souls at Mount Blackrock before throwing him in Mortemholdt so that Vidar could mock and humiliate him. Even to this day, Vulduin still could not get the image of the new Well out of his mind; it reeked of death and decay. "Medusa was born from blood and fire. She was created like you were brought back, Selena, except she wasn't born from a dragon. Vidar and Ashur showed me the memory of what happened through a giant crystal ball." The Oracle triplets possessed the same ability; some objects could help someone focus and foresee images from the past or future. "I never knew that Vidar had the gift of visions," Vulduin continued, "only very few can. That explains how he was always one step ahead of us, aside from his alliance with the Lich. But I digress.

"Medusa was already a fully grown being encased in this strange and slimy membrane pod. I'm not even sure what to call it—the Lich brought this *sack* to the Well's swirling blood pool to give her life. I've never seen anything like it. Then I saw the black flames erupt around this pod, consuming her and the Well. By the next day, amidst the smoke, Medusa emerged forth, and the Well of Souls remained unscathed."

Selena couldn't imagine the horrific and sickening tale of Medusa's creation her father had witnessed. Rahim shuddered and said, "Medusa didn't turn evil. She was just born bad."

"I'm afraid you're right, Rahim. She already knew the purpose of her existence, which was to take over Snowhaven, help the Lich reclaim Thor, and…." Vulduin's voice trailed off as he gazed upon the look of horror displayed on Selena's face, "and to kill you."

Thor roared and turned sharply, making his riders jolt from the saddle. Following his thunder, a fire blast erupted from his maw, threatening to reduce the sky to a smoldering pile of ash. His rage grew stronger than Selena's; she consoled her heartbroken dragon as he unleashed his requiem upon the shuddering heavens. After he had stopped, she wrapped her arms around his neck and ran her fingers across his scales. *It's okay. Medusa is gone now.*

That still doesn't take away the pain of what she did to you.

Vulduin brushed back his greasy hair while ignoring Silver's random ramblings and outbursts. "She grew off the Lich's poison and dark magic. Her entire existence has been spent in shadow; she knew and wanted no other way. It was her desire for Thor to be the one to kill her, thus unleashing the dark Aether that would—" his stoic and nearly insensitive explanation was wholly interrupted by Thor's continued agonized growls.

That will never happen to me.

Selena was a little unnerved by how aggressive he was beginning to act. *That's why we will talk to Ulrich when we get back.*

I will talk to him, but there is nothing wrong with me. Thor made another sharp turn and howled in torment, his lamenting song making the heaven and earth weep.

"I'm sorry, Thor." The distraught dragon snarled and sneered at Vulduin's words, and the former Shadow Emperor realized his error. "I had hoped that Vidar was a liar and that you two would be safe." He looked at his daughter with cumbersome eyes. "I refused to listen when he said it was a matter of time before Medusa caught up to you, but I knew our worst fears had happened when I saw your hand. Vidar described Medusa as the first success, and now, the Nidhoggr dragons are the perfect creations."

All Selena could say to this dreadful news was, "And now, of course, the walking dead."

"Sadly, many more Dreygur await to storm our world from Oblivion."

Rahim dropped his head as he and the others gathered together in their melancholy atmosphere. "What else can go wrong?"

What could be judged as arrogance, insensitivity, or lack of remorse, Vulduin wasted no time answering Rahim's question. "This: during the eclipse, the Lich will use the Nidhoggr to rain dark Aether over the land, and black magic will consume and destroy everything. His army will commence their journey across the earth's surface with their cataclysmal torrent of destruction, as, I'm sorry to say, there would be no escape."

Selena's aghast expression deceived her. "I can't believe this. What are we going to do?"

"The plan hasn't changed. We still need to do whatever we can to stop the Lich before the eclipse. We need to return to Dark Blood Hold and deliver this information to your father immediately, Your Highness—"

Selena's head snapped up. "Wait, you're going to leave again?" Both Rahim and Silver jolted from her thundering question, though it sounded like a demand from their standpoint.

Even Vulduin flinched. "Lord Godfrey plans on fighting by our side to help us stop Venexus. I hope you realize that the Shadow Templars will benefit from the eclipse, too. The others will need to know what's happening."

Instead of acknowledging his explanation, Selena returned to her seat and stared over the horizon as Thor remained on course. Their plans were no longer appealing; they conflicted with her chance to spend time with family, but she felt abandoned by her parents, not to mention the forced responsibility of ruling an empire. She never wanted the throne. The anger burned, growing into a brewing storm with each passing second, her wrath waiting to unleash. It took all of her strength to keep from lashing out.

"Silver," Vulduin began when confident that the worst had passed, "We should all prepare to Lord Godfrey's fortress."

Selena's lips trembled as she answered instead. "Silver is supposed to take us to meet Ulrich first, and that's what we're going to do."

There was a pucker in Vulduin's brow. "Ulrich? The Divine secludes himself at Heaven's Tear with no interest in mortal affairs. We have a war to plan—"

"Then pray tell Lord Godfrey that Thor and I must train with Ulrich to master our powers." A single drop drifted down her cheek as she whispered to herself, "I wish you would listen to me."

Vulduin looked as though she slapped him; he couldn't control how much he opened and closed his mouth in a wasted effort to find the right words to comfort his daughter, but his mind remained blank of any sympathetic remark. "Silver," he finally began, "Damien and I will wait for all of you at the castle."

"We will meet you there as soon as we're able."

"Do you have a way for us to get there from Heaven's Tear?"

"Yes, of course. I believe I still have your old zeppelin secured and ready for use."

Vulduin and Damien resumed talking about their plans once they reached Dark Blood Hold, as if Selena's outburst didn't happen earlier. Rahim crossed his arms and leaned over the saddle's edge, staring across the sky as if expecting to see Niamh again, but he remained disappointed.

Selena was too focused on calming her stormy thoughts, not noticing when Silver came over to sit beside her, but her eyes shimmered as he slipped his arm around and pulled her close. The two didn't speak, but Silver's presence was all she needed at that moment. Even Thor kept his words to himself, but having him and Silver there in silent empathy was more than enough.

The quiet trip back to Heaven's Tear was much faster than it was to Mortemholdt; the group enjoyed their rain-less flight as the days passed; they admired Armageddon's burning green and orange sky in the clear, cold evenings. If it weren't for the Day of Eternal Darkness, the world would feel at peace.

When they returned to Silver's library at midday after nearly six days of non-stop flying, Vulduin and Damien wasted no time preparing to depart for Dark Blood Hold; not too far away, its location down the mountain near the coast. Selena watched them in dismay as they prepared their zeppelin Silver safely hid behind his tower. It would take two days, perhaps three, on dragonback, but she was upset that her father was eager to leave after everyone had just reunited. She understood his directive, and he was anxious to see his wife again, but she neither wished to be forgotten nor left out. When they said their goodbyes, Selena didn't say a word when Vulduin hugged her and whispered, "We will see you soon. I promise."

Damien bowed and said, despite her objections earlier, "Farewell, My Queen."

Selena's chest swelled, and her heart throbbed as she watched the two sail away from the summit, the airship vanishing into the beckoning clouds.

CHAPTER 12: A BROTHER'S TALE

While Silver and Rahim discussed when the group should meet with Ulrich, Selena separated herself. She followed the weaving mountain's pathway, slithering through deep opulence, leaving Thor behind at his pavilion. Growing angry for leaving him so suddenly, Thor dashed from the marble archway to chase her down, his thoughts stinging at her like a thorn throbbing from her side. **Where are you going?**

Away.

Please tell me that you are coming back soon.

Eventually.

He didn't like her one-word answers. Growing uncomfortable, he took flight above the sea of pines to hunt her down, ignoring her careless and reckless behavior as she sought solace to mend her shattered heart; yet, her parents' abandonment reopened the wounds.

She disappeared through the thick pine lush, her steps crunching the old snow that had arrived the evening before. A shadow of a dragon shot through the heavens, and Selena guessed that Silver's sister was returning to meet with Thor; as much as she didn't want to admit it, the stinging pain of jealousy returned.

Selena hated that Thor could read her mind when she wanted solitude; he continued pestering her. **Ebony and I are coming to find you.**

I don't care.

Yes, you do, and besides, you owe her a duel.

Selena huffed as she leaned against a tree and looked at the sun-filled sky. This daylight may be the last time they would see the clear heavens for a while, as the gesturing winter storms would continue to worsen in the days to come. She chuckled at the fact that she couldn't be happy when the world seemed to be.

Her vision grew blurry, and pain erupted across her back once more, but it returned worse than before. Selena convulsed as she fell to her knees and vomited tremendously over the open ground before her, leaving an acrid stinking mess.

What happened?

I'm fine. Selena wiped the bile from her trembling lips, and the urge to retch made her hurl stomach acid. After a few dry heaves, she finally caught her breath, leaving her throat burning and sore.

No, you're not—you're ill. I'm coming for you now.

Please, I'll be okay. Selena forced herself to her feet, but she stumbled backwards and sat against the tree while careful not to touch her disgusting puddle of body waste. The pain eased, only to flare up again after a few seconds.

Yet, holding in her stomach contents, she stood up as she saw two dragons circling above her, the gale from their wings bending the trees. Thor dove and touched down beside her, ground quivering from his landing, with Dragonheart dangling from his claws. Through her still blurred vision, she looked upon him in admiration of his massive size and the rainbows shimmering from his ruby scales, contrasting the deep hue from his harness sapphire.

His strength wasn't exaggerated, as his mass was comparable to a twenty-gun first-rate ship.

Ebony followed his example and landed beside him, her smooth onyx hide glimmering in the sunlight. She transformed to her black-suited guise after Selena retrieved Dragonheart from Thor, pulled out a vial hiding in an inside pocket, and handed it to Selena in the mid strut. Selena watched the azure liquid swish within the glass as she held it to her face; she was used to Silver's many elixirs he had offered to her, but she was ashamed not to trust his sister. "What is this?" she asked Ebony.

"I believe you're familiar with this sort of brew, though its coloration may not be the same: it's a potion of stamina restoration. Though I'm not as proficient as my brother, I've been practicing my alchemy, and I pulled this from my private selection when Thor told me you were ill. It will help you feel better."

Selena felt hopeful that the concoction could heal her completely. "Will this cure my wounds, too?"

To her dismay, Ebony shattered her expectations. "I can't do that, but I believe only Ulrich can help you. This potion will temporarily allow you to regain your strength, and I've been waiting for you to fulfill your promise." Her eyes sparkled in delight and eagerness for their upcoming battle.

Selena bit her bottom lip after giving her sword a few new swings with her mechanical hand, as she was somewhat reluctant to take the potion. Her fingers tightly wrapped around the glass. "We had a prior engagement at Mortemholdt."

"I know. Are you free now?"

"I suppose I am."

"Good. Please, drink that."

Selena spun around and faced Thor, who only dipped his head in agreement. As soon as she brought the bottle to her lips, the sweet nectar immediately soothed and calmed her convulsing muscles. Within seconds, she felt the strength of ten dragons return to her.

Unheralded, Ebony drew her curved blade and dashed forward. Selena barely had time to respond, but she held up Dragonheart and parried her attack. "I'm not sure if Silver told you, but I've traveled across the world and learned different fighting techniques. Now, I wish to learn yours."

While the two sword masters were engaged in a clash of metal, Thor remained to the side and watched them with keen interest. Selena couldn't help but notice her dragon was paying a little more attention to his mate than to her, but she kept her mind on the duel. Ebony only used one sword, but she was quick and dangerous. She was an armed wasp who showed no mercy, with a temper to match. Selena was forced to take more defensive measures; she kept dodging Ebony's flurry of blows while looking for the first opening to strike back.

Show her what you can do.

I'm trying.

I don't think you are.

Having enough of playing the defensive side, Selena found her chance. She remembered when she and Silver last dueled together after crafting Dragonheart, and without realizing it, she teleported and reappeared behind Ebony. The black dragon spun around to block her blade, but Selena grew faster, and soon, Ebony was forced to take the defensive. Yet, she was amused and couldn't help but dote on Selena's skill. "So you are a user of Aether, then."

"I'm not skilled enough to practice the art."

Ebony paused her attacks. "You just vanished. The only way you can do that is by using Aether."

"If I did, I can't freely control it yet...." Her voice grew faint as she recalled her previous experiences, such as her last duel with Silver and how she fought the guards in Mortemholdt. She had no justification for how it came to her. "I can't explain it."

"No need. That's why my brother and Ulrich will help you two." Ebony nodded to both her and Thor. "Let's continue."

Silver and Rahim eventually found the three after following the sound of clashing swords, but they didn't interrupt. Instead, they joined Thor on the sidelines and watched as the two dueling dragons remained locked in their contest for the next few hours. It felt good for Selena to channel her anger and frustrations through her sword, taking it as a nice distraction and therapy session that she needed.

Thor took note of her behavior change and chittered in approval. **Are you feeling better?**

Better.

When Ebony was satisfied, she withdrew her blade and stepped back. "That was insightful. Thank you for sharing this duel with me." Selena nodded. Her breaths were quick and heavy, but she didn't want to show Ebony that the clash winded her. However, she could tell that Silver's sister was also sodden, but Ebony was too prideful to admit it. Ebony slowly sheathed her weapon, the blade's thirst for battle now satiated. "My brother was true to his word. I've battled sword masters throughout history, and every one of them fell to my blade, but you're different. You and I could have an ageless battle, and neither would waver. You are, without a doubt, my greatest adversary."

Twittering in delight, Thor made his way over and dropped his head over Selena's shoulder. **And that is still with your handicap.**

I don't have a handicap. Selena lifted her mechanical hand to show Thor.

That's not your usual hand.

Understanding their conversation through Selena's gestures, Ebony looked at the two and nodded. "That was you at a real disadvantage, too. Take pride, and keep honing your skills. The world will need them." She turned around to face Silver and Rahim. "Thank you for your hospitality, but it's time for me to leave before my presence becomes too much of a hindrance." Tight-lipped, Silver didn't offer any response; Selena and Rahim shared an awkward glance as the two felt the tension rise between the siblings. "Take care of her, brother. When all of you reach Dark Blood Hold, I will make sure to send a falcon."

Expressionless, Silver nodded. "We will look forward to it." Despite the silent unchecked hostilities, Silver and Ebony continued to remain civil.

As Ebony resumed her dragon form, she made her way to Thor, and the two dragons nuzzled each other before she took to the skies. Thor, however, remained looking heavenward with a loving gaze. Dismissing the pit of jealousy that brewed within her, Selena reached over and stroked his neck. *She will come back to you.*

I know. Still, Thor wouldn't tear his stare away.

I thought dragons took on many mates.

We do, but—

You love her.

I think I do.

Silver's demeanor brightened once his sister vanished beyond the horizon, and he clapped for Selena's performance. "You were amazing, as always." He looked back at Rahim, who gave Selena a thumb's up in approval. "And she was supposed to be the best sword's master the world had ever seen, but you were on par to her sixteen-thousand-years of skill."

"I couldn't imagine," Rahim began, "but she stands no chance in defeating a Divinity Dragon."

Selena laughed, but her chest and back hurt too much. If time weren't of the essence, she would allow herself to collapse right then and there to sleep for days on end. However, she held her stance, and when Silver noticed her discomfort, he said, "As promised, I will lead you three to Ulrich. Are you ready to meet the mad god who tried to kill you?"

After the trio removed their guard disguises and donned their usual attire, they rode with Thor to the very top of the mountain in wariness of the thickening and violent plumes of clouds protecting the summit. Selena and Silver manipulated the air around them, creating a bubble shielding Thor, allowing them to fly through the vehement weather safely. Her back pain slowly returned during their journey, and Selena did her best to endure it. It wasn't easy, but she remained focused on the task and what awaited them within Ulrich's fortress.

That potion Ebony gave you seems to be wearing off. Will you be all right?

I have to be.

That's not what I'm asking. We don't have to do this right now if you aren't.

Selena caught herself too trusting of Ulrich, now doubting if she genuinely was ready to face what was needed to help her overcome her pain. Yet, Thor's unstable power was what she feared the most. As Ulrich's lair grew closer, her concern for Thor's uncertain future weighed upon her like a crushing boulder, but she didn't dare share her fears with her dragon. Upsetting him was what Selena hoped to avoid.

The clouds dispersed as soon as the group reached the mountain peak. Silver and Selena halted their casting as Thor balanced himself upon the icy fortress. His claws clicked against the slippery slope, but he dug his nails deep into snow and stone and pulled himself forward.

Ulrich's lair was a harsh winter tundra; his crystallized cave was large enough to house ten dragons the size of Thor—his eyes dazzled in a gleam from seeing the treasured cave. The Divine's fortress was made of turquoise ice formations glimmering in the light. Upon further admiration, Selena noticed how the diamond christened glaze was caused by the waterfalls that froze unevenly across the surface. From what Silver explained, Ulrich used magic to force the blocks to be pushed up onto the surface of the frozen falls, thus creating his gem-like lair.

As Selena and her group dismounted from Thor's saddle, Rahim took a peep inside but withdrew himself and shivered. "You three go first." Thor went ahead of the others. Despite Silver's assurance, she and Rahim remained on high alert. After all, they were going to meet one of the Divines.

Selena's eyes were drawn to the countless scrolls and books stacked upon the stone shelves gracing the walls as they entered. "I see where you draw inspiration from, Silver."

"I think it's the other way around. Ulrich borrowed some of *my* books." Silver took it upon himself to dig through Ulrich's collection and began pulling out titles he recognized as his.

"Well, yes, but only a few books, *Silver.*" Selena and Rahim looked at each other as neither one of them spoke. Silver didn't seem bothered by the unfamiliar voice, and instead, he waved his hand to dismiss that earlier comment.

The great Emerald Dragon himself came from the other side of the cave, the gems from his fortress making his scales sparkle and gleam. Ulrich kept his wings half furled against his sides with every heavy step he made; the leaf-green leather-textured membrane chipped along the edges due to age and battle were dabbed in specs of yellow, orange, and blue. The dazzling crystals reflected upon his wings, making them look like stained glass. Selena couldn't help but admire the resemblance between him and Thor: their crown-shaped horns, but she shared Ulrich's emerald eyes. The now-sane Divine approached the four and bowed his head in greeting.

Selena and her friends returned the gesture, unsure how to address the mad god. "Ulrich, it's good to meet you under better circumstances."

Unlike Thor and how other dragons communicated, Ulrich verbally spoke. He had a calm and deep voice that was very easy on the ears, like auditory honey. "Yes, it is I, Liongod. After my mind cleared, I've been waiting here for you and Thor."

Thor lowered his head. **It's an honor to meet you, Divine One.**

Rahim emerged from the shadows and attempted to conquer his fear. "I hope we didn't keep you waiting too long after you, well, you know, destroyed Rhumbek."

Ulrich sat down and flickered his massive tail. "I cannot help that. Every era, I lose my mind and control over my powers. I try to fight it, and each time, I fail. There is no stopping Rhumbek's dark fate."

"How can we still remember when the rest of the world doesn't?" Selena asked.

The great dragon's emerald eyes shimmered as he blinked. "Because I allowed it so. When I saw you and Thor there, I had a brief moment of clarity, and I willed it for you and your friends to remember in hopes that it would help end my curse. However, I couldn't fight it off for long, and I became insane again after my short interval of sanity."

"I couldn't imagine such a fate." Selena spun around and placed a hand on Thor's shoulder. *What do you think? Are you ready for this?*

I've been ready.

Ulrich read their thoughts. "We shall see, Young Ones."

Selena's head whipped around. "Wait a minute. Can you understand Thor?"

"Of course, I can. As one of the Divines, I can understand all creatures and mortals. I commune with all living and non-living things." He arched his neck and stared directly into Thor's eyes. "You have grown, Divine One." Gleaming in delight, Thor adjusted his shoulders and straightened out his neck more as he puffed out his chest.

Selena smiled. "How big do dragons get? Thor is still young, but he's larger than any dragon I've seen."

"We never stop growing, Young One. You should have met the Ancient Ones. The mighty dragons from the Mythic Flight attained that status before entering Niflheim, growing as big as mountains and able to hold their breaths for hours. When it was time, the ancient souls joined the Aether streams that help sustain life. We eventually lost the need to hunt for sustenance and soon evolved to where the Aether energies preserved us. We are all part of this great cycle, and one day, you will reach enlightenment, Divine One."

I would have loved to meet the Ancient Dragons.

As would I.

"The Ancient Ones have never left us. We are all part of each other." Ulrich bowed his head. "Liongod, once you gain control of your powers, you will be as much of a dragon as Thor and I, and we are the most powerful creatures known to exist. No magic or artificial ward can stop us or our breath abilities as we are the ultimate form of magic—magic comes from us dragons, and mortals learned how to harness the elements upon watching us.

Our energy runs through your veins, and you are a dragon through mind, body, and soul. Please, allow me to examine you two." Ulrich's eyes locked on Thor's, the two dragons locked in an unblinking battle. All communication with Thor was severed for a few seconds, but before Selena could argue, Ulrich broke away and swiveled his head to challenge her unbroken will.

Her shoulders trembled as the Emerald Dragon sniffed her hair and face, but what terrified her more was the sudden absence of sound proceeding his judgment. Over the agonizing growing seconds, she heard her heartbeat pounding against her chest as if it wanted to escape, and the ringing within her ears grew deafening. She listened to her bones grinding against each other with any slight movement she made. Then, after Ulrich pulled away from his unyielding stare, Selena's senses finally returned, and she could breathe in sweet relief.

Without warning, Ulrich swung his massive body and marched directly over to Silver before Selena or Thor could ask what happened. "I've warned you, *demigod*, that I feared it was too late." Silver, however, only shrugged and ignored the bombardment of questions the group fired at him. Unsatisfied, the Divine hissed through his clamped fangs and swished his tail, crashing against the crystals growing from the ground; even Thor took a step back to avoid Ulrich's strikes.

"What do you mean by too late?" Selena asked.

The Divine entity unfolded his wings and let out a long groan in despair before shooting another smoldering glare at Silver for lying to him about the severity of Selena's and Thor's situation. After Silver did his best to explain his actions to save the pair, no matter the cost, Ulrich's chest swelled, and he dug his nails into the dirt. "Your wounds are too far gone, Young One, and

Thor, your mind has become tainted. I can no longer help you two."

A meteor could have struck Selena, and she would still have felt the same; Ulrich's devastating blow almost knocked her down as she panicked and immediately looked over to Thor, who snarled and unfurled his wings to retaliate against Ulrich's lies.

When Selena couldn't bring herself to ask, Thor challenged the Divine on her behalf: **You're a god, aren't you? You should have the power, for I will not lose her again.**

"I would if it were not for the Day of Eternal Darkness." Ulrich sounded offended, his voice reaching a roar, but his shoulders and wings relaxed with every deep breath he took. When Thor still didn't back down, the Emerald Dragon continued explaining, "Every day that passes, I grow weaker. Even if I was at my full strength, purifying dark energy is not easy, and cleansing a Divine entity is nearly impossible." Ulrich arched his neck over Thor and barely nudged his snout against the crimson hide. "You must take care if you don't want to repeat your mistakes from Snowhaven, Divine One."

Selena's glistening eyes laid upon Thor, her expression nearly begging for an explanation of what Ulrich meant. Was he too far gone to be saved? *What happened to you in Snowhaven? What did you do?*

Thor hung his head in shame and swung his body away. **I....**

"Snowhaven is now nothing but a rubble of ice and stone." Ulrich snarled as he flickered his tail.

Thor roared through his clamped fangs and swiped at a nearby crystal growing from the ground after Rahim dashed away from the rampaging dragon, shattering the gem with his sharpened claws. Selena recalled his threats of destroying a city if harm were to befall her, but she never imagined he would do it; her heart sank to her feet as she reached out to touch him, but Thor recoiled further.

You never told me that you destroyed the capital. Selena turned to Silver and Rahim, who were both twiddling their thumbs. "Neither of you thought to mention what happened to the city?" Rahim bit his tongue, but he didn't have a proper response.

Silver turned pale, and his lips shuddered. "You've been dealt with handling such a heavy burden. You shouldn't have to worry about whether you would lose Thor, too."

Thor's low growls turned to deep rumbles as he snaked his head around to meet her teary gaze. **I was angry with myself. I'm so sorry.**

While Thor and Selena attempted to reconcile with what had happened, Silver cleared his throat and approached the snarling Ulrich with extreme caution. The Divine's eyes turned to slits and lifted his lips to reveal his serrated fangs, but Silver clapped his hands once and said with a cracked voice, "I understand that I wasn't *entirely* truthful," but the green dragon interrupted him with a sharp growl. Silver clicked his tongue against his teeth but continued, "But please, is there anything you can do to help them? If anyone can, it's you."

Seemingly appeased by his slight groveling, Ulrich straightened his neck and shoulders but said, "Selena and Thor may be too far from being saved."

"We won't know unless we try."

The Emerald Dragon dipped his head and twirled around; Selena and Thor paused in the middle of making their amends and watched the Divine with pleading expressions.

The Divine snorted as he raised his wings over his head, the tips brushing and bending against the ceiling of his lair. "I cannot guarantee your success, but if you are to withstand my training, Divine Ones, you will need to face your anger and let it go. As I see it, the only possible way to cleanse the dark Aether that now corrupts you both is for you two to unleash your powers. I may not purify you two, but I can at least show you how and the rest will be up to you." Ulrich stepped forward and lowered his head to make eye contact with Selena, addressing her directly. "I know that Silver passed on Revelation's secrets to you, but you're still far from ready to face the Dark Master." Ulrich reclined his neck back and inched his snout close to Thor's. "I'm still unsure about your success, Divine One, but...." The dragon's voice trailed off as he sighed. "I believe Silver is correct, and right now, it's the only chance we have if we are to face the Dark Master."

They were interrupted when Rahim mumbled under his breath. When he looked up and saw that Ulrich was snaking his head towards him, he screamed and tripped over his feet, but the Divine remained undeterred by his fear; Ulrich stopped and sniffed the top of Rahim's head with no regard to his apprehension. "I know that you're burning with questions, Little One. What were you trying to ask?"

Rahim relaxed his shoulders and straightened up, eyes darting over to Selena. "Before you start training Selena and Thor, I wondered if you knew what happened to my father." He hung his head. "I thought we saw and fought him before, but I didn't believe it was him."

Ulrich backed away and turned around to face a stone basin filled with crystal clear water on the other end of his cave; many colored gemstones jutted from the edges, the calm and undisturbed pool serving as Ulrich's looking glass. "I'm sorry, young Rahim, but I'm afraid your worst fears have been realized. His is a dark tale."

"I still don't believe that. Please, tell me that my father didn't become one of those *things*. I want to know what happened to him and what will become of him." Selena bit her lip when Rahim wouldn't accept that his father was now one of the Dreygur. She wasn't sure if Ulrich confirming it would make breaking the news any better.

The Emerald Dragon sighed and hung his head in defeat when Rahim wouldn't back down. "Very well, but I can't tell the future—just mere glimpses. The future is hard to predict. As you all know, the outcome can change based on your choices." He made his way to the bowl and gestured with his claws for the others to follow him. Silver was the last to join, but he had a few scrolls stuffed away in his jacket. "Will you please put those away? You know that they belong to me." Silver muttered inappropriate comments under his breath, but he did as Ulrich asked.

Thor approached and sniffed the azure water, his snout barely dipping its surface. **What is this?**

"This allows me to see visions and the thoughts and memories of others, Divine One. It can also help me see what's happening in different parts of the world. It takes time and patience, reflection and focus."

Rahim squinted his eyes at the dragon god and held his hands to his head. "Okay then. What am I thinking now? What about now?"

Selena elbowed him. "Rahim, stop it."

Ulrich's nostrils flared, but he ignored them and stood in front of the pool. The azure waters swirled towards the center, and a figure of a strange man began to appear on the surface. "Wait, something is coming into focus." The four leaned forward to see the Divine's vision. "I can't see where your father has gone, young Rahim, but all I see is the darkness surrounding him." The image faded, and the silhouette of the Lich appeared riding a dragon in front of his massive Dreygur army.

"What does that mean?" Selena swallowed hard, but she didn't want to state the obvious if Rahim were to lash out. She did her best to pretend like their previous meeting with the Nidhoggr rider didn't happen.

"If it is what I believe it is, it seems as though Rahim's father swore himself to the Lich and is now part of the Obsidian Order as a Dreygur with powers over necromancy."

Rahim's eyes shimmered when he realized that what he feared was, in fact, reality. "No...."

Ulrich inched his head closer to the water. "You must understand, Young One. After leaving you and your mother, he was taken by the Lich and his followers. He was poisoned and corrupted and has spent the most recent years in darkness. He now knows no other way and was made to do the Dark Master's bidding."

Rahim backed away from the vision pool and held his hands to his mouth to keep from making a sound. "No, I don't believe in that. Why would he join them? *THEM!*"

Ulrich's voice filled with deep sorrow. "Your father didn't have a choice. No one can resist the dark magic."

Rahim couldn't hold back his tears. "Just like they did to Niamh. Is there no hope for her, either?"

"I fear the worst for her."

Rahim's jaw trembled, and he stumbled backwards as if Ulrich had swiped at him. His breathing became harsh and quick, and his eyes flooded over. Selena rushed over to hold him and let him weep over her shoulder, but instead, he pushed her away and wiped his tears with his sleeve. "No, I don't believe in any of that."

Selena sucked in her cheeks. "There must be hope for both, right?" Rahim sniffed but nodded. "Then we can still try, no matter what." She turned to face Ulrich. "What about Azrael?"

"I'm afraid for my brother."

Selena and Thor exchanged surprised glances while Rahim lifted his head halfway; Silver, meanwhile, remained unfazed, and she assumed he probably knew. "Your brother? Then you, Xyaxon, Azrael, and Artio are siblings."

"Indeed, we are."

Rahim pointed at Ulrich. "Who is Artio? I thought there were only three gods."

"Our sister watches over those in the Hinterlands. That is her domain."

"I met her once," Selena began and twirled her wolf necklace in her fingers, "when the Aynu accepted us into their pack."

Rahim raised a brow when he looked down at his fox pendant. "How did you meet her?"

When she realized that Rahim shot her an angry and questioning glance and Thor was tapping his claws against the stone in irritation for keeping a secret from him, Selena stumbled through her story: "It was after the ceremony. Time froze for a moment, and I heard her voice. I asked Azrael about it, and he told me she was his sister, but I had no idea that Xyaxon and Ulrich were his brothers."

"It sounds like all of you went on loads of adventures during your trip to Snowhaven." Silver smirked.

After Rahim was satisfied with the answer, he, Selena, and Silver shared a few hearty laughs, but Thor was not amused. Instead, he snarled. **You've been keeping secrets from me, too.**

Selena kept her response cold. *It's not as bad as you not telling me about Snowhaven.*

Eyes turning to slits, Thor growled, and his head spun away. Selena, still feeling betrayed, ignored him. She reached into her pocket and twirled the watch that hid Revelation's true nature in her fingers. "Is there anything that we can do to save Azrael and Niamh? You say that you fear the worst, but we have to do something."

Ulrich's tail swished over to his other side. "I can't stop you from doing anything. However, if there is a chance against the Lich and his army, you will need to learn much more. Now, come with me. I have something for you two."

Before following the Divine dragon, Selena took one last peek into Ulrich's pool of visions, as the previous image still rippled across the water. The dragon seemed oddly familiar; a stone dropped in her stomach when looking at Thor.

*****

CHAPTER 13: HIS SOLEMN HOUR

"**Y**ou and your crew are highly qualified for the mission I have in mind, Captain Battleraven." Vidar clasped his hands together as he leaned forward against his desk. The band of mercenaries wasted no time in meeting with him after returning to Rune Citadel. Their fleet of flying airships docked around the mountain metropolis, overlooking the smoldering remains of Alfheim. A lamp stood between the half-elf and Dante Battleraven, the fearsome sky pirate captain of the *Blood Diamond*, an awe-inspiring ship capable of carrying up to forty fifteen-ton dragons. The sixty-gun heavy frigate was considered the largest and most powerful vessel ever constructed.

The captain's wide-brimmed hat shrouded his chiseled and scarred face in shadow, veiling Battleraven as he twirled his richly jeweled necklace with his bony fingers. "You know I don't do anything for free. Everything comes at a price." Vidar cleared his throat as he reached down and grabbed a sealed trunk that he threw down on the table and pushed towards the captain. Battleraven snatched it and popped open the top, revealing a pile of glowing riches inside. Confident in officiating this deal, Vidar watched as the sky pirate captain grabbed a single gold coin and inspected it. "What do you need me to do?"

A vicious sneer played upon Vidar's lips after capturing his attention. "Are you familiar with Selena Liongod?"

"Aye. Your gormless companion wouldn't keep his bloody trap shut about her."

Vidar stood up and paced his office, ignoring the captain's complaint about Ashur Bel. "Word has spread of her surviving Snowhaven. I didn't believe it until recently, and now she has declared herself the 'Queen of Dragons.' But she's not the one sitting upon the throne."

Battleraven scowled and pinched the bridge of his long, crooked nose. "Sod off, or get to the point."

"She recently paid a visit to my lovely Mortemholdt and helped my special guest escape, not to mention killing a bunch of my guards and prisoners. I want you and your crew to find and kidnap Liongod by any means necessary. I have no qualms if you must kill her, but I prefer her alive for now."

Battleraven burst into raspy laughter. "You want me to waste my time chasing down this brat because she freed your prisoner. Please, I have more important matters that require my attention. That's not my problem."

Vidar sneered. "What matters are those, if I may ask? More important than your illegal fighting arena?"

Captain Battleraven growled and scoffed at Vidar's insulting comment. "It doesn't matter what's legal or not. I have a business to run here, and it doesn't involve chasing down little girls. The point is, there's a lot of gold involved. Besides," he turned and nodded to the floating ships, "with how anxious and pent-up my crew is, there probably wouldn't be much left of the girl to give you once they're done with her. Again, this isn't my problem."

"It will be soon if she isn't dealt with now." Vidar turned around and placed both palms on his desk to face the captain. "The Council and I now serve His Dark Majesty. Since I hired you and your band of mercenaries, you also serve the Dark Master. Selena Liongod is the only one who poses a threat to the one we serve and any ongoing contracts and dealings between you and me in the foreseeable future. If you and your crew help us deal with that trouble, there will be more gold: half now, half later. As you've said so yourself, Captain, everything comes at a price."

Slightly intrigued by the promised fortune, Battleraven rubbed his chin, and his dark brown eyes sparkled from the lamp's fire. "We've heard of her dragon. How do we deal with it?"

"You don't need to worry about the dragon: the problem will soon solve itself." Vidar spun around on his toes and glared at the captain. "And tell your crew to leave something to give to me. I don't care if they want to have their fun, but I prefer you keep her alive and in one piece. The Dark Master wants to deal with her himself."

*****

As Ulrich spun around, the wall behind him rumbled and sank into the ground, revealing a hidden pathway, dimly lit by blue crystals jutting above their heads. The winding passage swirled deeper within the mountainside, the gem light fading into the encroaching darkness awaiting them.

Rahim rolled his eyes and gestured at Silver. "Oh, more training sounds wonderful."

The Divine spun his head around and snarled. "This isn't like any training you've seen. You and Silver will remain here. Selena and Thor, this way. It is time to unleash your true power."

Thor followed the Divine without question, but Selena dragged her feet as the image from Ulrich's pool still haunted her. The lingering threat of the Lich snatching him away was almost like walking down the stairs in absolute darkness and missing a step, tumbling into the abyss. Yet, she fought through the burning inferno waiting to be unleashed; it was hard to forgive their crime of secrecy concerning Snowhaven's fate, as she had every right to know.

Silver reached over and cupped her hands, but Selena withdrew from his touch. "I'm sorry, my dear. I don't know what you want me to say."

"I hardly know what I want to hear."

"You can be mad at us later. Promise me that you'll return when you two finish magic school, okay?" Rahim lightheartedly added and laughed. After fighting through her boiling wrath, Selena was thankful to see he perked up after accepting his father's fate.

Enchanting as the corridor was, she heard Ulrich's voice echo before she could look at Silver and Rahim one last time. "Do not look back, Young One."

Not heeding the god's warning, Selena spun around to find the way back was blocked and shrouded in obscurity. She then faced forward, and Ulrich and Thor vanished; the crystals above faded, leaving her trapped in the devouring darkness within her lonely world. Her breaths quickened until she backed against the wall, focusing on keeping herself grounded and not succumbing to fear. Her only company was Ulrich's voice ringing throughout the tunnel. "You must face your fear. What are you most afraid of?"

As Selena made her way through the gem passage, her mind raced to Xyaxon's challenge in Niflheim after destroying Ragnarok; she immediately fell into despair upon blaming herself for failing to stop the Lich. Because of her, the Dark Master will destroy their world, and Thor and Silver will be lost to her forever. The mere fact she was the one responsible made her recoil in the gloom. "You've led yourself to believe in failure. You must let your fears go."

The Divine's gentle voice beckoned her to look up at the flickering blue crystals, threatening to extinguish because of her hopelessness. *Have I learned nothing from Xyaxon's teachings?*

The gems sparkled to life, like twinkling stars, from the other end of the passageway; Selena noticed her shadow dancing across the ground and stretching up before her until it took her form. Much like Xyaxon's original lesson about self-acceptance, her copy mimicked her moves and voiced every word she said. "I'm not a failure."

The shadow clone shattered like glass. Selena immediately dashed through the vanishing shards towards the glimmering lights; she entered a crystal cavern with gemstones growing in mineral pools, a fairytale-lovely rock of rainbow. Selena became attracted to their enchanting aura, and like a dragon allured to treasure, her eyes ravenously took in the delightful sparkling scenery.

Ulrich's voice twinkled in her ears, a sound she imagined the glittering gemstones themselves could speak. "Good. If you are to bring about a new age of peace to this world, you need to be a positive force for yourself and others. You will need to forgive yourself."

Like a deadly firestorm, a pang of burning guilt ached in her chest. She condemned herself for all the misfortunes her friends and family had to endure because of her, and she could no longer hold back tears as she began to relive every mistake she had made. She never forgave herself for losing Helshire Village to the Obsidian Order; it was her fault for Alfheim's downfall and the death of innocents and her comrades. Armageddon fell because she hand-delivered the dragon eggs to the Lich, the final key to his gambit. She was the reason for the Empire's demise. "I-I did this…."

"Let your pain and grief flow. Accept your choices, but do not allow your emotions to consume you, or you will never hope to move forward."

*****

Thor's ivory talons clacked with every step he took as his eyes drew to every sparkle the gems gracing the walls made. He admired the various colors, never seeing such a flawless display of iridescent rainbow glittering upon the tunnel rock. Yet, Thor focused on following Ulrich, but he felt an itch throbbing in his mind that he couldn't scratch.

My dear, I hope you can forgive me for what I've done. I'm sorry. When Selena didn't answer, he stopped and whipped his head around. His tail thrashed against the walls when she and Ulrich were nowhere to be found. **Selena, my dear one? Where are you?**

Thor was again alone with his thoughts; he swore never to allow their mental link to sever again. His chest swelled, and he dug his claws into the dirt as his eye color flickered between red and a deep purple.

"Clear your mind, Divine One," Ulrich's voice called out, "you've indeed felt a great loss and pain. You must learn to control your emotions if you can tame the true Divine powers within you."

Where is Selena? What did you do to her? Ulrich didn't answer his demands. Thor's nostrils flared, and sparks of fire erupted from his mouth.

"You have so much love for her, but you're still stricken with grief and doubt." He recalled the very first moment he and Selena met. All he remembered even

183

within his egg was her endearing presence; their energies always linked the two.

The scene played out before him in a vision, and he watched himself hatching from within the Lich's lair at Mount Blackrock, his baby self stumbling out of the shell to be by Selena's side. He neither knew her name nor his connection to her, but Thor never wanted to be apart. His heart filled with the love and warmth that burned for her. **I never want to leave you.**

"If you are to face the Lich and his army, you will need a clear mind and heart to withstand the evil that now consumes Armageddon. Lay all your grief out before you, and let it go."

Thor shut his eyes and spread out his wings to create a protective barrier, his thoughts drifting to when Silver and Selena first kissed: the first time he ever felt jealousy. Despite its revolting and poisonous thorn threatening to pierce his heart, he didn't want to interfere in his rider's love life but only wished for her affections; he believed that no one else deserved them but him.

His vision changed, and Thor recalled the moment when Silver first approached him for his blessing to ask Selena for her hand in marriage. He was, of course, more than willing to be supportive of their love, but his selfish behavior became his familiar taste of poison. **You were supposed to belong only to me.**

"You must let your pain flow away. You have grown possessive, and therefore your love for your rider was toxic. Accept that Selena can share her affections with both you and Silver. Her love for you will never leave you."

When Silver first proposed, Thor felt neglected and replaced. He knew she tried including him in all she did, but it wasn't the same; he convinced himself of the impossibility that she would make time for him. Yet, in his companionship with Ebony, Thor somewhat understood, but his grief grew when realizing that *he* was the one who abandoned *her.*

Their final fight against Medusa and her army in Snowhaven began replaying before him, and he saw himself after Selena fell in battle. The way he felt, the ruin he wanted to cause; all Thor wanted to do was kill and destroy. Even if Rahim and Azrael had intervened, he would have struck them down.

Ulrich's voice rang like the tolls of a bell: "Selena's love for you would never leave this world. It will always reside in your heart."

A light shimmered from the other side of his tunnel, and Thor rushed to it without hesitation. **Selena, are you there?**

His head throbbed like it was about to burst. To his disappointment, the glow led him to a crystallized cavern crafted to mirror Ulrich's lair, the turquoise ice formations glittering across his crimson hide. His steps were slow and heavy as he looked around with extreme caution, ignoring his attraction to the gemstones surrounding him.

"You need to let go of what you fear most and control your wrath."

His surroundings melted away, and Thor found himself standing in the middle of Snowhaven, fighting against Medusa and her undead army. His desperation crept in as his heart almost exploded from his chest upon watching Selena tossed into the growing violent Turquoise Ocean, threatening to tear her limb from limb. **My dearest one, no....**

Thor attempted to charge in after her, but he couldn't; his paws froze to the ice, his muscles refusing to obey no matter how hard he tried. He watched in horror as the scene played before him. Although Selena was in the middle of casting a massive maelstrom of ice and water, once more, Thor stood by as Medusa sliced off her left hand and prepared her final blow, and Selena's chest and back tore open. Her blood splattered all over the ice, and Thor's brewing rage grew to the most violent storm the world had ever seen.

As Thor began yielding to his despair and fury, Ulrich's voice interrupted his destructive thoughts: "If you are to control your Divine powers, you will need to restrain your emotions. Let it go."

Thor was finally in command again, but he completely ignored Ulrich's lesson and tapped into his dark energy as he did before, unleashing his catastrophic wrath. The black magic released and killed Medusa and her army in ever-expanding concentric circles of power, and his surroundings faded after finishing his onslaught. When all returned to focus, Thor found that the harrowing scene began repeating itself.

Again, turning a deaf ear to Ulrich's teaching, Thor gave in to his power and anger upon watching Selena's death, destroying his enemies. His corrupted thoughts and emotions slowly consumed him while enduring eternal torment; with every recurrence of the memory, Thor began slipping into insanity. His vision would reset, and he would make the same choices each time, watching Selena die repeatedly; his eyes kept flickering between red and purple, and his blood-diamond scales flashed red and black.

"Let your anger go."

No, I will never let it go.

*****

Could I bring peace to this chaotic world?

Breathing deep, Selena closed her eyes and imagined her friends and allies with her, all in smiles, and she saw hope and the willingness to keep moving forward in each of their faces. Her eyes glossed over like a frozen lake, and her face beamed like a beacon in Armageddon's darkest hour.

Ulrich continued: "Very good. The Divinity Dragon can bring us into the dawn of a new age." However, Selena's smile faded, and her copper-skin tone turned pearlescent white when the Divine added, "If you are to protect the ones you love the most, you will need to detach yourself from them. Only then will you be able to unlock the true dragon within you."

All her friends and family: Rahim, Chaliss, her parents, everyone whom she formed an acquaintance with, the idea of casting them away from her heart and mind was as impossible as counting grains of sand from the beach or the infinite stars. Her fragile heart shattered when she imagined severing emotional ties to Silver and Thor, and her emerald eyes glimmered from an uncontrollable stream of tears. "But I love them."

"You must learn to let go of those closest to you if you're to control the Divine energy flowing through you. Let them go."

Before she could object to Ulrich's teachings any further, two shadows emerged from the corner of her crystal cave; Selena took a defensive stance as she prepared for an attack without hesitation. However, her shoulders relaxed, and her arms dropped to her sides when Thor and Silver approached, and she immediately wiped her eyes dry. "I'm so glad to see you two again. Pray forgive me for how I reacted, but please, promise that you two won't keep secrets from me." Selena opened her arms to them, but they didn't return the gesture.

Instead of exchanging words and pleasantries, Silver sneered and summoned his reaper scythe of azure and gold, while Thor snarled and hissed at her, unfurling his wings while flames plumed and boiled from his maw.

Selena winced and recoiled from their sudden hostility; it seemed as though the world around her vanished, and she plunged into the void.

Ulrich's voice twinkled like a gentle tune being carried by the wind. "Let your attachments to your loved ones go, and allow your Divine energy flow."

Selena backed away and gritted her teeth, having enough of what Ulrich had to say. "No, I will not let them go—I love them."

Silver followed Selena's statement with a swing of his weapon with no regard to her profession of love, but her betrayed trepidation kept her trapped in position. He was too quick for her to evade, and with great reluctance, she ruefully held up her left hand in a wasted and foolish effort to block. She had to choose between him cutting at her midsection or her mechanical hand, and she didn't have much time to debate. His blade descended upon her prosthetic, and it was sliced clean off in one swipe.

Her Aether source severed so suddenly felt as painful as Medusa chopping off her natural hand. At first, her arm tingled, and it burned like it was on fire. Selena dropped to her knees and held her amputated arm to her chest while she screamed and convulsed, staining her clothes and the ground crimson. However, she didn't have time to nurse her arm as she had to react fast; she was in the way of Thor's oncoming attack. He reared up and swiped with his sword-sharp claws, but Selena moved out of the way with nary a second to spare.

Yet, it was too soon to celebrate her small evasive victory; she was slow as Thor spun around and knocked her down with his tail. Her eyes flooded when she knew he and Silver would not ease up on their attacks. She mouthed the words, "But I love you," and couldn't bring herself to attack back. "I promised to love you both."

Ulrich resumed pleading, "Surrender yourself. Let them go."

When both Silver and Thor were upon her, she finally gave in and spoke. "I'm sorry." Then, she got down to her knees and closed her eyes as she bowed. Time stopped when she began concentrating and meditating: Silver and Thor froze in mid-pursuit. Even the floating dust particles couldn't escape its timeless prison.

Within the deepest confines of her subconsciousness, she saw herself surrounded by stars, drifting across the infinite cosmos. Among the swirling stars adorning the nether sky—like diamonds emblazoned in a crown—an aurora light flashed across the void and solidified into a radiant platform beneath her feet.

Selena turned from her world below and saw a massive entity standing on the other side, her spectral Divinity Dragon form reveling in absolute glory, beauty, and power. She set out towards it with much caution, her mouth open in awe and appreciation; as she neared her dragon self, its eyes shone brighter than the surrounding stars. The celestial being was as brilliant as the three Divines themselves, wisps of blue Aether pluming from its body and around the massive ruby engraved into its chest. Azure fire writhed around its crown-shaped horns, reflecting against the gem's crimson shine that painfully reminded her of Thor; even the dragon within her always carried his memento close to its heart. *How can Ulrich say that I must let him and Silver go?*

She reached out with her only hand to touch it, but the Divinity Dragon reared its head back and roared, its thunder quivering the eternal ether. She flinched and stepped back as it expanded its enormous spectral wings, preparing to attack with claws and fangs at the ready. Selena fell backwards and crawled away just as the dragon stood on its haunches and slammed its front paws down, its long, sword-length claws clicking against the ethereal glass.

I don't know what I'm supposed to do.

All she could do was run, as she neither had a sword nor shield to help fight back. Her inner dragon swiped at her with its talons, but she rolled out of harm's way; as the celestial being swept its tail across the platform to knock her down, Selena sidestepped again and switched to using magic. She summoned fireballs and followed with icicle shards targeting her dragon self, but to her dismay, the dragon absorbed her attacks and continued with its cataclysmal course.

Ulrich's voice echoed in her thoughts. "The only way to tame the dragon within you is to let them go."

Tears rolled down her face. "I...."

A distressed cry suddenly distracted her, and as the Divinity Dragon was upon her, Selena saw a vision of Thor standing alone in a crystal cavern, issuing his destruction as his dark Aether consumed him. Before realizing it, her Divine Dragon state lunged forward with its claws and knocked her off the platform, casting her into the endless abyss. Selena began to plummet, watching as the Divine entity and the ethereal path vanished; she fell through the starry void and crashed down to her world.

Selena jerked awake, and Thor and Silver disappeared from her cave. They were only illusions, and she had to run and fight. "Thor is in trouble—I must help him."

Desperately reaching out to him, she could hear Thor's suffering roars. Still holding her severed arm, she ran towards the exit, but she halted when Ulrich called out. "No, you must let him go. If you don't, your dragon state will corrupt and destroy you."

Selena paused as if to heed the Divine's warning, but she dashed ahead without the slightest care for her safety—Thor was in danger, and he needed her. She didn't know where she was going but did her best to follow her dragon's roars trembling throughout the mountain, and eventually, the tunnel brought her to where she wanted to be.

She paused in her tracks at the sight of her dragon's solemn hour; shrouded in a black aura, Thor hung his head, his chest swelled with each breath he took, growing deeper and heavier. Ulrich emerged within the gem cavern from the other end as the peak quivered, but he kept his distance.

Thor, stop!

The distraught dragon ignored her and summoned violent, screeching winds circling him. The brewing storm threatened her; however, disregarding her safety, she trudged onward to join his side, regardless of her fate.

As his rampage grew, Ulrich neither intervened nor said a single word. Instead, he sat and watched in despair and dismay as the dark Aether slowly devoured Thor. His growing rage pushed Selena back with a wave of energy, and she pleaded to Ulrich for assistance. "What are you doing? Help him." The Emerald Dragon only shook his head and swished his tail.

The screaming windstorm surrounding Thor turned to black energy, and soon, the deadly maelstrom immersed the dragon. When the magical vortex faded and dispersed, his scales became like the void, and dark Aether danced upon his hide like wisps of fire. He unfurled his wings, and to Selena's horror, the now onyx membranes became like shadows leaving tendrils of black magic with every movement. When she made eye contact with him, her heart sank to see Thor's irises clouded in a dark purple veil.

Thor, no.... His mind was twisted and corrupted, and he no longer understood her. When the screaming storm completely dissipated, Selena rushed forward. Thor made no attempts to respond when she reached up to touch his muzzle. *No, this isn't you. This darkness isn't who you are. Please, answer me.*

He didn't flinch. Selena's chest ached, and her heart shattered; she dropped to her knees as a harrowing tune rang through her ears, holding her only hand to her head as she heard a voice call out: *Join me, Destroyer of Worlds. The time has come for you to serve the Dark Master.*

Thor snaked his head upward and roared obediently. Dark Aether boiled within his maw, and he unleashed a black beam with lightning pulsating around the energy, blasting a massive hole through the rock ceiling, opening to the grieving heavens. Selena watched him launch upwards in one leap away from Ulrich's fortress, black ribbons of dark magic trailing behind from every wing flap.

Still holding to her severed arm, Selena threw herself to where he stood previously and looked at the sky in despair, his shape slowly disappearing into the night. Watching him succumb to the Lich's dark magic was more painful than losing her hand ten-fold. *No, please, answer me. Come back.*

Ulrich flickered his tail and lowered his head. "It's no use, Young One. Thor now belongs to His Dark Majesty." She refused to listen as she kept calling out to him, hoping to hear his voice again but failed each time. *No,* she thought, *Thor would eventually answer. He had to.*

As Ulrich watched Selena continue calling for her dragon, Silver and Rahim finally reached them. The two looked to the dragon god, then to the distraught Selena; Silver pointed a shaky finger at Ulrich. "What happened here?"

The Divine remained still as a statue, his sea-green eyes beginning to shimmer in anguish for Selena's sudden loss. "It was just as I feared. They were not ready."

Rahim stood beside Ulrich as he could not offer any words of comfort. On the other hand, Silver inched his way to Selena, reaching out to touch her shoulder, but she moved away. Instead of acknowledging her friends' return, she spun around to face Ulrich, ready to explode at any moment. "What did you do to my dragon?" When he didn't answer, she swung her only hand, casting a fire blast, obliterating the crystals on the other side of the cavern. "What did you do to Thor?!"

Silver's rage boiled, matching hers. "What happened?"

All the indifferent Emerald Dragon could say was, "Selena and Thor needed to learn how to control their powers, and I was showing them how. There was no other way."

Selena allowed herself to give in to her ever-growing fury. A ball of light shrouded her, transforming into her spectral dragon form; her eyes glowed crimson like the ruby upon her chest, the unstable energy risking rendering her to pieces. The dragon trembled as the rage continued stirring and growing.

"What did you do to Thor?! Tell me what you put him through!" Her voice was no longer hers, as if it didn't belong in their world. She summoned a lightning storm swirling around her, growing and billowing with each heavy breath she took.

Rahim escaped through the tunnel he and Silver came through, and Ulrich lowered his head, but he offered no explanation or fought back. Silver, however, stayed and faced Selena's wrath.

Her storm grew and spread rapidly throughout the cave as he made his way through the violent screaming

wind and reached her. As he wrapped his arms around
Selena's exposed neck and hugged her, the storm lessened,
and tears streamed down her snout. Silver did his best not
to let her go, even as she reverted to her human form, and
returned his embrace. The two grieved in the somber
silence, weeping for their terrible, sudden loss.

CHAPTER 14: WELCOME ABOARD THE BLOOD DIAMOND

When all was still again, Ulrich led the three back to his lair. Selena did all she could to keep from lashing out, but her anger burned inside her every time she looked at the green titan. He still had yet to tell her precisely what brought Thor to madness, and Selena deserved an answer now.

After cleaning and bandaging her severed arm, Silver stayed by her side, but Rahim remained behind, stuffing his hands in his pockets. Whenever he attempted to help Selena, Silver shooed him away, so instead, he followed them from a distance. Growing flustered by his guardian role, Selena pulled her arm away. "Silver, please stop it."

"But now you'll need a new one. And after all the work I put into—"

"I don't give a damn about my hand." She moved away from the startled Silver to confront the Emerald Dragon. "How could you let the Lich do that to Thor? Why didn't you stop it?"

There was no remorse in Ulrich's voice, and Selena's anger swelled; his explanation lacked genuine concern. "Once you two began my trial, there was no stopping the outcome. This test was something that Thor had to face and control, as did you."

"You still should have gotten me. I could have stopped him from—"

"No, you couldn't." Ulrich's voice turning to thunder made Selena flinch and step back. "You couldn't even save yourself. Your dragon form would have overpowered and corrupted you if it weren't for Thor."

Selena stomped away from them to avoid hearing anymore. "I don't care. I'm going to find him and bring him back."

Silver reached out for her, but she shrugged him away. "No, wait."

Ulrich grunted, his eyes turning to slits. "Young One, you are in no condition to go after Thor. If you should have any chance against the Lich, you must remain here and complete your training."

"To Oblivion with your training. I'm going, and nobody is going to stop me."

"How are you going to do that?" Rahim's eyes darted between Silver and Ulrich; his shoulders trembled as he feared she would strike him down out of blind rage.

Selena squinted her eyes as she peered to the cavern's exit. "I'll fly."

Silver's jaw dropped. "You have no control over your dragon state yet."

"Then you can fly me. Take me, now."

"No, I won't." Selena couldn't bring herself to face him, and it took all of her strength not to cry again. "My dear, I understand. No matter what I say or do, I know I cannot change your mind. If you want to go, we can't stop you, but I will not be the one responsible for you getting hurt."

Ulrich's roars made his mountain quiver with fear. "This is foolish. Young One, you will kill yourself if you continue."

"I don't care. I just want Thor back." Selena reached the edge of the cavern and focused on forcing her transformation. However, she couldn't bring herself to change, except for when she was enraged or in danger. She was angry now, so why couldn't she alter her form? Her eyes began flooding with every failed attempt. Silver and Rahim watched her as she grumbled and stomped, but her efforts remained vain.

Eventually, she gave up, sat over the edge, and turned her gaze upwards at the stars; her mind was devoid of all thought except for Thor's torment. *Ulrich allowed this to happen. He's supposed to help us, but he didn't intervene.* "And he had the gall to tell me to let him go? I will never let him go. Thor, I promise I will find you and bring you back. You told me you would never leave my side." Selena brought up her knees and buried her tear-stained face into her thighs with only the strength to scream and cry.

Minutes turned to hours as she slipped further into depression. Silver had already taken Rahim down the mountain, but Selena didn't want to move. Silver returned for her, but he gave her what he thought was much-needed space while she dealt with her grief.

On the other hand, Ulrich retreated to his lair, his steps slow and falling with heavy dread. "I must remain in solitude and meditate on what transpired here."

Silver refused to meet the dragon god's gaze and asked for a third time, "What did you do to them?"

"The only thing that I could do. Thor needed to overcome his anger, and Selena had to detach herself from everything she knew and everyone she loved."

Silver's face boiled like a whistling tea kettle. "You can't do that—I've warned you."

Ulrich snapped his fangs and fixated his pupiled-slits on the non-flinching Silver. "As I've warned you, *demigod.* You insisted that I train them, and I did as you requested. You brought this upon them, not me." Silver didn't buckle down to the Divine's wrath but instead watched from the corner of his eye as Ulrich made haste and sought refuge within his cave to stay in seclusion. Even after Ulrich was gone, Silver kept his post by the entrance and watched Selena as she kept whispering and pleading for Thor to return.

When morning came, the two hadn't moved. Silver only broke their distance to offer Selena some water and food, but she denied those luxuries. But he stepped back as she shuffled to her feet and made her way towards the trail leading back to the library. His eyes widened as she marched on without regard to the danger of the swirling clouds defending Ulrich's peak. "My dear, stop."

Ignoring him, she summoned wind gusts surrounding her in a protective barrier against Ulrich's violent clouds. *Thor! Thor!* Her pleas and calls went unheeded; Thor's silence and emptiness unnerved her.

Selena continued her low, depressing march before leaping off the edge, tumbling below without considering the consequences. Perhaps, she believed, her impending doom would trigger her to change form. Selena didn't fear the fall, not after her first flight with Thor ended with her slipping off his back when flying without a proper saddle, unafraid but rather mesmerized by the scenery. She admired the endless green sea expanding over the horizon and the terrain moving like ocean waves.

Silver wasn't too far away. He morphed into his serpent dragon guise and dove in pursuit to catch her. He snatched her with his ivory talons, trapping her in his clawed cage, and when he brought her back to Ulrich's lair, Silver leveled his snake-like muzzle with her face and roared between his bared fangs. **What in Oblivion are you doing?! Killing yourself won't bring Thor back.**

Selena slipped through his tightened talons. It didn't daunt her in the least that Silver could speak to her directly through telepathy, and yet, it was the first time she heard his voice boom through her mind. "Don't do that."

Do what?

"That—talking to me. That mental bond is supposed to be between Thor and me."

Silver hissed, and Selena knew she struck a nerve, but her unrelenting emotions clouded her regard for others. **You know I'm not like the other dragons, and I'm not bound to a handler. I can talk to whomever I wish and do as I please.**

"I don't care."

Yes, you do. Why are you trying to kill yourself?

"I wasn't," she snapped, "I hoped that maybe I could...." her voice trailed off.

That you could do what? He paused before coming to the realization. **Did you think that throwing yourself off the cliff would trigger your powers?** When he saw that Selena's face flooded upon catching her true intentions, Silver recoiled and softened his tone. **That's not the way to do it, my dear. You must trust Ulrich.**

"After what he did to Thor?"

You know Ulrich was trying to help him and had nothing to do with what happened.

"No, he wasn't." She stormed off. *He wasn't trying to help Thor.*

Silver snaked across the ground and stood between her and the cave. **If you intend to find him, I'll**

at least go with you. He lowered himself to the ground, defeated and undone.

Selena paused before accepting his offer, and she climbed over his back and grabbed his golden horns. Unlike Thor's jagged and rough scales, Silver's were smooth as silk. With serene grace, he slithered upwards, and the two were airborne. Whenever she rode with Thor, the flight was a bit more linear. Flying with Silver, however, she had to adjust to how his elongated body swayed back and forth; he flew like how a snake moved across the ground.

Silver held his tongue when Selena repeatedly called out for her dear companion, not wanting to interfere if her voice could reach the fallen dragon. He circled the Aurora Peaks to catch a glimpse or even a shadow, but their search remained futile. Yet, Selena didn't want to give up.

Thor! Where are you? Thor! She looked out over the horizon, and her chest tightened when he was nowhere in sight. *No... no!*

The furthest they flew until the Opal River was well within their aerial view. It was already midday, and Silver knew that Selena was growing weary. Despite her escalating protests, she eventually agreed to turn back; Silver slithered around and made his return to the mountain. He avoided the peak, and the pair landed by the library tower at sundown, with Rahim waiting for the two outside.

Noticing how their search accomplished naught, Rahim approached them with care to avoid triggering Selena's depression. "I'm sorry. I understand this is hard for you right now, but we'll eventually find and save him." She only mumbled under her breath as she dismounted and made her way back inside.

Silver, transforming back into a human, dusted off his jacket and cleared his throat. "I'm sorry for your loss, my dear. But right now, we must focus on getting you to Dark Blood Hold."

Selena paused mid-strut before reaching the tower's front door. "I won't abandon Thor."

Rahim flinched from Selena's harsh and cold tone. "We still have to prepare for the eclipse."

"It doesn't matter. It's not going to help me get Thor back."

"It can if we can stop the Lich," Silver began, but she wasn't listening. She kicked some rocks and swaggered inside the main room, leaving the dismayed Silver and Rahim behind. "We'll leave in a few hours."

The long night was upon them. Silver did his best to give Selena the space she needed, but it disturbed him when she first turned away and stayed on her side for the entire evening. All he could do was leave again for his laboratory and work on building a new hand to replace the one she broke during Ulrich's training, but he would check on her every few hours. He had hoped to finish it at Lord Godfrey's fortress without using his laboratory.

Before the sun was even up, Silver went to wake her, but she interrupted him before he could even touch her. "I couldn't sleep."

Solemn, he withdrew his hand. "We need to leave if we're to reunite with your parents. Lord Godfrey will be expecting us to arrive soon."

Selena slumped out of bed and trudged down the stairs. Her face was pale, and her eyes were swollen and red from hours of silently crying. However, she paused and jolted as the floor suddenly rumbled, and they heard explosions erupting and blasting from a distance. "Silver, what is that?"

Sharing in her confusion, he shook his head; Selena snatched Dragonheart leaning against the pavilion columns, and they rushed outside. However, a hole blasted through the ceiling, and a bomb landed not far from the two, exploding upon impact. The pair flew back from the force, and before they could brace themselves, more explosives fell and destroyed parts of Silver's library.

A large fleet of rusting metal and solid oak flew above them—about thirty-six heavy frigates ranging between twenty-eight to fifty guns. Solid masts upon the heavily-armed airborne ships were adorned with grey and tan sails, but Selena gritted her teeth when realizing they were the dreaded sky pirates Rahim warned them about prior. Silver bit his cheeks and cursed their luck. The ceiling collapsed from more dropped bombs, and boulders caved in the bedroom. Selena shielded her face from the scattered debris. "Rahim is still out there; we need to find him."

Silver didn't argue; the pair ran out the exit before another boulder crashed down and sealed them out. Several bombs plummeted before them, and a band of mercenaries marched from the smoke. Selena's eyes jumped over their round knitted caps to the single golden earrings they wore in one ear.

One whom Selena presumed was their leader stepped forth. A single rope of cloth tucked down into his vest was donned around his neck. "The Queen of Dragons," he shouted and pointed at her through the clash of their swords. Ignoring Silver's and Selena's snarls, the leader ordered two men to charge by gesturing with his gun. One of his nearby comrades leapt forward; the other refused to budge, and the leader used the pointed end of his weapon to push him down. Silver pulled out an Aether sword from underneath his sleeve and sliced through the first pirate with a sharp gleam twinkling in his eye. Cleaved in two, it was like cutting melted butter.

Dragonheart whistled upon unsheathing, and its copper-tinted blade shimmered from every strike Selena made while dodging as best as she could. Back to using only one hand again, she could no longer use a shield to protect herself like she used to. Her opponent currently outmatched her in speed. The mercenary parried Selena's blade and surprised her with a sneak attack by pulling a hidden dagger from his belt. However, before he made his blow, Silver spun around and thrust his sword deep into the pirate's chest and threw his twitching body down into a pool of his blood.

The leader and the rest of his gang rushed forward. Frustrated at how slow she was with her blade, Selena swept her foot to the side and made parting motions with her arms; the floor grew unsteady and crumbled. The pirates did their best to keep balance as they approached, but the ground caved in, trapping them in the bottomless pit.

When Silver consoled Selena, she pushed him away and made haste down the destroyed hallway. Yet Rahim was nowhere to be found, but they heard the distant sounds of gunfire and Rahim screaming inappropriate words at his enemies. As the two made their way towards the entrance, they saw several sky pirates fighting Rahim. He shot one, only to be greeted by three more from behind. Silver rushed to his aid and countered their attacks with a stream of Aether flowing from his hands, forming icicle-like lances striking through his opponents.

Tethered ropes dangled from the airships surrounding Silver's tower, and more pirates arrived while bombs rained down and balls of fire arched like meteors.

Soon, the pirates had the three cornered in an enclosed circle of men and thieves.

She had a brief moment to look up and scowl at Ulrich's lack of interference yet again; Heaven's Tear trembled and shuddered, but the Divine remained ensconced within his lair. Swearing under her breath, she sheathed Dragonheart and summoned a whip made of fire, lashing it at the brutes' legs. They broke formation, and Selena beckoned Rahim and Silver to follow her.

However, from a nearby docked vessel came more fiendish felons jumping from ladders and swinging on ropes. The impressively sizeable heavy frigate of sixty guns drifted overhead, nearly blotching the morning sun from the sky. A heavily armed marauder wearing a wide-brimmed hat watched the action from the deck as the cannons fired and his crew of over eighteen hundred scrambled to prepare for the queen's capture.

She focused on powering her attacks to clear their path; her breaths were deep as she gathered the surrounding energy. When Silver and Rahim dove for cover, she unleashed it. Concentric rings of blue Aether exploded in a shockwave wiped the ground clear of pirates, but her magic knocked over parts of the library, and the debris separated her from Silver and Rahim. Manipulating Aether was such an exhilarating feeling but also terrifying.

Even as she stood there, sparks of Aether zapped across her body like tendrils of lightning as Selena continued tapping into her rage: the only haunting thought that drove her was losing Thor. Before she unleashed her fury and retaliated, Selena spun around just as the pirate captain was upon her; his massive crew swarmed and threw heavy metal chains, pinning her to the ground within seconds.

Silver and Rahim fought their way into the fray, but the captain grabbed Selena's hair through the tangled mess of metal and placed his sword's tip against her neck. "Unless you want your queen's head on a platter, I suggest you back away right now."

Silver and Rahim exchanged glances before heeding the captain's warning; the gang of thieves kept their weapons pointed at the two as they dropped to their knees and raised their hands in surrender. Silver never tore his gaze from Selena's, even as the captain ordered his crew to search their pockets and take what the trio had on them at the time. Rahim took issue in them liberating him of his revolver and Aynu necklace; he held on to both for as long as possible, but when the captain threatened him again, Rahim finally yielded. Silver remained stoic as the brutes searched his jacket and snatched the pocket watch that showed Aydin's memories.

Selena bit her tongue when the captain grabbed Dragonheart but fought against the captain's hold when two pirates searched Thor's pavilion and returned holding his golden diamond bracelets and ruby chain, and her face flooded over. "No, those were Thor's. Put them back."

The captain yanked on her hair and spat in her face. "Your dragon ain't here, now, is he? Take your spoils back to the ships and leave these two here. We've got the queen."

Silver and Rahim stepped to the side as they exercised with great caution in not provoking the sky pirates any more than their already unpleasant exchange. However, Rahim hissed through his teeth and raised a fist as if to challenge the captain. "What do you scoundrels want with her?"

"Our business is not with you, *boy*." The captain threw Selena down, face planting into the ground, and ordered his men to bind her arms and legs. Her vision blurred, and she drowned out the captain's voice. A deep ring buzzed through her ears while the pirates dragged her on board the massive, sinister black ship of oak and steel, cluttered with crates filled with illegal cargo.

Silver stomped forward as the gang finished packing their plunder, but the captain's crew posted by the boarding plank pushed him back with their weapons, preventing him from stepping a single foot aboard their vessels. He snarled through his teeth and raised a fist. "I swear by the Divines I will murder you all."

The captain laughed. "Go ahead then. If you do, she dies as well."

One of his mercenaries yelled. "We're all set, Captain Battleraven."

"Capital—let's be off, then." Selena's eyes swelled as the pirates removed their plank and set sail skyward. She maintained eye contact with Silver and Rahim for as long as possible as the captain's large fleet flew away from Heaven's Tear. Battleraven marched to her and leaned on one knee. "I offer you my humblest apologies for the rude welcome, *Your Grace*," he mocked, "welcome aboard the *Blood Diamond*."

*****

CHAPTER 15: PROMISES TO A LOVED ONE

Blackheart Village stood against the unforgiving wind and torrential rain. Despite its small size, the village was a fortress. The whipping wind pushed and shoved the residents as they moved food barrels and other supplies. However, as their thick-furred dogs whimpered, everyone turned to the source of the shrieking noise shattering the tense atmosphere.

When rumors first spread about the dead coming back, the residents built a massive wall surrounding the town, only opening the gates to allow their shipments through. The smell of rotten flesh laden the air, and the ear-shattering screeches grew close. Fearing that the Dreygur would overrun their hamlet, a group of men charged over, placing large, thick planks to hold shut the door. There was a loud crash against the other side of the gate without warning, and based on their lookouts' expressions, the Dreygur arrived and attempted to break in.

Yet, another undead creature attempted to climb underneath the gate, clawing and digging through the dirt. While a warrior lopped off its hands, another stepped forth and peered through the cracks in the wall, and instantly, a rotting hand busted through the gap, thrashing wildly. It scratched the man in the face, but he pulled back and chopped the arm off.

The guardsmen keeping watch nocked their arrows and fired; their barrage of attacks rained over the vast horde of the undead swarming towards their settlement, trying to get through their wall. However, their efforts were futile as more Dreygur crawled even further under the gate while others began clawing holes into their wooden fence.

All the warriors rushed forward to fight off the impending doom surrounding Blackheart. However, the holes grew by the second and were soon big enough for the Dreygur to break through. Flying overhead was a Nidhoggr and its rider, Arawn Branwen—when he used to walk among the living—commanding the oncoming wave of undead ransacking the settlement. It didn't take long for the Dreygur to tear the residents apart: men, women, and children alike.

After Medusa's defeat in Snowhaven, Arawn was ordered to take her role in assembling the Lich's army among the mortal realm. He had been moving from one place to the next, gathering more undead forces to prepare for the eclipse, bringing some back to Alfheim while others roamed freely across Armageddon. Once Arawn carried out Blackheart's cleansing, a group of robed zealots from the Obsidian Order emerged from the shadows, as the village was now theirs. The rider shrieked, and with the dark gift given to him from the Lich, Arawn raised his hand to reanimate the fallen corpses. Their bodies twitched, and their eyes opened, glossed over by a faint blue film. The recently deceased stood up, walked with Arawn's Dreygur army away from Blackheart, and marched for Alfheim.

Meanwhile, watching them from a distance was a group of fifty rogue Nidhoggr witnessing the entire scene. The largest weighted masked dragon hissed and growled at its saddled kin, but instead of attacking, the flight took off towards the northwest, hunting down the ones who stole one of their newly hatched whelplings.

*****

Eyes fluttering open, Selena found herself locked up in the dark, damp, lonely prison cell aboard Captain Battleraven's ship. Barren of any furniture or cot, only a chamber pot and a pile of hay scrunched in the corners of her dilapidated quarters. Her sharp breaths stabbed through her lungs; Selena had hoped that she would never find herself locked up again, but here she was. *And all for what?* The captain never did say, but he was after the 'Queen of Dragons' for some reason. However, she immediately assumed Vidar was responsible for her capture, and her face burned with rage. *That conniving rat is behind this. Maybe they want to collect a reward on my head.*

Selena hissed and spat on her dirty floor, kicking her empty chamber pot and screaming through her teeth as she reached over and rattled her metal bars. Growing sodden, she stopped, resting her head, and slipped to her knees. *I lost Thor, now Rahim and Silver.* Her eyes shimmered, and her chest tightened when she recalled how she lashed out at them. It wasn't their fault, and Selena knew that. Now, she may never get the chance to apologize for her irrational behavior.

She stood up and continued pacing towards her cell door, only to realize that the pirates may have rummaged through her clothes for treasures as they did to Silver and Rahim. She traced her neckline, now devoid of her obsidian wolf necklace; her hand sunk into her pocket, and her face drained of all color when she couldn't feel

209

Revelation. She fished through her other side and patted herself down as best as she could with one hand, but her pocket watch was missing. Selena cursed and swore, only stopping to look down the dark and damp corridors and note a shadow of a whelpling dashing across the rickety floors.

Upon noticing the small dragon's different mask as it moved closer, Selena asked herself, *Why is a baby Nidhoggr onboard a pirate ship? Is he smuggling the whelplings?*

It looked up at her and paused. The youngling sniffed the air, and without thinking about it, Selena reached out from her cell to pet the curious creature. Her hand almost made contact with its snout before it opened its mouth with dark Aether boiling within its tiny maw. She stepped back as the hatchling exhaled its blast over the metal bars but abruptly stopped and fled the way it came.

The bars slightly bent to her touch when she inspected the creature's handiwork, and Selena understood the whelpling was assisting in her rescue. However, heavy footsteps shaking the floorboards interrupted its mission, and from the end of the corridor emerged Captain Battleraven. Selena moved back from her cell bars, but she was not intimidated by the commander's towering shadow. Instead, her eyes remained fixed upon the massive mercenary like a dragon ready to strike.

Keeping his hands clasped behind his back, Battleraven sneered when he reached her prison. "Well, well. It is such an honor for you to grace us with your presence aboard my ship, *Your Majesty.*"

"I'm assuming Vidar set you up to this. Where are you taking the smuggled Nidhoggr and me? What's in this for you?"

"As they are no longer under Vidar's command, we capture ferals to compete in my arena fights, as those beasts make worthwhile entertainment. However, I have different plans for you. Everything comes at a price, and believe me, I intend to collect the rest of my promised reward. No hard feelings, and nothing personal—it's just business."

"What about taking me to my family? I'm sure they would offer you more than Vidar is paying you; even Lord Godfrey of the Shadow Templars will make you a deal."

"With what gold? Your family no longer holds the throne." Captain Battleraven spat on the floor. "I don't do business with vampires. There's quite a large bounty on that lord's head that will soon belong to me. My crew and I will be set for life between you."

Selena furrowed her eyebrows, and her chest swelled. "My offer meant your life. That sounds more valuable than gold to me."

The pirate captain laughed and mocked her. "You're funny. I like that." He leaned down until his crooked nose touched the metal. "Maybe before we make port in Alfheim, my crew and I could use a little fun. Perhaps we'll all share you."

"Then I will show you Death's mercy by making sure you die first."

"That's the spirit. If you'll excuse me, I have a tournament to host. It would be rude of me to keep my guests waiting any longer. Oh boy, do they love the bloodshed." The captain spun around and made his way back down the corridor as he continued with his bellowed laughter.

Selena bit her lip until she tasted blood, unable to withstand his thirst for animal brutality and his threats of rape; she made a silent vow not to allow Battleraven to survive, no matter the cost. The world would be much better off without him and his band of brutish mercenaries.

When she was sure the pirate leader was out of sight, she reached out to the metal bars again, and her hand burst into flames—hot as dragon fire but only tickling against her skin—her magic sizzled against the steel. Her cage bent to her will as she pried it open, but a familiar voice called her before she slipped out. "I suppose you don't need us rescuing you, my dear."

Selena whipped around, her hand extinguishing the flames. "Silver!" He had his arms crossed while leaning against the cell wall, but he rushed to meet her embrace. "Thank the Divines you're here. I'm so sorry. I...." She lost her voice as she dug her face into his jacket.

If Silver was angry with her, he didn't show it. Instead, he returned her hug. "I was never angry with you."

"How did you sneak in here?"

Silver raised a brow. "Shapeshifter, remember? I turned into a beetle and hid in your cell until the time was right. You didn't think that Rahim and I wouldn't follow these barbarians, did you?"

Selena's head spun when she heard a stick rattling against the metal bars, and a wave of relief washed over her. Rahim paced back and forth outside her bent cell door and laughed when he saw her reaction. "We chased you down after the pirates left, but getting on board was rocky. Too bad for that unpleasant conversation, but it's time to go. We can deal with that oaf later."

Selena shook her head. "Not yet. Have you two seen a Nidhoggr whelpling running around the ship? It ran by here before the captain arrived."

Silver met Rahim's confused gaze. "We didn't see anything. Why would Captain Battleraven have Nidhoggr whelps?"

"To fight for the pirates' amusement."

"But that would mean its parents would try to find the imprisoned hatchlings," Rahim bit down on his nail, "I don't know about you, but I don't want to be around when those goop dragons appear."

Selena declared, "I'm not leaving here just yet. I have unfinished business to attend to."

Silver sighed as he met Rahim's terrified gaze. "My dear, Rahim is right. If they act anything like real dragons, they are very protective of their hatchlings."

"Then we will leave the sky pirates to them, but I must find our trinkets. They took Revelation." Silver's face turned pale, but Rahim was confused. "Rahim, I don't have time to explain—"

"It's in a pocket watch form." Silver winked at him. "There, now you don't need to explain any further, my dear. Damn, it feels so good to talk about it and not have that blasted curse get in the way."

Selena could still tell that he didn't fully understand, judging from Rahim's expression, but he nodded. "After what I've seen, I believe it. Escape now, explain later."

Silver and Selena slipped through the bent bars, and the three rushed down the hallway past the other countless empty prison cells. Captain Battleraven's muffled voice echoed throughout the ship, but his words were drowned out by the cheers from the fighting arena above deck. Selena's stomach stirred at the thought that another match was about to begin. Her eyes shifted from one door to the next in hopes that she would find the baby Nidhoggr, but it was nowhere to be found.

However, the trio paused their pursuit when the ceiling rumbled, and the corridor became shrouded in dust. True to Rahim's fears, the group heard a roar thundering from above the deck, and the frigate shuddered. Rahim coughed. "W-what's happening?"

Another shriek bellowed throughout the ship, and the boat began rocking back and forth. The roars sounded like dragons, but the trio suspected otherwise. The ceiling caved near where they once stood, and a torrent of black Aether blasted a hole through the heavy frigate. Silver grabbed Selena's and Rahim's arms, pulling them away from falling debris, but she yanked herself free and rushed ahead as soon as it was clear and safe.

From the opening, she saw a flight of Nidhoggr attacking the *Blood Diamond*, their black flames of energy scorching the ship and consuming all its path; the vessel slowly descended to the ground from the irreparable damage. Cannons fired relentlessly in retaliation, but the undead dragons were too quick and avoided the meteor volley.

Silver shoved Rahim further down the corridor and yelled for Selena to follow him, but she remained transfixed on the Nidhoggr raid. "We need to get off the ship, now."

She ignored him and hurried further down the hall with Silver and Rahim swearing and following her. Her ears stung with the cries and screams of the mercenaries above, but they could rot in Oblivion for all she cared. Silver and Rahim caught up, but she interrupted their objections and repeated her wishes to retrieve their trinkets and settle matters with the captain. "Take Rahim out of here, and I'll join you later."

The shadows shrouded Silver's look of defeat when Selena wouldn't yield. "How? You'll be stuck on the burning boat."

"You must trust me. Please." Before he could muster another protest, she continued down the corridor. The pell-mell pirates overlooked her as they rushed to the flying lifeboats tethered to the *Blood Diamond*, yet, the captain was nowhere to be seen.

She shot around a corner and ran into two armed pirates with swords and pistols at the ready. The vessel rattled from the ongoing attacks, and the mercenaries almost lost their footing. Selena collected her bearings and demanded, "Where did Captain Battleraven take my sword and my friends' trinkets?"

When the pirates only grunted and charged forward after regaining their balance, Selena inhaled deeply and breathed a chilling frost freezing the floorboards beneath their feet. She ran up and around the buccaneers along the walls and ceiling, reaching the other side using air magic. Ill-prepared, the two felons slipped and fell as Selena fled and vanished around a corner.

As more time passed from exploring the ship, she eventually found herself in a colossal treasure horde down on the lower deck. Her eyes shimmered over piles of gold and gems pouring from chests stacked against the walls, but her heart stopped when she saw Thor's diamond bracelets and ruby chain tossed into the assortment of jewels. Next to his jewelry were Dragonheart, Revelation, Rahim's revolver, and Silver's pocket watch thrown on top.

She snatched the firearm and Dragonheart and tied them to her belt as best as she could one-handed. After a few seconds of searching, she plucked and donned the Aynu necklaces hiding underneath the gold coins and the two timepieces to hide in her pockets. However, she couldn't help but tear up when touching Thor's jewelry; the bracelets and necklace reminded her of him so much that her chest nearly exploded.

When she heard footsteps approaching from behind, Selena linked the gold together and lanced her arm through so she could carry them out; then, she wrapped them within his gold and ruby chain. Before becoming too emotional, she caught a glimpse of the familiar and dreaded figure in the brimmed hat.

Captain Battleraven's deep-throated chuckle made the hair on the back of her neck stand on end. "It's astounding how much of a nuisance you were. It was a clever trick to bring the Nidhoggr with you and attack my fleet."

"I didn't bring them, but I wish I did."

"You crazy bitch. It doesn't matter, as the only way you will leave here will be as my prisoner. I will still collect the bounty over your head after my crew and I take turns with you. Whatever is left of your body will be given to Vidar."

"I never said I was going anywhere. You and your crew will go down with your vessel."

Captain Battleraven launched for her with his pistol at the ready, but she avoided every attack he lashed out. In between his next volley of bullets, Selena shut her eyes and drew the surrounding energy. Time froze, and she again found herself standing on the aurora stage in the Divine cosmos. The spectral Divinity Dragon appeared before her, eyes glowing as it reared its head back with a thundering roar and lunged forward. However, instead of fleeing, Selena stood her ground.

All I have to do is to let go of Thor and Silver. It should be simple, right?

The celestial dragon continued with its rampage, claws and fangs ready to tear her to pieces, but she wasn't intimidated. Ulrich's words echoed through her mind, but Selena pushed his lesson away with fleeting memories of her childhood that always brought her back to Silver. All she saw was him and how he made her happy, and Selena knew she loved him from the moment he proclaimed his affections. Whenever thinking about Silver and how

Ulrich wanted her to say goodbye, her love grew so strong that she couldn't contain it.

As for Thor, he stood by her side since he hatched, choosing her as his life partner. Their Aether energies had always connected them, and no Divine force could ever pry them apart; Thor was her other half, making her complete and whole. Her love for him would never leave this world, no matter what the Lich may do.

Her dragon form was almost upon her. It lifted its claws to strike her down, but Selena didn't cower. Instead, she held up her only hand. *But how can I? There's absolutely no way that I can ever let them go. Every time I think about it, my heart wants to burst.*

The ethereal dragon stopped its attack and landed on all fours, snarling and snaking its head down, and it sniffed her open palm.

Thor, I couldn't take it to watch your wrath and rage consume you. That's why I will never let you go. I swear I will do whatever it takes to save you and never allow the Lich ever again to hurt or threaten anyone else: this, I promise.

As the dragon's snout brushed against her hand, her eyes were like the stars swirling around them. Both she and the dragon imbued themselves in a massive amount of blue Aether magic as the infinite void surrounding the two entities vanished in their light.

Time resumed, and Captain Battleraven stood in awe and dismay at the sudden maelstrom that rapidly appeared before him, drawing in the freshly fired bullets from his pistol. The growing storm formed a sphere of light, its energy turning into a shockwave of concentric circles expanding in all directions. A single white-blue beam shot up from the orb and through the ship's ceiling, blasting skyward.

The whirling vortex diminished, and Selena stood in the burned crater that her Aether created—as a fully-realized Divinity Dragon slightly smaller than Thor with eyes sparkling brighter than the summoned light energy. Her form no longer resembled the former spectral apparition; the tips of her celestial wings brushed against the tall ceiling. In fear and panic, the captain gazed upon her ethereal wings and her turquoise gem-like scales gleaming against the sunlight, then at the deep ruby emblazoned upon her chest. With her left paw restored, Thor's diamond bracelets were upon her wrists, and his gold and ruby chain draped around her neck; wisps of blue Aether graced her spine, pluming and wafting from her body like Divine fire.

Captain Battleraven stepped back as his jaw fell to the floor. In a state of panic and alarm, he fired one shot after another. The bullets disintegrated to dust once they touched Selena's celestial shield encasing her body, protecting her from most—if not all—melee attacks. She unleashed a roar that made heaven and earth cower; Battleraven fell and recoiled from her thunder. Tilting her head back, clouds of blue Aether swirled from within her maw. As she opened her mouth, Selena released a blazing hot torrent, her Divine jet wholly incinerating the pirate leader within seconds. When her fangs snapped shut and interrupted her azure stream, she saw all that remained of Battleraven were the scorch marks of his footprints beneath a pile of ash.

Instead of escaping the burning boat, Silver and Rahim caught up to the Aether dragon and flinched, hesitant in approaching the Divine entity. When Selena and Silver locked gazes, she began speaking in their newly shared mental bond. *I'm so sorry. I've been going through such a horrible time. All I want to do is to protect everyone I know and love. Ulrich kept telling me that I needed to let go of Thor and you, but instead, all his training did was remind me of how much I love you both.*

She swung around and blasted another torrent of Aether, shattering the wide window behind, and emerged as her wings swept through the heavens with aurora ribbons following every flap. Selena soared high above and set forth an eruption of blue Aether, destroying one of the vessels closest to face her wrath. Nearby were the saddle-less Nidhoggr encircling what remained of the captain's fleet like a murder of crows, randomly striking down lifeboats eagerly escaping from their boiling fury.

The pirates' incompetence in dealing with the dragonkin attack led to their easy downfall. Before the brutes could prepare the surviving cannons and ballistas capable of bringing down a dragon, Selena made her pass as she held her Aether breath, and the frigates made their fiery descent as they were caught within her deadly torrent. She flew past the Nidhoggr with inhuman speed, obliterating another ship before arcing over with a second blast. Each vessel fell from the sky and met the ground with blazing destruction.

Silver changed into a dragon and carried Rahim off the *Blood Diamond* as the ship sank further until Selena swept by with a steady torrent, incinerating what remained of Battleraven's prized heavy frigate; the vessel, unable to withstand her fury, exploded upon contact with the ground.

Fidgeting upon his back, Rahim objected that the two needed to intervene, but Silver only shook his head. The two settled that she neither wanted nor needed assistance taking down the entire fleet—the largest pirate armada in recorded history of thirty-six ships. Yet, in alarmed amazement, they watched Selena wipe out another handful of vessels with one belch while strafing another row. The Nidhoggr were drawn to her like flies to honey, following all that she did, and soon, the flight worked on coordinated attacks; their black and blue

Aether magic streams conjoined in perfect harmony and deadly display.

Yet, while they were busy distracted by the pirate slaughter, nobody paid attention to the disappearing silhouette of a dragon speeding away. Selena couldn't feel its presence beyond the dark veil donning the desperate creature.

With their onslaught finished, all that remained of the sky pirate ships burned on the ground. Selena kept aloft by the beat of her wings and eyed the Nidhoggr surrounding her as if they awaited her following command. The whelpling she saw earlier on the ship zipped by her head and made chirping noises before joining its brethren; an identical hatchling pushed its way through the row of heavy-weighted ferals to meet with its twin. They circled each other, and the undead dragons roared through their teeth, celebrating their reunion, but before leaving, the largest weighted creature locked its massive, glowing red eyes upon hers. Through a series of low growls and clicks, the Nidhoggr flight spun around and fled south, ignoring Silver and Rahim as they zoomed by.

Selena joined Silver's side and met his admiring gaze. **Nothing is more powerful in this world than a Divinity Dragon. Where are they going?**

I don't know. Her head swiveled outward to watch their disappearing shapes descend over the horizon, and Selena smiled when a brilliant idea came to her.

CHAPTER 16: NOCTIS

Battleraven's grim defeat dyed the vault of heaven crimson. Selena kept her dragon form, and during their flight, Silver could not contain himself at how she was able to do so. **You learned how to manipulate your energy to transform at will.**

When you first taught me about Aether and how to manipulate others' energy, I realized I could control mine.

Ulrich said the only way you could purify yourself and use Aether was to detach yourself and be free.

I found a different resolution.

Selena sailed forward while Silver eyed her in wonder and admiration. **I love you.**

She soared in a heightened state of awareness, enjoying the new senses that beguiled her; sight, sound, taste, and so on. She could hear the patter from all creatures across the ground, from the crawling ant to the pirouetting deer; Selena enjoyed listening to the earth's sweet ballad of life. She carried the strength of a hundred dragons—Selena wondered if Thor always felt that way—but immediately, her attitude spiraled downward, unsure of how she could enjoy her awakening when her companion remained lost.

The sunlight shimmered across her Aether scales, reflecting glimmering turquoise specs. Selena even caught Rahim admiring her beauty as a dragon on several occasions, which gave her the gleaming pleasure of knowing that no other dragon could compare except for Thor. She allowed a small stream of Aether flames to slither and twirl through her serrated fangs as she thought to herself, *One day, Thor, our Divine fire will reign.*

Although he couldn't hear Silver's and Selena's previous conversation, Rahim still spoke to the two dragons. "As much as I may regret saying this, I remember when you first brought up the idea of getting an army of Nidhoggr, Selena. They must have gone rogue, or they would have attacked us back there. We should figure out where they went and form an alliance with them."

Silver swung his head and moaned. **I'm not sure Lord Godfrey will appreciate a flight of undead dragons knocking on his castle door, but if we can convince those creatures to join us, why not?**

Rahim's eyes widened, and he clenched his teeth. "I… did you just talk to me, or am I losing my mind?"

Silver chose not to reply, allowing Rahim to believe the latter. However, after Selena arched her neck around and growled with a snap of her fangs, Silver finally explained how the mental bond worked. Meanwhile, Selena considered herself pleased when Rahim, although hesitant because it had to be Silver, accepted this new form of communication.

Before Silver could explain how she could do the same by opening her thoughts to others, Selena already began speaking with Rahim in the same manner before addressing Silver directly. *Thank you, but I've done this before with the She-Wolf, Kiba of the Aynu.*

Silver groaned, and Rahim kept shaking his head in disbelief. "Err, you two are too much for me." After staring at the two snickering dragons, he clicked his tongue against his teeth. "Anyway, how will we find that group of ferals?"

They looked to be heading towards Blackheart Village. We could always stop and ask if they've seen them.

"That will take us a little longer to get to the keep."

But wouldn't it be worth it if we came with reinforcements? It wouldn't hurt to try.

After a few painful groans, Rahim eventually conceded to Selena's line of thinking and fell deep in thought for a while before his eyes widened and sparkled at a sudden revelation. "By having those goop dragons fighting alongside the vampires and us, and with the added firepower from the eclipse, we should be able to launch an invasion to reclaim Alfheim. We can stop the Lich's army from making their apocalyptic journey." He leaned over Silver's horns. "I have an idea of how to do that. When we get to Dark Blood Hold, I want to help Lord Godfrey work on the battle plans."

Selena dipped her head in agreement. *I trust that you will come up with a great strategy.* Rahim's face beamed from her expressing full faith in his ideas.

The three made their way back to Heaven's Tear, but only briefly to grab their provisions, weapons, and armor. Selena braced herself and prepared for the worst at seeing so great of a library destroyed, but she was pleasantly surprised that Silver's tower was back in one piece as if the pirates were never there. **It took me a few minutes to rebuild my sanctuary before we chased down the fleet, but it's still difficult to remember how I had everything.**

You never cease to amaze me.

I'm just an old shapeshifter. What can I say? The group shared a hearty laugh, but Selena couldn't help but gaze upwards at the swirling, violent clouds protecting Ulrich's peak. She wondered if Ulrich knew she would ultimately figure out how to conquer her powers, but the Emerald Dragon remained in solitude within his crystallized fortress.

The trio landed in front of Silver's freshly rebuilt tower. Selena placed Thor's bracelets and gold and ruby chain beside his pavilion before resuming her human guise; Silver and Rahim were astounded by her sudden appearance change. Not understanding what the two were gabbing about, Silver eventually redirected her inside to find a full-body mirror in the same apartment with the grand piano. To say she was stunned was an understatement; her face was now as smooth and angled as her mother's—an elven maiden most fair whose beauty could never be matched—emitting a faint glow as if kissed by sunlight.

Selena's right hand reached for her soft and shiny turquoise blue blending to a snow-white hair that had suddenly grown to her waist; the tableau of gradient colors matched those of her brilliant, gem-like scales. She ran her trembling fingers across the new pointy tips of her ears. Although her parents were elves, unfortunately, due to the effects of the Well of Souls, her race changed to human. The only resemblance that connected her was the tan skin tone she and her mother shared, but now, from Silver's theory, by controlling her Aether, she was able to revert the Well's mistakes. Her emerald eye color, magnified by the sheen from her new hair, was the only feature that hadn't changed. According to Silver, she was as beautiful, if not more so, than any elven maiden he had seen, though Selena assumed his opinion might be biased.

When Silver looked down at her left arm, her eyes immediately followed, and the two saw how she no longer had a bandaged stump. Instead, Selena had fashioned herself a new left hand made entirely of Aether—a spectral limb with Divine energy wafting from her fingers. Silver rushed to her side so he could examine her beaming appendage. "This is amazing—you're brilliant."

She wasn't sure how she accomplished this new creation, as her mind had subconsciously crafted the new limb. Maintaining her Aether in this manner was the same as breathing or her heart beating; she didn't have to think about it. Silver asked if making one of flesh and blood was feasible, but Selena expressed satisfaction in sporting the new, ethereal look. After seeing Silver's defeated expression, she only added the future possibility, but his eyes wandered to the floor as he fell deep in thought. "I wonder. My dear, how is your back feeling?"

After permitting him to examine, Selena immediately undid the back of her blue dress and allowed Silver to see. While he was busy assessing, his jaw almost dropped to the floor. Her back no longer bothered her, and she hadn't felt ill since before she and Ebony shared their duel. Yet, per Silver, her skin was as soft and unscathed as a newborn babe's, and Selena saw the results on her chest; the scars and marks from Medusa were gone.

"Curiouser and curiouser. Neither Ulrich nor I could do that, but you somehow cleansed Medusa's corrupted magic. You astound me." Silver couldn't stop his grin from spreading across his face, his happiness contagious as Selena couldn't help but smile herself. Her fingers of flesh and Aether wisps fumbled as she redid her dress, still at a loss at her accomplishment that a Divine said would be impossible. Silver's excitement knew no bounds. "You're remarkable. Not only did you fashion yourself a new, fully functional Aether hand and purify your wounds, but you managed to reverse the effects of the Well of Souls. Absolutely brilliant, my dear."

Selena ignored Rahim as he dashed into the room moments later but couldn't push away the badgering about the sudden racial change that ensued. The moment felt more like a dream; Selena eventually explained what she achieved following Silver's brief report of the Well's mistakes. Rahim couldn't help but stare in wonder when Selena clarified that, through manipulating her energy, she corrected the errors and restored her appearance.

While Rahim babbled about her new form after blushing twice, Silver playfully argued against Rahim falling in love. Rahim and Selena exchanged disgusted expressions; Selena wondered at her capabilities when an idea sparked. Expressing her desire to test her theory to Silver, she then strutted back outside with her enthusiastic and cheering audience. She waved her fresh hand, and the magic erupted like a spike of ice taking a sword's shape. The ethereal blade glossed over like a frozen lake; the air kissed it with a cold mist.

Rahim jumped and bounced in his spot like a child anticipating a gift, while Silver's face glimmered in the absolute delight of this discovery; Selena couldn't tell who was more excited. "That's like when you first learned magic, and you made that fire scythe," Rahim said.

She swung her Aether blade at a nearby tree, grinning wide, leaving a notch with every lash she made. Being able to manipulate her energy made her feel like she had the power of a thousand suns coursing through her veins.

Selena unsheathed Dragonheart with her other hand and began practicing dual-wielding her weapons as she followed Azrael's former instruction. Silver and Rahim saw a flurry of metal and light emerging from Selena's swings that struck down the ancient pine tree with lightning-speed attacks. The thick tree couldn't withstand her onslaught, and it fell before her, the mountain yielding to its great weight. Breathing deep, she released her Aether sword and sheathed Dragonheart when satisfied.

Remembering that she still had Silver's and Rahim's trinkets with her, Selena distributed them to their rightful owners. Rahim hadn't smiled so big since Selena first bought him the Aynu necklace and revolver, cradling them before draping his leather charm and tying the holster to his belt.

"Thank you, my dear." Silver bowed and smiled before accepting his watch back. He slipped it into his pocket, and, once he confirmed Revelation remained safe in her possession, the three made haste to grab their newly repaired belongings for their trip.

Yet, Rahim asked her to show him Revelation. Sighing, she pulled out the golden watch, and his face glimmered. "Whoa. How does it work?"

"I have to say a certain phrase to unlock its true form."

"Can you show me?"

She glared at him and stuffed the timepiece away after affirming it should only be saved for her fight against Venexus. Rahim crinkled his nose at the sound of the necromancer's name, but he neither argued nor protested against hearing it. Instead, he grudgingly agreed and went to join Silver.

When he finished, Silver marched outside with his packs thrown over his shoulder and took on his dragon form with his possessions tied down to a small, makeshift harness already strapped over his back for Rahim's benefit. Rahim carried their last pack of provisions he needed and, after thanking Silver for the new accommodation in wearing a saddle, ensured all their belongings were safe and secure. Selena was still hesitant to leave as everywhere she looked reminded her of Thor, and she didn't want to abandon her memories.

Her mind was so clouded and hazy that she didn't hear Rahim calling her name. "Where are you? It's time to go." She grabbed her shield and strapped it over Dragonheart as her friends impatiently waited; she marched outside but paused when peering at Thor's jewelry, unsure if she should leave or bring the treasures.

Will you ever return to Heaven's Tear? Her heart broke every time she received no response.

Silver interrupted her growing grief by walking over and nudging her shoulder. **Why don't you bring them and just wear them when you're a dragon?**

Selena thought about it for a moment but shook her head, as the bracelets and necklace weren't for her. If she continued to wear the jewelry, it would be disrespectful to Thor. Instead, she rummaged through her property until finding his gift from the Aynu. As her eyes became like glass, Selena brought Thor's obsidian dragon totem over and laid it beside the golden jewelry before kneeling and muttering a small prayer for his safe return; if he ever did, his treasures were waiting for him.

After taking one last look at Thor's pavilion, and when she was ready, Silver stood back as she transformed into a dragon in a burst of swirling light, he and Rahim watching in awe. Launching herself towards the heavens, she unfurled her iridescent, ethereal wings midair, dust billowing from every flap she made. Silver followed her, slithering off the plateau's edge, and made the steep climb skyward.

Selena's flight was soft and steady and as graceful as a bird's; she rode upon the breath of the Divines themselves as she and her friends moved onwards between the heavens and the earth. The only time she ever felt this free was when she flew with Thor, and her heart ached.

Rahim pointed outward towards a massive score of people marching like they were in a parade, behaving oddly similar to the patrons from the Grand Exchange. "Those are the Dreygur, aren't they?"

Silver opened his mouth and let out a long groan to confirm Rahim's suspicion, as he was too lazy to speak directly through the new mental link. As the trio approached, they could see rotting flesh falling off their exposed bones. The clothes on their backs were tattered and blotted with old blood, while a blue film covered their eyes, and stringy and greasy strands of hair plastered upon their faces. The three watched the Dreygur march in the opposite direction with a dark purpose.

Selena heard the whispers again when they first encountered Rahim's father, and moments later, they could see the Nidhoggr and its rider flying with the herd of Dreygur. However, the undead dragon was too far away to see Selena's group, and the rider was busy guiding the deceased forces to their destination.

"Should we do something about them? About…?" Rahim couldn't bring himself to finish what he was going to say.

Selena arched her neck back and growled. *Leave it be for now.* Rahim sighed, but he couldn't tear his gaze away from the monster his father had become.

When Blackheart Village was in sight, Silver and Selena made haste. However, as the three flew closer, they noticed a wall built around it, but the front gate looked like it had been clawed open. Silver and Selena circled its perimeter a couple of times but stopped and hovered when two armed citizens standing on the wall called them from below.

While Selena remained aloft, Silver landed where the guards pointed and allowed Rahim to dismount. He shapeshifted back to his human form and greeted the hostile village. The two residents standing guard marched forth; to Selena's surprise, they didn't react to Silver's transformation or care that a massive Aether dragon was watching them closely.

None of this seems right, Silver. Please be on your guard. Silver still heard her; he peered over his shoulder and grinned.

"State your business." The first guard ordered.

"Our business," Silver began, "has nothing to do with yours. We're weary travelers. Nothing more."

"Why do travelers such as yourselves need to carry weapons?"

"To defend ourselves against anyone who swore an oath to the Dark Master."

The two men aimed their pistols at Silver's head with fingers on the trigger. "You're not welcomed here. Leave now before we shoot."

Silver squinted at them, put his hands to his hips, and leaned over to whisper in Rahim's ear. "Us turning into dragons doesn't faze them, but they noted our weapons. How odd."

Rahim cleared his throat and stepped forward. "If you shoot us, you'll have to deal with our powerful dragon. She destroyed an entire fleet of sky pirates, you know. What do you think she'll do to your little village?" The guards made as much effort as they could to ignore Selena. However, she roared to catch their attention, pleased to see them shaking in their boots when they finally noticed her power.

Silver smirked. "Mind I ask, what's with this atrocious abomination that you call a wall?" He meandered close enough to flick the deteriorated wood. "It looks like someone or something already destroyed it for you."

The second guard's hands tightened around his firearm after getting Silver well within his sights. The watchman growled when Silver didn't pay him any mind.

"Since those *things* rose from their graves, nothing has been right. We had to build this wall to protect what remained of Blackheart."

Silver raised a brow as he remained undaunted by their idle threats. "This wall won't keep the undead out." Despite Selena's warning snarl, the guards didn't let up on their promises to shoot. Instead of arguing with them anymore, Silver sighed and turned to his party and gave them a firm nod. "All right. Have it your way. I hope the Lich doesn't come by and take you tossers." The guards didn't respond to his sarcasm, and Silver spun on his heels, beckoning for Rahim to follow.

One guard finally followed Silver's remark, "I hope those weird dragons drag you off."

Rahim paused in his tracks. "Weird dragons?" He turned around and walked back to the destroyed gate. The guards yelped and pointed their weapons at him instead. "What do you mean by weird dragons? Are they around here?"

"A-aye. They've been camping by the mountains, waiting to torment our village and pillage our supplies like they do every night. Now, off with ya."

As Rahim and Silver strutted away, Rahim grumbled, "Piss off." Silver only chuckled.

Selena swiveled her head around and fixated her attention on the possible location of the rogue Nidhoggr while Silver, now back as a dragon, and Rahim rejoined her. "We need to find those undead goop dragons. If what those twats say is true, the creatures can't be too far away." Rahim looked back at the village and shuddered. "Still, something didn't seem right about this place."

Selena snarled and hissed in agreement as the three leapt to the sky. *Blackheart reminds me of Snowhaven.* She could have sworn Rahim immediately reached down to grab his revolver but snapped his hand back after having second thoughts; instead, he ushered Silver and Selena forward.

It didn't take the two dragons long to reach the south mountain peaks. They made sure to land before the silver and black clouds caught up. The gentle storm spun and weaved the land a brilliant white fleece, with arctic's embrace protecting the pine trees. Heaven's porcelain glitter dressed the landscape in a crystal-white gown.

The three made camp at the highest point of the canyon that overlooked the sea of green and white. Silver made a fire while Rahim pulled out some cheese and bread to share, and Selena leaned against a boulder to observe heaven swirling overhead, watching the glowing snowflakes perform their playful dance before gracing the ground.

Selena's ears twitched to an air-breaking screech as a shadow zoomed through the charcoal grey sky at lightning speed. Before she could see what it was, the silhouette disappeared as quickly as it came. "What was that?" she asked. Rahim and Silver looked at each other and shrugged. Selena squinted at where the object vanished but turned away when she knew it wasn't coming back.

Rahim cleared his throat as he handed Selena pieces of food. "So, uh, do you know how we'll find these weird dragons?" When Selena began eyeing one of Rahim's packs, he ran over to his stash and shoved it behind some nearby bushes. "No, you're not going to use my jerky."

"I don't think bread and cheese will entice them."

"Then find a different way to train them."

Silver, both amused and intrigued, clapped his hands. "Rahim, will you try to be a bit more supportive? She just lost Thor and—" Rahim quickly pressed his fingers to his lips, interrupting Silver before he could finish his sentence.

The two glanced up at Selena in fear of how she would react, but to their surprise, she didn't lash out. Instead, she wrapped her right arm around her drawn-up legs while holding her Aether arm to her chest. "I'll be okay. I'm sorry for being upset about losing Thor before and getting angry with you two. Right now, I just want to focus on finding the Nidhoggr and getting to Dark Blood Hold."

Rahim's eyes widened. "Very good." However, the three jolted from their spots when the trees behind them moved. Before they could prepare to attack, a small black dragon emerged from the verdant lush. Selena's eyes drew to its facial mask, giving away its true nature. The moonlight shards pierced through its oily onyx hide, and Selena was in awe to see its scales radiating rainbow colors across the ground. She wasn't sure if it was the same hatchling from the *Blood Diamond*, but regardless, that meant the rest of the horde were nearby.

With a furrow creasing his brow, Rahim bit his bottom lip to keep himself from giving in to past anger. Not taking notice of the three, the baby sniffed around their campfire and clawed at the ground. The undead dragonet waddled over to Selena, and, as it smelled her feet, its head bobbed up and down, and a chirp erupted from its throat. It shivered as the snowflakes kissed its slimy hide.

Silver's eyes darted between Selena and the whelp, and he inched his way forward with much-needed care. He bent down and allowed the Nidhoggr to smell him in turn. "I will admit, it is adorable. It behaves just like a freshly hatched dragon." Silver scooped it up in his arms and ran his hand across its back. The hatchling twisted itself within Silver's embrace before positioning its front paws over his shoulder, tail twitching from side to side like a cat ready to pounce. "But where are its parents?"

Silver didn't need to wonder long; a myriad of large shadows zipped across the ground. It was a flight of feral Nidhoggr, big and small; about fifty landed among Selena's group. Their deafening screeches pierced the air, and the rhythmic flap of their colossal wings made the earth and sky quake.

The whelpling responded to its brethren by jumping out of Silver's arms and soaring upwards with its razor-like wings to join the others. While Silver stood quizzically to examine and study their new guests, Rahim rushed over to hide behind Selena as if she were his shield.

Silver was more amused. He crossed his arms over his chest and observed them with a tilt of his head. "If they wanted to kill us, they would have done so already." He turned to face Selena. "Isn't this fascinating, my dear?"

She only nodded and looked up as the largest in the group descended upon her, the same creature that shared in their silent farewell after battling the pirates. The undead dragon was almost the size of Ulrich, and Rahim wobbled behind her back. The creature tucked in its razor-blade wings as its paws touched the ground—although their wings were as sharp as a two-edged sword, Selena noticed they were light and limber as feathers, allowing them flight. Her gaze met the red glow burning through the Nidhoggr's eye sockets as a deep rumble escaped from its throat; to everyone's surprise, it was purring.

The rest of the undead flight joined their alpha and encircled Selena, to which Silver clarified, with no intent to harm. Rahim scrambled to his feet and shoved his way through the blitz of curious creatures, regardless of Silver's reassurance. Silver reached out and helped him stand after Rahim clawed at the ground as a means to escape.

Meanwhile, Selena raised her hand and backed away as she suddenly felt claustrophobic from the crowd.

The undead dragons paused and turned their attention to her raised arm. "Rahim, I need your pack now."

"No, it's mine."

Selena gnashed her teeth and repeated her demand in a slow, deep tone. "Give it to me, now."

Before Rahim could object further, Silver elbowed him in the ribs and gave him a shove forward. While muttering profanities under his breath, Rahim eventually gave up his particular jerky; he pulled out his luggage from the bushes and brought it to Selena's side, sticking his tongue out when she was busy unpacking the meat.

The Nidhoggr remained entranced between their exchange. Yet their eyes snapped open when Selena waved the food around; the creatures huddled together and nipped their fangs but recoiled when Selena scolded them for their behavior. "Enough. I can share a little with each of you. Er...." Her words trailed off when she wasn't sure how to provide enough to keep them interested.

The largest weighted feral stood up on its haunches and spread out its sharp-looking wings. "We... understand."

Selena's heart stopped, and her jaw dropped to her feet as she whipped her head around and met Rahim's and Silver's gazes. It spoke like Fafnir, and she began wondering if they all possessed the ability of speech.

Silver shared in her surprise, but Selena expected Rahim to be more composed. Indeed, he wasn't jumping in his spot like Silver was, but Rahim's face burned. He locked eyes on the feral leader like a wolf stalking its prey, and Selena stood directly in between him and the alpha with the hope of redirecting his unchecked rage. She felt Rahim's heated glare burning the back of her neck, but he kept his tongue in control. Selena opened her mouth to speak, but her dry throat made her voice crack. "C-can all of you...?"

The Nidhoggr bowed its head and dug its talons into the ground. Its mouth twisted and curved open, where its speech sounded like a series of intelligible shrieks. "M… me on…ly. I-I s-speak… for others."

Before she could restrain him, Rahim sidestepped and pointed at the Nidhoggr leader in accusation for the raiding of Blackheart. Thumping its tail against its side and whipping up a dust cloud of dirt and powered snow from each flick, the alpha snarled as it wholly extended its wings to their full length. The rest of the ferals copied their leader, and Selena feared they would attack at any moment. Recognizing their warning, Rahim backed and hid again, ignoring the growing intensity of the ferals' fury and the fire burning in Selena's eyes for unnecessarily provoking them.

However, instead of directing its anger at Rahim, the leader began clawing deep gashes into the ground while growling, "Black… heart," in-between breaths. The larger weighted ferals hissed and roared while the hatchlings unleashed a small torrent of black fire mixed with a poisonous cloud that threatened the trio; through gentle waves of motion, Silver and Selena summoned gusts of wind to carry the lethal haze away from their camp.

Selena and Rahim took a step back as the alpha swung its head to and fro before arching his neck to face the flight, hissing at each other like cats. The leader remained indignant, but through Selena's efforts, he and his flight eventually relaxed their wings, and their roars lowered to tiny grumbles vibrating throughout their bodies. The feral hatchlings snapped shut their dainty maws, cutting off their breath streams, and continued sniffing her in great interest.

Not wishing to invoke their unexplained anger, Selena divided up the jerky she had and shared it with each of their new allies in hopes of easing their growing aggression. Her plan briefly worked; however, they fought to reach her as they snatched a piece. Selena feared for the safety of her fingers—even with her Aether hand, she could still feel pain—but much to her surprise, the Nidhoggr left her unharmed.

Still keeping an eye on Rahim so he wouldn't act rashly again, Selena dusted off her hands before reaching out to the alpha. She could feel Rahim quivering as he kept his body pressed against her back when the leader stared at her before snaking its head closer to meet her palm. When the two made contact, they shared a brief, silent communion. Silver and Rahim watched with mouths agape, but they observed the profound interaction in fascination. Selena asked, "Do you have a name?"

The alpha hung his head, and his slimy lips curved into a snarl. "N-Noctis...."

Selena drifted her fingers across his hide with a feathery touch, and she heard the same rumbling purr from before. "It's a pleasure to meet you, Noctis."

After Noctis cleared away from her touch, Silver stepped forward and cleared his throat after asserting his succinct visual analysis. "Noctis, you say? May I ask you a question?" The alpha swiveled his head and grunted. Though Selena reassured Noctis was harmless, Silver's lips twisted as he searched for the right words. "How did you and your kin come about nesting here?"

The creatures snarled and roared at Silver's question, and Rahim tripped over his feet, but he regained his stance. Silver backed away, but the leader approached him with heavy steps. "C-cast... away. Weaker than... the s-strong... ones." If Silver had any further questions for the ferals, he remained tight-lipped.

On the other hand, Selena scanned the desperate creatures, and her heart almost burst from her chest as their faces reminded her of Thor. She inched closer to

Noctis' muzzle with her hand out, and the feral leader welcomed her affections. "Why did you help me fight the sky pirates, Noctis?"

He hissed in between his fangs and lowered his head. "S-saved one… of… our own. You are… one… of… us. In… d-danger. We… s-sensed… your p-presence."

Silver lifted his hand to the air for a chance to speak. "My dear, do you remember my journal? I faintly recall that other creatures of magic can sense other essences. You're both creatures of magic, and they are no different. The Nidhoggr share the same lifeblood as Thor, and so they recognize your magic, too."

His explanation was interrupted; without warning, Noctis' head whirled around, and he roared as his head struck forward in Selena's direction like a snake. She twisted around to avoid his sudden attacks, and Rahim and Silver rushed over to move her. Yet, Noctis ignored them completely, and he sprinted before taking to the skies with his flight of ferals following.

As the three were left to wonder, Noctis swooped down and belched out a black blast of Aether that incinerated the ground near them. Although the attack wasn't directly aimed at them, the group still got into position to attack, but they saw that their flames consumed secret stalkers hidden in the trees. Selena's heart sank when she saw the dreaded zealot robes and wondered how the Obsidian Order found them. Yet, despite Noctis' flames devouring the initial wave, to the trio's dismay, their enemies were large in number; Selena guessed as many as fifty, perhaps more.

Silver and Rahim spun around to meet the surrounding masks reflecting with the moonlight, and without sharing additional unpleasantries, the cultists rushed in with weapons and magic. Silver cast streaks of chain-lightning that struck one, then another. Rahim got his revolver ready and took out a few more while staying to Silver's back, avoiding the ropes of Silver's summoned lightning.

While her friends were preoccupied and noting how the Order purposefully singled her out, Selena stomped on the ground. Her magic sent a shockwave erupting like an earthquake while the cultists mustered swords made of black fire and slashed waves of dark Aether blasting in her direction. A few zealots rolled away from the attack on the ground, but an unfortunate group got caught in Selena's magic and fell through the pit.

With accurate and quick precision of his revolver, Rahim mowed down another line of zealots before they could prepare themselves; Silver tore through each of his foes by channeling and untwisting their Aether strands, causing their bodies to shred like grated cheese.

However, their group of attackers dwindled and added to another wave rushing with their barrage of magic to help their comrades subdue Selena. She sidestepped their attacks and waved her hands, summoning stones from the ground, and with the flick of her wrists, parts of the rock broke into tiny pieces and shot through the air like bullets from a pistol. The Order dove for cover, but one of the Lich's followers pulled a large boulder hiding behind the trees and hurled it at Selena. Yet she was faster; she waved her Aether hand and shot a blast of azure spirit energy shattering the rock into pieces.

Although Selena didn't need much assistance, Silver created fire rings that expanded outward until the flames reached their foes. Three from the Order broke formation and focused their energy against Silver, breaking through the smoldering concentric circles with a slash from their black Aether swords.

The others changed their tactics by punching the air and shooting black fireballs aimed directly at Selena's friends. Selena slammed her foot against the ground, causing it to ripple like water, and pillars erupted underneath where the Order stood, but they dashed away to avoid her attack.

"My dear, over here." Silver reached out to pull her close while warding off another Order wave.

Growling through her teeth, she prepared to take her dragon form, but the group suddenly heard Noctis' roar above the trees, catching the zealots off guard when they saw the feral leader circling overhead. As the trio took cover to the ground, Noctis reared his head back and breathed his torrent of dark Aether consuming all in its path.

With no chance at taking down one of their own 'failed' creations, the Order fled as Noctis landed beside Selena's friends and raised his wings, sheltering the three from the black fire. The other ferals emerged from the darkness and exhaled their shadow flame streams, creating a protective wall separating the Order from the group.

Noctis roared, and the Obsidian Order attempted to strike him down with magic and firearms, but their attacks bounced off his hide as he swung his body around and addressed Selena directly, "C-come...."

She didn't question the leader and climbed on his back. Before Silver and Rahim could join her, Noctis launched himself through his brethren's flames—both he and Selena unharmed—as he flapped his wings and took off from their campsite.

The remaining Nidhoggr chased off the Order after Selena was whisked away, but Silver, already morphing into a dragon in mid-leap and snatching Rahim in his talons, pursued Noctis, but the feral leader was too fast. **My dear, pray tell Noctis to wait for us.**

Selena reiterated Silver's plea, but Noctis ignored her and roared, her hands trembling as she gripped his crowned horns. His massive wings swept them through heaven's divine sea, with each beat putting more distance between them and the others, and before she knew it, Silver and Rahim disappeared into the shadows. "Why did you save us?" Noctis didn't respond. "Do you know where the Order came from?"

Noctis snorted and finally grumbled. "Black… heart."

Selena's face turned pale when she realized why the village seemed odd; the Obsidian Order had taken Blackheart Village. *They planned on attacking us after we approached them for food and shelter.* "What about the innocents within the village? What became of them?" When Noctis only hissed and grunted, the air pierced her lungs from each agonizing breath she took, and her heart drowned in a sea of sorrows.

Silver's voice beckoned her once more. **Where are you two?**

I don't know. If Noctis' flight is following us, fly with them.

Are you hurt?

Not at all. Silver remained unconvinced and demanded a better reply. *You know how capable I am. I will not let Noctis harm me.* Selena didn't mean to sound harsh, but she was not helpless, as Silver had first-hand seen the power she possessed. Eventually, he reluctantly withdrew and ruefully agreed to follow the ferals after they finished tracking down the rest of the Order.

Suddenly, her previous plan to acquire a Nidhoggr army was within reach. She and Noctis savored in the silence as she worked out a way to convince the leader to ally against the Lich. "Join us, and we can strike down the Dark Master and his Order."

"Your efforts… will be… f-futile."

"But we must fight back." Selena's eyes glossed over like their winter tundra, but Noctis remained silent, not surrendering to her request. Although Selena could have left him, she stayed by his side, hopeful that she could persuade the feral leader. Together, they flew for about an hour, and when Noctis was sure they were far enough away from Selena's ambushed campsite, he made his descent and landed near a small waterfall and a pond enclosed by snow-dressed pine trees.

She dismounted and looked around to see if she could see Silver and Rahim or any of the others from the alpha's flight, but she and Noctis were alone. "Where did you take me?"

"S-safe…."

Selena reached out to pat his nose, and Noctis touched his snout to her outstretched palm. "Can you take me back to Silver and Rahim?" He grunted and snorted before turning away, whipping his tail across dirt and rock.

*****

CHAPTER 17: THOR ALONE

Three days ago, in Ulrich's lair, Thor was trapped in his pandemonium of madness. He gave in to his anger and was again surrounded by his swirling maelstrom of darkness. Ulrich's voice was the last light before extinguishing within the blackness. "Let your anger go."

No, I will never let it go.

A purple cloud covered his raging eyes as lightning struck across the surrounding ground. He flapped his wings, and Thor's storm grew violent and heavy like the purple aura glowing around his body. He summoned a black ring of dark energy that orbited him; with his final cry, he released it. It stretched outward in a shockwave, and Thor's wrathful magic destroyed Medusa and her army from his memory.

His vision brought him back to the fairytale-lovely crystallized cavern, and soon two unrecognizable entities appeared before him. Perhaps he knew them, but Thor no longer perceived them as friend or foe. To him, they were nothing.

Thor, stop!

Thor didn't react, as the voice was no longer familiar. Instead, he hung his head as his chest swelled, with each breath deeper and heavier than the last. The screaming storm continued circling him until he was entirely consumed by it. When his magic dissipated, his once ruby scales had turned to ebony; wisps of dark Aether tickled his hide as Thor's wings became wafting shadows. The purple veil over his eyes glowed eerily through Thor's unblinking trance, and all that he saw from that point forward was darkness, and all he heard were whispers from demons and the void.

Thor, no.... His mind was twisted and corrupted, and he no longer understood her. He felt a light touch on his snout, but he didn't know who was there. Was it a friend? A foe? Instead, he remained idle. *No, this isn't you. This darkness isn't who you are. Please, answer me.*

The stranger's words jumbled together, but clear as crystal, another voice entered his mind: *Join me, Destroyer of Worlds. The time has come for you to serve the Dark Master.*

Yes, Master.

Thor didn't even try to fight his new master's orders, and he was more than obliged to obey. He lifted his head and roared before opening his massive jaws, exhaling his new and terrifying breath. His once Divine fire changed to a black Aether beam with writhing ropes of lightning, and he blasted a hole through the side of the mountain; once the falling rock debris cleared, Thor launched himself skyward in one leap and flew away from the Aurora Peaks.

The dark voice echoed through his subconscious again: *Yes, come to me, Fallen One, and join me at the ruins of Alfheim. I shall be waiting for you.*

The brilliant blue ore moon rose above Thor as he continued his predestined course. He floated for hours until the sun hovered over the horizon behind him. However, his eyes snapped open when he heard a voice calling out from the light: *Thor! Thor!*

His wings struggled to keep him adrift, and Thor's head thrashed about as he moaned and groaned. He rocked himself back and forth as he began spinning out of control. Yet, his head filled with a harrowing ring, and he was back under the dark influence that drove his purpose. However, Thor could no longer continue to abide by the Lich's control when the voice cried out again. *Thor! Where are you? Thor!*

The dark purple veil vanished, and Thor's eyes returned to normal as he stopped in mid-flight. He whipped his head around, thrashing about in place by clawing at his horns, and let out a roar that made the heavens cry. The distraught dragon attempted to return his handler's call, but his mind was still addled. He could hear Selena, but he couldn't answer her; Thor was in a constant battle fighting off the Lich's magic.

No... no!

Selena's voice twinkled within his subconscious. He turned around and saw a slithering shadow disappear into the fading mountains behind him, and Thor immediately flung himself after the silhouette. **My dear one, is that you? I'm here. I'm right here.**

His futile effort to communicate with her made him give in to the anger that brewed within him. She was right there, and he couldn't speak to her, let alone sense her presence. He knew it had to be her with Silver, and they were looking for him. Fear and dismay made his heart race as Thor realized that Selena perhaps couldn't feel his aura, too.

The Lich's dark and sinister voice filled his thoughts. *You belong to me, Destroyer of Worlds.*

The necromancer's black magic continued its ever-consuming hold over him, and Thor began his long descent into the Black Bog Forest as he struggled to fight back. He flared out his wings to slow his fall, but his eyes drooped, and he came to a sliding crash onto the forest floor. The earth rumbled and quaked, and Thor's vision darkened and blurred.

He wasn't sure how long he was out. Minutes? Hours, maybe? All he knew was he heard chirps and growls. Thor's eyes fluttered open to find that black whelplings surrounded him, and he recognized they were feral Nidhoggr hatchlings: he counted four. He tilted his head as one of the younglings inched closer, bobbing its head up and down, sniffing his snout. Thor growled, and they scuttled away—he couldn't help but think they looked cute. Thor's nostrils flared as he fell to disbelief that these hatchlings were the same monsters that attacked Alfheim, and he remembered Tiamat, the hatchling that gave her life to save Selena.

One of the whelplings approached with slow steps, ignoring Thor's fixated and curious gaze. As it got close enough, the dragonet sniffed him again. When their noses touched, the baby Nidhoggr twittered, and the other three moved forward. The hatchlings ran around Thor after they each took a turn to smell him, and after satisfying their curiosity, they dashed ahead and ran in circles.

Thor turned his attention heavenward as the whelplings chased each other through the emerald sea of pines. The Lich's voice was gone, but his magic was still there. Thor could no longer hear Selena calling for him, but he was back in his right mind for now, and his colors changed back to normal. **What have I done? I am so sorry, my dear one. I promised that I would never leave your side.**

His heart swelled, but his head snapped up to the unusual sounds echoing in the distance. Without warning, the Nidhoggr hatchlings scattered through the green lush in fear of the booming voices. "Listen up, maggots. Spread out. Captain Battleraven only wants prized fighters."

Thor crawled on his belly and inched his way closer to the strangers and, through the thick and twirling branches, witnessed a flock of mercenaries wandering across the clearing. He did his best to remain hidden—as much of a dragon his size could—behind a nearby large thick tree root slithering out from the ground.

One pirate caught sight of the fleeing hatchlings, pulled out a blowgun, and fired it at the closest feral Nidhoggr whelpling. It staggered and dropped to the ground after succumbing to the tranquilizing dart; the pirate bagged the whelp in a sack and threw it over his shoulder. "These nasty little beasts will put on a good show in the coliseum. Double the bounty for the bigger ones."

Out of anger, dark flames plumed from Thor's closed maw. His snarls and growls, however, drew the attention of the mercenaries. The pirate that snatched the baby Nidhoggr ordered a few of his men to scout ahead and investigate the sound source. As they crept closer to the root, Thor emerged from the shadows and let forth an eruption of black Aether fire.

The pirates dodged his deadly conflagration, and the rest of the crew leapt from the trees and surrounded the dragon. "What have we here? Captain Battleraven would triple the bounty for your capture."

He had enough of their nonsense; Thor roared and swept his tail across the ground, creating billows of dust that made the pirates stagger back and rub their eyes. However, as he unfurled his wings, several mercenaries pulled out their blowguns and fired brown darts that were strong enough to pierce his rock-hard hide.

Instantly, Thor's eyes began to sag, and his muscles melted as he lost all motor control and slid back down. His vision blurred, and Thor's last sight was the pirates throwing heavily weighted chains over his limp body.

"Rise and shine, dragon." His eyesight recovered, and Thor jerked awake, greeted by cage bars while a strange man stood post to his prison cell door. Without meaning to, the jeweled mess hanging from the man's neck attracted Thor's attention, and his wide-brimmed hat hid part of his greasy old face in the shadows.

Thor whipped around and found himself trapped in a large jail cell—stripped completely barren, minus a large pile of hay stacked in a corner—made entirely of metal on board a massive, wooden vessel of black oak and steel. His wings were tied down to his sides by chains, and adorned around his neck was a thick collar tethered to the floor, banging against the sapphire from his harness.

He bellowed, and fire erupted between his fangs, but the strange man shook his head, clicking his tongue against his teeth. "I wouldn't do that if I were you. You see, we're airborne on the *Blood Diamond*. My ship and fleet are currently as high as the mountain tops. If you burn down my boat right now, you will plummet to your death while trapped in that metal cage." Thor snapped his fangs but held back his readied attack, extinguishing his ember fury in plumes of smoke. "That's much better. I trust that your living quarters are to your liking?" Thor's eye twitched as he assumed this man to be the unfortunate Captain Battleraven began pacing in front of his prison cell. He snarled as the brute pulled out a brown dart his crew used to bring him down. "Do you want to know why these are perfect for bringing down dragons? They're crafted from dragon bones and can pierce through anything. You were not an easy haul."

Thor roared through his clamped fangs. **I will kill you all as soon as I get the chance.**

Of course, he knew that the captain couldn't hear him. "That's a nice little piece of treasure you have there. Too bad we couldn't remove that gem. Believe me; we've tried. However, your enchantments to protect that saddle don't mean anything to me, Thor." The captain snarled when he saw the dragon's shocked reaction. "Oh, yes. I know you: the queen's precious commodity, Thor, the Divinity Dragon. I was disappointed at how easily we could capture you, but hopefully, you will be worth our while.

"You see, I run sort of a… business. My crew collects prized fighters to battle in my stadium—entertainment and gold. You, too, will be made to compete in the arena fights just like my other prisoners." Thor snaked his head around to see a horde of pirates coming from down the corridor and encircling their captain; he was disappointed when they ignored his growing growls, but they made haste when the captain pointed to the imprisoned dragon. "Get ready because it's time to fight." Battleraven turned around and took his leave while his minions approached Thor's cell to escort him out.

Despite Thor's large size, the *Blood Diamond* was a magnificent ship that could easily accommodate forty dragons his size. The pirates led him by the leash with his wings still chained to his sides, preventing him from flying to freedom out of the arena. They made their way to the circular hall open to the natural elements packed with pirates.

Captain Battleraven occupied a throne directly opposite the stadium entrance; he stood from his seat and spoke over the mass of cries. "My fellow felons, welcome to the arena. For the first event of the evening, we give you an exciting battle. Introducing two extraordinary creatures of magic and might, prepare yourselves for Thor, the DRAGON!"

The arena gates opened, and Thor stepped forward towards the fighting area. As the crowd saw Thor emerge, they cheered madly; these brutes were ready to embrace the upcoming bloodshed. "And his opponent, who you know and love, I give you the Many-Eyed Giant!"

The beast stepped forth into the coliseum. When Thor whipped his head around, his jaw dropped when he saw it was a massive gryphon with hundreds of eyes all over its eagle head. **The All-Seeing Argus.**

Its beak opened while it squawked and screeched, digging its talons and hind lion paws into the dirt. Its feathered wings were chained down to its sides, like Thor's. His thoughts flashed to when he and Selena first fought another Argus during their search for Ragnarok, and his heart yearned for her companionship.

The audience's cheers edged the beast on; the Argus swiped at Thor, but he backed away and prepared himself for the fight. Feeling remorse for the gryphon, he didn't want to fight back, but his rage grew as the beast threw strike after strike. The Argus pecked at him with its long beak and launched a flurry of slashes, but Thor continued backing away, his back arching like a hissing cat. He remembered his first encounter and how elementary his skills were—as Thor was now thrice his opponent's size, perhaps more.

Thor made a warning slash for the Argus to stand down, but the creature wouldn't listen. Leaving him with no choice, he let forth his deadly torrent of black Aether, but he aimed his blast past the gryphon. It recoiled but then launched itself towards him in a desperate attempt to win the fight. Thor dodged and directed his breath attack directly at the beast, the dark Aether incinerating the All-Seeing Argus, and when he clamped shut his maw, a pile of ash remained of the creature.

The fiendish audience applauded and cheered for Thor's flawless victory, but he refused to take a bow for his performance. However, Battleraven sneered. "Well done. Come forward, dragon, and bask in your newfound glory. We may have found ourselves a new champion. Pray don't disappoint us, dragon."

Thor hung his head as Battleraven's crew escorted him back to his cell. He felt horrible and wished that the gryphon didn't have to attack in a blind frenzy; he dreaded what other creatures the captain had planned for Thor to battle. **Is this to be my new life?** He feared he would never see Selena again.

The pirates abruptly left after locking him up, but before Thor could make as much of another step, his head grew fuzzy and light. He saw two of all before him before fainting to the sound of the Lich's dark command: *Come and find me, Destroyer of Worlds. I will be waiting for you at Alfheim.*

When he awoke, Thor was greeted by Captain Battleraven banging on his metal bars. "Rise and shine, dragon. It's time for you to make me more gold." Thor snarled, but the captain ignored the dragon's threats and returned to the arena as his mercenaries arrived to lead Thor out of his cell.

The stadium grew packed and ready for the next fight as it had before, and Captain Battleraven had already taken his seat on the throne above the pit. "My fellow fiends and felons, let's welcome back Thor, the dragon!" Thor stepped through the opened gates, only to be greeted by the howling fans. His lips curled into a menacing snarl, which seemed to add to the audience's anticipation. "It's time to bring out the creature of death itself."

Thor turned around and shook his head in disbelief when he met with a smaller weight Nidhoggr; the undead dragon wasn't much larger than the whelps he had encountered previously, but it still hissed upon seeing its massive adversary. The creature advanced to the arena, ready to make its assault. Soon, the two dragons threw themselves upon the other in a melee of claws; the clash amused the spectators as the two dragonkin broke away and circled each other.

The young feral was surprisingly strong and quick; shaking off the pain from the fresh gashes, Thor got into a defensive stance by showing his unscathed side, but the Nidhoggr paused its attack and began sniffing him with curiosity. While the area was stunned in confusion, a small whelpling—the one the pirates bagged before Thor's imprisonment—ran from the shadows and joined its companion. It exhaled a small black Aether stream that melted the chains binding its friend's wings.

The crowd began yelling their boos when the fight paused, and before Captain Battleraven could intervene, Thor heard a sudden roar over the coliseum. The once impressive frigate trembled and rocked. Several Nidhoggr around his size flew overhead, belching their black Aether blasts that decimated the audience and parts of the ship; black meteors rained over the sky pirates.

While the captain and his crew made their escape, the two ferals rushed towards Thor and used their Aether breaths to melt the chains that bound him. Through the combined might of their magic and Thor's strength, the metal snapped off his body, and they assured him he was free with chirps and clicks before flying away to join their brethren.

Stretching out his muscles for the first time in a long while, Thor unfolded his colossal wings, swept himself skyward, and soared into the night. During his hasty escape, he didn't look back to see the massive Aether dragon leading the flight of Nidhoggr and burning down the pirate fleet, nor did he witness Captain Battleraven's grim defeat. Thor couldn't feel her Divine presence due to the dark magic still consuming him. Instead, he kept moving forward and flew away from Battleraven's smoldering ships as fast as possible.

Yet, the Lich's voice returned to him. *Come to me, Fallen One.*

Thor snarled as he struggled to remain aloft, but the deathly ring shattered his ears, and his flight caught turbulence. His slits rolled into the back of his head as the Lich's command overcame his mind, but Thor continued fighting for control.

Growing tired and weary, he suddenly spiraled again from the sky; after gaining a slight moment of sanity, he focused on catching his flight and strained his wing muscles. However, the fall was too great, and Thor slid and crashed back down into the earth, his massive weight making the ground shake. With the lingering darkness threatening to overcome his subconscious, he felt like he was hit with the captain's sleeping darts again as he faded into slumber.

As his eyes fluttered open, Thor caught the faint rays of sunshine glistening through the dull clouds. He shook his hide like a wet dog and flinched from his aching muscles and wings, but Thor desperately wanted to make it back to Selena. Fighting through the pain, he took to the skies again, determined to return. That necromancer could not hold him back forever.

Much to his relief, the harrowing call remained silent during his trip back. Thor was still far from Heaven's Tear, and he pushed himself to the limit as he increased his speed; the desperate dragon flew as fast as his wings could carry him. Even as the evening soon settled upon the world, his muscles burned like they were on fire, but Thor saw he was almost at the summit and pressed on through the night.

Finally, he made it back to Silver's library while it was still the early dawn, but to Thor's dismay, Selena and the others were already gone. He peered over the horizon to see if he could spot them, but his friends were nowhere to be found.

Sodden and stricken with grief, Thor made his way to the pavilion. He started pawing at the dirt until his eyes scanned over his golden bracelets and chain, along with the dragon totem the Aynu gave him, and he immediately bellowed in despair. Thor collapsed to the ground beside his old treasures and lapsed into a deep slumber in exhaustion, only for his dreams to remind him of her:

"It seems that the hatchling has developed… an attachment to the girl."

"Women are not allowed to become part of the Force."

Thor recalled those words of doubt as he and Selena spent many evenings together in Alfheim. There was no war, no Lich, no Silver. It was just him and her.

"I will never let you go… I promise I will find you and bring you back." Selena's voice was the light that chased away the darkness tormenting him.

As it reached midday, Thor was roused by the flutter of beating wings. He snaked his head around to see Ulrich, jumped to his feet, and stared down at the descending Divine. Ulrich made no reaction to Thor's sudden hostility as the green dragon landed close to the tower and fixated his glimmering emerald eyes upon him, his wings still fully extended. "It's good to see you again, Divine One." Thor didn't want to speak to him and greeted Ulrich with a long, menacing growl, but the Emerald Dragon didn't offend by the rude welcome. "You are still so twisted up inside. You're full of love, but your mind has been tainted."

Where is Selena?

"As far as I know, she and the others left to Dark Blood Hold." Thor's heart shattered from this dreadful news. "She and Silver did their best to find you after I sought solace in my fortress. I've been deep in meditation and isolation since your unfortunate absence. Still, I saw how Selena didn't want to abandon her search for you." Ulrich bowed his head to Thor. "Yours and Selena's energies are intertwined, and the bond you two share is unyielding. Your Aether connects you two."

Drawing back his building rage and vehemence, Thor paused for a moment before bending. **As it should always be.** He glanced at his pavilion and treasures before leaving, as he didn't care for them anymore; all he wanted was to find Selena again, and no amount of gold or jewels could ever replace her.

As he made his way heavenward, he heard Ulrich say, "Farewell, Divine One. We Divines shall watch over you two. Until we meet again."

Thor soared down the peak and through the ice-kissed air. Flurries of pure white greeted him as a newly black-blossomed sky sailed above and bequeathed the world with a bounty of snow. He attempted to reach out to Selena once more as a final, desperate act. He expected his call to go unnoticed. However—

Thor? Is that you?

Thor's eyes widened, and he came to a halt. Her voice at last, though it sounded a little different, he didn't care. His head thrashed around to look for her. **My dear, where are you?**

I'm at Blackheart Village.

He didn't question that she didn't seem very talkative, but instead, his heart filled with joy to communicate with her again.

He felt light as a feather, and Thor dove towards the settlement like a fired bullet, flying so fast that it made the air scream. He plunged through the clouds and began his descent as he drew closer, and the village was soon well within aerial view after escaping the cold cloud's embrace. His smoldering amber eyes shifted to a shade of red, and his pupils dilated into slits as he approached Blackheart's walls, but he noticed the heavily armed residents who guarded the top watched him like a hawk.

Thor hovered over the town as he looked around for any signs of Selena. **I'm here. Where are you?**

Instead of receiving an answer, he spun around when the citizens surrounded him. Before the dragon could brace himself, the residents attacked and threw a series of weighted chains to pin Thor down systematically. His roar shook the earth, and he fought back as best as he could, clawing at the ground and shackles, breathing out a barrage of magic attacks, but his efforts to escape came to a halt when he heard the familiar death ring that made him cower. Thor resisted as much as he could, but his mind and body weakened, and he was quickly captured.

The voice Thor thought was Selena's evolved into the Lich's familiar sneer, and the demon mocked the dragon. *Where are you, Thor?* Thor snarled at the cruel trick, and his eyes zipped past the faces of his captors. *I told you that you belong to me.*

One by one, the residents of Blackheart unveiled themselves as members of the Obsidian Order. The first guard on top of the wall laughed at Thor. "You missed your rider by *hours*. Don't worry; we will go after her next."

Thor barely had the strength to curl his lips into a snarl as his mind began to drift out of his control, and the Order finished binding his chains. A shrill shattered the air, and two large saddled Nidhoggr appeared over the horizon and landed beside the subdued dragon.

He conceded to the Lich's final calling; his vision blurred and faded to darkness when the Nidhoggr worked together by snatching his chains and carting him back to what remained of Alfheim.

*****

CHAPTER 18: THE CASTLE BY THE SEA

Joining Noctis' side in the thick of the evening, Selena knelt before the feral leader and stroked his neck, his ebony hide as smooth and slippery as fish scales. "Please tell me what happened to Blackheart. What became of the villagers?"

Noctis snaked his head around and sniffed her face before letting out a low grumble. "Gone...."

"What do you mean gone? Were they...?" A tear drifted down her moon-kissed cheek, but her grief was soon replaced by the blazing fire burning within her; her wrath was about to erupt like a violent volcano. "If Blackheart is nothing more than those zealots, I will burn it to the ground." Noctis snorted and flickered his tail across the dirt before wrapping it around his body, creating puffs of dust from each sweep.

Growing weary of waiting, Selena decided to take matters into her own hands. Noctis stayed ensconced within his coils, but she had already assumed her dragon form, heaved herself upward one full-body leap, and sailed through heaven's sea of stars. She was the light chasing away the darkness that consumed Armageddon, and time eluded her as she made her way towards the shadow over Blackheart.

As the village drew close, the mountains could hear Selena's roar. The guards who gave her group the rude greeting now donned the Order attire. As she closed the distance between her and the settlement, Selena snarled when she saw Blackheart crawling with the Lich's atrocious worshipers—their dark blue bone masks made her almost retch.

Upon spotting the Divine blue dragon, the zealots rushed about in pell-mell fashion, taking up arms in retaliation, firing a combination of magic and bullets as Selena flew close. Yet, she danced around their attacks as she swooped downward, her fury knowing no bounds. She breathed a line of blue Aether fire into a row of cultists, and she paused mid-strafe to watch the men from the Order burst into flames.

Pleased with her work, she circled and wafted more flames across the wall, destroying what remained of the wooden structure, her wings fanning the fires as her blazes burned. Steering herself along the perimeter, Selena spewed another torrent that ravaged both infrastructure and Order alike, with buildings and supplies exploding into pieces; barrels and body parts flew through the air.

Soon, the Order stopped attacking the rampaging dragon and began fleeing for their lives; Selena dove through and burned them down with a single breath, finishing her onslaught with one final strafe of the burning village and unleashing her deadly azure inferno. The Divine Aether Dragon reduced all her enemies to piles of ash. Satisfied, she flew away, not taking note of some talon prints left in the ground at Blackheart's center that belonged to Thor.

It didn't take her long to return to the ensconced Noctis. The lazy Nidhoggr leader looked up as she landed before him; black smoke plumed from his nostrils in greeting. To Selena's dismay, her friends still had not arrived. She was about to look for Silver and Rahim herself, but she was hesitant to abandon Noctis again after forming a new acquaintance. Noctis snaked his head across the ground to face her as if he read her thoughts. "Wait… for… them. T-they… will come."

Trusting in his words, she wrapped herself up within her coils and draped her wings over her head, only accompanied by the sound of Noctis' breathing as steady as the ocean waves. Grieving over the fallen villagers, with the lack of graves or, as much as it pained her to consider, a pile of bodies, Selena could only surmise that the Dreygur Rahim pointed out were the risen residents from Blackheart.

However, she heard a whistle, like a drawn sword. Her head shot up, pupils turning to slits as she prepared herself for a possible surprise attack; a bright flutter of sword-sharp wings caught a glimmer in Selena's sparkling emeralds, Noctis' rapidly descending dragonkin with their spoils from the Order's ambush. Their snouts and claws were dyed crimson as they gorged themselves immediately upon landing.

Shortly after their arrival came Silver, with Rahim in his clutched claws. Only after Silver dropped Rahim to his feet did Selena unwrap herself from her coils, and the two dragons changed form to resume their mortal guises. "Are you hurt?" Silver lingered skeptical, however, despite Selena's reassurance of her wellbeing and that Noctis meant no harm. At the mention of his name, he swung his head over and yawned wide enough that he could swallow them whole.

Rahim said, "It reminded me of what happened to Niamh; we were worried about you."

Selena squinted at the two and placed her hands on her hips. "You seem to have forgotten that I annihilated an entire fleet of ships—thirty-six frigates, the largest armada of pirates ever assembled, as I recall. You've said it before, Silver. I'm a Divinity Dragon like Thor, and I have the power of a whole damn army."

Recoiling from her assertion, the two still couldn't help but smile at her confidence and agreed with a firm jerky nod. Slithering his neck and body along with the dirt like a snake, Noctis slid over to Selena's side and nudged his snout against her wispy Aether hand; the deep rumble from the back of his throat made the mountain quiver. Silver stroked Noctis' muzzle and briefly mentioned the bonfire that now consumed Blackheart. When Selena didn't offer her involvement, he furrowed his brow and tilted his head curiously. "I know that's your doing."

She felt no shame; instead, she held her head high and reiterated the news Noctis shared with her before her friends' arrival. "I did what needed to be done."

It was Rahim's turn to be impressed. "Brilliant. Remind me not to cross you."

Spinning around on her heels, Selena met the intriguing gazes of the Nidhoggr as they paused mid-meal and watched her with deep interest upon hearing of her remarkable exploits; even Noctis began chittering with glee. "You've helped us fight the sky pirates and now the Obsidian Order. Allow us to make our pact and help us fight against the Lich, and together, we can save our world and live in peace. What say you?"

Noctis' sudden snarls made the trio back away as he stood up entirely on his haunches, towering above the ground and his pack of ferals, his bladed wings unfurled to their full length; his flight hissed and stamped their bloodied paws against the earth. "We... s-serve... no one."

After sharing a few awkward side-ways glances with Silver and Rahim, Selena chose her following words carefully as she bravely stepped forward to approach the leader, ignoring the growing intensity of Noctis' growls. "I'm not asking you to serve but to form an alliance. You and your brethren saved my friends and me from Captain Battleraven and his crew, and now I'm willing to fight for you. Wouldn't you and your flight wish revenge against the Dark Master for what he did to you? First trapped in chains and made to serve, only to be cast and thrown away."

The very mention of the Lich's atrocities invoked their wrath, and Noctis unleashed a thundering roar followed by a long stream of black Aether lancing through the metal-hued clouds. Selena watched the ferals' reaction in satisfaction as they spewed their breaths in despair; at that moment, she felt confident the Nidhoggr would give her no other answer but yes. "Will you fight alongside me?"

After Noctis interrupted his stream of black flame, he fell to all fours—wings still unfurled—and growled through his clamped fangs; he reminded her so much of Thor that it hurt. Sharing a few low growls, twitters, and snarls from his flight, Noctis flickered his onyx tail, thumping it against his sides. "We… w-will… fight beside y-you… Divine One."

Pleased, Selena stretched out her Aether hand to meet the alpha's snout, commemorating their newly formed pact, and Noctis lowered his muzzle while chittering in delight. A thick, rancid cloud plumed from his nostrils and tickled her cheek—Selena half expected the smoke to burn her skin, but much to her elated surprise, it brushed against her like an ocean spray before dissipating into the evening air.

Silver grinned and gave them all a congratulatory clap as the flight of ferals roared in unison—not in anger, but to memorialize their treaty. Rahim, however, needed more convincing, judging from his squirming and fidgeting, but reassured Selena when she confronted him about his behavior. Nervous and cautious as he may be, Rahim still maintained the position of allying with the feral Nidhoggr. Yet, he flinched and swore under his breath when the twin hatchlings flew in circles around him, twittering in playfulness.

When he deemed it safe after gesturing to the whelplings to leave him alone, Rahim stepped lightly and made his way to Selena and Noctis, keeping a close watch on the ferals to prepare himself in case of an attack. "I know I said we should do this. I trust you, but I don't fully trust them."

"They're not the ones who took Niamh."

Rahim's nostrils flared. "It doesn't matter. We have to be careful."

"Yes, it does matter. You can't condemn Noctis and his flight for a crime they didn't even commit."

Defeated and undone, Rahim grudgingly helped Selena and Silver make their new campsite. The snow had already stopped, but the blizzard clouds still lingered overhead. The three—Rahim ruefully—decided to rest with the Nidhoggr for a few hours before continuing towards Dark Blood Hold. Silver already made a big fire and pitched up a warm tent that was large enough for the group.

Rahim complained under his breath about how close their camp was to the ferals. Instead of sleeping under shelter, he snatched his blankets and picked out a sleeping spot as far away as possible from their new and, in his opinion, 'questionable' allies. Bemused, Selena watched him as he mumbled and stomped around. "This was partly your idea, Rahim."

"I know, but I was thinking about it from a tactical standpoint. Now that it's happening, I-I dunno." He threw his sleeping bag down while muttering, "I'll never fall asleep with those *things* here." Yet, it didn't take long before Selena heard him snore.

Silver agreed to stand guard outside so that she could rest her eyes. It seemed like she barely shut them when it was time to pack up and leave, yet Selena felt awake and alert; she was ready to face the day with a clear mind and a set purpose.

While the trio folded up the tent, the Nidhoggr returned from their morning hunt; even as they picked through their deer and elk bones, the group's actions allured the undead masked dragons. After Noctis finished his meal and cleaned himself of the blood and gore, Selena approached and explained their route and destination. She felt slightly uneasy about how Lord Godfrey would take to see a flight of about fifty Nidhoggr approaching his castle, but Noctis swore that he and his kin would not attack as long as the Shadow Templars didn't retaliate.

In his dragon form, Silver waited for Rahim to finish packing. Rahim's swollen eyes drooped, and, in between yawns, he finally brought his bags over to strap down to Silver's harness. Selena, however, was kept busy by the Nidhoggr: they were interested in any movement she made and any task she completed. The whelplings rubbed up against her legs like a cat around its owner. She snickered when she heard Silver growl and snarl. "What's the matter?"

Silver turned his head upward and snorted. **I don't like how they're so attached to you. That's all.**

While she teased him for jealousy of the sudden affections, Noctis paid no mind to their playful banter; he bowed to her before taking flight. "We… are… r-ready."

After Silver and Rahim affirmed their preparations, she transformed by channeling her Aether in front of an enthusiastic watchful audience. Selena swept her wings and climbed the skies, and the others followed. The metallic clouds came as sunlit glitter. The blue-grey haze adorned the heavens like a velvet curtain; the soft, filtered light kissed the earth and sparkled across the dazzling array of different colored scales as Selena flew with the flail of wings trailing behind her.

The group traveled for hours in silence until they finally crossed the crimson ocean of an ancient grove lining the small mountains guarding the coast, shielding Ghost Lake from their aerial view, and the trio reached the castle by the sea: Dark Blood Hold. The bold fortress of tower and stone stood as the crown at the edge of a massive cliff, transient turquoise waves rising and falling as they slammed against the sheltering rock.

The group flew above lines of tents and over the assembling army camped outside the castle when they crossed the crimson grove. Men and women had gathered around as they prepared for the upcoming battle, exchanging horses, armor, and weapons. The aggregation stretched over the horizon; the battalion wasn't intimidated by the group's passing shadows darting across the ground.

Much to Selena's surprise, even the horses weren't spooked by the flight of dragons and Nidhoggr; upon further examination, hoods draped over their heads and pouches covered their nostrils. Silver explained that Lord Godfrey possibly trained the horses not to frighten easily by stuffing the pockets with herbs and dried flowers to keep them from smelling dragons and even Nidhoggr, thus giving them the advantage to use their calvary during dragon-fire.

Selena asked Silver, *how many fighters do you think he has?*

I'm not sure. Silver flew up a little higher and surveyed the land.

Do you believe we'll have enough soldiers?

I-I don't know. Let's pray that it is enough.

Selena looked to Rahim, who was busy watching their allies below, and their battalion was greeted by the ballistas lining the walls of Dark Blood Hold, loaded and ready. Bolts large enough to take down a dragon were aimed at Selena's chest. Selena came to a halt in mid-flight, and the Nidhoggr followed suit. Her wispy lips curved into a snarl, and even her feral army grew restless; their growls shared her vehemence from the rude welcome.

Rahim tightened his grip around Silver's horns. "They don't look too happy to see us."

Selena swiveled around when Silver approached. **Allow me to speak with them first, as Lord Godfrey is familiar with my guise.**

Withholding reluctance and dubiousness on her part, Selena agreed; Silver snorted and slithered through to meet the armed guards. The archers hustled into position and held their bows taut, ignoring the white dragon. Noctis and his kin inched forward, but Selena spun her head around, snapping her fangs, to which the flight snarled in response. The smaller ferals zipped around in inpatient circles, their anxiousness growing every second.

"Stand down."

Selena's head whipped forward to find the one who spoke. Her eyes landed upon a prominent, ominous figure, a mysterious man reminding her of Prince Damien, strutting along the wall and surveying the newcomers. The winds swept his shoulder-length raven black hair while sunlight glistened against his ebony skin and black armor; a gold-trimmed cape followed the man's movements as he made his way between the ballistas. When his glowing crimson eyes pierced the darkness from under his hood and landed on Silver, the man raised a hand in the air.

The guards shuffled around, and the metal gates clicked open. Silver landed before the sentries and resumed his usual appearance after Rahim dismounted. All the armed soldiers within the fort lowered their weapons and bowed. As satisfied as Silver was with the new treatment, his demeanor switched when he heard someone calling him. "It's about time, Genesis."

After the guards backed away from the loaded bolt-guns, Selena and her undead dragon army landed behind Silver just in time for Vulduin to emerge from the blitz to see them inside. His long, crimson coat made him recognizable from a distance, contrasting the deep blue hue of his eyes. Two long, thin strands of braided hair draped over his pointed ears past his jaw, leaving the rest combed back, rustling in the breeze like raven feathers. Much to the trio's relief, Vulduin was a much better sight since his escape from Mortemholdt—clean-shaven and devoid of any imperfection that would disgrace his former regality.

Rahim made his way over while avoiding the uncomfortable stares from the guardsmen. He, Silver, and Vulduin watched as Selena controlled her Aether to transform back, and her father almost fell from shock as he no longer recognized her. At first, she almost forgot that the others hadn't seen her since she fixed the Well's mistakes, and the guards surrounded her and the Nidhoggr with weapons at the ready.

Noctis growled and fidgeted in his spot. His tail swayed from side to side, and she knew he was contemplating fighting back, and the others were growing as eager for a possible skirmish. However, the tiny hatchlings hunkered down between their parents' large talons. Selena peered over her shoulder, making eye contact with Noctis. "Stand down. They will not attack us if we don't provoke them."

Noctis opened his maw to reveal his ivory teeth as long and sharp as a battle-ready sword. "They... t-treat... us... like mindless... b-beasts." His bellowing roar made the soldiers cower and quiver.

Rahim bit his bottom lip and turned to face Silver and the frozen Vulduin. "You two can help us right about now."

Still recovering, Vulduin staggered as he stepped forward and parted the sea of soldiers to look at Selena's new form, his voice shaking and echoing like thunder. "Lower your weapons—Lord Godfrey ordered you to stand down." Hesitating at first, the guards pulled back, but a few maintained their hands near their belted pistols in case. Noctis and his flight refused to move or relax, keeping their eyes fixed on the nervous soldiers if they grew trigger-happy.

Vulduin rushed forward, and after his eyes danced from her new hair color to her facial features and the pointed tips of her ears, he wrapped his arms around his daughter, but Selena did not return the gesture. "It's you. W-what happened to you?"

Selena's voice remained stoic during her brief regaling. "It's a long story, but I reversed the Well's mistakes after learning how to control my powers."

Vulduin pulled away and ran his fingers over the edges of her new ears. "I can't believe it. Your mother and I loved you, even when you were human. I...." his voice trailed off as he spun around to look at Silver with his jaw dropped to the ground, convinced that he was involved with her transformation. Silver only shrugged and declined before pointing back at her, reaffirming Selena's new power. "Y-your mother will be thrilled to see you the way you're supposed to be, but," Vulduin looked down at her Aether hand after the two stepped away, "what happened to the device Silver made for you?" He looked at the Nidhoggr, and his face turned pale when he realized that Thor wasn't with them. "Where is your dragon?"

Silver lifted his hand and shook his head, but Selena said, "It's okay. Thor has been missing for a few days," and she continued to explain how it happened, including the tale of how she attained her new hand and appearance. Both Silver and Rahim exchanged grim expressions for Thor's loss during her story.

All Vulduin could say after Selena finished was, "I'm so sorry. We promise to get him back. There has to be a way, like how you managed to change your form and create your new hand." He looked to the Nidhoggr that were patiently waiting on Selena's following command. Much to her surprise, Vulduin didn't detest seeing the same creatures that destroyed Alfheim. She wondered if he suspected a possible future alliance or considered it after discovering they shared the same essence as Thor. He confirmed her suspicions. "I see you brought an army of your own, though I'm not surprised at their taking a liking to you. How did you train them?"

Noctis snapped his fangs at the insult, throwing his tail across the dirt, but Selena held up her hand to his snarling snout and spoke softly to him. "They're not dogs or slaves. They're as intelligent as any dragon I've met. The Lich abandoned Noctis and his flight, and they agreed to help us fight as long as we treat them with respect. Like dragons, they serve no god or king." She turned to face Noctis' smoldering eyes glowing from the mask, chattering. "We are not their masters but allies."

A deep rumble escaped Noctis' throat as Vulduin stepped forward to touch his muzzle, keeping his eyes locked on the alpha as he rubbed his hands across the undead dragon's hide. The feral leader's growls turned into chittering purrs as he accepted Vulduin's apologetic touch. "With Lord Godfrey's permission, your new allies may stay here."

The group was interrupted when Lord Vincent Godfrey approached them. The guards immediately dropped to their knees as the Lord of Vampires made heavy strides to meet her and her friends for the first time. Prince Damien himself was not too far away, standing on the marble steps to the inner keep with his hands clasped around his back. A line of armed soldiers with spears stood behind, slamming the butts of their weapons as Damien's eyes scoured the scene.

A posse of his soldiers followed Lord Godfrey in two unified rows, and Vulduin, Silver, and Rahim stepped back as the Shadow Templars marched, their firm footsteps striking the ground in unison upon approaching Selena and the Nidhoggr. They stopped, and everyone lingered in uncomfortable silence.

Before Selena could bend the knee, Lord Godfrey and his militia bowed before her and her new friends. "It is an honor to welcome the Queen of Dragons herself, though I must admit you know how to arrive with flair. I almost didn't recognize you; my sincere apologies for the hostilities. As your father said, we welcome your new allies here as long as they do not attack my men. I shall inform my butchers to open the feeding grounds to them at once." He looked up and examined the masked dragons. "Where is the Divinity Dragon deemed Thor?"

"The Dark Master took him." Selena's throat turned dry as she saw Prince Damien shift uncomfortably from the corner of her eye, and the courtyard filled with gasps of disbelief and despair.

Godfrey's face drained of all color. "This is very grave news, indeed."

"That's why I must save him before he's lost to me forever."

"The Shadow Templars will stand beside you, as we have done for your family for generations. I have raised an army in your name, Your Majesty."

Noctis roared and spread out his wings, not out of intimidation but in acknowledgment of Selena's right to the title. She turned to him, the rest of the ferals, and then her friends. Damien called her that before at Mortemholdt, as did the captain of the *Blood Diamond*. Queen of Dragons? She never wanted any title, let alone her parents' throne. Selena made that clear, but her allies had already named and accepted her as queen. Rahim gave her a thumbs up; Silver smiled, and both he and Vulduin bowed in respect. Her people believed in her, and although hesitant if she was fit to rule Armageddon and take the throne, she needed and wanted to do what was suitable for the Empire and save her people.

Selena turned to Lord Godfrey and his gathered army within the hold. "Then, as your queen, we will take back Armageddon from the Dark Master and his forces. We will fight together."

"May your Divine fire forever reign." Godfrey smiled a toothy grin while his soldiers screamed and waved their weapons, affirming their pride in their new queen. The guards who stood behind Damien repeatedly slammed their spear butts onto the ground in perfect sync. Noctis led his flight in unified thunders that shook the earth and terrified the heavens, unleashing a row of black Aether fire over the courtyard.

CHAPTER 19: IF YOU SHOULD DIE

Selena walked with Lord Godfrey and Vulduin through the keep of Dark Blood Hold, flanked by a large contingent of bodyguards and soldiers. Silver and Rahim remained close behind, chatting about what she could only assume. Blacksmith work stations lined around the fortress; her ears rang from the clang of the artists' hammers. Her stomach rumbled when the perfume of roasted beef and potatoes graced her nostrils.

Noctis and the rest of the ferals were led towards the open fields outside the gates by Lord Godfrey's appointed soldiers. Several butchers and chiefs zipped by Selena's group, some carrying steaming cauldrons of food, to meet with the dragonkin flight and offer cattle to gorge on to their hearts' content. The whelps swooped downward and circled the cooks as they chirped in delight.

Lord Godfrey guided Selena and their group around the militia lines and artisans preparing for their counter-attack against the Lich. Meanwhile, Rahim's head kept whipping around to see how many vampires there were within the keep, and Selena could hear him mutter under his breath, "I knew the Shadow Templars were real.

I knew it." He reached out and grabbed her shoulder. "Why didn't you tell me about them before?"

"About vampires existing? You found out when Kain rescued you. Remember?"

"Yes, but I mean when you first discovered you were the Crown Princess."

Selena shrugged her shoulders. "It was on a need-to-know basis, and you didn't need to know at the time."

"Still, you could have mentioned it whenever I brought up the Templars. Maria and Niamh thought I was mental."

Selena couldn't control her laughter, but Rahim was not amused, offended by her lack of support. "I'm sorry, and you're right. I should have told you—I promise not to keep secrets from you anymore."

Yet, Rahim still wasn't happy. "Is there anything else that I should know? Like if Maria was a vampire the entire time and that she wants to suck my blood?"

Rahim tightened his lips when he saw that Godfrey's piercing eyes were upon him, making him shake in his boots. "You should be a little more respectful to the Dark Lady Maria. She's betrothed to one of our own, Lord Kain Vanguard."

Shocked and dumbfounded, a huge grin appeared on Selena's face. "That's so exciting." Kain was a captain from their initial meeting, but now Selena assumed he earned a new title since returning to the keep. Either way, she knew that Kain was a highly regarded Templar. "But, Lady Maria told us she was going to Winterguard."

"My escorts brought her to Winterguard safely on behalf of your mother's request, Your Grace. Shortly after, however, Lady Maria and Lord Vanguard grew close, and, after arriving here, the two were soon to be engaged." Godfrey turned his attention to Selena with sparkling yet deadly crimson eyes. "We are aware of your and Silver's engagement, and we offer our congratulations, Your Majesty."

Selena and Silver turned to each other, but the two silently agreed that the war came first. They smiled and bowed before Silver said, "Thank you kindly."

Selena asked, "How many fight for us, my Lord?"

"Around twenty thousand have pledged their blades to you, Your Grace." When he noticed the hopeless look on Selena's face, Lord Godfrey added, "We've been actively working on our battle plan, as numbers do not always win a fight."

"My Lord, how were you able to acquire such an army in only a short while?"

"When we heard what happened in Snowhaven, I immediately called upon all our allies outside Armageddon. We have connections to Runefell and Mirrorhold, and many you see here have answered our call for aid. They've traveled a great distance to serving you and us."

Rahim grabbed his chin. "My Lord, if I may be so bold, I would like to help with the battle plans. I have a few ideas that I think would work."

"I've left that with the Shadow Emperor, General Araneus, and Lord Vanguard. You must ask them."

Rahim spun on his toes to face Vulduin. "May I please help, Your Imperial Majesty?"

Vulduin grunted but nodded. "Yes, you may join us, but do not call me 'Your Imperial Majesty' again. Only my daughter deserves that right."

Selena turned away from the two and crossed her arms over her chest. "No, he doesn't have to."

"Your people already call you their new queen, and you've accepted the title."

"But that doesn't mean everyone has to continue addressing me as such."

"The formalities are to show you the respect you deserve." Vulduin's voice remained calm and reassuring, but she was still angry; they still wouldn't open the invitation for a proper discussion.

Lord Godfrey continued leading the group towards his castle. Damien stepped aside and bowed as his father walked by, then fell to one knee when he and Selena made eye contact. The soldiers behind the Prince of Shadows cleared the way into the keep as the vampire lord drew close, and they followed Damien's example by showing the appropriate greeting fit for royalty.

Selena admired the castle's majestic splendor. Her eyes scanned the raised banners that bore the Shadow Templars' sigil: a pair of folded bat wings forming a diamond shape. Godfrey continued: "A call went out to your new friends: Kiba and Maru of the Aynu pack. It came from your mother, Your Grace."

Selena felt light as a feather, but her voice cracked within her dry throat. "Where are they? A-and my mother, where is she?"

They followed Lord Godfrey down the stone corridors before pointing at a closed room. "Your mother and the Aynu alphas are there, Your Majesty."

Vulduin quickened his steps. "I will stay with my family before joining Lord Vanguard and General Araneus at the command table. Rahim, go on ahead and meet with them so you three may start making plans."

Rahim nodded before Godfrey began addressing him directly. "I believe your mother, Chaliss, is here as well."

Rahim's eyes lit up like the sun. "Where is she?"

"She's currently on the other side of the castle, but I'll send word for her to meet you in the war room. Her Imperial Majesty's right hand, Neith, escorted your mother here from Nuvak by traveling with General Araneus while he transported supplies."

Both Selena and Rahim smiled at each other to learn Chaliss was safe and sound. However, Selena had other matters requiring her attention and wouldn't have the opportunity to join her company. It was only fair for Rahim to reunite with his mother first; she didn't mind.

Selena looked at the thick oak door in despair and disbelief. The color drained from her face, and her heart sank with every heavy step she made to the room. Lord Godfrey asked Rahim to follow, but he gave Selena a quick hug before leaving. "Will you be all right without me?"

"I don't know. Go on ahead."

"I'll try not to let Kain and Maria skin me alive, but I'll help develop a good plan." Rahim kept his voice low so Lord Godfrey wouldn't hear and laughed, but his chuckle faded when she didn't partake in his joke. "Will you come and see mum?"

"Of course, I will. Tell her I said hello and that I miss her."

He grinned and gave her a firm nod. "Let me know if you need anything." The two broke apart, and he bid them farewell.

Silver, sharing in her rueful disposition, reached over and put a comforting hand on Selena's shoulder. "You're not all right, are you?"

"No, I'm not okay." Selena's glistened eyes turned to her father. "I've been angry for so long that it's hard for me to refer to you two as my parents." Vulduin looked as though Selena had struck him across the face. Before her father could object, her face boiling red with rage, she marched forward and swung the door open. However, she immediately ducked, avoiding a thrown teapot smashing and shattering against the wall.

Inside, Kiba and Maru growled and snarled, in wolf forms, at Aryl Aurora, Her Former Imperial Majesty, sitting calmly across the table from the alphas. Her fair complexion was paler than usual, magnified by the deep blue hue of her dress and eyes, and Selena assumed she would soon succumb to her incurable ailment. Yet, her mother still possessed the beauty, grace, and poise of any elf she had seen, with hair as fine as silk and burning like a white flame.

Between her and the alphas was the rest of the broken tea set, smashed under their heated tempers. Selena saw an orange ball of fur curled up in the corner; Loki, the fox, was safe with them. Silver slithered in and took Selena's side, but Vulduin rushed forth to join Aryl. Silver's eyes darted to the cowering fox, but he made no inclination to go after Her Former Imperial Majesty's messenger. Instead, he remained put and ignored Loki.

Kiba's snarls turned violent as she snapped her fangs and barked. Maru had backed away, but the black wolf kept his focus on his snow-white mate in preparation to protect her. Selena noticed a white bandage wrapping his right paw, and when Maru saw her staring, he gave her a light gruff and leaned in to sniff her. After recognizing her scent and the wolf necklace, Maru gave her a jerky nod and swished his bushy black tail. Usually, Kiba did all the talking, so she didn't expect an explanation or salutations from Maru.

Selena regained her composure. "What is going on?"

Kiba whipped around to the sound of her voice and immediately growled from seeing her new elven form. Yet, like Maru, she wagged her tail after exchanging scents and spotting her donned totem, and her loud voice boomed within her subconscious in eager excitement: *What happened to you? You look just like them now.*

Her mother squinted at them, studying their civil discussion. However, Aryl's eyes widened when noting Selena's totem necklace. Selena grasped her obsidian wolf charm, ignoring her father's worried expression over hers and the Aynu's exchange. *It's a long story.*

You better explain it to us, but now is not the time. You finally arrived, and we've been waiting for you. We thought you were the one who sent us aid.

I will be more than happy to tell you the tale, but what do you mean?

Kiba's lips curled back as she bared her large, sharp fangs. *Someone sent that general of yours to rescue us after those undead things attacked and took our home.*

I'm so sorry for your loss. I wish I knew, and I would have helped you myself, but who—? Selena was wholly interrupted when Kiba snarled as she and Maru shapeshifted back to their childish figures wearing masks. When they faced the former Empress, Selena had to muster the strength and return her mother's gaze; Aryl's expression matched Vulduin's upon seeing her new transformation but withheld all opinions.

Loki unfolded himself and, upon remarking his new queen's prompt entrance, rushed over to hide behind Selena's legs. "Your Majesty, it's so good to see you again." Still trembling, Loki looked up from Selena's feet and gave her a toothy grin, but the fur along his back bristled in fear until he sniffed her feet. "Would you look at that? Now, you're a lovely image of—"

Kiba's growls disrupted Loki and grew and billowed with extreme vehemence—Selena feared she couldn't hold her back from unchecked rage—and she pointed at Aryl, who still couldn't shift her eye from her daughter. "Did you think that sending us aid would make us forgive your crimes?"

"What are you talking about?" Selena faced Silver and the others when she realized she was the only one asking questions. That was when she understood—

The She-Wolf hissed through her teeth, her eyes locked upon the former Empress like a wolf ready to take down its prey. "She was the one who betrayed us. She joined the elves who drove us out of our city."

Aryl hung her head in shame at the accusation. Silver and Vulduin exchanged glances, but Selena suspected that Silver knew her mother's secret, judging from his expression. Her stomach churned that Her Former Imperial Majesty was part of why the Aynu were cast into exile. "I won't deny it," Aryl began, "and I knew that it would come back to haunt me one day."

Selena's fists trembled at her side, her anger growing like a storm as she shared Kiba's and Maru's justified fury. "Mother, how could you have done that to them?"

"The Betrayer is your mother?" Snarling, when looking her up and down, Kiba snorted. "Now, you look just like them."

"I shouldn't be condemned by what she did to your people." Ignoring their side glances as the alphas contemplated the irony of the Betrayer's daughter joining their pack, Selena came forward and placed both open palms against the table. Aryl's eyes drew to the pulsating Aether hand, but she held her tongue. Selena's voice cracked like a porcelain vase when she asked, "Why did you do it?"

Aryl's voice was as calm and as smooth as glass, but one mishandling could make it shatter at any moment. "After we rebelled against the dwarves, we sought refuge in what is now known as Alfheim until other elf outsiders came and drove us from the city. My father led the Aynu at the time, and during our short, peaceful union with the interlopers, Artio blessed us with our wolf powers."

Selena asked, "Aydin was from your clan, wasn't he? That's why you two were so close."

"Yes." Aryl's throat swelled to learn of Selena's knowledge behind the man who became the Dark Master. Kiba and Maru growled.

Vulduin put a hand on Aryl's shoulder and explained: "Before the schism, the outsiders arranged the marriage between your mother and me to unify our race. However, her family and many others left the Aynu to remain in the city—we were barely your age when this happened.

"After establishing the hierarchy and forming the Empire, my father and your grandfather, Enyalius Xyrrion, began the Xyrrion Dynasty and became Armageddon's first Emperor when Aryl and I married—thus solidifying our family's rule. Your mother insisted upon carrying her mother's maiden name, Aurora. It was considered untraditional as women were supposed to take their husbands' names, but I never cared."

Aryl nodded. "Emperor Enyalius Xyrrion ruled for many years. Then, your father and I took the throne shortly before the One Hundred Years' War when he passed away. The rest, I'm sure you know." She looked up at Kiba and Maru with shimmering eyes.

Selena bit her cheek so hard that she thought she tasted blood. Too angry and upset, she almost didn't care to know more about her family, for the Empire was built on war and betrayal.

The She-Wolf kept her eyes locked upon Aryl, ready to attack at any given notice. "We've always believed in Artio. Both of you were there when we prayed for her strength and protection before the schism. For our loyalty, she blessed us with masks and wolf powers." Kiba pointed at both Aryl and Vulduin. "You two turned against us after the blessing."

"My husband and I lost our masks when we renounced our oaths to Artio, but we were still wolves." Her sparkling sapphire eyes forced their way to meet Selena's smoldering emeralds.

"And Aydin—?"

"Him, too." Amidst their brief silence, Silver placed a gentle hand on Selena's shoulder to subdue the rampaging dragon within, but she refused to tame it.

Kiba and Maru snarled. "The worthless wolves without the mask should have kept their oath."

"We had to choose."

"You chose wrong." Before anyone could prepare, in one swift movement, Kiba lunged straight for Her Former Imperial Majesty until Silver intervened; he stepped in the way, but the white wolf tackled him down, attacking like a rabid dog foaming at the mouth. At a loss for his mate's uncontrollable bloodlust, Maru assisted Selena in prying her away; Kiba avoided the two, pushed herself off of Silver, and made another attempt for Aryl's throat.

However, Vulduin marched forward and summoned his chains, binding the two alphas in place. "Enough! We will not do this here." The tangled mess of metal squeezed Kiba and Maru like a snake after catching its prey.

In a wasted effort to pull his steadied arms back, Selena pleaded for him to release his magic, but his chilled heart and expression unyielding, her father remained still as a stone. Kiba stiffened her muscles to fight the constricting magic, and Maru squirmed, but Vulduin only considered Selena's request after the two alphas agreed to stand down. Kiba and Maru dropped to the floor when his chains withdrew, sodden and gasping for air, but they remained true to their word once they fully recovered.

Silver readjusted the fittings of his jacket before clearing his throat, mumbling under his breath but recoiled when Maru growled at him. After ensuring their injuries were only minor, Selena quizzically stared at the two at the vexing conundrum when asking, "I thought you said before you didn't remember who betrayed you."

"I forgot her name, but I will never forget a scent." The She-Wolf only shrugged when Selena wasn't satisfied with her explanation. "What? I'm terrible with names. Sometimes I have trouble remembering yours."

"I didn't know my parents are wolves," Selena said, "but that's another secret you two have kept from me."

"Our past wasn't important." Vulduin eyed the alphas like a hawk, ready to intervene if they broke their verbal agreement. "I was the Red Wolf, and your mother, Silver Fang. I've only recently used my powers to remain hidden from the Council."

"The same goes for me," Aryl continued, "the last time I took my form was when Loki and I fled Rune Citadel right before the attack." Her face soon grew wet from the uncontrolled flowing tears. "I'm not sure what I can do to make things right, but I promise to find a way."

Kiba snorted. "We want our land back."

"That's not up to me."

"To Oblivion, it isn't."

Selena had enough and slammed her fist against the table to silence both sides. The room immediately turned eerily silent, and all eyes were upon her. "If I'm the new queen, I will be the one making that decision." She turned her heated gaze over to her mother. "But first, you and father owe me more than words describe."

"We were only trying to do what we thought was right and protect you." Aryl's words sounded like metal scraping against stone.

Selena hissed through her teeth but whipped her head away. "I wasn't mad at you or my father for that."

Vulduin let her words sink in. "But you are mad at us."

Unsure if it was because of the subdued anger from losing Thor or a combination of, Vulduin and Aryl became her victims to endure her fury. Selena's eyes began to flood, and once she opened her mouth, her words poured out like the Raging River. "Of course, I'm mad at you; I'm more than furious. It's difficult to call you my mother and father. After rescuing you from Mortemholdt," she pointed to Vulduin, "you weren't concerned about my welfare. Yes, you asked me about what happened in Snowhaven, but to immediately disregard me in favor of the Empire—"

"My dear," Vulduin whispered, but Selena wholly scorned his endearments.

"Your reassurance of love for Thor and I meant nothing; we felt alone and unwanted." She could have struck Vulduin and Aryl down, and it would have been the same; her wrath continued flowing with little regard for her words' consequence. "I understand the suffering and torment you two endured, but since reuniting briefly in Alfheim upon reporting for duty, right damn there, the two of you pretended I didn't exist until Azrael stepped out of line. Silver was the only one with the decency to help me understand," Selena directly addressed her father, "and he had to ask for your assistance to help me with my sword and see me for my birthday; otherwise, I'm certain you wouldn't have come. Before my hearing, you," Selena then accused her mother, "just stood there. Even when Vidar and the Council threatened to hang me, you said nothing." Kiba and Maru flinched from her rage and took a step back, while Silver hung his head, but he held his tongue.

"Selena…." Aryl's dry voice died out.

Discounting her mother's plea, she waved her Aether prosthetic and continued. "I noticed how you flinched when I came into the room, Mother. Did my father tell you the story?"

"Of course—"

"Then you know exactly how it ended." Selena's cold and bitter tone chilled the tense atmosphere. "My friends and I were captured and tortured for about a month in Snowhaven—a bloody month!" Hot tears poured down her face, and her body began to tremble. "All I wanted was to know my parents, but you two remained absent when I needed you most. Chaliss acted more like a mother to me.

"Yes, I may have finally fixed the Well's mistakes and restored my appearance and form, but I still don't remember anything from my childhood, and I doubt that I will. I understand that all I can do is make the most of it by moving forward and creating new memories." Selena lowered her head, focusing every ounce of energy on keeping herself propped up over the table. "Do you know what the worst part is? It's that my parents are expecting me to take over the mistakes that they've made. You two already decided I would take the throne without consulting me first, not wanting to hear what I thought or wanted." Overlooking her sobbing parents, she swiveled to face the wolf leaders. "After the war is over, the Aynu will return to Alfheim, and we will all live together in peace. As the new queen, you have my word that I will fix my parents' faults." Both Kiba's and Maru's eyes sparkled from her declaration.

Vulduin's hand tightened around Aryl's shoulder as her eyes glossed over like a frozen pond; yet, they kept their opinions to themselves during Selena's firestorm. "I've had a few fleeting memories from childhood, but they're never about you, my parents. I can only think of my new family with Chaliss and my adopted brother, Rahim, Thor, and Silver. I can only remember them, but not you; I feel like I mean nothing to you two." She stormed out, leaving her parents to weep.

Selena wasn't sure where she was going, but she knew it was best to be as far away as possible, and her steps quickened when she heard Silver calling after her. After wandering around the castle, she found the top of the eastern tower, the wind cutting across her face like daggers and the moonlight shimmering through her gradient hair —the turquoise blue and snow-white melting colors gleaming like her dragon scales. The sound of the crashing waves was soothing against her ears; the sea's mist sprayed against her skin.

I wish I knew where you were, Thor. I need you here now more than ever. As always, shadow and darkness cloaked his mind. Tears streamed down her face whenever she tried to contact him, but Thor was gone.

Training dummies and archery shooting posts waited for her along the rooftop. Still drowning out Silver's call, Selena pulled out Dragonheart belted over her back and swung her blade at the first heavily stuffed target. She arched her Aether hand, summoning her magical sword, and began throwing her flurry of blinding blows. Silver caught up to her but halted, hesitant to interrupt, and watched her deadly dance of attacks.

"Don't worry. Those dummies are enchanted to withstand blows of any caliber for training. It's a pain to keep remaking them." He stepped to the side and saw Lord Kain Vanguard dwelling in the shadows; a single white stripe streaked across his black hair, glowing in the moonlight with his eerie crimson eyes. Silver was somewhat alarmed to see him more adequately dressed, as Kain never followed the Templars' traditional garb. Yet, the new lord sported a formal black jacket clasped by gilded buttons and buckles—its collar brushing the underside of his lean and chiseled jaw—and his best breeches and black hessian boots to complete the attire. The vampire lord leaned against the stone wall, arms crossed over his chest, and observed Selena's newfound power with a satisfied sneer. "I knew the princess had a lot of fight in her. That look suits her."

"She's your queen now."

Kain grinned, flashing his pearly-white vampire fangs. "Damn, it's been a while, Silver. I missed having you around."

Silver gave a hearty laugh. "I heard the good news, and I offer my congratulations. How are you and Lady Maria?"

"As good as you can expect while preparing for a war." Kain chuckled. "We will probably hold off on our celebrations afterwards when things go back to normal."

"You should know that there is no such thing as normal," Silver smirked and fixed his glasses, "What are you doing up here?"

Kain nodded to Selena. "Half the damn castle heard the commotion. I left the war room to meet you all here, but D told me what happened."

Silver squinted at him. "Even with using the shadows to move around, you're quick."

"Be that as it may, I've never been allowed to give D a piece of my mind. I was always afraid the bastard would tear me limb from limb if I ever did," Kain cringed, "I must admit, I've come to respect her tenacity."

"Vulduin would never do that to his daughter, and he knew she was angry." Silver couldn't help but look upon Selena in admiration. "I don't think she realizes it yet, but she has begun to embrace her new role as the queen that her people want her to be."

"Our new queen, huh? I think Lord Godfrey was too excited when the announcement was made." The two looked up just in time to see a shooting star fire across the heavens. "Did you ever think we would wind up here?"

Silver shook his head. "After being alive for so long, nothing surprises me anymore."

"Huh." Kain closed his eyes. Silver was right; life was full of surprises, and all Kain could think about was when he first turned. Only nineteen years old, Kain grew up as an orphaned child who turned to a life of crime in a small village in the Fire Kingdom province. It was the only way for him to survive with no home. Kain's thoughts drifted to when he met Prince Damien for the very first time. It never bothered him that Damien was a vampire; instead, he was fascinated. Damien had invited Kain to join the Shadow Templars on several occasions with a simple bite upon the neck, but Kain refused to join the undead.

However, Kain's luck of thievery ran out, and one of his heists turned sour. Kain pushed an older man out the way while attempting his escape from pursuing authorities, but the innocent's frail body could not withstand the fall. Kain had accidentally killed the bystander who caught him; he flinched when he recalled the sickening crack of the person's skull as it struck the sharp rocks on the ground.

Kain grimaced from getting caught as he was convicted of murder: sentenced to hang by the neck until dead. Prince Damien came to his rescue that day, saving Kain just before the floorboards dropped and freed him of the noose. Using the shadows, the vampire prince killed all the guards and civilians, screaming for Kain to die, and offered to extend the gift of vampirism once again; this time, he accepted.

That was about two hundred years ago; Kain rubbed the bruises around his neck that would never fade, the marks a constant reminder of when he first joined the Shadow Templars. After all those years, he served Lord Godfrey and was eventually appointed captain. Now, with his pending engagement to Maria, Kain earned lord status. There was no higher honor. Even after all this time, Damien's words that day still rattled Kain. "If you should die."

Selena stopped attacking the training dummy and closed her eyes, ignoring Kain, but she spun around as Silver finally approached her. "If you're coming here to tell me that I need to go back and apologize, you wasted—"

Silver shook his head before wrapping his arms around her, and she sobbed into his jacket. Selena buried her crimson face deeper into his shoulder. "I just want my parents to care about me." Then the source of her true misery exposed itself, "I want Thor back." Silver didn't interrupt and continued cradling her to his chest, listening to her mournful cries.

CHAPTER 20: HOW TO BECOME A SHAPESHIFTER

The azure waters were surprisingly calm. Returning inside with Silver and Kain guiding her, Selena heard the shrill cries of the sea lions from below their cliff. Though she felt better, her eyes were still red and swollen, overwhelmed by fighting for her companion, and she was utterly lost without Thor by her side. Yet, she had accepted her role and was prepared to face the Lich no matter what happened.

Silver continued inquiring about her comfort, but she reassured him she was better. *But I still need you, Thor.*

Kain ran ahead to greet a companion hidden in the shadows at the end of the ornate hallway, and Selena's face lit up when she saw it was Maria. Nearly ghost-like in her evening gown decorated in red lace, the moonlight kissed her cold, pale skin and long black silk hair, her lips as red as a rose; she was a true beauty of the night. Before exchanging the proper pleasantries, the two ran over and hugged. Maria spoke first. "Kain told me you and your friends were here. Thank the Divines." When they broke apart, Selena saw the vampirism in Maria's eyes as they bled crimson. "Don't let my appearance frighten you."

"Not at all."

Upon further inquiry about Maria's recently changed nature, she happily obliged by detailing the painful transformation before arriving at Dark Blood Hold. "It wasn't easy, and I couldn't quench my insatiable appetite for the first week. With Lord Godfrey's help and assistance, I learned to control my new behaviors." As the four walked down the hall together, Maria continued, "Your recent development has been one of the conversation highlights since you and your friends arrived. Even upon seeing your dragon form is now considered a blessing from the Divines." She paused and pulled out a sealed letter from her evening gown's pocket. "A falcon arrived earlier with a letter addressed to you and Thor, Your Majesty." Maria paused, but Selena held up her hand and shook her head. "I'm sorry, I didn't mean to sound insensitive."

"There is no need, and you weren't. Who was the letter from?"

Lady Maria handed it over for Selena to see, and Silver recognized the handwriting; it was from Ebony. Selena ripped it open and held the letter up for her and Silver to read.

I pray that this finds you just as you arrive at the keep. I heard about the dreadful news, and my heart breaks for you. I was hoping to meet both you and my beloved at Dark Blood Hold, but it seemed as if the Divines had other plans. I've been in pursuit of tracking down Thor, and I learned of his capture and forced return to Alfheim. I will continue lurking in the shadows and help in any way. I pray for Thor's safe return and your success, our Queen of Dragons.

As much as she was glad to receive news of Thor, Selena felt her stomach lurch at the reminder of his inevitable fate. Immediately, her mind reached out to his, but Thor's remained unyielding; her tendrils of thought poked around the darkness, and she did the best she could to keep from wallowing in despair. She and Silver exchanged dreadful glances, and Selena swallowed her grief. "I know that your sister is trying to help, but we could use her assistance down here in preparing for the war."

"This isn't even her war to fight." She sensed his ambivalence towards the idea, but Silver added dubiously, "Besides, I've never been able to count on her for anything. I'm surprised she's willing to do this much."

"This is everyone's war when our very existence is threatened by it." Selena turned to Maria and bowed. "Thank you for delivering this."

"Of course. We'll show you to your quarters, Your Grace."

Still growing accustomed to the new formalities, she and Silver followed Kain and Maria around the corner and up the grand staircase where the grandfather clock graced the wall, touching the ceiling. It reminded Selena of the Pyre, and for some reason, she missed the grim clock and its deathly hourly chimes. She made sure not to drag her feet across the blood-red rugs and admired that the carpets remained untainted.

The Lord and Lady brought her and Silver to a magnificent apartment fit to house royalty, where Selena was greeted by the moonlight shimmering through the stained glass windows. Intricate designs lined in gold weaved across the baseboards and embroidered cushions and pillows, contrasting with the room's deep crimson hue. Lord Godfrey's servants displayed bread, different cheeses, and mouth-watering fresh fruits upon a golden platter on an oak table, ready to be served with a bottle of red wine. Lady Maria gestured to their quarters. "Please let us know if you need anything, Your Majesty."

"You don't need to keep addressing me as such."

"You are our queen. Since Emperor Enyalius Xyrrion, the Shadow Templars have served the imperial family."

Kain snickered, but he nodded. "You're not exactly the frail princess I first met. You have a lot of guts, and I pray that the Lich doesn't rip 'em out of ya, Your Grace."

Selena grinned, recalling her first meeting with Kain and silently agreeing that she was no longer the timid young woman she used to be. "Next time I face the necromancer, I will bring him down and save Thor."

After sharing a few smiles at the thought of victory, Kain and Maria took their leave. Silver made himself at home by snatching the wine bottle and filling the glasses next to the food platter. "Let us toast to joining forces with the Nidhoggr and the Shadow Templars. Tomorrow, we'll reconvene with everyone." He poured Selena a cup and offered it to her.

"Thank you. Here's to all of us, and for the Empire." Their glasses clanked, and they drank.

Silver sat down after quenching his throat, and after he and Selena shared a light conversation, the two indulged in the Templars' history. Vampires were initially from Mirrorhold, and when Lord Godfrey and his brethren arrived in Armageddon, Selena's grandfather sought to eradicate their race. The Lord and the Emperor dueled, and His Imperial Majesty bested Godfrey, who came to respect Emperor Enyalius Xyrrion, as he was the first to win against him. Godfrey swore loyalty to His Imperial Majesty and his future descendants, and in exchange, the vampires would be granted a haven within the Empire. "Your grandfather agreed and thus dubbed them the Shadow Templars," said Silver, "the two made this pact about seven hundred years ago."

Vampires fled Mirrorhold to avoid persecution and prevent a war from breaking out. The citizens there feared their race and pursued their destruction. A massive mob killed the first vampire, Lord Druk, and his wife; thus, his successor, Vincent Godfrey, took control and vowed to save his people, avoiding further misfortune befalling the others.

"The public remained safe during Lord Druk's two hundred year sovereignty, but once they discovered their true nature...." Silver couldn't bring himself to finish, and he sighed. "As you can see, fear brings out the worst in others." Selena immediately thought of Rahim's previous prejudice and became overrun with guilt by association. "By pledging their services to Emperor Enyalius Xyrrion, Lord Godfrey created a refuge here where vampires can now live freely without fear. Those within the Shadow Templars are directly descended from Lord Druk and are of the purest bloodlines: the most powerful and prestigious; every vampire here is royal in their own right."

"How do you become one of pure-blood?"

"You have to be bitten by one who is. Other vampires outside the Templars have watered down bloodline connections: one Templar possesses the strength of a hundred vampires."

As their conversation wore on, Selena couldn't help but hang her head in shame for unleashing her blazing temper upon her parents. Their mistakes have cost her dearly, and the only way they could atone for their sins would be to share parental affection; even asking for that felt like pulling teeth. Still, she understood an apology was in order. Silver didn't argue when she expressed her melancholy manner but took another gulp from his wine glass. "It would be best. Maybe tomorrow you will have your chance."

Selena pulled out the letter and scanned the message again. "If I sent a falcon back, would your sister join us?"

"Not likely. Angel only did things for her benefit." Selena couldn't ignore the deep scorn from his tone; Silver poured himself another glass.

"I don't think the end of the world sounds like fun. Protecting it would be to everyone's benefit." There was a furrow on her brow as she looked at him inquisitively. "Wouldn't you agree?"

Silver only shrugged, but when Selena was displeased by his lack of answer, he tightened his lips and bit his cheeks. "You could try, but I wouldn't count on her. Ever since we were little, I remember she was never around. Bits and pieces come back to me now and then."

Selena held her chin. "Wouldn't you wish to see your past with your enchanted timepiece?"

Silver immediately declined the idea; given his prompt refusal, Selena wondered if he considered doing so before reaching his absolute resolution. "I don't care for it." Silver paused, and his eyes wandered towards the ceiling as he fell deep into thought. "I recall caring for our sick little brother, and Angel never helped. Our parents abandoned us, and I was the older sibling who handled everyone and everything. I remember being a carpenter, as I had to be the provider." He turned around and looked out the window towards their private balcony, and the uncomfortable silence stirred the tense atmosphere. "Do you want to know how to become a shapeshifter?"

It was hard for Selena to swallow. Figuring it was a great secret, she still asked. "Please, tell me. How?"

"By making a deal with a demigod and signing a blood contract with one." His answer came freely; she was surprised that she didn't have to pry for more information. "When my brother got sick, I remember meeting a demigod who promised me that I could find the cure, but for a price. He never told me what that meant, but I was young and took the offer without thinking about the consequences. Yes, he gave me the powers, but it took me many years to control them." Silver paused for a moment. "When you become immortal, you no longer possess the concept of time.

"I realized that, even though I made this deal to become a shapeshifter, I still had to research the cure myself. So, I went straight to work. I didn't realize how long I was stuck reading book after book on different known diseases, working relentlessly to find a treatment that would work on what ailed my brother. By the time I found out what he had and the remedy, I realized that so many years had passed, and my brother had died of the illness long ago. It was pneumonia—now treatable thanks to my research—but I was so consumed with finding the answer that I didn't realize so much time had passed. That was my price."

"Silver, I am so sorry." Selena shed tears for his little brother, but he shook his head. She finally understood why he dedicated his time to alchemy, to prevent others from suffering as his brother did.

"It happened so long ago, my dear. I've never been able to track down that demigod that cursed me; they could be anyone or anything, and I gave up finding that spiteful creature long ago. Like how you told your parents about your fleeting memories coming and going, mine do the same. Meeting my sister again brought back so many repressed recollections, and I had hoped never to see her again, but the Divines have a sense of humor. I suppose I will never be rid of her." Silver laughed when he took another drink.

Selena fingered her glass. "Have you offered this deal to anyone before?"

"No. I had yet to meet anyone worthwhile and responsible enough to use those powers." He immediately paused when meeting Selena's questioning gaze, and his face burned. "Err, I mean—"

"Please, it's all right. Your answers are merely satisfying my curiosity and nothing more."

"My dear, if you weren't already a Divinity Dragon, I would have offered the gift to you long ago once you were more magically adept as an apprentice. However, you're already more powerful than I am, and we share immortality." He laughed in between sips. "There's nothing else I can offer you."

She grinned at his reasoning but was still not wholly convinced that Silver had found his resolve regarding his past. "Perhaps it'll be time for you and your sister to make amends and move forward. I'm sure she feels guilty for not being there for you and your brother."

"I highly doubt that."

"I don't think so. Maybe that was why Ebony came back after all these years. Why else would she return after so long?"

Silver hung his head and clapped his hands together. "I dunno. She never did say, and quite frankly, I didn't care."

"I'm sure you do." Selena set her cup down. "I will send a falcon to her tomorrow."

"As you wish, my dear." Silver looked up at her, and the room grew tired of their conversation. "Did you mean what you said back there, or were you speaking out of anger?"

Selena couldn't tear her thoughts away from Silver's brother's fate, but she allowed the discussion to change. "Both." When he pressed for a better response, she ruefully continued. "I've been so angry at them. You saw how my father treated me after we rescued him from

Mortemholdt. He was more concerned with what needed to be done than seeking reconciliation from his daughter." Selena returned Silver's glistening gaze. "Was I wrong? Would you have been angry with them too?"

"No, you're not wrong. I was furious for you and at your father for keeping so many secrets." He bit his bottom lip, considering trudging through what he believed to be dangerous waters. "But what I meant was, did you mean what you said about your memories?"

Selena finally understood what he intended and nodded. "Every time I've tried to remember anything about my past, I can only think of my new family—and you. You were the one who was always there, and I realized that when I finally learned how to control my powers. That's why—" After springing from his seat, Silver pulled her close and kissed her deeply. Before she could say another word, he picked her up and brought her to the bed, and the two became passionately engaged.

Just as dawn's diamond rays peered over the horizon, Selena awoke to the pleasant surprise of Silver passed out beside her; it was the first time she caught him in a deep stupor. Being a demigod meant he didn't have to, but sleep was one of life's pleasures.

Yet her smile disappeared as she and Silver rose and dressed. The eclipse wasn't too far ahead; only a matter of days. She could feel the lingering dread and gloom spread across the land as the winter solstice drew close. It made the hair on the back of her neck stand on end, her skin crawling with goosebumps as she donned her navy blue dragonscale dress and clasped her golden buckles around her waist. She slipped her fingers into her pocket, ensuring that Revelation was still safe; her hand grazed over the cool touch of metal from the timepiece, helping ease her nerves.

Selena belted Dragonheart, but she left her shield behind. With her dress to protect against most melee and magic damage and the ability to use Aether for dual-wielding and guarding herself, she no longer needed it. Instead, she was now the ultimate weapon thriving on the offensive.

Before the two left the room, Selena forged the message she planned to send back to Ebony, pleading for assistance. Though unsure if she would comply, Selena wouldn't know without trying. She and Silver navigated through the castle and made their way to the mailroom, where messenger falcons were lined up and ready to take off from their perches. Selena found one and tied her parcel to its claws, and the bird immediately launched itself out the window in the course of its destination.

Silver smiled at her, and the two left to meet in the war room. Kain and Maria joined the pair halfway, and they entered the massive chambers at the top of the keep. Welcoming them were Lord Godfrey, his son Damien, Vulduin, Aryl, Loki, General Araneus Morleth, Colonel Theron Cyres, the Aynu alphas, Rahim, the Oracle triplets, and—

"*Matu.*" Selena rushed forward. After recovering from the initial shock of seeing her new appearance, she and Chaliss clashed into an embrace. "I'm so glad you're safe." Chaliss beamed in warmth like a mother waiting to reunite with her child as she returned Selena's affection. "Rahim told me everything. I'm so happy to see you here." Her beauty remained unyielding to the ravages of a mother's worry; Chaliss was a lovely human woman with long black silk hair sweeping with every step she made, her face as fair as porcelain, accentuating her hazel eyes. From the corner of Selena's eye, she saw her mother's tear-stained face and her torn and defeated father.

Emerging from between the two former monarchs, General Araneus Morleth stepped forth and, after taking in her sudden burst of beauty, gave her a firm salute and a huge smile that grew from ear to ear. After sharing a fleeting glance with her grief-stricken parents, Selena returned the general's gesture; Colonel Theron Cyres looked like he had aged another fifty years in the last few months. His dark, maroon skin hue looked pale, and silver streaks lined his light sea-green hair. Yet, he still smiled and greeted her without hesitation.

The Oracles and Neith Anahita stood behind them, their arms crossed and folded within the sleeves of their formal robes, and they bowed. The triplets still dressed to differentiate their identities: Nona, whose hair swept past her knees, donned a high-waisted satin blue gown, extravagantly trimmed and decorated with lace and ribbons. Cassandra tied her hair with a red ribbon, matching the color of her embellished dress. Lastly, Morta, clad in green fashion, adorned her hair with a series of braids meeting in a single, thick ponytail. Together, their hair burned like smoldering white flames.

Neith stood next to her wooden staff leaning against the wall, the pole's top a carved claw holding a deep ruby. Her familiar fox mask hung from the right side of her face, her pointed ears parting fire-kissed hair. From Selena's memory, she still wore her thick crimson hair in a single large braid decorated in golden chains and tiny jewels gleaming against her crystal pendant and obsidian dragon tooth necklace. Yet, Neith's green eyes couldn't match the brilliance of Selena's. "It's wonderful to see you again, Your Grace." Neith smiled brightly.

The triplets' cold, pale faces grew warm like the rising dawn during their exchange; Nona, Cassandra, and Morta said in unison, "May your Divine fire chase away the darkness. It's an honor to grace us with your presence, Queen of Dragons."

Selena hadn't seen them since she first left for Snowhaven; she was partly tempted to ask the triplets if she and her friends had any chance at winning the war, but the Oracles had an odd way of avoiding her questions. Rather than asking about their future, Selena resolved that everyone controlled their fate; relying on the triplets would be folly.

Loki scurried about on the floor and found a higher place to share eye contact, orange bristling tail wagging like a happy dog. Selena's heart fluttered and burned like a tiny ember, and she couldn't help but smile at being surrounded by her friends and allies; she wouldn't have had it any other way.

Everyone in the war room bent their knee to her in unison, including Silver. With the formalities finished, the room echoed the same questions regarding her recent changes and if the rumors were true about Thor; as much as it pained her to repeat the tale, Selena still recounted all the past events leading up to arriving at Dark Blood Hold.

The chamber fell silent at once until Rahim broke the dreary air by summoning the party towards the table with his sketched-out battle plans for all to read. Loki jumped up to the tabletop and sat in the corner to join her side. Kiba and Maru veered at both Aryl and Vulduin with venomous glares but kept their distance, upholding their promise not to lash out like before. Instead, the alphas remained hopeful in their alliance with Selena.

Rahim stood by Selena's side, followed by Kain and Maria; he nodded at the two vampire nobles, but Kain said, "It's your show, kid. You came up with most of these ideas, not me."

He smiled at Kain's recognition and scratched his head, looking somewhat confused, but he cleared his throat and found his needed words. "Everyone knows the eclipse on the winter solstice is coming. That's why we're here, right?" He scanned the room, only to find nobody laughed at his crude attempt at making a pun. His smile faded, and he pressed on. "Right now, we have around twenty thousand soldiers, not including the Nidhoggr. The Lich's army outnumbers us by…." Rahim began counting on his fingers, but he shook his head. "Look, I'm sorry, but I'm not too good with math. It's one billion against a ragtag team of twenty thousand; it doesn't look too promising when I put it that way.

"However, Kain and I came up with an idea: launching an invasion force to take Alfheim back. The Day of Eternal Darkness is only a couple of weeks away, but we should easily overrun what remains of the city. Selena, our Divine Queen," Rahim laughed when she rolled her eyes at the new title he came up with, "the Lich will be your fight, but we will be around if you need help."

"I'll handle Venexus. Don't worry about that."

Surprisingly, Rahim didn't flinch from hearing the necromancer's name this time. Selena wondered if he slowly came to terms with referring to a demon by their actual name, as he and Chaliss always considered it bad luck. "Very good. Next up, since we have our Nidhoggr army now, and to make it to Alfheim in time for the eclipse, they can help us carry our soldiers." General Araneus squirmed when considering working with the same creatures that destroyed Alfheim and the Her Imperial Majesty's Air Force, but he never shared his opinions; instead, he accepted his previous orders from Lord Godfrey and Vulduin without complaint. Colonel Cyres shared his disposition, but he still hung his head in defeat.

Lord Godfrey stood up as Rahim waited, and all eyes were on the vampire lord. "Before your arrival, Your

Majesty, my best metalworkers and blacksmiths labored for weeks building vessels large enough to carry a thousand soldiers each. We originally planned to travel and transport the ships by train, which would have brought us to Alfheim by the Day of Eternal Darkness if we had left today. Your alliance with the Nidhoggr, My Queen, bought us more time and strength to our numbers, and they should have no issues in their invaluable assistance to carry our ships and supplies."

The room all nodded in agreement. With the eclipse so close, Selena knew that the vampires and Nidhoggr grew in strength daily; the ferals would carry the force of ten dragons each, thus easily making the trip to Alfheim with Lord Godfrey's army at Divine's speed.

After Godfrey permitted Rahim to speak, he continued: "We will need at least two middle-weight Nidhoggr to carry one vessel, while the smaller and younger ferals can help us move and transport crates with our provisions and supplies. Although we haven't much time, we need to train the ferals to feel comfortable enough to carry riders. The plan involves our first battalion of goop dragons and their handlers staying close to the Lich's opened portal and keeping the Dreygur corralled by the wall's remains. We can't let them leave Alfheim." Rahim then pointed to his drawn diagram. "Then, our second group of Nidhoggr riders will attack the Dreygur from above as they emerge from the gate; it will be like shooting fish in a barrel. This strategy will help keep our soldiers from getting overwhelmed on the ground.

"We'll have General Araneus and Aracania lead their forces to deal with the Dreygur on the ground. Our separate battalion will handle Ashur's air fleet from above and stop them before unleashing their fiery offense. Lord Godfrey, Prince Damien, and I will lead that unit. That way, we can at least keep them distracted long enough to prevent them from commencing their journey. The eclipse will last for the entire day, so every moment counts. If we succeed, the war will finally be over, and the Lich will be defeated and destroyed."

The room echoed with cheer upon hearing Rahim's proposed plan; Lord Godfrey and Prince Damien were amused and impressed, while General Araneus and Colonel Cyres were impressed, admiring his ideas. Rahim and Selena looked at each other and smiled, and even Silver came over and patted him on the back. Chaliss squeezed her son's arm and gave him a firm nod of approval as she endlessly repeated how proud she was.

Selena remained at the table while the others cleared out with her eyes fixated on Rahim's notes and Armageddon's spread-out map. Her parents sought a meeting with Neith and the Oracles, discussing seeking safe refuge for those who will not fight—Aryl herself, Chaliss, Neith, the Oracles, the hatchlings too young to help, and so on. She ignored their conversation; when he saw the grave look on her face, Rahim came over. "What's the matter?"

"I'm worried about Azrael and the dragon eggs. If we can destroy the portal, will they be all right?"

"I would assume so."

"We can't assume, Rahim."

He bit down on his tongue and raised his head towards the ceiling, searching for an answer. "What else can we do? Besides, you can't kill Death."

Selena closed her eyes and recalled her father's words from Starsong. "You can still kill a god."

"I believe it will take more than that to kill Azrael and the eggs. The Mythic Flight hatchlings are powerful creatures, next to the Divinity Dragons—I don't believe they'll be so easily destroyed. I know we will save them once we defeat the Lich."

"Niamh and your father, too."

Tight-lipped, Rahim nodded. "Niamh and my father."

Before taking their leave, General Araneus and Colonel Cyres approached and bowed, interrupting their conversation. "It is an honor to serve you, Your Majesty."

Selena turned to them and smiled. "General, there is no need to address me so formally. I'm still Liongod."

The general shook his head. "Nonsense. I am yours to command, Queen of Dragons."

"I don't give commands. I will be out on that battlefield like you and everyone else fighting together." She straightened up, and General Araneus rose to his feet. "I pray that Aracania and Onyxria are doing well."

Colonel Cyres went stone-cold as he stood up, his maroon skin tone turning pale. "Onyxria was killed in the line of duty at the Red Rains of Alfheim, Your Majesty."

"My condolences for your loss, Colonel." She couldn't imagine his pain nor understand how Cyres upheld himself so well after losing his partner of more than forty years. The Onyxian Steelbellies were valued heavy-weighted firebreathers, and as far as she knew, Onyxria was his first companion.

Cyres met her with a somber gaze. "It was a bloody shame, and Onyxria was the best partner you could ask for. She saved my life at her sacrifice—I will commemorate our victory in her name."

"It will be a lovely memory, and Onyxria will be with the other fallen soldiers, praising for our success from Niflheim," Selena turned her shimmering gaze to Araneus, "And Aracania—?"

"She is doing well, Your Majesty. After your news, our hearts broke for you, and we offer our sympathies."

Selena shook her head. "This isn't goodbye for my companion. I will save him. Thor will return to me after I destroy the Lich." Her sinking stomach made her feel like she was spiraling from the sky upon thinking of ending the Lich, but she remained convinced there must be a way to save Aydin from the clutches of the necromancer. However, if she had to kill Venexus, she would destroy Aydin.

"I have no doubts, and I pray for our victory and Thor's safe return." General Araneus then faced Silver, and the two gave each other a salute followed by a firm handshake. "It's damn great to see you again, Admiral Altessa."

"Sir, likewise. If you two will have me, I wish to help you and Colonel Cyres work with the Nidhoggr."

"It wouldn't be the same without you, Admiral. Lord Godfrey's leatherworkers are growing sodden from the sudden huge order of saddles, but they are very much needed. Aracania has already met the one called Noctis, and they've been practicing maneuvers and drills all morning. By the end of the day, we'll need the ferals to get used to wearing a harness and carrying riders. We don't have much time, but I hope it will all be enough."

"Sir, we will make it enough."

Colonel Cyres and General Araneus bade them farewell and slipped out to meet with Aracania. Selena remained behind, however, when she overheard Rahim talk to Chaliss about his father and Niamh. Not wishing to partake in the unpleasant conversation, she remained afar but saw how Chaliss turned pale, and tears flooded down her face. "I haven't seen Arawn since after you were born."

Her shimmering eyes widened when Rahim recounted meeting with the Nidhoggr rider. "I think he's still in there. Wouldn't you want to try and save him?"

"Is there anything left of your father to save? You told me he's already been turned into a Dreygur. There is no coming back from that."

Selena looked over her shoulder and saw Rahim hang his head in defeat. "I still want to try and save him and Niamh."

Desperately wanting to keep her promise to save his father, Selena feared the unavoidable. *What if we can't save Arawn?*

Silver poked her arm to get her attention and beckoned her to follow him down the corridor, greeted by the sight of the Aynu alphas talking to her parents in civilized conversation. "I'm willing to let go of what happened, but don't think I will ever forgive what you two did. However, I only trust the new queen. She's the sole reason I'm prepared to move past your betrayal." Kiba snarled through her clamped teeth.

"And I stand with my She-Wolf," Maru added. "History will never forget, and neither will we."

She witnessed how calm her mother remained, and Selena couldn't help but be amazed; it took so much of Aryl's strength to maintain her relaxed demeanor. "Vulduin and I can never make amends for what we did. I don't deserve your mercy."

"Nor do I," Vulduin began, "but I pray we can all live together in peace once the war is over." Kiba and Maru growled, but they bowed their heads in respect, and Selena's parents returned the gesture.

Silver placed a comforting hand on Selena's shoulder, squeezing as a tear drifted to her jaw. "I think it's safe to say that they've all made their amends, my dear, even if there is no forgiveness."

Selena sighed, her glistening gaze fixated on her parents as they strolled away. "We need to all work together if we hope to win this war."

"Do you not have any faith in Rahim's plans?"

"Of course I do, but sometimes our plans don't always work."

"Then we'll just have to hope for the best."

Kiba and Maru took their leave. Selena quickened her pace forward when her parents ambled away, her throat cracking when she called their attention. The two paused and looked over their shoulders in shock, replaced with sad smiles as they spun around. Instead of words, her mother opened her embrace, and Selena fell into her hold. Vulduin wrapped his long arms around his wife and daughter, and the three were together at long last. "I'm so sorry for what I said. I'm so sorry...." Her voice grew too hoarse to continue.

"We were never angry with you," Vulduin began, "what you said reminded us of all that we did wrong by you."

Aryl couldn't contain her tears any longer. "We are so happy to have you here, safe and sound. For that, we are grateful."

Before it reached midday, the group made their way to the fields outside the castle, only to be well received by Aracania leading her battalion of Nidhoggr and teaching them and their riders different flag signals. Their v-shaped formation reminded Selena of how she and Thor trained together while in the Force—how she missed those simpler days. Rahim was a surprisingly fast learner; General Araneus and Colonel Cyres had come to rely on his skills.

General Araneus strutted forward with his head held high and arms clasped behind his back. He nodded up to his dragon and watched Aracania's team practice unified breath attacks on far-away targets. The ferals were surprisingly quick at grasping flag signals, and Selena was confident they would have them all memorized by the end of the day.

Godfrey and Damien were already on the field and observing the Nidhoggr. The sun may be hiding behind the clouds, but Selena could see the nobles fidgeting a little in their spots; their hooded cloaks could only do so much to shield them from the sun's deathly glare.

Noctis was right behind Aracania; whenever he treated it like a race and sped up to pass her, Aracania would whip her head around and hiss at him to remain in place. He bared his fangs but slowed his wingbeats to maintain position.

Stirring above the formation were the twin hatchlings Sethak, the brother, and his sister, Rhasydra, the dragonet Selena met from the *Blood Diamond* per Noctis. The squabbling siblings hatched from Kayda's—a smaller weighted female sharing the same dainty build as Aracania—and Vyrilion's—a larger weight male among those practicing maneuvers—second clutch. A young feral from their first, Volterion, circled with the twins until Kayda called the three from the ground through a series of clicks and growls, sweeping her slick tail across the dirt in impatience. Selena was amused to see Kayda scolding the hatchlings for interrupting the training.

The general shook his head, but he laughed. Colonel Cyres, however, remained melancholy. "My main concern is dealing with Ashur and Jade, as Jade now has other powers besides his venom. His Former Imperial Majesty told us he's seen Jade use similar magic to the Nidhoggr—it's just darkness and shadow."

Araneus clicked his tongue against his teeth. As an Imperial Pearlscale, Jade was a rare species like the Aracania Venomtooth. They were the only known breeds in Armageddon capable of using acid and venom. The general looked up and met Selena's worried gaze. "Aracania and I will deal with Ashur and Jade when it comes to battle."

Aracania flew above them with the undead still following, and the formation made its way towards the hills away from the group. Selena instantly recognized the red Fire Ridgeback dragon Vulcan and his two riders—the Steelmane brothers Gromm and Beck—among the flight.

Another from the battalion was a blue-grey Typhoon Wraithclaw, its stormy hide iridescent in the sun. Its rider was someone Selena had least expected: Volt White, a former muscular cadet whose head was as empty as a flower pot. He had harassed her during basic training until Silver intervened and stopped their brawl, but prior to her leaving for Snowhaven, a rare Typhoon Wraithclaw had hatched for Volt. Though the youngling was about five months from the egg, the Wraithclaw had already outgrown Aracania.

Volt peered over the saddle, and his face turned pale upon seeing her again, possibly not recognizing her. The Wraithclaw chirped as it sailed with its silver glinted wings, edges dabbled in specs of yellow and blue. The two circled and landed near the gates, keeping their distance in fear of invoking Selena's wrath for their past hostilities.

Selena ignored Volt and the Wraithclaw and waved at the Steelmane brothers, hoping they saw her. They almost fell overboard when they glanced down, and as she expected, they didn't identify her immediately until she announced her name. Gromm Steelmane—the physically built of the two—gave her a firm salute, and Vulcan dipped his head in a bow; Beck Steelmane, the scrawny sharpshooter, leaned over and returned her gesture. If it weren't for the two sharing the same sandy hair and blue eyes, Selena wouldn't have been able to tell they were brothers.

Araneus smiled. "I was happy to see more survivors from the assault on Alfheim; I found them with Volt and Skyfyre and Colonel Cyres while transporting supplies to Lord Godfrey. They joined us after the Aynu." Selena's heart soared as she shared in the general's glee, even to see Volt's surviving the Red Rains of Alfheim. The Wraithclaw—Skyfyre—opened his maw and let out a long groan, wind gusts wafting from his slender snout.

Aracania joined Araneus after the Nidhoggr were dismissed from their training, and Vulcan steered himself around to meet with the others, his solid crimson scales matching Thor's gem-like hide. Selena rushed to greet the brothers, as she hadn't seen them since the initial attack on Alfheim. "Oi, is that really you? It's so good to see you." Beck dismounted and walked over with his hand extended, but Gromm came up from behind and yanked on Beck's ear.

"Is that the proper way to greet the queen? Please, forgive my brother, Your Majesty. He forgets himself, sometimes." Gromm dropped down to one knee. Beck, rubbing his ear, realized the error of his mistake and followed suit.

Disgruntled, Selena shook her head at their ridiculousness. "You two know me. I'm just happy to see you again and that you three survived." The two looked up, waiting for permission to stand. Through the pit in her stomach, Selena raised her hands. Beck's eye caught the glimmer of her Aether energy and began bombarding her with loads of questions, but Gromm threatened to pinch his ear again if he couldn't contain himself. Selena had to explain her new hand and her recent transformation to fulfill Beck's inquisitiveness. "Believe me when I say I don't mind answering your questions. Please don't deem me a merciless tyrant."

"Not at all, Your Grace." Gromm cleared his throat. "We only mean to show you the proper respect. You are our new queen, and we are here to serve you."

General Araneus let out an ear-shattering whistle and mentioned the two over to him. "That's enough. Make sure that Vulcan is well rested and fed before tomorrow. We will have a long flight ahead of us."

Gromm and Beck gave him a salute. "Yes, sir."

"Dismissed." The two brothers were excused from Selena's presence at the general's command, tending to Vulcan's needs.

Noctis, however, remained grounded. He greeted her but growled when Damien approached, raising his bladed wings halfway. However, after she stroked his snout, Noctis snaked his head around her as he took more interest in Damien, even as the prince recoiled slightly. Selena smiled and nodded at Noctis. "It's okay."

Damien's eyes widened as he looked at the feral leader, unsure of what to do. Chittering, Noctis inched his massive head closer to the young vampire prince. "C-come." Selena may be used Noctis' speech, but the rest of her friends still couldn't fathom meeting a verbally outspoken dragon, or Nidhoggr, for that matter.

Noctis lowered himself to the ground before the Prince of Shadows, but Damien remained unsure as he swiveled around to meet Selena's gleaming gaze. "My Queen, I don't know how to ride a dragon."

"You'll learn." Selena stepped forward as she became imbued with Aether, transformed into a dragon, and lifted off from the ground through the rhythmic beat of her ethereal wings. Maintaining her hovering, she surveyed the reactions of her friends and allies, and everyone looked upon her in awe and amazement as whispers of "the Queen of Dragons" bounced between them.

Volterion remained close to Kayda, but Sethak and Rhasydra zipped over to examine her Divine aura. Their tiny bladed wings flapped nearly as fast as a hummingbird's to keep them aloft. The twins took turns nuzzling her snout before their mother called for their return.

Noctis extended out his foreleg, allowing Damien to pull himself into the small hollow between his shoulder blades. After the prince was safely seated, Selena flung herself skyward with a single flap. Noctis followed suit, but he left poor Damien tightening his arms around the dragon's neck as Noctis continued climbing.

The two dragons flew higher and fought through the icy turbulence. Noctis kept swaying side-to-side and almost bucked Damien off his back, but the young prince held on. Together, he and Selena flew over the soldiers stationed outside the keep and past Lord Godfrey, Silver, and the others until they turned to dots. Selena sped ahead of Noctis and continued soaring higher before tucking in her wings and launching downward into a nosedive. Noctis copied her maneuver, and the three disappeared into the metal-hued clouds.

They continued twirling through plumed spires, reaching higher than before. Once they were close enough to touch the sky, Selena and Noctis slowed down and sailed across heaven's sea. Damien's hands couldn't stop shaking with excitement. "I never want to go back."

Selena grinned, and both she and Noctis roared in unison; they opened their maws and let forth a torrent mixture of black and blue Aether fire blazing across the sky like a shooting star.

*****

Black clouds swirled across the crimson sky over Alfheim's remains. A massive Dreygur army emerged from the debris and Hinterlands, heeding the call of the swinging bells from the Pyre. A dragon's screech bellowed from the darkness, followed by Death's shrill. Ally and foe followed the dark rings like flies drawn to a rotting corpse.

The Dark Master watched and waited by the wide window within Vidar's office as the necromancer and the Council surveyed the smoke wafting from the burned buildings. Despite the city's downfall weeks ago, black Aether flames continued to flicker among the debris in an eternal blaze. The Lich's skeletal hands burned with an eerie green fire blazing against his voluminous layered black cloak. Two dragon horns had grown and torn through his cowl; horrific red pupiled-lights peered through the empty eye sockets of his grisly nose-less skull, his once white mask now wholly shattered. The necromancer's pale, undead skin frayed away from his lips, revealing a wicked and perpetual grin.

Vidar paced about in his office as he bit down his nails. The Lich hadn't said a single word, and Vidar grew worried. Yet, Venexus kept calm. The Dreygur marched around Alfheim with no course or direction. The undead rose restlessly without the Lich's command, but they dared not to act on their own accord. Their corpses and what remained of their minds belonged to the necromancer.

The bells upon the Pyre began to sway and ring; two Nidhoggr flew in their direction, carrying their precious chained cargo. Before Vidar could utter a single word, the Lich vanished from the office and re-appeared outside, flying with the shadow wings sprouting from his back to meet with the dragon that would soon be his.

The two Nidhoggr had traveled faster than normal dragons, making the trip from Blackheart Village in days rather than weeks. They laid the dragon's unconscious body down on the ground as Venexus approached the one called Thor and touched his snout. Thor stirred, and his now dark, purple eyes shot open.

*****

*****

CHAPTER 21: THE BELLS

Damien and Noctis remained sky-borne for hours more, even after Selena returned to begin her drills. Lord Godfrey, Colonel Cyres, and General Araneus worked with some of the top fighters from the Shadow Templars and assigned them a Nidhoggr to train. One by one, the ferals chose their handlers. Vyrilion agreed to align himself with Kain and Maria, and Obsidian, a male close to Noctis' size, partnered with Lord Godfrey. While still battling through much reluctance after recently losing Onyxria, Colonel Cyres partnered with a large-weighted female named Ysyra.

Ignoring his disposition, Rahim ruefully worked with Eshara, a large-weighted female part of the formation. As he was still young and too small for combat, Volterion and the other whelps around his size and age assisted with moving supplies as part of Rahim's plan. Sethak and Rhasydra were far too small to be of any real help and instead stayed with their mother.

As the general wanted, the ferals took direction well, and the new riders began forging their unbreakable bonds with the undead dragons—including Rahim, though he didn't want to admit it. Skyfyre and Volt worked directly under Gromm, Beck, and Vulcan as they would cover their left flank; during their drills, however,

Volt briefly broke away and approached Selena before she broke away from Silver, Araneus, and Cyres. She squinted at him, and her former superiors eyed Volt suspiciously, but Volt acknowledged her as queen by bending the knee. As he apologized for past behavior, Skyfyre approached, tucking in his wings and chittering in agreement. Yet, Volt kept a watchful eye on Silver, who wrapped an arm around Selena's shoulder. "Please, forgive me," was all he could say.

She and Silver nodded, though Volt couldn't help but dote on her blossomed beauty; he only averted his gaze when Silver growled at him. "Don't you have somewhere to be, Mr. White?" Volt scrambled to his feet, and he and Skyfyre rejoined Gromm and Beck.

Selena and Silver laughed, and she excused herself and returned where the training dummies were and began her practices; many other ground soldiers were there and joined in. As powerful as she already was as a dragon, she still chose to practice her melee attacks. She didn't want to turn into a dragon if it wasn't necessary, and it never hurt to be prepared.

Selena would shoot out blue Aether blasts from her punches between sword swings; she repeatedly persisted with her techniques. Everyone stopped their training and watched as her deadly dance turned into a blinding inferno flurry of strikes, but she ignored their stares; Selena was too focused. All she could think about was perfecting her techniques, but her attacks became faster as she fell victim to her worries. The eclipse was only days away; Selena knew they would have to leave Dark Blood Hold by tomorrow's end if they were to make it to Alfheim in time for the Day of Eternal Darkness.

Already, General Araneus busied with arrangements. The Nidhoggr assisted with carting over the newly crafted metal airships, fit to carry Godfrey's estimate of a thousand abled bodies; simultaneously, the daintier and smaller ferals moved crates holding weapons, armor, and other supplies like food and water. As big as many ferals were, the powerful flight would have no issues transporting their precious cargo.

Selena stopped her practices and left the dummies and archery targets, ignoring the other soldiers behind with their mouths agape. Making it down the tower, she strolled through the war preparation commotion until reaching beyond the castle gates, traversing beyond the edge of the black sandy beaches until she had approached Dark Blood Hold's crimson dream. The thick trees twirled their branches, creating a tunnel of red and orange; even in late autumn, the leaves stood firm against the coming chill.

A faint and delightful tune twinkled in Selena's ears as she freely transformed into her Aether dragon state; her turquoise gem-like scales glimmered a rainbow from the peeking sun. Selena kept her ethereal wings, glowing like the northern lights burning Armageddon's evening sky, extended and unfurled as the celestial membranes passed through the guardian trees like a ghost vanishing through a wall.

The twisted branches were no match against the weight of her massive paws and quickly gave way with each passing step with a loud crunch, but Thor would still be the larger of the two; she would only stand to his shoulders. Yet, Selena exercised extreme caution when small animals and rodents crossed her path. One rabbit paused in its tracks and looked up, only to greet her sparkling emerald gaze. To her surprise, it wasn't afraid of her presence. Selena lowered her snout while maintaining her soft demeanor, ensuring no harm to the rabbit. The creature leaned upon its haunches and brushed its nose against hers before dashing away.

Weaving through leaf and limb were fairies shimmering all the colors of a rainbow. Selena extended her neck for a closer look, as Rhumbek was the only place she saw the lovely creatures, but the fairies floated freely here. The sun lanced through their crystal-cut wings, beating like those of a butterfly.

Selena arrived at Ghost Lake within an hour on foot, where the water line met the sky beckoned her. She passed through its donned misty curtain and stepped in its icy black waters. Even as she fully submerged the lower half of her body and used her wings to row herself across the surface, all she could think about was when she and Thor last went swimming together at the Ankoku Pass. She curled her neck back until her chin rested upon her breast, like a heartbroken swan. *I need you here.*

Tears rolled down her scaly face when her calls went unanswered, and she slowly sank to join the underwater world. Selena summoned an air bubble encasing her snout; she could stay under for eons. She felt like hours passed her by as she slithered through the dark depths like an ancient sea serpent without the need to come up for air. *Someday, you will be by my side again, and we'll be masters of the sky and sea.*

She plunged through the lake's surface, followed by an explosion of water; her exit was like a volcanic eruption. She propelled herself heavenward to hasten her way back to Dark Blood Hold, her celestial wings leaving ribbon trails of iridescent Aether.

Her return journey lasted only minutes. Upon arriving at the fortress, Selena watched Noctis and his flight follow Aracania to practice combat maneuvers and maintain formation. However, the Nidhoggr paused when they saw the Queen of Dragons arriving with a rainbow flair. Ignoring them while making her slow and graceful descent, as her paws touched the ground, Selena switched to her elven form and headed towards the keep's entrance. However, her parents stood post to the giant doors, waiting for her return.

Selena almost rushed by them without a word, but she paused when her father greeted her. "Silver is waiting for you in your room. There is something he wanted to discuss with you in private."

Selena bit her inner cheek. "I take it he didn't say what it was." Aryl turned to Vulduin, and the two shared a small smile. Only from their odd silence did Selena realize that with the final battle coming up soon, she feared the worst: she and Silver may never get married.

She rushed back to their apartment, only to find him standing before the window with his hands behind his back. He looked over his shoulder and smiled at her. "My dear, if I may be so bold," Selena half-expected his hasty proposition, "would you think it too soon if we were to have the ceremony tonight before the battle?" Her heart soared from the idea, but Selena had to hold her tongue; despite the circumstances, she was afraid of a rushed and botched event.

However, she shared his concerns that they may not have another opportunity, and this moment may be their last chance. After much consideration, she ultimately agreed, and Silver said, "Allow us to have at least one evening to ourselves before the world ends." The two laughed before pulling each other close into a passionate kiss.

"Do you think Lord Godfrey would have an issue hosting a last-minute wedding?"

"Not at all. You're the queen, and I'm sure he would do anything you commanded." Silver laughed, but she wasn't too thrilled with his jest; she despised being compared to a tyrant.

"You know I don't issue commands."

"That's why we're confident you will be a great ruler." Silver and Selena made haste to reach outside the keep, only to find Lord Godfrey returned to the castle with Aryl and Vulduin. Kain was among their company, but Damien remained outside the gates and tended to Noctis. At first, she was reluctant to approach Godfrey about planning the wedding with Kain there—she didn't want to appear insensitive to his and Maria's wishes. However, Kain suspected their reason to seek the lord's audience and was more than approving their plans.

Godfrey was surprisingly delighted to make last-minute arrangements for their wedding when Silver proposed their wishes; she clarified it was only a matter of officiating the ceremony. "I will do it at dusk, and I will marry you two right here, on the steps." Lord Godfrey smiled and immediately took his leave to prepare while Aryl and Vulduin remained behind, discussing how to proceed with this arrangement.

Selena bit her inner cheek and inspected Kain as her face drained of color. "I'm so sorry, and I hope we haven't offended you and Lady Maria."

He dug his hands into his pockets and smirked at the two. "Don't worry about us. We've already decided to wait until the war is over. Besides," Kain's eyes drifted to Silver's smoldering gaze, "I don't think we'll ever hear the end of it if we got married before you two."

"I beg your pardon." Silver's nostrils flared. "I would never—"

Selena stepped in between them. "Enough. There will be no arguing here." Kain and Silver exchanged glances and nodded in agreement before shaking hands in a truce and sharing a hearty laugh afterwards.

Despite Selena's simple request, Aryl ushered her directly back to hers and Silver's apartment. Vulduin, however, pulled Silver to join him in the opposite direction. Selena heard Kain snicker before he returned inside while murmuring about the mischief Silver would find himself in under imaginary circumstances and confronting "the big boss if anything were to happen to her."

Upon returning to Selena's room, Aryl immediately ordered one of the wandering chambermaids to bring the dress from her quarters. "Your father and I were already working on putting together your upcoming wedding, but we thought it wouldn't happen until after the eclipse." Selena doubted whether she or the others would be victorious or if any of them would come out of the battle alive; yet, her mother clung to that hope but made no further comment on the matter. "I had sewn your dress myself, and I need to make the finishing touches and fit you." Aryl eyeballed her up and down to get a better visual. "I remembered you were a little smaller. You're still thin but more...." She paused before adding, "becoming. You've blossomed into such a beautiful woman." Immediately her eyes looked like glass as she grinned, a mother proud of seeing how much her daughter had grown.

Selena couldn't believe her mother of unmatched beauty would give compliments to someone of less splendor; when she gazed at her mother's facial features and the pointed tips of her ears, she reminded herself she now shared these characteristics. Aryl spoke of her daughter's loveliness like she was the fairest elven maiden to walk this earth, and when she refused her mother's claims, Aryl urged her to look at her reflection in the full-body mirror. "You possess the beauty of an elf and a dragon that none would ever hope to compare. Even before you amended the Well's errors, you were still a lovely young woman."

Selena couldn't help but run her fingers through her gradient blue hair, nor could she stop examining her narrowed cheekbones, her copper skin kissed by starlight. Her mother brushed her hair back over her new pointed ears, mentioning pieces of jewelry she could wear over the tips if Selena wished.

Lord Godfrey's chambermaid returned with the sleeveless ivory dress, bodice embroidered with jewels, donned on a headless, wooden mannequin. Other than slight modifications that she could quickly fix within a couple of hours with magical aid, Selena found the dress rather lovely and fit for royalty: it followed the curves of her body before flaring at the hips like a ball gown, the hem sweeping the ground.

Despite Aryl's fears, the fairytale-lovely off-shoulder dress was almost the right size, if only a tad bit snug: her mother took the measurements needed. "We may not be able to do a full ceremony right now, but at least you will look like the queen you are," Aryl continued, "If you and Silver wish after the war is over, we can do a proper wedding fit for the Queen of Dragons."

*****

Vulduin and Silver sat across from each other, a bottle of brandy and a platter of food between them, trudging through the suspenseful phase of the upcoming nuptials: waiting for the bride to finish. Even from within the confines of the apartment, the castle bustled with activity as Lord Godfrey ordered his servants to make the final preparations.

Bathed and clean-shaven, the two were already dressed in their best formal attire: Silver donned the same black suit with a matching jacket when he asked Selena for her hand. The gleaming gilt trailing the edges of his long coat and his golden chain stretched diagonally from shoulder to hip caught the fainting sun's rays as it prepared to vanish over the horizon. A golden brooch of a dragon head rested upon his shoulder, set with sapphires for its eyes, holding the gold links in place. He and Vulduin wore their best breeches and hessian boots; their shoes polished to an eye-catching shine. Vulduin swapped his usual long, red coat for a black jacket with gold trimmings, nearly matching Silver's. His raven hair was neatly combed back, sweeping past his pointed ears. Typically not one who wore jewelry, His Former Imperial Majesty bore a simple gold crown weaving together like grapevines for the occasion.

Sitting within Silver's pockets were two rings of white gold. His a plain band, but two soldered together for her: the outside guard embedded with tiny diamonds delicately weaved around the inside ring, faceted with a grander gem and smaller diamonds lining the sides. Initially discovered from a fallen meteorite by a dwarf chemist named Firbead Moissan, he thought he accidentally unearthed diamonds until later determining that the crystals were differently composed. Only a handful of these space diamonds, now called moissanite, exist, thus making them rarer than an actual diamond; the gem's rarity gave Silver the idea to use for jewelry. When held under proper lighting, the stones glimmered rainbow flecks.

Upon hearing the news, General Araneus, Colonel Cyres, and Aracania finished training with the ferals after properly fitting them with new harnesses. Much to their delight, Noctis and his flight accepted the saddles on the condition their leader tried it first. While Selena took her afternoon flight in solitude, Silver used magic to embed a jewel into each harness as Thor had, and Noctis paraded himself about the camp with his new treasure. The ferals caught in their envious blitz impatiently waited for Godfrey's soldiers to securely strap down their saddles as they, too, wished to brandish their bestowed wealth.

To celebrate their alliance with the feral Nidhoggr, Vulduin poured himself and Silver another glass. "Thank you again for your fine work, Admiral Altessa. Here's to a much-needed victory and your upcoming marriage." The two drew their glasses to a toast, and the smooth liquid amber drenched their throats. "I have to remind myself that she's no longer a child."

"Whether she wanted it or not, Selena has certainly grown into her new role. Being a queen is natural to her."

"She made it very clear to us that she never wanted it. Even on our way back to Mortemholdt, she loathed the idea." Vulduin sighed. "I wished that her mother and I could have done right by her."

"But you did all you could."

He shook his head and waved his hand to Silver's claim in dismissal. "She said Chaliss was a better parent than either of us: she was right." The two sat in uncomfortable silence, only accompanied by the castle's anticipation and preparation. "When did you realize you loved her?"

Silver was a little concerned with how much Vulduin had to drink, as his face was already flustered. The two had been indulging in food and brandy since Aryl and Selena separated to prepare, and a few hours had already passed; sunset would soon arrive. "Since she and Azrael had their last brawl. I didn't recognize it until Kain confronted me."

"Have you ever loved another before her?"

Silver leaned forward and looked down at his feet while twiddling his thumbs. "Honestly, no one I can remember."

Vulduin squinted at him. "You never forget your first love."

"If I had one, I forgot. I barely even remember what my childhood was like." Silver looked up to see the unsatisfied look on Vulduin's face. "Try being alive for as long as I have, and then you come back and tell me if your memory serves you any better."

Vulduin only smirked, and the two shared a light-hearted laugh in between drinks before the two indulged in more brandy. "Fair enough. I want to make sure you're what's best for her."

"When have I not been? I love her more than life itself. I would give up my immortality and powers for her."

*****

The sun sank over the horizon. The bells upon the top of the keep began to sway, and their rings resonated across the heavens.

Noctis and his flight stood like statues along the courtyard perimeter, watching the upcoming ceremony. Yet, he growled when the younglings grew rambunctious, and he snapped his fangs to gather their attention. Immediately, they withdrew; Kayda and Vyrilion extended their protective arms and pulled the twins close to the behaved Volterion. Aracania, Ysyra, Skyfyre, and Vulcan circled overhead before perching near the feral leader, their contrasting ruby, blue-grey, and black scales glimmering across the ground.

Lord Godfrey's soldiers—Gromm and Beck among them—formed an aisle up the stairs. Silver waited beside the lord with Prince Damien by his father's right side. Standing a few steps down from the three were Her Former Imperial Majesty donned in her midnight blue dress and the decorated triplets next to her.

Rahim, Chaliss, Colonel Cyres, General Araneus, and Volt stood ground-level; Loki rushed over and wedged between the two, and he and Chaliss shared a small smile. Opposite of them was Lord Vanguard and Lady Maria towering over the short-statured Aynu alphas. As Kiba and Maru refused to dress, it was only appropriate to join by keeping their wolf forms, much to their delight.

A faint musical tone played from a flute tinkled from above by the fairies from the crimson forest zipping over the aisle, and Selena and Vulduin entered from the main castle gates. Before the courtyard filled with guests, Aryl whisked her daughter away through the side entrance so she wouldn't be seen until the ceremony, as was the custom—even fleeing as a dragon still counted.

Her bridal beauty, of course, was the center of attention. The sparkling gems embroidered into her bodice glimmered like the fairy crystal wings fluttering overhead. Gracing her ear tips were delicate gilt-plated pieces embedded with mother-of-pearls. Upon her head was a golden tiara faceted with sapphires, amplifying the hue of her gradient hair decorated in thick braids taking a floral shape, leaving the rest in long and elegant curls. She held onto her father's arm with her porcelain gloved Aether hand as she carried a small bouquet of white roses in her right, her flower of choice since her birthday gift from Silver.

Vulduin took his spot next to Aryl after reaching the top of the marble stairs, and Lord Godfrey stepped forward. "Two souls, two hearts come together before the Divines this evening. The Dragon Queen, Selena Liongod, and Admiral Genesis Silver Altessa come here to be wed and seek the blessings of the Divines." After sharing blissful smiles, Silver gently took her hand in his and pulled out the bands from his jacket in the middle of Godfrey's recitation, hers first to slip on her ring finger, followed by his. "We all stand here together with the insight of the three Divines to witness the union of man and wife. I seal these two and bind them as one heart and soul, now and forever."

Preceding directly after their ceremony, Lord Godfrey arranged the festivities involving dancing, eating, and drinking wine. Musicians blared their enchanting and upbeat music enticing the hall while a magnificently cooked large boar serving as the oak table's grand centerpiece drew everyone's nostrils. Aracania, Skyfyre, Vulcan, Noctis, and the ferals were given an extra pig or cow—their choosing—to participate in the celebrations.

Both she and Silver occupied the end of the table while Godfrey and Damien took the other side; Kiba and Maru eyed the stuffed beast with mouth-watering angst but waited until the kitchen maids served the guests of the hour first. Rahim proposed a toast in their honor, and everyone clanked their glasses before sharing the over-stuffed platters. The great hall echoed with the sound of laughter for the joyous occasion.

With drinks still in hand, many guests joined in on the dancing while doing their best not to spill—Silver and Selena took their spots at the center of the lined partners, circling each other with outstretched arms and wrists touching. They modified the steps and moves from the first dance they shared at the ball in Dragonstone; they weaved around the other dancers before returning, and Silver finished the tango by spinning her around, only to bring her back for a kiss.

The entire reception burst into cheers and whistles as the newly married couple clashed their goblets and shared another drink, celebrating before the end of the world.

CHAPTER 22: THE BROKEN MAN

Winter's dread drowned out the nuptial bliss after the new couple shared their last evening. Two plates of untouched food sat cold on the table as Selena lay restless —clothed in only blankets—with her eyes fixated upon her new ring emblazoned with the meteorite diamonds, and Silver enjoying what could be his final slumber. All her thoughts raced back to Thor, and she couldn't stop the tears swelling within her eyes, unable to imagine his torment: day after day, night after night, she never gave up hope that one day, he would finally respond.

Please, talk to me—even one word would suffice. Again, her calls went unanswered, and Selena silently wept from drowning in her sorrow when all she felt from him was darkness.

Her head whipped over the pillows to see her new husband sleeping peacefully and happily before the final battle, and she wondered what swirled within his dreamland. As a demigod, Silver probably hadn't slept since his initial transformation. Selena smiled and leaned in to kiss him on the cheek before slipping out of bed and taking advantage of their private balcony beyond the window, seeking solace in the cold evening. She looked heavenward to watch the black and silver clouds wafting overhead.

The winter solstice was nearly upon them, and the castle shuddered from the lingering eclipse creeping behind; the allies planned on leaving for the assault in the morning to make it on time. The Nidhoggr were fast fliers and would have no issues bringing their armies to Alfheim within a fortnight. Yet, Ebony still returned no response, but Selena hoped she would ultimately make the right decision.

She welcomed the chilling air kissing her naked body, her dragon blood keeping her warm even as the snow began drifting.

Thor, please know that I will be coming to save you. I promise.

She took a couple of steps back and sat on the cold stone with her legs crossed, eyes closed, and hands together as she bowed her head in silent prayer. *Xyaxon, I need your wisdom.*

The Divine made no hesitation in granting her an audience. Within seconds, the world paused, and Selena was whirled into the ethereal realm: Niflheim. She stood before the desolate castle of glass glimmering from the burning cosmos, but the god's gentle voice whispered across the empty air. "And you shall have it. My help is always available to you as long as you ask."

Selena remained puzzled and troubled as she looked around at the sparkling cosmos floating above her. "I need to figure out how to save Thor and the others. I know Thor isn't lost to me yet, and everyone keeps telling me Aydin is dead, but I don't believe that."

"Aydin is only but a broken man."

"That's not true. I know there is more to it. Silver showed me a few of his memories, but they were after Aydin began yielding to Venexus' control."

"Venexus is a primordial creature, older than existence itself; his task is to kill and destroy life. I watched young Aydin suffer, and it didn't take long for Venexus to possess him. Even before he met your mother, Venexus waited for the perfect moment to strike, and Aydin was his perfect vessel to help further his plans before the man was ever conceived. His fate remained sealed."

"What should I do?"

"If you wish to save Thor and the others, you must end the Lich once and for all with Revelation. Death is the only solace that Aydin seeks."

Selena's eyes shimmered, but they widened. "Aydin is still alive."

"He's only a shell of the man he used to be."

"I know, but I want to save him, Azrael, Thor, and everyone else. Nobody, not even Aydin, deserves this agony."

"I understand your reluctance, and your heart is in the right place, but Revelation will end Aydin's torment. What is the fate of one life to millions more?"

"But it was his life."

Xyaxon remained indifferent to Selena's gentle nature, and his answers sent a cold shiver down her spine. "His will be a noble sacrifice. You must do whatever it takes to protect your world." The Divine's voice vanished, and, with a flutter of her eyes, she found herself sitting on the balcony at Dark Blood Hold once more.

She swiveled her head to see that Silver was still sound asleep, and the world resumed spinning. With her new resolve, her breaths and steps grew heavier as she returned inside and made haste in scribbling out a letter intended for Silver, hand trembling and struggling to hold the quill: *Please forgive me, but I have to do this.*

After folding up and displaying her small letter on top of her pillow, she rushed over to the washroom and cleaned herself before donning her dragonscale dress. Satisfied once ensuring Revelation remained safe within her pocket, she tied up her waist-length hair and belted Dragonheart to her hip but purposefully left her shield propped against the wall, no longer needing it.

Selena had to meet the Lich on the battlefield and save Thor before Lord Godfrey's army arrived; she wanted to find Rahim and tell him of her plans, but she paused as she reached for the door, hand frozen mid-reach for the handle. She feared never seeing her friends and family again, but—no, they would stop and convince her to stay until their planned departure.

Instead, she hurried to the balcony, looking back at Silver once more before shifting into her dragon form and sweeping herself through the brewing winter storm, ribbons of Aether following each flap from her celestial wings.

*****

Hours later, when morning came, Silver awoke, but he panicked and scrambled around to find his wife missing. Only when he paused did he bother finding and reading the note she left on the pillow, and his face became like porcelain; he then noticed the opened window to their balcony, and his heart sank faster than a dragon spiraling from the sky.

While Silver jumbled in a frenzy to clean up and dress, Lord Godfrey and his allies prepared for their long trip. Among the clatter of preparations, Lord Godfrey, Colonel Cyres, and General Araneus repeated their planned stops supporting their schedule, allowing the army some rest before the eclipse. Satisfied, Araneus and Aracania led their newly harnessed Nidhoggr and riders towards the rest of the group from the nearby deep hills, the ferals admiring the massive gems blazing from the middle of their chests. Araneus couldn't excuse himself from laughing at how much they acted like dragons when hoarding treasure, but Aracania grew impatient; she clicked her talons against the rocks in anticipation as she ordered the ferals to take up formation, tail flickering and swishing side-to-side.

After Aracania cleared him from yesterday's maneuvers, Noctis took his position as leader of the second battalion that would handle Ashur's aerial raid. The only rider he would accept, aside from Selena, was Damien; the Prince of Shadows, with Rahim's help, ensured the new saddle was securely fastened and packed with weapons and provisions. Noctis swung his head and nudged Rahim's shoulder with his nose in between the deep-rumbled chittering vibrating from his throat.

As much as Rahim attempted to ignore Noctis' affections, eventually, he sighed and reached out to pet the feral leader. "You know what? You lot aren't so bad." Before he could brace himself, Eshara dove down from the circling flight above and joined in on his newfound friendliness, chirping to Rahim's touch. He grew nervous and stepped back as the two circled him, but eventually, he couldn't help but grin when the ferals rubbed their snouts against his open palms like cats showing affection.

The last of the suited soldiers—Kiba, Maru, and the rest of their pack—boarded the large metal ships lined with rows of benches covered in thick furs for comfortable seating. The rest of the ferals waited for General Araneus' command to carry them off. Lining the vessel walls were a plethora of weapons and extra armor, the extras carted off by the smaller weighted dragons in boxed crates. The Aynu, in wolf forms, followed their alpha leaders proudly into the ships, ignoring the others still wary of their presence. Maru snarled as the fur bristled upon his back when he noticed one soldier staring grimly at one of his pack members; immediately, the warrior averted his gaze.

The ground soldiers serving the general's formation assisted in loading Godfrey's trained warhorses inside their stable designed frigate with no regard to the blitz of activity; the beasts remained indifferent to the restless Nidhoggr, lining up calmly within their stationed stalls.

Meanwhile, Gromm and Beck ensured that Vulcan was ready for the long flight ahead, as they were part of the general's battalion and would help cover the right flank. Behind them was Volt harnessing Skyfyre as he was in the middle of gulping his last cow down to the hooves. Nearby were Lord Vanguard and Lady Maria; the two agreed to fight against the swarming Dreygur right at Oblivion's open gate. They and Vyrilion were instructed to use bombs and ranged aerial attacks to keep the undead detained and occupied for as long as possible. While Maria packed her supplies, Kain and Rahim discussed the possibility of Vyrilion creating a wall of dark Aether flames to barricade the Dreygur within Oblivion. However, the two feared the Dreygur would remain unharmed by Nidhoggr attacks, but it was worth the attempt.

Silver shapeshifted into a falcon through mid-leap off the balcony and dove towards the group of allied leaders to deliver the grave news. Their Former Imperial Majesties, Chaliss, Neith, Loki, and the Oracles were caught in a deep discussion, presumably continuing their previous plans of finding shelter during the upcoming battle.

Kain and Rahim paused in mid-conversation to see Silver descending upon them and morphing back to his usual guise. Loki rushed to hide behind Vulduin's legs through high-pitched howls and squeals and became ensconced within his bristling tail, but Silver ignored the scared fox. Before Rahim could give him an eye roll over his dramatic display, his knees buckled when he made sense of the delivered news. "Why would she leave now?"

Everyone froze, minus the smirking Oracles, and looked to Silver for a better explanation or hoping that he was playing a cruel trick. However, they shared horrified gasps when he paused mid-sentence, shaking his head while waving Selena's note in the air.

Lord Godfrey, overhearing the demigod's alarming message, excused himself from General Araneus and Obsidian, marched over, and snatched the parchment away to see for himself. "This doesn't change anything," he said after reading the letter, "the Queen of Dragons will still face the Dark Master. The eclipse is arriving soon, and our plan remains the same."

Silver, still unconvinced, paced, only to stop and point at Vulduin, questioning why he remained calm when Selena was missing, to which he and Aryl reaffirmed their complete confidence in their daughter's capabilities. Eshara stood on her haunches with wings completely unfurled, snaked her head back, and let out a series of chirps and clicks in approval; Rahim added in his assured opinion through a small smile, "Selena will be fine. She's a Divinity Dragon and a one-person army. Plus, we'll be right there if she does need us."

Kain clapped Silver's shoulder, tightening his grip to keep his old friend grounded. "If she was willing to save your arse by picking a fight with me, that necromancer won't stand a chance." He gave a hearty laugh, regaling in Selena's failed attempt at knocking him down with a tree branch upon their initial meeting.

"I couldn't imagine Her Majesty sitting back while Thor was in danger," Maria chimed in, "she will save him, and those two will be unstoppable."

Vyrilion joined in Eshara's glee and released a victorious roar. However, Silver counted their celebration unwarranted, but he couldn't help but grin when the others burst in with Selena's courageous stories, reassuring each other that she would succeed. After the group settled on the matter, Lord Godfrey dismissed himself to join General Araneus and Obsidian. Despite his rising faith in her power, Silver still loathed that she left in the middle of the night without saying a word; he hoped it wouldn't be the last time he would ever see her again.

Instead, he approached Rahim, watching and waiting as he strapped down his belongings and sacks to Eshara's harness after polishing the massive pearl gleaming upon her chest. She couldn't help but stare at the gemstone, a happy dragon owning a new treasure. When Rahim turned around, the silent Silver extended his hand as a truce, making amends for their past hostilities and discrepancies. Tight-lipped, Rahim bit down on his tongue but accepted the gesture with gratitude, and the two shared a smile. "Don't die out there, or I'll bring you back to kill you myself. Selena wouldn't forgive me if she lost her new husband."

Silver laughed, but his grip tightened. "I'm a demigod. Remember? I'll be a difficult kill."

"I suppose. Welcome to the family."

The smile faded from Silver's face when Vulduin demanded a private audience with him; Chaliss rushed past when Silver dismissed himself and waylaid Rahim for one final hug before leaving with the others.

"Genesis, I have a favor to ask." Silver scowled but didn't have the energy to fight Vulduin, not even when he asked to use his library as a haven for Aryl and the others. Silver agreed without hesitation, and Vulduin nodded to his wife; she beckoned the others seeking shelter to follow away from the main party.

Before the Oracles left, however, they turned and bowed to Silver in unison. "May your queen's Divine fire forever reign." Thinking of their remark as an act of respect, he accepted it, but his face beamed when given a moment to ponder.

When Chaliss left her son to finish saddling Eshara, Neith waved her over to Kayda, waiting on a nearby hilltop to ferry their group to safety. Those too small to fight—her twins included—circled the small female, impatient to fly away. Both Silver and Vulduin watched as they mounted Kayda and flew away from Dark Blood Hold. The hatchlings and younglings trailed behind their mother's party, nipping and squabbling. "Now, I have a second favor to ask."

Vulduin's demands put a pucker in Silver's brow. "I seem to recall more than two that you've asked of me."

Not taking his eyes away from Kayda's faint silhouette disappearing over the horizon, Vulduin, unamused, ignored Silver's sarcasm. "You will fly me directly to Vidar's office. I have a score to settle with him."

"Are you sure that's wise?"

Vulduin's heated gaze made Silver flinch. "I can handle Vidar."

"That wasn't my question. I don't believe that's the best idea, and he will fall once Selena defeats the Lich."

"That won't be good enough. Vidar will pay for his crimes, and he will answer to me. I want you to enchant my chains so I can attack him."

"Now, thrice you've asked for a favor, and that's just today alone." Silver moaned when Vulduin's expression hardened at his witticism, but he didn't argue; instead, he touched the thick crimson jacket, imbuing the fabric with a touch of blue Aether energy. "With this," Silver began explaining, "you should be able to penetrate any of Vidar's wards."

Vulduin raised a brow. "Even if it's the Lich's magic?"

"Light Aether will nullify the darkness."

While Silver and Vulduin made their separate preparations, General Araneus and Aracania landed near Colonel Cyres, the two vampire nobles, and their battle tactician with their air fleet right behind them, ready for taking off. The general dismounted, giving them a hearty salute while Noctis ensured Eshara, Ysyra, and Obsidian were in position.

After settling on their plans, Silver looked to every one of his allies and gave them all a firm salute. They returned the gesture. "Goodbye, everyone. Today, we meet destiny. Let us hope she's kind." He transformed into his wing-less dragon character with a small harness, allowing Vulduin to climb aboard.

General Araneus bowed to everyone. "Today, we work to fight for Alfheim."

"For Armageddon," Lord Godfrey corrected.

"Aye. For Armageddon, and the world."

General Araneus mounted Aracania, and the two took to the skies after His Former Imperial Majesty and Silver; their battalion snatched the metal vessels with their long, sharp talons as the soldiers within closed the doors from the inside.

After Vulduin gave the signal, Silver slithered skyward away from the cheering and roaring camp. When everyone separated into their assigned formation groups, they followed the general's air fleet for the final battle in Alfheim.

*****

Concurrently, in the fallen elven city, Thor and the Lich watched and waited over the next fortnight until it was time: Oblivion's portal ready to open, and the unconscious Azrael impaled between the two spires that would support the gate. While the Destroyer of Worlds perched on the wall's debris, wispy shadow wings unfurled, Fafnir and Jade circled above, gathering the Nidhoggr army behind the mountain metropolis of Rune Citadel. Arawn and his companion remained close to the Dark Master's side until it was time to lead the Dreygur.

The black crystals, already powered up from the dragon eggs, were set to power open the portal: two in the mortal realm and two in Oblivion. The gems floated above Azrael's pinned heads with dark Aether pulsating and writhing around the stones, tethering them in place. The Mythic Flight eggs were kept within Rune Citadel in Vidar's office for now, waiting to join the Lich's undead creations eventually; the Dark Master's new Mythic Flight would be unstoppable.

Venexus, while riding Thor's new saddle, gave the command, the smoldering red pupiled-slits burning from his frayed skull. *Open the portal.*

Thor's eyes flickered as he opened his jaw and unleashed a black blast at Azrael; what remained of the fallen Divine's Aether energy contorted around his body, then to the pillars, creating a swirling maelstrom of dark magic erupting in between the bloody circle. "Dark fire will cleanse this stagnant world, and a new one will be reborn from the ashes." In response to the necromancer's declaration, Thor's terrifying roar made the earth tremble in fear at announcing its dark fate.

The sky burned red and orange as the dark morning arrived. Meanwhile, haste was Selena's only ally, and she was right on the outskirts of Alfheim's ruins. The blazing sun burned fiercely over the horizon behind her as the moon began draping it in darkness.

CHAPTER 23: THE ECLIPSE

The Day of Eternal Darkness was upon them. The eclipse streaked across the ground, its dark energy destroying the clouds in its path, leaving Armageddon cloaked in an eerie shadow. Selena emerged from the eclipse and dove through the sky just as the portal opened, her eyes transfixed on the dark Aether radiating from the black glass spires. Her wings parted the crimson spires swirling into a brewing storm forming above Alfheim's ruins, and she looked like a shooting star streaking across the blackened heavens.

Selena breathed deep, and her lips curved and twisted into a snarl upon Azrael's ghastly fate; this was the first time seeing Death's proper form, and her boundless rage threatened to incinerate the world to ash for his torment. Yet, her fury grew to that of a thousand rampaging dragons when she saw the tainted Thor coated in dark Aether energy, eyes glowing purple, the dark magic dancing off his hide like fire. She swooped down and looked outward towards Rune Citadel—the keep her family built now littered with red banners lined in gold and black bearing the Lich's insignia. How dare Vidar and the others reside in what was rightfully hers?

All she endured and lost ensued her brewing firestorm; she reared her head back and unleashed a massive roar making the earth shudder and quake. The Lich and Thor turned their focus to the giant Aether dragon heading in their direction, the dark light from the eclipse shimmering across her scales. Trails of rainbow Aether followed every flap from her wings, and her iridescent hide still managed to glimmer like polished gemstones through the swirling darkness.

Venexus stared at Selena in surprise but smirked. Thor bared his fangs before making a full-body leap and landed on the crumbling wall, roaring through clamped teeth. She circled and landed on the other end of the wall's debris, her sword-length nails clacking against the stone, her paws shoving pieces away during her balancing act.

Yet, she cringed from seeing how Venexus had evolved since their last direct encounter; now remarkably large, his once eerie mask was wholly gone, revealing his pale, undead, frayed skin stretched against his nose-less skull. Dragon horns matching Thor's design ripped through his torn cowl. Bristling, Selena snarled from his tiny, burning pupils glowing from his sockets; the necromancer's shrill laugh made her grimace. "It's quite fitting that you should be here as we witness the dawn of a new world. I was afraid you wouldn't arrive in time."

Through flicking her massive tail, Selena manipulated her Aether and resumed her elven form; if Venexus was shocked at her recent transformation, the necromancer didn't show it. She wrapped her fingers around Dragonheart's grip in preparation for a blow. "I wouldn't miss it."

"Then please, sit down and join us." Following the Lich's words, Thor roared and swiped at her with his claws. Selena dodged his attack, but just barely; his talon left a single tear in her clothes, but her skin at least remained unscathed as she staggered back to her feet. Selena gasped to see that her armored dragonscale dress couldn't withstand Thor's attacks. "Please, Aydin, you don't have to do this."

Venexus sneered, his eternal grin widening. "Oh? Aydin is dead. It's only me now."

"No, you're not. I know you're still there, Aydin."

"You can try all you want, but I'm the only one who remains." The Lich dismounted and walked towards her, and Thor unfolded his titanic wings that spread behind the necromancer's back; Selena shivered at the unsettling image. "I've warned you before that this was the fate of your pathetic world. Here you are, trying so hard and refusing to accept that this is our duty. It's our destiny to bring about the cycle of destruction and rebirth."

"I don't believe in that."

"It doesn't matter what you believe. Look down there." The Lich pointed to the portal with his skeletal hand, and as the eclipse rose higher, the tethered crystals attached to Oblivion's gate caught the black sun's dark light and began to shine. Ropes of lightning writhed down the spires and absorbed into the ground. The magic cracked the very foundation of the quaking earth, and the portal collected the swirling vortex of crimson clouds gathering above the city. It came into focus, and the gate opened up to the desolate plains of Oblivion.

The Dreygur emerged from the powered passage, massive in size and numbers. Selena's eyes widened in horror as the snarls of the Lich's undead army preceded them. She watched as they swarmed Alfheim like a tidal wave, unable to stop herself from marveling at their sheer force.

The Lich said, "You brought about the end of the world. You fulfilled your destiny by your actions and choices to avoid it. Soon, I will destroy your world, and you along with it."

"No…." Selena made eye contact with Thor to communicate with him, but his thoughts were as clouded and tainted as the dark Aether that now consumed him. *I'm here—please, come back to me.*

The necromancer's mocking laughter screeched from her failed attempt to reach Thor's twisted mind. "You want him back? Then get him back." Jet-black feathered wings sprouted forth from the Lich's back, and his following command echoed in both Thor's and Selena's minds. *Kill her.*

Thor roared in obedience. Satisfied, the Lich launched himself into the bleeding heavens, making his way for the portal.

Thor, don't do this. The bloodlust was apparent in his tainted eyes; when Thor didn't heed her plea, Selena took to her dragon form and flung herself skyward in one full-body leap. He blindly went after her, and just as she feared, Selena knew she would either have to run or fight back.

*****

The reinforcements arrived as soon as the portal opened. General Araneus and Aracania zoomed over the broken wall, with the Shadow Templars and their Nidhoggr clutching to their vessels. Following Rahim's strategy, the pair led their formation towards the Dreygur pouring from Oblivion's gate. Lord Godfrey, Prince Damien, and Rahim remained airborne, preparing for Ashur's air fleet, which had yet to arrive; they focused on ensuring Araneus and his battalion wouldn't be overwhelmed on the ground.

Damien and Noctis dove side-by-side with Rahim and Eshara as they closed in on the city, but while guiding Eshara into the fray, Rahim couldn't shake away the horrific wave after wave of Dreygur swarming from the portal. As soon as they were upon the stampeding horde,

Damien and Rahim relied on gunfire to shoot the unharmed Dreygur as they invaded. While their riders became snipers, Eshara and Noctis retaliated by spewing forth a conjoined attack of black fire and poison cloud of destruction upon the undead army; to Rahim's relief, the Dreygur caught in their venomous inferno melted and disintegrated from their magical torrent.

The dragons swept through the freed Dreygur tsunami wave with another painful and brutal inferno pass; Rahim signaled Kain and Maria to move ahead with the plan to use Vyrilion's fire and block the gate's opening: *Commence fire barricade.* Roaring in approval, Vyrilion broke away from Godfrey's contingent and swooped closer to the portal. He strafed a street filled with Dreygur, belching a deadly torrent of fire and shadow, decimating and consuming all in his path. Kain and Maria readied their weapons while dropping bombs, blasting upon contact with the ground; Vyrilion avoided as the explosives blew the Dreygur to pieces. As he landed before the massive Oblivion gate, he spewed another blast of dark fire, creating a wall blocking the doorway. Satisfied with the Lich's forces now trapped within their sepulcher prison, Rahim spurred Eshara, maintaining formation while looking for Niamh and Fafnir, but they were nowhere in sight.

While Lord Godfrey's formation was busy controlling the sky, General Araneus sent up the flag signals. His battalion had already landed outside the city with their precious cargo, the Aynu pack—with Kiba and Maru at the front—and Lord Godfrey's soldiers burst forth from their metal ships, the two armies clashing at full speed. Releasing their vessels, Vulcan, Skyfyre, and the allied Nidhoggr circled the ground; upon the general's signal, they exhaled large jets of combined red and black flames, creating a wall of dark fire corralling the Dreygur from reaching beyond the city limits.

Engage the enemy closely. Aracania spun in circles, spitting out clouds of acid, catching the Lich's undead soldiers before they could overwhelm her and her rider. Araneus dismounted and covered her exposed flank, lopping off their heads one after another. Gromm and Volt joined their commanding officer on the ground, swords at the ready, while Beck remained on Vulcan's back, all the firearms under his disposal as he mowed through the enemy contingent. Ysyra hovered above and, upon Cyres' signal, decimated a surrounding wave to keep them from being overwhelmed. When it was clear to do so, Cyres descended and joined the general's defense team, dual-wielding blood-thirsty twin broadswords, slicing and dicing through their opposition.

Forming a protective circle around Araneus, Cyres, and their dragons, Kiba and Maru led their Aynu warriors; the straggling waves of undead crashed over the wolves, shrieking and snarling. They stabbed and sliced each rotting corpse as they barreled through their ranks with claws and teeth, but some Dreygur landed gruesome blows against the general's and the She-Wolf's fighters; the fallen had their flesh picked off and eaten, their frayed undead pale blue skin dyed with crimson gore.

General Araneus and the Aynu alphas did their best not to allow the ghastly screams to torment them, but the wolf leaders rallied with newfound vigor. Kiba and her soldiers immediately switched to magic and summoned pieces of rock and metal from their ships, casting deadly earthly shards striking and impaling their foes by flicking their wrists. Then, the wolves cracked the ground in two. The earth split, the fissure webbing around the base of the firewall, creating a deep trench to protect their division's dwindling numbers; the rushing Dreygur burst into flames before plunging into the abyss.

Maru joined his mate and called forth the tree roots growing deep underground from the Hinterlands, and the thick, slithering vines erupted from the ground, trapping the incoming Dreygur wave. The vegetation collected until Maru was wholly consumed by a controllable foliage behemoth. The Black Wolf alpha snatched and swung groups of animated corpses, its vine-like limbs whipping and slicing through skin-frayed limbs and bones. The others followed his example by utilizing Artio's blessing, calling the forces of nature in their time of need, helping their soldiers from being overwhelmed through crowd control tactics using tangled tendrils of vines and metal.

Araneus smiled when all seemed to be going well, looking quite pleased. The dragons from his and Godfrey's units now acted out of instinct, their strategy advantageous to their efforts. However, their victory didn't last long; his face drained when he and Aracania thought they saw a ghost dash across the darkened sky. General Araneus recognized it right away; Jade and Ashur had arrived with their aerial fleet, and behind him were Niamh and Fafnir, a colossal behemoth close to Noctis' size. The venomous Imperial Pearlscale's strikingly white hide magnified the deep-hued sapphires faceted from Jade's solid gold torque emblazoned upon his neck and piercing emerald eyes. The gems from his neckpiece and golden headdress reflected the eclipse's contrasting, malevolent glow.

Rahim paused midshot and spun around, and his eyes immediately glossed over. However, he swallowed hard and guided Eshara to meet Niamh in combat. Thankfully, his father didn't make his appearance, but when Arawn would inevitably arrive, Rahim knew that he would be the one to confront him; he had to if he wanted any chance at saving him. But before Eshara could break formation, Damien and Noctis intercepted her, and Rahim hissed through his teeth. "Let us through."

"Her Majesty will never forgive me if I let you kill yourself." Disregarding the prince's warning, Rahim urged Eshara to continue; she swooped downward and made haste for Niamh and Fafnir as they broke away from Ashur's formation and began their destructive rampage over the buildings, progressing towards the general's army.

As Rahim followed through with his pursuit of Niamh, General Araneus' face twisted into a snarl when he saw his former captain leading his death fleet. Soon, they were upon the allied troops, but Ashur and his battalion ignored them and flew past the battlefield. Jade's chest swelled as he inhaled deeply, spreading out his ghostly white wings and tilting his head back like a venomous snake ready to strike. A small but intense black and red flame ignited within his maw, growing steadily larger until it erupted into an enormous blast igniting the earth below.

His fighters followed his great stream of dark fire as they unleashed their intense torrent of black flame downward in unison, their blasts burning the ground beneath, creating immense amounts of smoke. The hills and nearby trees from the Hinterlands instantly became emblazed by their cataclysmic inferno spreading with each passing second until it looked as though the whole world had caught fire.

Significant swaths of field and trees continued burning where the enemy Nidhoggr laid waste, endless flames unyielding with no other purpose but to destroy. Noctis and Obsidian led their formation and rode above the devastation, taking stock of the general's battle; upon Godfrey's signal, *Prepare to intercept,* the vampire nobles spurred their companions and began their descent upon Ashur's airstrike.

Araneus and Aracania dashed for their targets, ready for the next phase. When Aracania locked in on Ashur and Jade, she snarled as plumes of venom and acid built up around her maw, her wings snapping hard against the wind as she gained speed. **Shall we give our old captain a proper greeting?**

General Araneus made sure his pistol was loaded and that his sword was at the ready. *With pleasure.*

Ashur looked down below to savor the damage and allowed his former superior to intercept him. Aracania caught Jade in her talons, and the two dragons engaged in an aerial melee of claws and fangs. Both Jade and Aracania battled and roared, spiraling and jerking towards the earth. The general pulled hard on his reins until his knuckles turned white as he did his best to stay in the saddle, but Ashur readied his sword. Araneus fidgeted as he went to grab his pistol, but the swirling dragons made it difficult as they bit and raked one another with claws, slicing significant wounds and leaving deep furrows along their necks and sides.

Disengage now. Let go!

Ignoring her handler's command, Aracania snapped at Jade, but the Pearlscale clamped his fangs on her neck and sank his teeth in. Jade then ripped his maw away as venom boiled and built up in his mouth while Aracania attempted to push him away with every ounce of her strength, but her wounds weakened her considerably.

While Araneus struggled to hold on, Jade bit at him next; the general twisted and avoided the dragon's snake-like strikes, plumes of green and black venom puffed from Jade as the dragon continued snapping and biting. Aracania did her best to keep her rider out of harm's way, but the dragons soon became entangled as they spiraled. Araneus saw the built-up neon bile in the back of Jade's throat when his maw opened wide, like the entrance to Oblivion itself.

Then, when the general least expected the salvation, Silver, in wing-less dragon form, swooped in from the veil of black smoke and grabbed Jade in his talons, prying him away. Vulduin gripped Silver's golden horns tightly, not having faith in his belts and carabiners.

Ashur spun in his seat and swung his sword wildly, leaving nary a nick against Silver's hide, but Vulduin retaliated with a wrist flick and summoned a tangled mess of chains, tearing through Ashur's defenses. The straps of his saddle strained against the twists and turns, and Vulduin's chains ripped through its thick but damaged buckles; when the general noticed, he pulled out his sword and sliced through the frayed leather. His blade made a clean cut straight into Jade's exposed side, and the harness couldn't withstand the Pearlscale's sudden bucks and mid-air thrusts to shake away the pain. The saddle slid off Jade's back, and Ashur fell and plummeted to the burning ground.

The general continued holding onto Aracania for dear life as she struck back; Jade was fully exposed against two rampaging dragons and a Chain Master, and Aracania sank her fangs into Jade's neck. Silver and Vulduin kept the Pearlscale detained, and Aracania chomped deeply with a sickening crunch and spread out her wings to catch her fall before the velocity grew too great, and they released Jade's body. They watched as the white dragon fell, and he joined his former rider in the void.

The general collected his bearings as he groaned and panted but put his sword away after Aracania re-positioned herself, allowing Silver to heal her quickly. He roared after finishing his work, and Aracania stretched and twisted her neck, reassuring Araneus she was well again.

The Shadow Emperor gave the general a firm salute once he withdrew his chains, and he and Silver made haste for Rune Citadel.

In the meantime, Noctis and Obsidian chased after Ashur's air fleet while General Araneus and Aracania remained behind to help Colonel Cyres, Volt, and the Steelmane brothers maintain control of the battlefield. Instead of dealing with the enemy head-on, the vampire nobles signaled to their formation: *Increase altitude and prepare volley.*

They soared above the clouds and out of sight. A sudden shriek pierced the air before Godfrey ordered their airstrike, and a regal black dragon emerged from the smoke and plumes of black Aether fire, dashing across the sky to join the allies. Lord Godfrey was about to set his targets on attacking the new dragon, but it faced Damien and Noctis, dipping its head to reaffirm its allied position; the dragon bellowed a deafening roar and took its place among their battalion. Silver and Vulduin turned back at the sound of the new dragon's call: it was Ebony. Silver felt slight relief to see that she had answered Selena's plea for help.

The enemy Nidhoggr paid no attention as they continued their widespread and devastating air raid. The black fire grew exponentially, sweeping across the ground and consuming the desolate land. Still retaining their v-shaped formation, Godfrey signaled to his riders: *Commence fire.*

Their battalion, Ebony included, made the nosedive. Following their mighty and thundering roars, they unleashed jets of black fire blasts upon widening their jaws, striking their foes from the sky, their meteors raining from the darkened heavens. Ashur's dragons were struck down, spiraling out of control towards the earth and meeting their explosive demise.

Amidst their catastrophic display, Damien signaled to his other riders, and they swooped downward, meeting the remaining enemies in close combat; both sides clashed and got caught in a flurry of claws and teeth. Both Noctis and the Prince of Shadows were the ultimate assault pair against what remained of Ashur's air fleet. The feral leader was much larger than the others, easily taking down one behemoth after the next through quick deep furrows along their sides and ripping their masks from their acid-drenched skulls.

While Noctis managed the physical offensive, Damien used shadow magic, taking down enemy riders before they could launch a single bullet or cast magic. He vanished from the saddle and reappeared on the enemy harness, slicing their throats in one quick movement. One after another, Prince Damien took down the enemy fliers, and Noctis delivered his final blow while the rival Nidhoggr was distracted by their handlers' deaths.

Noctis swiveled his long neck around, hissing through clamped fangs to see what remained of the opposing formation breaking apart. The enemy split into several groups of three and began targeting the vampire lord's straggling riders, one attacking the front while two came in from the side. The allied rider manifested tendrils of shadow magic twisting in circular motions, thrusting towards his attackers as his companion belched forth a massive and deadly torrent of ebony flames, consuming and destroying another enemy fighter. As the other assailants arrived, helping their singled-out comrade overwhelm the vampire soldier, allied reinforcements arrived. Their undead masked dragons fell before the ferals' flurries of claws and snapping fangs, their tenacity proving too great for the Lich's forces to handle.

The sky bled from Ashur's fleet clashing with Lord Godfrey's; the allied forces maintained their tactical advantage by following Rahim's battle plans despite the enemy's sheer numbers. Damien and Noctis swooped past their exposed riders when they sent their distress flags, baiting the enemy away before finishing them through their combined might.

Godfrey and Obsidian swept overhead, tearing through one fighter from the next with claws and magic. When a group of five from Ashur's dismantling air fleet surrounded Obsidian, Godfrey snapped his fingers. Five apparition doppelgangers of himself appeared behind and beheaded the enemy riders, their heads and bodies thrown overboard. As the Nidhoggr retaliated for their fallen handlers, they spewed intertwined streams of black fire and poison at the manifestation of flesh and blood. Through growls and hisses, Godfrey manipulated and countered their breath abilities ten-fold; the mirrored blasts struck them down from the sky.

Ebony joined beside Obsidian and Noctis, and before the enemy could swarm her like angry bees, her chest swelled, the air echoing and resonating from her ever-enlarging lungs. Once they recognized the similar display to Thor's previous power from Alfheim's initial assault, Damien quickly sent the flag signals to the nearby allies: *Take cover.*

The tremendous shudder made the sky quiver; once the others cleared away and upon opening her maw, Ebony released a terrible wave of noise and wind, her rampaging gale storm tearing the remaining enemy Nidhoggr to shreds. Her typhoon roared louder than thunder and ensued devastation of cataclysmic proportions against her adversaries, the flames and trees writhing and flailing as her squall ripped away branches and rocks. When she finished through the snap of her fangs, she met Damien's and Noctis' smoldering eyes. The prince and the feral leader tilted their heads forward in mutual understanding.

In the meantime, Kain and Maria made their way to rendezvous with General Araneus within the city. While Kain readied his bombs to drop on the Dreygur below, Maria held her bow taut with arrows nocked, firing one right after another with such quick precision that even their allies were stunned. Kain lit the fuse on another explosive and dropped it into a massive horde; the ground beneath them erupted within moments, and the Dreygur were blown to pieces.

As the two did their best to help while still airborne, Vyrilion spun around and returned to the portal. Tilting his head back and spewing forth another deadly conflagration of dark Aether, he strafed row after row of Dreygur to keep General Araneus' army from being exhausted.

Vyrilion dropped down when Kain and Maria ran out of ammo, pulled out their melee weapons amidst dismounting, and joined the grounded onslaught. Vyrilion leapt back into the air, adhering to Ysyra's chirps and clicks, and the two breathed black fire across the ground, adding flames to Oblivion's firewall. Holding his breath, Vyrilion swept his Aether flames across the land, wiping out a contingent of Dreygur rushing in. Ysyra crisscrossed her streams, still fixating her blazing eyes on Cyres, ensuring he remained safe; the colonel's stamina knew no bounds as he danced across the battlefield with his magnificent broadswords, chopping off heads left and right.

However, the alliance halted when a shrill shattered their ears; the necromancer himself appeared beyond the growing wall of dark flames burning around Alfheim, his raven wings carrying him above the chaos. Ignoring them, he lifted his bare-boned hand, burning with eerie red and purple fire, and extinguished the firestorm encircling Oblivion's gate. The Dreygur waiting within Death's realm resumed pouring forth from the portal as the firewall dissipated.

As the allies grew overwhelmed and hopeless, the Lich slowly swept his hand over the battlefield. The fissure protecting the general's ground troops had sewn itself back together, and the Dreygur and Nidhoggr that the allies defeated in battle reappeared in plumes of shadow, their reanimated corpses re-joining the cataclysm.

When General Araneus saw the massive onslaught of resurrected corpses, he almost lost hope; Aracania swept overhead, and he yelled and screamed words of encouragement for his soldiers to keep fighting. Yet, despite their efforts, the Lich's army remained relentless: sooner or later, General Araneus feared that the Lich's forces would wear the allies down, and there would be no stopping them.

*****

Thor ignored Selena's struggles in reaching past his tainted thoughts; Selena gracefully dodged torrents of dark Aether erupting from her once-beloved companion's maw and continued putting more distance between them. She flew over the destruction that brought Alfheim to ashes in the first place, and her heart shattered like glass to see the eternal blazes burning across the world, but another blast attack from Thor made her focus.

He relentlessly spewed his Aether breaths, and she strained against his black conflagration, threatening to swallow her. Weaving an evasive path, she brought her celestial wings in and created an air bubble, deflecting Thor's dark fire, and zipped over the burning city towards the forest of black flame. She made the steep climb heavenward, every sweep of her wings bringing her farther away from Thor. When she reached the growing and rumbling clouds, Selena searched anew for any signs of her dragon brother.

Lightning struck the sky, and she almost spiraled down in shock when she saw Thor below; his bulky maw opened wide, ready to clamp his fangs into her. Her tail skimmed across his corrupted hide, missed by barely a breadth's touch; Selena dodged and made a nose-dive, but the velocity proved too great as she made her sharp descent. She did her best to transition from flying to running, but she slid on her belly against the ground, leaving a massive gouge in the earth upon impact.

Thor's thundering roar bellowed above her. He crashed into the earth, but he caught himself and landed on all fours, legs wobbly as he kept his wings unfurled. Her vision grew blurry and fading, and Selena changed back into an elf as she recovered. Seeing Thor approaching her with heavy steps, Selena's sight focused, and she forced herself to stand up and face him. Her hand went straight for Dragonheart, but she paused her draw.

Thor, stop!

He came to an immediate halt; from within Thor's mind, there came a beacon of light amidst the darkness, beckoning him forward, and for the first time, the most beautiful sound in the world rang within his tainted thoughts. His nostrils flared, head thrashing around, and Selena finally heard his voice. **I-I can't....**

I know you, and I understand this isn't you doing this.

Thor lowered his head and roared to the ground; his irises swirled with the eerie, consuming purple mist upon peering up. He ignored her calls and approached slowly, snarling as burning black embers streamed from his nostrils.

Selena unsheathed Dragonheart, its rosy tint catching the sky's crimson hue, but threw her sword to the ground. As tempted as she was to use her blade, her love for Thor grew so intense that her heart would burst; she could never bring it upon herself to hurt him.

No longer fighting the Dark Master's control, Thor rushed to her with sparks of black Aether fire flaring from his mouth and nostrils, but Selena neither faltered nor buckled. *This darkness isn't you. I made a vow always to protect you.*

As he got close, Thor came to an immediate halt and tightened his jaw when she didn't retaliate. With his fangs bared, he lowered his head, plumes of dark Aether wafting from his maw. Yet, he withheld attack.

The Lich noticed from afar, and his voice boomed in their minds. *What are you doing? I order you to kill her.*

With no regard to the black flames threatening to burn her, Selena touched Thor's head, her sparkling emerald eyes meeting his fading purples. *You're my brother and my best friend, and I love you. Please, come back to me.*

His eyes flickered, and the fog lifted; the dark Aether fire that consumed his body vanished. His blood-diamond scales sparkled from the eclipse's glare, and his golden chest plate gleamed like his Divine fire that the Lich could never extinguish.

And you're my sister. I love you, too. Selena's heart felt like it was about to explode from hearing his voice; she couldn't hold back her tears as she wrapped her arms around his neck. Thor wrapped his neck around her body to hug her back, but he took a step back, and his now amber eyes widened in shock at seeing her new appearance for the first time. **My dear, what happened to you?**

It's a very long story.

Fluttering feathered wings demanded their attention as the Lich suddenly flew over the pair, interrupting their reunion. "So be it. You made your choice, and you will share her fate." With one massive wing flap, he soared high above the swirling storm.

Gritting her teeth, Selena retrieved Dragonheart, and Thor assisted her back onto his harness, its royal blue sapphire blazing against the dark energy radiating from the eclipse. As he was in mid-leap, her frantic hand fished about in her pocket to pull out the golden timepiece, and she whispered, "Vor'noctes." It immediately assumed the shape of Revelation in a flash of blinding blue Aether. She gripped the reaper scythe's icy handle, and the two pursued the necromancer in what they expected to be their final battle.

Are you with me, brother?
I'm with you, my twin flame.

*****

CHAPTER 24: INTO THE INFERNO

While Lord Godfrey and General Araneus resumed their offensive and stopped the enemy's rain of fire, and Selena and Thor took their fight to the Lich, Rahim pursued Niamh. She and Fafnir were upon the allies; when Fafnir belched forth his dark Aether destruction over parts of the general's army, Rahim spurred Eshara and held on tight as the two sped after the pair. The wind howled, and the crimson clouds swirled overhead as Fafnir moved with haste and purpose towards the city. Eshara flew through when he and Niamh vanished behind the veil. However, suddenly Fafnir appeared before Eshara, and the two dragons were set on a collision course.

"Niamh," Rahim called as the two masked dragons banked to avoid one another, Niamh grunting as her companion thrashed and bucked. Rahim checked to ensure that she was still safe as Fafnir and Eshara broke apart, struggling against the turbulence, and both Niamh and Rahim were tested by the jerky flight. Yet, Eshara remained steady and flew by Fafnir's side. "Niamh—it's me, Rahim."

She didn't answer but focused on the black fire consuming the world below as the newly risen undead army surged forward. His eyes froze like a pond in winter when she turned a deaf ear to his pleas. However, her head swiveled back to face him, and his lips trembled when he saw her eyes weren't hers; they glowed purple like Thor's after he gave in to darkness. "Niamh… No." Rahim's voice cracked.

When he saw that she readied her sword, Rahim and Eshara flew away to avoid direct combat. During their escape, the same ominous tone rang in his ears from when he first confronted his father. His head cranked to the side as he heard the slow flaps of a great dragon; his heart nearly burst from his chest upon seeing Arawn and his companion approaching through steady wing beats. Arawn's masked dragon shrieked, and Rahim prompted Eshara to avoid it. She roared with plumes of black flame erupting from her clenched fangs, but she dodged as the enemy dragon struck at her and swept herself across the burning sky to flee. However, Arawn hovered aloft, not giving chase.

Fafnir roared and made a terrifying sound that Rahim surmised was laughter; Fafnir's voice made the hair on the back of his neck stand on end. He and Niamh soared through the billowing clouds after the fleeing Rahim and Eshara; the two zipped past Arawn and his companion, who only watched the scene with a smirk.

The storm impeded Niamh's pursuit; Rahim and Eshara broke through the clouds to find the eclipse's illumination. They hovered, searching for any signs of their enemies, but an eruption of black fire burst through the crimson spires from below. Eshara veered away as Niamh and Fafnir flew upwards, and Fafnir belched another dark Aether at Rahim and Eshara as they escaped.

When Rahim thought they put more distance between them and Niamh, Fafnir intercepted the pair and clutched Eshara in his hind claws while snapping his fangs at Rahim. Eshara roared, slashing her tail against Fafnir's head while clawing at his exposed neck, black venom boiling within her maw. She released her breath attack, yet Fafnir only winced as he snaked his head around to strike at Rahim. Instead of fighting back, he squirmed away to avoid Fafnir's fangs. His hand grasped his revolver, but he didn't dare to use it against Niamh. "Please."

When it was clear she still wouldn't answer, Rahim gritted his teeth, but he withdrew his hand from his weapon and struggled to grasp Eshara's reins. His eyes caught the gleam of Niamh's sword as she unsheathed it and pointed it at him, and Rahim couldn't hold back any longer. "I love you."

Niamh stopped, her face twisted, and threw her sword overboard without warning. She snatched Fafnir's reins before placing her fists against her ears, screaming while their dragons tail-spun and spiraled towards the ground. Fafnir ignored Niamh's cry as he sank his claws deeper into Eshara's hide, but with one last effort before crashing down, Eshara twirled her body around and exhaled a torrent of black fire, scorching Fafnir's hind legs. He finally released his grip and recoiled while Niamh thrashed about, and Rahim got to hear her voice for the first time since Snowhaven, though disgruntled. "Ugh...."

His heart soared when he realized that Niamh was beginning to break free from the Lich's control. Fafnir's eyes widened; he roared and pushed himself away as the pair screamed and shrieked. Eshara strained against the fall, wing muscles burning like the fire that now devoured nearly half of Armageddon. To Rahim's dismay, it wouldn't be long before the entire continent burned in black flames and spread to Mirrorhold and Runefell.

Eshara finally caught herself before the speed grew too great, and she reached the ground. Fafnir roared above them as he swooped down and landed nearby, still swaying and fighting against the necromancer's control as he stood on all fours, tail swishing with his wings unfurled. Rahim looked up to see Niamh riding assuredly astride Fafnir; her big, teal blue eyes that he admired were back to normal, brightened under her sandy hair. His heart fluttered out of his chest, and his smile widened when she smiled.

She shamefully looked down to see her fully clad in black and red military attire, but Fafnir's faint guttural voice could only muster, "My dear Niamh." When his roars ceased, he lowered his head and laid down on his belly as she dismounted. Though Eshara snarled through her fixated gaze, prepared for another assault from Fafnir as black blood oozed from her fresh wounds, Rahim assured her they were well. He dismounted and rushed over to embrace Niamh without another word, ignoring the world's cataclysm.

Yet, their touching reunion was only short-lived when Rahim saw the shimmer of metal wings emerge from the smoke, and Arawn approached them through the smoldering grounds with a readied sword. Rahim pushed Niamh away as he pulled out his revolver, and both Fafnir and Eshara launched themselves at Arawn and his masked dragon.

Arawn, alerted by the dragons' pursuit of him from the crunching sound of their heavy steps, swung his dragon bone steel sword at Rahim's companion, the blade leaving a clean, deep wound through her neck. Rahim wasn't sure what kind of enchantments Arawn used on his sword, but they were enough to bring down a Nidhoggr quickly. Usually, their weapons wouldn't harm the undead dragons save by attacking their masks, yet Arawn brought Eshara down with one clean slice.

Out of retaliation for his fallen new comrade, Fafnir came from the side and slashed at him with long sword-like claws. Arawn lost his weapon arm, but he didn't recoil or flinch from the attack. Watching Fafnir hacking off Arawn's limbs disgusted Rahim, but he couldn't hold back his stinging tears when Eshara slowly succumbed to the fatal wound, her boiling black blood pouring over the ground like a waterfall. He rushed over and placed a hand on her snout, whispering words of comfort until she slipped into Oblivion.

To protect its rider, Arawn's dragon thrashed from the darkness and threw itself on top of Fafnir before he could make another strike. The two snarling undead creatures rolled around, biting and clawing at each other, and eventually, Fafnir reared his head back and sank his fangs deep into its grisly hide. He tightened his jaw to keep Arawn's companion from breaking free, and soon, it grew limp after one last sickening crunch, and Fafnir tore its neck and mask open, black blood splattering everywhere.

Niamh drew her sword and took Rahim's side, her hand trembling; Rahim gnashed his teeth as he had to watch Eshara pass away, and to his dismay and distraught, Arawn showed no remorse for the death of his friend but instead just cocked his head slightly. His father wouldn't react or show any human emotion, and Rahim finally accepted the loss of his father.

"Dad." Rahim's voice cracked and shattered like glass. Arawn grabbed his fallen sword with his still intact arm, striding for the two. He wheeled around and swung his blade at Niamh first; she dodged, but just barely. The sword's tip cut through her military garb and left a gash against her skin. Rahim roared and lunged forward as he whipped out his gun, using the butt of his revolver to bash in Arawn's head. His skull caved in like the Dreygur's weak rotting flesh, but Arawn's next uninterrupted swing aimed for Rahim's neck.

Niamh raised her sword and lopped Arawn's other hand off before he could make his blow. Rahim backed away, the revolver still ready, but watched as Fafnir snaked across the ground and spewed out a torrent of black Aether that consumed Arawn—his expressionless face as his blazes burned neither stirred nor faltered.

Rahim remained transfixed as the lifeless husk belonging to the walking dead was reduced to a pile of rubble and ash. He pulled Niamh into a hug before closing his eyes; Fafnir wobbled over and extended a protective arm, bringing the two close to his chest while groaning in despair.

*****

In the meantime, after saving General Araneus and Aracania from Ashur and Jade, Silver and Vulduin continued their course for Rune Citadel. Vulduin hadn't uttered a word since they began their invasion, but the closer they got to Vidar, the edgier he became.

As they approached the wide window leading into Vidar's big office, Silver reared his head back and spewed out a torrent of azure fire, shattering the glass and setting the furniture inside ablaze. Vulduin transformed into a massive red dire wolf in mid-leap before Silver entered, his sleek and shiny pelt shining in the eclipse's dark light. His claws clicked against the broken glass, crimson fur bristling along his spine and tail.

The Red Wolf sniffed and searched for any trace of the Council leader, but to Vulduin's dismay, Vidar wasn't there. Silver resumed his usual guise upon landing, but he stood by the destroyed window while Vulduin took it upon himself to search. His efforts weren't all for naught, as the two found a trunk sitting by the wall; Silver's flames wouldn't touch it. When Vulduin rushed over to open the chest with his snout, his eyes lit up when he saw the four dragon eggs from the Mythic Flight.

Vulduin peered at Silver from over his shoulder and nodded to the precious cargo. *I want you to take these eggs and bring them someplace safe.*

"Of course. I hope these little ones weren't affected by the Lich's dark magic." Silver came over to observe their shells, but Vulduin shut the lid before he had the chance and bolted away. Silver huffed as he grabbed the chest and moved it by the window. "What exactly do you think this will accomplish?" Vulduin shook his head. "I understand how you feel. I felt the same way after what happened to Alfheim and Snowhaven."

Vulduin paused when he finally caught Vidar's scent, and he immediately changed back; his head whipped around, but he ignored what Silver said. "Are you sure that your enchantments on my equipment will break through Vidar's wards?"

Silver sighed. "Yes, but I hope you will choose forgiveness. Otherwise, you'll only hurt yourself while watching your enemy fall." Vulduin only grunted and turned away, dashing through the fire and out the door, and Silver remained behind, hanging his head. "Please do the right thing, my friend."

Vulduin rushed through the dark tunnel before reaching the main floor with the glass dome covering overhead. The sound of the crystal-clear running water from the mermaid fountain splashed in Vulduin's ears, and the looming eclipse painted the marble floors red. Vidar emerged from behind the spring with a huge smirk. "I see you're still alive."

Vulduin's mouth curved into a sneer when his eyes landed upon the wretched half-elf. "It's time to settle this once and for all. After we take our home back, I want you and your associates to leave and never return."

"You want Rune Citadel back? Fine. Come and take it from me. It's just you and me."

Vulduin wasted no time; he flicked his wrists and summoned his magic chains from his jacket's sleeves. The metallic gleam sparkled in Vidar's eyes, but his expression changed when he realized the chains were upon him, wrapping around the plump official like a snake coiling around its prey. Vulduin turned his hands into fists and dug his nails into his palms until they bled, his links tightening to an inescapable death grip.

Instead of begging him to stop, Vidar embraced the attack and sneered. His arm quivered, and Vulduin's eyes widened when his chains shattered like glass, and Vidar was free once more. "How clever of you to figure out how to break my wards. Was it Silver's doing? However...." Vidar's voice trailed off as he looked up at the ceiling. Shadow figures—eleven in total—dropped below and landed before him. "The Council still has other secrets."

Vidar's posse kept themselves consumed by a dark veil. When the shadows rushed at him, Vulduin spun around and ran. A black beam erupted beneath his feet, but he dodged it by jumping away and flipping forward. Two of Vidar's followers flung a couple of dark Aether blasts at him, but his lightning-fast reflexes countered by using his chains and deflecting their homing attacks. Gritting his teeth and his face burning, Vulduin summoned another set of metallic tendrils targeting each member, but the figures vanished in a puff of smoke and reappeared on the other side of the room.

Yet, their battle abruptly paused when the mountain trembled from a dragon's thunder. Silver busted through the glass dome in his dragon form, landing between Vidar's associates, and spewed forth his deadly blue conflagration, catching the shadow figures within his sapphire inferno and turning to dust.

Vulduin evaded the raining diamond shards and made a u-turn at the end of the room; sidestepping the snake-like dragon, he lunged straight for Vidar, unleashing another volley of chains. The metal cut and slashed at the vile creature in different areas of his body, bloody when he was bound. Vulduin clenched his teeth as he focused every ounce of energy on squeezing out what remained of Vidar's pitiful life. Before his surviving subordinates could help, Silver stood in their way and created a wall of blue flames, separating them from their leader; two drew too close to his fire and incinerated upon contact.

To Vulduin's surprise, Vidar let out a whimpering noise, and the chains paused their mortal coil; Silver flickered his tail, keeping his gaze fixed upon Vulduin, anticipating what his friend would do next. Vidar spat out blood. "I did so many bad things, and you deserve revenge. Do it. Do it, now!"

Vulduin tightened his grip again but stopped. "As much as I hate you… I just can't." With quivering hands, he released his chains, and Vidar, now a bloody and broken man, fell to the ground. The half-elf cowered, but he scrambled to his feet and limped to the other side of the room, escaping from the castle as fast as he could.

Convinced they no longer posed a threat, Silver released his fire prison, and the rest of the Council followed their wounded leader as he and Vulduin watched them like a hawk. Once the Council fled, Vulduin finally snapped at Silver. "Where are the eggs?"

Silver changed back to normal and readjusted his spectacles, ensuring they remained in place. "They're still safe in the office." He reached over to put a comforting hand on Vulduin's shoulder. "I'm proud of you."

Clinching his fists to his sides, the Shadow Emperor remained tranced by Vidar's escape, perhaps contemplating his mercy as a weak mistake, but he shook his head and returned to the office with Silver and retrieved the chest.

*****

Meanwhile, Thor and Selena flew above Alfheim, chasing the necromancer into the inferno. Gripping Revelation, Selena peered at the blood-red clouds swirling into a devastating maelstrom swallowing the three. The eclipse vanished behind the black sky, a ferocious gale enveloping the pair, and the Lich disappeared.

Selena lost her bearings and struggled to remain aloft as the two fought through the tremendous ensuing storm. Yet Thor remained in control of his flight; he arched his neck around and shuddered when he saw the peril that he and Selena escaped. She could no longer see the battlefield but did her best to guide Thor through the churning clouds. Thor relied on his instincts when she couldn't, keeping himself level amidst the tempest sky.

Lightning erupted, and the two saw a silhouette of the Lich flash through the ensuing darkness, his smoldering pupiled eyes burning against empty sockets. The necromancer soared higher than his pursuers and summoned his solid black reaper scythe. He spun, creating circular waves of dark Aether that grew to massive proportions, expanding outward in shockwaves, parting the squall. Thor dove to dodge, and Selena held up her Aether hand, creating an azure shield protecting her and Thor, absorbing another black Aether blast shooting through the crimson clouds. Thor spewed forth a torrent of flame when the Lich's shadow neared them, but the necromancer followed up his attack with concentric rings of black fire erupting from swinging his scythe.

The attacks grew more prominent by the second, and Thor brought his wings together, protecting himself and Selena from being hit directly, and the force pushed the pair back. He then unleashed a blast of light at the

366

Lich as he straightened himself in the air, aiming his pulsating beam at the necromancer and sweeping it through the atmosphere. Ignoring the howling winds cutting through her face, Selena whirled her right hand and summoned streaks of light encircling her, flowing through the air in serene grace. When she slashed her hand down, the specs of Aether energy turned to rapid bullets firing directly at the Lich, the diamond-like shards parting and piercing the swirling plumed spires.

Instead of attacking back, the Dark Master encircled himself in a black sphere absorbing their magic and launched after the pair, his blades aimed directly at Selena. As Thor dodged again, Selena jumped off the saddle, resuming her dragon state to avoid the Lich's blades; her Divine light shattered the darkened storm as she arched her head back and exhaled a stream of blue Aether that bounced off the necromancer's dark shield.

Thor didn't have time to admire her new power, but he floated by her side, his eyes catching the gleam of her turquoise scales. **How will you get Revelation close to him?**

I don't know.

The pair were interrupted when the Lich screeched and imbued himself in a black aura. The darkness expanded and consumed all in its path, and when it vanished, Venexus changed into a different form: a massive skeleton cloaked in black wisps, the dark Aether dripping from his bones like oil. The monster's raven wings expanded three-fold and swept through the brewing storm. Coils of poison mist writhed around him like smoke and fog while fire erupted from his skull sockets and mouth. Selena's breath quickened, sweat dripping down her neck, and her jaw dropped in a silent scream.

His eerie voice rang like the tolls of Death's bell: "My reign has just begun."

Venexus swiped his newfound claws at Thor, who evaded quickly. He then aimed for Selena, who leapt at the necromancer instead of dodging, casting a beam of Aether at his striking hand from her maw. Their attacks collided in a fiery explosion, and the shock pushed the three back, but before Selena and Thor could collect themselves, Venexus suddenly reached for the pair.

Watch out!

Selena and Thor flew out of harm's way just in time; the two hovered above the Lich and countered with streams of Aether erupting from their jaws. Venexus held up his arms to block their attacks and followed it by shooting bursts of black fire with a wave of his hand. Selena and Thor flew in opposite directions to avoid his magic, and she exhaled another beam, aiming the blast at the necromancer. Thor cloaked himself in Aether flames and directly charged at the Lich's backside, but he grabbed them both with inhuman speed as they were upon him, his claws squeezing the two in hopes of crushing them to death.

Don't let him—

Argh!

The two broke free from his grasp with all their strength, spun around midair, and concentrated one last conjoined Aether blast to the Lich's chest, an eruption of blue energy shooting through and parting the crimson storm. Selena and Thor veered away as the necromancer made his downward spiral from the azure conflagration, vanishing through the squall. The two dragons dove through the clouds to look for signs of the Lich, and what they hoped was his defeat.

The speed was too incredible; the necromancer's crash left a crater at the site of impact, the earth rippling like the surface over water, and a shockwave of dust and destruction expanded outward—the buildings left standing crumbled and fell. When Selena landed and morphed to her elven guise, to hers and Thor's dismay, the Lich, now sodden and breathless, only reverted to his weakened state. "You cannot defeat me. I'm immortal and eternal—the death of all things."

Thor circled overhead, preparing for another attack, as Venexus showed no signs of giving up, although Selena knew he was growing weary. The eclipse peaked through the dark clouds, but she noticed how close it touched the horizon line; the Day of Eternal Darkness would soon end.

The Lich growled when he noticed it, too. His Dreygur army had dwindled, but hundreds of millions more still waited in Oblivion. However, the portal behind them began to shake violently, growing more unsteady with every passing moment. The mass amount of magic used to sustain it couldn't be contained and held for much longer; the earth would soon cave in and destroy the battlefield. Selena's friends were in immediate danger, but they were distracted and busy fighting off the released Dreygur to notice their impending doom.

The undead still waiting within Oblivion stopped rushing in when the earth quivered beneath their rotting feet. Cracks spiderwebbed across the ground, and the land caved in; the massive earthquake spreading across Oblivion swallowed the remaining Dreygur waiting to storm their world. Selena suddenly sprouted an idea, but she knew that Thor would detest it.

She threw Dragonheart down and did her best to keep Revelation steady. As much as she loved her sword, Revelation was her only chance at stopping the Lich, and she had to concentrate her efforts on maintaining Death's weapon.

Get out of there, now. Thor dove down like a falcon going after its prey. He stretched out his claws to snatch her away, but she rolled out of his reach. She grew imbued by Divine's light and took on her Aether dragon form, ignoring Thor's snarls as she flew after the tired Lich. **What are you doing?**

This war needs to end once and for all.

More cracks appeared underneath the portal. Before the Lich could react, Selena snatched his frailed body in a single scoop with her talons, trapping him in between her clawed prison. Grimacing at the thought of crushing and squeezing him like the dangerous insect he was, the Lich kept himself protected from any melee damage by shrouding himself in his dark Aether bubble. His magical pressure slowly pushed apart her paws, which eventually would force her to release her grip; before Thor could protest further, Selena dashed through the gateway.

Oblivion was desolate and endless. Rings of vaporous mist reflecting orange and green circled above in the abyssal sky, pouring into the empty spaces between the giant red rock towers scattering the lifeless realm. Selena was unnerved by the sepulchral silence compared to moments ago. The portal stood its ground, the chasm splitting in an eternal line across the domain.

Thor's growls turned as violent as the storm brewing around the gate, ready to explode at any given moment. An idea came to her upon noticing the mirrored placement of the black crystals tethered within Oblivion and their world. *What if I...?* Hesitant at first, but she saw no other way. *Perhaps I can—*

What are you playing at?

Selena deflected his boiling questions and dropped Venexus over the abyssal crack as the pressure grew too much. Before the necromancer could retaliate, she dashed towards the portal, snarling and turning a blind eye as Venexus soared from the cataclysmic void and pursued her. *Break the crystals from your side. We need to close the portal before it explodes and kills everyone.*

No, absolutely not. I will not help trap you in there. I'll find Silver, and we'll figure out what to do. Selena didn't ease her speed, and Thor's head frantically whipped around to find another solution that she had missed.

Lightning flashed from the tornado of clouds surrounding the portal, and the gate began to crack and crumble. Thor roared and dug his claws into the dirt before throwing himself at the gateway, preparing to make his way through until Selena said, *There's no time—leave me. I promise I will find my way back as soon as I can.*

No.

I'm not giving you a choice. Save Azrael; find and save the eggs after you destroy the crystals.

No! I've lost you once. I'm not going to lose you again.

The Lich was almost upon her, and she needed to make her decision. Even if she could defeat Venexus within Oblivion, she had no way of returning; Oblivion would serve as her eternal prison. Selena reared her head back with azure Aether erupting from her maw, and the Lich's shrill shattered her ears. "Stop—no!"

Before Venexus could impede her self-sacrificing act, Selena unleashed her torrent, shattering both gems on her side completely. *I'm sorry, my dear one.*

The gateway began crumbling from the sudden loss of energy. Selena's last image of Thor was his huge pupils dilating into slits and his lips raised over his sword-length ivory teeth. He roared to the bleeding sky in a beautiful and horrifying tableau upon unleashing his rage; nearly yielding to his despair, Thor destroyed the crystals on his end with a torrential beam of flame.

The gate's foundation exploded within Oblivion once it closed from their realm, and the portal vanished. Waves of dark energy blasted in every direction in concentric circles; she dropped down to avoid the aftermath, but the Lich was caught in the shockwave of destruction and flew backwards. The clouds above dissipated, and the lightning ceased.

Did I save them? Selena's heart crushed upon believing the worst, but she shuddered when the Lich laughed, a deafening screech slashing through her ears. Her eyes swelled when she could no longer hear Thor; he just returned to her and was lost again—the barrier between realms was enough to silence the two forever.

Selena gritted her teeth and forced herself to communicate with the dreaded necromancer, pushing through the ensuing darkness threatening to render her in pieces. *I'm not afraid of you anymore. You can't endanger or hurt anyone else again.*

The demon cracked his neck and looked at her over his shoulder, his everlasting frayed grin making her bristle. "*You're* trapped here. The Day of Eternal Darkness may be over, but I will find a way back. I always find a way, and I will get my dragon back. But first, I will enjoy tearing you *limb* from *limb!*"

Torrents of black and purple fire erupted from his mouth and hands. Selena flexed her claws and bared her fangs, battle-ready, as Venexus spun around, building circular waves of dark Aether flames expanding outwards. He then propelled himself after her, his raven wings sweeping across Oblivion.

Selena unleashed her azure blast upon widening her maw, and the Lich punched forward, shooting a fireball. Their two attacks collided into a fiery explosion, and the force of impact blasted the two away. She caught herself and landed on a stone pillar but raced upwards when Venexus returned with another black Aether blast, deflecting the attack by summoning a spherical barrier of celestial energy.

Selena dashed towards the necromancer; he dodged, but she spun and brought her wings in, gathering the Aether around her and unleashing it in circular waves upon unfolding her wings. Her attack slammed the Lich against the stone towers, and in fear and dismay, Venexus rocketed away. However, she launched at him, and her surrounding energy caught and carried him across the Oblivion wasteland.

As she flew with the necromancer caught within her energy like a fly in a spider's web, the two crashed through several rock spires before Venexus broke from her force. He flew to the top of a nearby tower, and before he could recover, Selena bounced off her paws and leapt from one side of the pillar to the next. With an ear-shattering roar, she summoned Revelation in a plume of smoke, swinging through her mental control and will. She almost made her death blow with Azrael's scythe, but the Lich's trembling fear made her buckle. Instead, the blade struck the rock beside him, and Revelation vanished; Venexus looked up, surprised by her sudden mercy.

Selena hovered beside him with her spectral wings still fanned out. *I will not end it this way, Aydin. I know you're still there.*

As if she anticipated his actions, the Lich reached out to cast another magical attack, but she maintained her position; with inhuman speed, she sliced his skeletal hand clean off with her ethereal claws. He cried in agonizing pain while cradling his severed arm. "How could—?"

Swallowing her fear, Selena reverted to her elven guise, hoisting Revelation over her shoulder while hovering over Oblivion's abyss; each step she took lit up with blue energy that kept her levitating midair. She found the courage to look straight into his smoldering eyes as she joined him on his rocky platform. "I should be asking you: how could you? All the horrible things you've done, all the people you've hurt and killed—Aydin, I know you're still there, and it's not you who's doing this."

Venexus laughed at her, his arm pinned to his chest. "You're weak, just like he is. Aydin is dead; I killed him hundreds of years ago."

"I don't believe that. You're not a demon, and you're still alive, Aydin. Come back."

The Lich reached up to backhand her away, but she waved her Aether hand within a single blink and summoned her energy sword; with one swift strike from the ethereal blade, his last intact arm suffered the same fate. "Curse you, little bitch! I will… I will not die so easily."

Selena ignored him and held her head high, knowing that the battle was over and that the Lich couldn't hurt her anymore. "Aydin, my mother forgives you," she continued, still flouting the Lich's taunts, "she is sorry to have caused you so much pain. My mother may not have loved you as you loved her, but you were still her best friend. She cared about you. Please, come back. It's time for you to wake up."

The Lich screeched once more and heaved over. What happened next took her by surprise: he was crying. "No, please. No more…." His trailing, hoarse voice no longer carried the grave's shrill; now, it sounded human.

Transfixed, she watched what remained of the necromancer collapse before her in his weakened state. His voluminous cloak vanished, leaving a broken man—arms now intact—in tattered rags for clothes trembling before her. Standing over a precipice and giving her once feared nemesis pity, her chest tightened; when he looked up at her, his dragon horns and skull evaporated in a plume of smoke. She saw the Lich's frayed and tired self for the first time. Now human, his greasy, long black hair flowed over his chiseled dirty face, dangling over his swollen, amber-colored eyes; his fragile voice trembled as he crawled across the rock, begging for her mercy. "No more. Please, just kill me."

Selena extinguished her Aether sword and tightened her fingers around Revelation, her eyes glistening with tears. "Aydin...."

"Yes, but not for long. Please, put me out of my misery. I-I can't... I don't have much longer before that *thing* comes back."

Her heart squeezed as she couldn't bring herself to do it. There must be another way. "This isn't right. I'm trying to save you." She dissented the choice. "No, I won't do it."

Aydin pushed himself up and dragged his feet to reach her; she stepped back as he threw his hands upon her shoulders to keep himself upright. "Do it before that monster comes back. Please, I beg of you. Kill me. Revelation will trap and eat that foul demon's soul. Let me finally rest in peace."

Even as Xyaxon's words chimed within her mind, Selena still couldn't be his executioner. He deserved a chance for salvation, but as she used Revelation to block him from approaching further, he reached up and gripped the blade until drawing blood upon his palm. "I want to help you."

Aydin smiled faintly. "You're just like her. Selena, was it? I kept hearing your name and your voice pulled me from the darkness, if only briefly—I thank you. I'll be fine. Please...."

Her look of trepidation betrayed her as her face glistened, and she pulled Revelation back after Aydin released his hold. Her head whipped around as she desperately wanted to escape Oblivion with Aydin and find Silver for a solution. She couldn't; she wouldn't. "You didn't deserve this."

"Who are we to decide on what we deserve? I've been waiting to greet Death like an old friend after so many years of torment and pain."

Death is the solace Aydin seeks. Her lips quivered as her cheeks grew drenched from tears, but she sputtered, "May you find peace."

A serene smile chased the darkness imprisoning his hopeless face; Aydin stood back and tilted his head up with both arms spread open, inviting Revelation's final strike.

I wish there were another way. Her trembling hands nearly released the scythe as she mentally prepared herself, but she tightened her grasp. She brought Death's weapon up to a full swing. Finally defeating her hesitation, she sliced the blade through Aydin, like a heated knife cutting through butter. *Goodbye, Aydin.*

The scythe glowed sky-blue upon the strike, and Aydin said with his last breath, "Thank you, Selena. I'm coming, Death, my old friend." The broken man faded to dust and ash as he fell, carried away by Oblivion's sepulchral gale across the desolate wasteland.

CHAPTER 25: BAPTISM OF FIRE

She froze, with Revelation still trapped in mid-swing as the song of Aydin's final hour chimed within her ears. The glow from Azrael's weapon flickered before extinguishing like a candle's flame, and Aydin's light from the endless diamond sky went out. *I'll always care and remember.*

Coming to terms with her new predicament, she lowered the scythe; Oblivion was now her eternal prison. "At least everyone else is safe. Maybe that was enough. I am sorry, Thor and Silver—I tried." As Oblivion's silence served as her new companion, Selena dropped to her knees and bowed her head in prayer for her friends' safety after setting Revelation down.

Yet, her head snapped upward upon hearing a lovely tune, as if someone played a gentle melody on the piano, and the most beautiful sound in the world returned to her: **My dear, can you finally hear me?**

Her heart was about to burst from her chest when Thor's voice twinkled within her consciousness like glittering starlight. *I'm so glad to hear you again, but how? Where are you? What's happening out there?*

I'm right behind you. Please, turn around. The landscape faded out of existence when she glanced over her shoulder, and Thor was there, his crimson hide blazing against the black velvet curtain. Her eyes flooding, she ran over and embraced him. Thor extended out a loving arm and drew her close to his chest; when the two broke apart, he allowed his long, crimson tongue to flow from his maw, and he licked her cheek. **You will never do that to me again.**

Hopefully, I won't have to. How did you get here?
I don't know. Somehow, I wound up here after we destroyed the portal.

Selena's eyes fell upon Revelation, and her guilt slowly overpowered her. *He was just a broken man. Did I do the right thing?*

You did what was necessary.

He may have been the one who caused all our misfortunes, but I didn't feel like that was the right way to defeat him.

Thor rubbed his snout against her back. **Allow me to send Aydin's soul a triumphant roar.** He stood on his haunches, reared his head back, and released his thunder while unfurling his wings.

Selena wiped her eyes and picked up Revelation, but the hair on the back of her neck stood on end when she suddenly sensed the two weren't alone; Thor fell into a deep growl as he picked up her uneasiness, tail swishing. "Indeed, that was most admirable." The two paused when their instincts were proven correct and looked at each other, for neither spoke.

The darkness melted away like spilt oil, and sudden light beneath their feet blinded the pair. As their visions adjusted, large numerals appeared upon a colossal ethereal platform manifesting itself into existence. The scene cleared, and Selena and Thor stood upon a giant clock face etched into the circular celestial glass—expansive as the ocean—floating freely in the night sky. A ticking sound echoed in their ears, and the clock's hands slowly drifted behind them, counting down the seconds. The cosmic ether adorned itself with infinite sparkling diamonds, stars dotting the black blanket; plumes of nebula clouds of blue and green burned like the northern lights—they wafted in Divine's vast pool. Together, they stood in ominous unbreakable silence.

My dear, look over there. Thor nodded to a giant blue and green orb floating in the nether below them.

What is that?

"That is your world," the voice said again. Both Selena and Thor spun around and flinched when they saw a giant standing across from them on the clock platform. The titan made Thor look tiny by comparison, towering over the two like a mountain. Its diamond-white full suit of armor trimmed in gold magnified the color of the eternal flames shaping its lion headdress helm. Spectral, feathered wings made of light protruded from under its flowing, black cloak, their massive length enveloping the divine cosmos.

Its left hand held a golden shield, shined to capture their perfect reflections like a mirror, while wielding a sword with the other. Ethereal amethyst wisps danced like flames across the wicked-looking ebony blade, shimmering against its black diamond pommel, and the carved grip matched the very image of the massive titan.

That sword looks familiar.

Thor snaked his head and snarled upon closer inspection. **It's Ragnarok, but how?**

Confusion enveloped the two as Ragnarok had been destroyed within the abandoned dwarven ruin. Selena took a step back and held up Revelation in defense. "Who are you?"

The giant strutted forward with Ragnarok pointed away, its footsteps making the ticking glass clock platform tremble and quake. "We've met before. Don't you remember?"

She squinted her eyes, a deep crease in her brow when the titan sounded familiar. "That voice... I know that voice."

Only when she came to the startling conclusion did he confirm: "Yes. It is I, Xyaxon."

Both Selena and Thor immediately bowed before the Divine after realizing their error and misjudgment. "What is happening? Where are we, and why are we here?"

"We are currently outside your world. I summoned you both here to congratulate you on finally defeating the Lich, Liongod. I must say, what you two did was quite admirable. Thanks to your efforts, I'm finally restored to my full power, and now, it is time."

The Divine's words unnerved her as her mind raced to different conclusions behind his meaning. "What do you mean? Time for what?"

Xyaxon ignored her. Instead, he looked out towards the void. "Time is an illusion. It's nothing more than an idea that events occur in a linear direction—always moving forward, never back. It's our endless symphony, and now, I believe that the time has come."

Selena's face turned pale, her heart beating like a ticking clock trapped within her throat. Thor growled through clamped fangs when Xyaxon avoided giving an immediate answer, ember shards blazing through his nostrils. **For what?**

Before Selena could repeat his question out loud, Xyaxon calmly replied. "For my will to be done."

She dreaded Xyaxon's possible implications, and her voice cracked. "What do you mean? What will?"

The Divine pointed his sword at the floating ball of water and land, and Ragnarok shimmered. "My will as it has always been: you two will bear witness as I create a new world by issuing the destruction of this one."

His devastating news struck Selena and Thor as the two had been fighting back for so long to prevent this from happening; at first, she believed she misheard the Divine, but as he raised Ragnarok, the harsh reality of his words began taking root. *Was this Xyaxon's cruel trick?* "Wait, no… No! We were trying to avoid that by stopping the Lich. This isn't right—you can't do that."

"Yes, I can." In an instant, Xyaxon slashed Ragnarok at their world; the Divine's baptism of fire created a crack of light that spread across its sky, growing with each tick their clock stage made. "Your world is dying; it's grown stagnant. Its destruction will be the start of a new beginning."

"I don't understand. You first told me that if I wanted to save our world, I would have had to defeat the Lich before the eclipse."

"Indeed, yes." Xyaxon's stoic voice frightened her.

Selena couldn't understand it and refused to believe that what he said was true. Still, they deserved an explanation. "Then… why?"

"You see, I allowed Venexus to possess the one you called Aydin and for him to overthrow Azrael, watching and waiting while he took over Oblivion. I foresaw your existence as a threat to my gambit. Initially, I planned on you not surviving your birth, but Silver intervened. Then, Venexus was supposed to sacrifice you to awaken Thor as the Destroyer of Worlds. When that failed, the demon's blood poison was your next intended end, but somehow, you fought it off—time and time again, you and your friends seemed to save your pitiful life. Yet, when the time came in Snowhaven, I realized that you proved invaluable.

"Because of your efforts, you returned Ragnarok to me by destroying its physical form." Xyaxon held out his sword and tilted the blade, examining the wicked ebony metal. The black diamond pommel gleamed with eerie intent. "It wasn't until after Snowhaven that I foresaw the Lich's defeat by your hand, Selena Liongod. By his demise, I, Xyaxon, have become more powerful than the other two Divines combined. The Lich was my vessel, and he became my sustenance with his death. That is why I allowed Azrael to bring you back from the Soul Gate, as his pathetic promise to protect you set all my plans into motion.

"Now that Venexus is gone, I am back to full strength. Everything you two did was in the pursuit of restoring my power to me. You brought about the destruction of your decaying world, and everything that happened was all part of my will. I warned you before, Liongod: remember in our first meeting? There is no stopping it as it has been foretold. Would you two sit here and stop the next world from being born?"

"Yes. We like this world, and we want to continue existing."

The next world will have to fend for itself.

"Perhaps, but how do you two know or understand the will of a god? It is my right alone to decide and change the fate."

Selena snarled. "I don't believe in that, and I don't believe in you," Xyaxon growled, but he staggered back as if Selena struck a blow, "that's not fair for you to toy with us—you're treating us like playthings. We all deserve the right to decide what kind of future we want. What about Aydin? His torment and pain were just for you—he was never given a choice."

"Aydin was just a pawn in my game, as are you and Thor."

Selena trembled as hot, angry tears streamed down her face. Her knuckle turned white over Revelation, but Thor gave her a warning growl, extending an arm to pull her away, helping soothe her fiery wrath and keeping her from lashing out at the Fallen Divine. Yet, she slipped away, allowing her fury to simmer. "This is just a game to you? A *game?* How could you allow these tragedies to happen? There is no justification for Aydin's agony. None of my friends deserved to suffer, and neither did I."

"That's how it's always been and will always be. Aydin was a noble sacrifice, and he did not die in vain. What you three have done for me shall be used for the betterment of all."

She held Revelation closer to her chest when Xyaxon's earlier argument of one life compared to millions suddenly made sense; she screamed and cursed his name when she never discovered his true intentions behind his various hints. "Did you not care about us at all? Your creations—we meant nothing. What was the point of creating us and our world?"

"Purpose? Your existence was just part of my experiment—nothing more." Xyaxon remained poised and indifferent to her anger as he explained without remorse.

Her voice shattered. "Experiment?"

"Your world was a result of my curiosity. I wanted to see what would happen if I made life in my image, or maybe I was lonely and wanted friendship. But I was wrong, and my creations were mistakes, yet I was sustained through controlling life. Destroying your broken and stale world to create a new one will allow life to resume and flourish, just as I've done many times before."

Selena made one final attempt to plead with the Fallen Divine. "That's not how it's supposed to work, and only we have the right to decide for ourselves. Life can continue to grow and evolve if you allow it."

Thor's snarls and growls made the ethereal platform tremble. **I serve no king nor god, and we will not grovel at your feet. We live by our will alone.**

Xyaxon turned away when he realized he couldn't sway them. "I see. It was foolish of me ever to think that you would understand. It is such a shame, as I've always admired you both. Pity. It will cause me great pain to end you, but so be it."

"We won't let you destroy our world. We will stop you." Selena held up Revelation, and Thor roared in agreement.

Xyaxon held up Ragnarok and his shield before suddenly vanishing and reappearing right behind the pair; he slashed his blade at Selena's back. She spun on her toes and blocked the attack with her scythe, but the impact from the massive sword pushed her back as she slid across the ethereal glass.

Thor summoned a cloak of fire mixed with lightning protecting his hide and charged after Xyaxon. The god dodged and remained fixed on defending himself against the rampaging dragon; Selena used this to her advantage and ran straight for him at inhuman speed, Revelation at the ready; she sliced through him, but to her dismay, it was like cutting the air. "Death's blade cannot harm me." Xyaxon bashed her away with his shield, and she fell back, tumbling to her knees.

Thor rushed to stand between her and Xyaxon, snarling through his teeth; he draped his wings over her, ensconcing Selena within his coils. **Don't you dare touch her!**

"I had expected more from you two, but no matter. I will make this quick." Xyaxon stepped forward with Ragnarok raised over his head, the sword's shadow looming over the two. As soon as he made what would have been the final blow, his attack was blocked by another blade. Selena's sword—Dragonheart.

The one who wielded it—"Azrael." She never thought she would ever be happy to see him again. He stood over her and Thor in his human form with a ball of light circling above his head, flickering like a beautiful, golden flame.

"Don't forget Doragon." Azrael nodded to his spirit companion, and the glowing orb zipped happily around Selena and Thor.

"You two are okay."

"I've told you before that we'll be back. Death keeps his promises." Azrael winked and waved Dragonheart triumphantly over his head.

Xyaxon staggered back. "How can that be? I foresaw your destruction...."

"It looks like you're not as all-knowing as you think, *little lion*."

His brother growled and prepared for another attack, but Azrael blocked it again, Dragonheart on par with Ragnarok's strength. Their brewing battle was interrupted by a thundering roar; Ulrich, the Emerald Dragon, circled above and landed beside Thor, his massive weight slightly tilting the celestial platform. The Divine's sparkling green hide matched the wafting nebula clouds, his unfurled wings catching the ethereal light beams like stained glass. As if the current situation wasn't demanding his attention, Ulrich casually asked, "Am I late?"

"About bloody time, as always," Azrael smiled before nodding to his scythe and added, "Thanks for saving us."

Selena's eyes flooded as she stood up. "Thor and I should be the ones thanking you and Doragon."

"Don't be daft. I'll trade you; I've waited so long to get my weapon back." When Azrael and Selena exchanged blades, a smile of satisfaction played upon his lips. "Give my thanks to Silver when you return, will you? I wanted to keep Revelation safe from *him*." His chest swelled with each deep breath as the storming rage steeped within him at Xyaxon's actions. "I can't believe that you planned this to dispose of Ulrich and me from the beginning. You banished me from Oblivion, knowing that it was Venexus. What's worse is that *you* let him."

"You better watch your tongue, or your defiance will be the end of you right here and now."

"No, I will not take orders from you anymore. This time, you will listen to me." Xyaxon snarled through his flaming helm but did not draw his sword. "For so many years after you and Ulrich chose to banish me, all I ever wanted was to make amends. I wanted my brothers to accept me back again. But you lied to me, and you lied to Ulrich. We will stop you, for we can't exist without them. Have you truly forgotten that, brother?"

Xyaxon roared. "I am no longer your brother. Do you and Ulrich think you can stand against me? I am more powerful than all of you combined."

"Oh, how lovely. It's always fighting, fighting, and more fighting. I honestly detest hearing you ramble on— you're worse than Silver. Revelation couldn't harm you before because I wasn't the one using it. Now," before Xyaxon could react, Azrael jumped up at incredible speed and slashed through his right shoulder before landing behind him, "it can."

The fire lion titan knelt as he dropped Ragnarok and held his injured shoulder. "Curse you, Death."

Ulrich roared, unfurling his wings as they transformed, becoming like ethereal energy. An orb, burning as bright as the sun, floated above his horned crown as streams of fire writhed around his horns. He snaked his head down to the pair while flickering his tail.

"I never lost hope that you two would return. I feared you were too far gone, Divine One, but you two never cease to amaze me." Ulrich turned to face Xyaxon and roared, a thundering testament to his fury. "But you betrayed us—all of us! I've stood by and watched you control everything for far too long. Since the day you banished our brother, I remained by your side, and not a day passes by that I don't regret it. I neither opposed nor threatened you, but you still decided to curse me a mad god. All we ever did was to please you, and you punished us."

As Azrael stepped forward, Doragon zipped in circles above his head, and the two disappeared in an orb of black energy. Revelation awakened Death's proper form as he and Doragon combined forces when the magic disappeared: a seven-headed beastly dragon, his metallic scales radiating with purple and red Aether energy. Upon his main head were four crown-shaped horns similar to Ulrich's, while the other six only had one curved spike. Wisps of black and purple Aether plumed from the backs of his seven long necks, his onyx tail slithering behind him like a snake as he inched closer to Xyaxon. His seven heads hissed and snarled, and Azrael's voice, the embodiment of his and Doragon's together, thundered across their minds: **You have no right to decide our fate.**

Xyaxon neither faltered nor flinched; instead, he picked up Ragnarok and held it high as if to strike. "Things will be different now. I see that I made the mistake of granting my creations intelligence and free will and my pact with you two. I have the power to change all that. This time, no one will not stand in my way."

Ulrich turned to Thor. "Join me, Divine One. This ends here and now." The two Divine dragons shared a heroic roar, rallying their allies; he and Thor flew up and, together in unison, dashed straight for Xyaxon as flames boiled from their maws.

The fallen god retaliated and cocooned within a magical barrier, blocking their conjoined attacks. He thrust his blade upward and began channeling energy; Ragnarok grew three times its size, and he slashed the sinister sword directly at Ulrich and Thor. The two barely evaded the attack, but a matching cut appeared on their chest scales.

Fearful for Thor's safety, Selena gritted her teeth as she sped forward with Dragonheart at the ready, but Xyaxon swung his massive weapon towards her. With Revelation floating beside him, Azrael's heads roared in unison, his reaper scythe growing to match Ragnarok's mass. Right before the ebony blade was upon Selena, Azrael struck his weapon against Xyaxon's, the clash rippling throughout the cosmos. Death stood between her and Xyaxon, but she jumped up and ran along the edge of Ragnarok with Dragonheart at full throttle. **Get out of here, now.**

Before Xyaxon could react, she held up her wisping hand, drawing her azure blade of energy, and slashed at the god with lightning-fast dual-wielding attacks. Though Azrael growled and snarled at the headstrong and foolish Selena, he couldn't help but admire her limitless skills from teaching her during their journey to Snowhaven. She leapt up with a kick and a blow to Xyaxon's chin, knocking his head back, and as she disarmed him, Azrael took advantage and aimed Revelation for the titan's midsection, the blade slashing clean through his porcelain-white armor.

While Xyaxon was focused on fending off Selena and Azrael, both Ulrich and Thor shot at the titan like firing bullets from a revolver. The Emerald Dragon spewed out fire mixed with lightning, and Thor called the forces of Aether, and the energy rained upon the ethereal platform like a deadly meteor shower. Xyaxon blocked their attacks at the last second with his golden mirrored shield and countered their magic, but they swiftly evaded.

As he grew enraged and tiresome of their antics, Xyaxon flew straight up and began imbuing himself with a mass of energy. The other two Divines retreated, but Selena would not give up; she held up both Dragonheart and her Aether sword and sped forward as her final desperate act.

"No, don't. Get out of there." Ulrich reached out his claws to grab her, but she slipped through his ivory nails before he could scoop her away.

Liongod, stop. Xyaxon will kill you and Thor. Snarling, Azrael extended out his arms and trapped her in his clawed prison, but to his dismay, she vanished and reappeared beyond his reach. Heedless of his warning, Selena began tapping into her Aether—this must end now. *My dearest one, are you ready?* Thor's war cry made their platform quake and, ignoring Ulrich's pleas to stay, followed her to bring down Xyaxon.

When the light around the titan disappeared, two giant hands made of pure Aether emerged—no body, no face. The god's dark veil of magic blackened the area like a thick, velvet curtain. Selena almost tripped in fear when she came to a halt. *What in Oblivion is that?*

Before she could escape, one hand lunged forward and grabbed her, sparks of lightning writhing around both Xyaxon's fingers and her body. Her muscles and limbs ached and quivered as the Fallen Divine sapped her dry of Aether energy, and when he finished, Xyaxon tossed her away like a ragged doll. Selena's Aether hand and sword vanished, and Dragonheart escaped her grasp, sliding across the clock's illuminated, smooth surface. Thor dove in to catch her, as she barely had the strength to breathe or blink; he held her close to his chest and wrapped his wings around for protection before hitting the platform himself, and the two skidded towards the edge.

Azrael and Ulrich inched to the pair but recoiled as Xyaxon's voice rang. "Such a right to decide is mine alone. By opposing me, I will destroy you four with everything," The two brothers flinched when Xyaxon's power made the platform tremble beneath them, "The world doesn't need you two anymore." He lifted both massive hands and grabbed the two gods. Ropes of white energy surged through his fingers and traveled to the Divines, electrocuting them like powerful lightning bolts; Thor cringed when hearing their cries of anguish. When Xyaxon finished absorbing their energy, Azrael and Ulrich were left brittle and broken, and he threw them over the edge.

Thor grabbed Selena in his talons and rushed to the side, only to watch them tumble and disappear into the starry abyss below. **No....**

"There is no use for weak gods in my new world. Now, you two are next." Xyaxon reached out to the pair, indifferent to Thor's warning snarls and growls. Ensuring Selena's body remained safe while she recovered, wings unfurled, his maw opened wide to reveal the brewing firestorm ready to erupt from his throat. Thor unleashed his wrath and fury as he spewed forth different elemental breaths to attack the god: fire, lightning, ice, earth, and Aether, all intertwined in his deadly display.

Yet, the Fallen Divine remained undeterred, Thor's attacks passing through with no effect; one of the titan's hands lunged forward through the frenzied retaliation and snatched him away. The dragon struggled and struck blindly, but Xyaxon tightened his grip around his body as Thor's use of magic became folly.

Selena squinted through the pain rendering her abilities futile, dreadfully watching as Xyaxon squeezed the life out of her beloved companion. *No, get out of there.*

I-I can't. Argh!

To her horror, she heard his bones crack and break; the god crushed and squeezed, her dragon's dying screams of pain and suffering piercing through her mind, an ear-shattering shrill worse than death itself.

"You will no longer pose a threat to me, *Divinity Dragon.* Your species was my second biggest mistake. Never again."

Selena forced herself to stand and picked up Dragonheart with her only hand, shuffling forward with the blade dragging across the glass floor. "That... is... enough!"

Amused by her ambition, Xyaxon stopped squeezing and dropped Thor's limp body before her; he was alive, but barely. Selena tightened her grip around her sword and limped to his side, but Xyaxon's hand slid between and pushed her away. "You have no hope. Yield to me, and make way for a new world to be born."

Selena's chest felt like it would collapse from looking at her brother, and she wished she could carry his pain. His light would soon extinguish, and she would be ready to join him when it did. She again attempted her trek, needing and wanting to be by her dragon's side, but Xyaxon forced her away. She repeated her unyielding march, her resolve unwavering as she tried anew, but the god was as relentless; the Fallen Divine impeded each attempt to join her dragon in his final moments before entering the void.

Xyaxon finally withdrew his hand and watched in curiosity as Selena stumbled and fell short of her last journey to her knees.

Please, no.... Thor didn't have the strength to respond; with his eyes fixed on her, his pupils dilated as he took his final breath before being drawn into Oblivion. *No!*

CHAPTER 26: DANCE OF DRAGONS

"**Y**our dragon was a disgrace to the race of Divinity Dragons. I have obliterated their existence with his death, and you will soon join him in the void; I will enjoy watching you vanish into nothing. Thor's powers, including his ability to resurrect, have been returned to me."

Selena used her only hand to move across the ethereal platform, crawling her way to Thor's body as she continued calling him, but all she could sense was darkness and emptiness. She ignored her limbs as her arms and legs began fading—she completely disregarded her imminent fate, for she would be with him before long.

She collapsed on his neck when she got close and sobbed into his hide. *I'm sorry... I couldn't protect or save you. You promised me that you would always be with me. Please don't leave me.* His eyes glazed by Death, Selena tilted her head back and released a blood-curdling scream through every fiber of her being. "NO!"

The Fallen Divine maintained his stoic demeanor and watched her surrender as she dropped her head, condemned and defeated. Just as Xyaxon reached forward, she closed her eyes, accepting her inevitable failure: she was ready to die.

Yet, a sparkling tune twinkled within her ears; her eyes fluttered open when she heard a familiar voice. "Selena? Is she okay?" It was Rahim's.

Another echoed within her subconscious. "I-I don't know." *Niamh?* "I hope she is. I hadn't seen her since Snowhaven before that monster, Medusa, controlled me. Rahim, I want to tell her how sorry I am for what I've done."

"It's not your fault. Selena will come back—she has to."

She struggled to lift her bruised head as a vision of Alfheim appeared before her; Rahim and Niamh stood among friends and foes, Dreygur and Nidhoggr, near where the portal once held, watching Xyaxon's baptism of fire spiderweb across the fragile heavens.

Fafnir wrapped himself around the two and asked, "Is this… the end?"

Niamh held tightly onto Rahim and cried into his shoulder, but he remained strong for her. "No, it can't be. Selena, if you can hear me, don't lose. If anyone can stop this, it's you. You always believed we could change the future—it all begins with you."

Her body wobbling and nearly broken, Selena forced herself to stand up upon seeing orbs of white light surrounding her, each one whispering her friends' wishes and prayers; they twinkled like the diamond stars adorning the eternal cosmos.

"What is this magic and madness? No, only I can change the future." Xyaxon sought after her again, but an invisible barrier protected her and her fallen dragon from the god's lunging hands.

"We like this world, and we want to keep it," Rahim continued, "sure, it can be scary not knowing what will happen, but that also makes life exciting. We want to live. If you can hear me, I'm praying for you and Thor."

"What? No!" Xyaxon reached out to grab the two floating orbs drifting downward but to no avail as they slipped through his fingers. One light touched Selena, and the other went to Thor's body. She felt power like a thousand suns flowing through her veins, and her eyes shimmered when her dragon's body glowed like the stars.

"We believe in you two," Niamh rallied behind him, "You and Rahim gave me the strength to live my life and make my own choices. I'm praying for you both." The pair absorbed a second light orb each, followed by a third when Fafnir joined with "please, save my handler."

A series of guttural shrieks broke through Xyaxon's panicked shrills: "S-save... my... f-flight, Divine... Ones." She saw a vision of Noctis and his flight bowing their heads; wings extended as they caught the shimmering glint of Divine's light.

Another familiar voice chimed in her ears, and Ebony knelt beside Lord Godfrey and Prince Damien, all three huddled in chant. "I'm glad I decided to heed your call, Your Majesty. You and Thor are the only ones who can end this darkness, and I will keep praying for you two."

"May your Divine fire save us," Damien whispered.

Kain's cheer rattled in her mind. "If you were willing to take me on in a fight, evil will never stand a chance. Right, Silver?"

"Right. Remember what you've always told me, my dear? We have the resolve to live our lives and decide our fate. Use your power to change the world and find the strength to seize your destiny. It is our own, not the will of the gods or demons. We all have the right and freedom to choose our path. That is our future."

One by one, friends and foes alike shouted cheers and prayers; following each praise, Selena and Thor continued absorbing the glimmering energy circling them.

"Pull yourself together and face this head-on. You're a dragon with the heart of the wolf; now fight back like one!" she heard Kiba shout.

"Thank you, Selena and Thor. Because of you two, we will finally live in peace," her mother's voice sparkled.

"Please save us."

"Save Armageddon—"

"Save the world—"

As the final orbs drifted down, the two became imbued in a blinding light; Xyaxon bellowed out an ear-shattering shriek threatening to break their ethereal platform. "No!"

The Fallen Divine's scream vanished, and the darkened sky grew brighter than the sun as the once most beautiful star illuminated the cosmos: a heavenly voice she longed to hear again glimmered upon her subconscious, and her heart soared. **I promised I would never leave you. I stand with you, forever and always.**

And I with you.

The two Divinity Dragons stood together before the recoiling titan when the mass of light disappeared. Selena's Aether dragon stood the size of Ulrich, her celestial wings wafting through the divine cosmos pool, glistening stars dotting her ethereal membranes. Her Divine fire burning with the different colors of the rainbow writhed around her crown-shaped horns as an orb of infinite energy levitated above her head. Her gem-like turquoise scales sparkled from her Divine light, with plumes of blue Aether radiating from her hide. Xyaxon snarled and stepped back from the now brilliant white diamond emblazoned into her chest, glittering colorful flecks in his eyes.

Reborn and awakened, Thor no longer carried his crimson colors, but now his scales glistened like perfectly cut white diamonds, and his scaly chest plate and ethereal wing membranes shined like solid gold. His bone mask had transformed into an ethereal mist sweeping against his face, his golden eyes now glowing brighter than all the stars. Thor's horns strongly resembled hers and Ulrich's crown, with writhing streams of matching Divine rainbow fire and the blazing blue-green sapphire he carried upon his breast, reflecting her scale colors.

The two Divinity Dragons struck fear and panic within Xyaxon, but the god refrained from showing any emotion besides anger. "How can this be? I killed you and destroyed your pathetic race of dragons." The hands lunged forward to grab them. Both Selena and Thor reared their heads back and unleashed a unified terrifying and mighty roar that made Xyaxon tremble and quiver.

Together, as they beat their wings, concentric rings of light energy wafted from every flap and rippled in all directions. Their magic turned Xyaxon's hands into stone, and with one final wave, they shattered like glass. The Fallen Divine reverted to his titan form, and in haste and panic, he took flight and left them behind upon the illuminated clock platform.

Don't let him escape. Thor gnashed his pearly white fangs and arched his back like a cat ready to pounce its prey, and the pair made one full-body leap off the clock with one wing beat and flew through the celestial cosmos, chasing after Xyaxon.

Selena reared her head and billowed a solid beam of Aether light towards Xyaxon's direction from her maw, and before the god could evade, he was thrown back violently by her attack. The Fallen Divine collided with a rock flying through space, and he grimaced in pain. As the dust from the floating asteroid cleared, Thor emerged with a roar and cloaked himself in light, dancing off his hide like fire, fading between the rainbow colors writhing around his horns. Xyaxon, watching while covering his head with his arms, was burned by the colorful Aether flames when Thor drew close, and the titan held up his sword, ready to deliver a quick slice.

Selena flew in to stop it by reaching out with her claws, and she swiped Ragnarok away, redirecting a beam of light from the god's blade to the side. She opened her mouth and spewed forth contrasting colorful streams through her serrated fangs with a thundering cry that made the cosmos bow before her might; the Aether energy looped about and formed a revolving ring around her. Xyaxon's eyes widened when he saw their combined destructive power, and he held up his shield in a wasted effort to protect himself. Selena and Thor dove in after him, and the Fallen Divine became caught in their protective barriers, but he pushed himself out of their reach and flew away.

The titan spun around and summoned beams of light that shot after his pursuers; Thor dodged and roared in between his teeth, belching out a deadly torrent of rainbow flames. The blast aimed at the frightened god, carrying him some distance away, but the leftover magic wrapped itself around Thor and encased him in a sphere. Xyaxon fired more light rays that sought after him, but to his dismay, Thor's barrier absorbed his attack.

Selena tucked in her wings and nose-dived, then climbed straight up, launching herself directly at the Fallen Divine. Her ring of rainbow energy struck Xyaxon and carried him for a short distance before she swiped him away with her talons. As he flew out and escaped her wrath, Thor came close and brought his wings together.

His energy reserves poured forth from his body, and their water-like tendrils aimed for the fleeing titan.

Xyaxon paused mid-flight and held up his shield to block, but Thor's overwhelming power stunned him. After he recovered, the fire lion retreated into the swirling wall of asteroids nearby. He looked up to see the two dragons flying overhead and descending upon him, breaking through the rocky belt. The rocks spinning and swirling freely in the nether shattered upon contact with Selena's and Thor's protective barriers as the two dragons sliced their way through stone and rubble while Xyaxon dodged in haste and panic. Seizing a chance for retaliation, he spun and swung his sword blindly, but when he saw that Ragnarok left nary a scratch, he dove downward to escape from the dragons' deadly dance.

While in mid-pursuit, another voice reached out to her. **We knew you two could do it.**

Azrael? Selena was so happy to hear his voice again. *Where are you? Are you and Ulrich okay?*

We're fine, but don't let him get away. We'll try to catch up.

He won't. Today, Xyaxon will fall.

Selena roared and raced after him while Thor picked up speed and knocked the titan away once he drew close. The god changed direction to avoid his swipe, but the Divinity Dragons followed him tightly. Xyaxon looked back fearfully as Thor rushed forward and head-butted him into a stun. Clinching her jaw in anger, Selena moved her paws in a circular motion, pulling the streams of rainbow energy from her protective ring, and the magic looped around Xyaxon's body. He looked at Selena and Thor with fear and dismay as she pulled him back, her arcane rope slamming him against the nearby rock.

Reiterating all of their friends' hopes and dreams, the two dragons roared together: *This ends now. Today, we take back our world from you and our right and freedom to choose our path—that is our future.*

Together, she and Thor made a weaving motion with their claws, and streams of their Aether energies interlaced to form a massive blade twice the size of Xyaxon. Their rainbow Aether sword rapidly descended upon the Fallen Divine with a slashing motion. Then—

Their conjoined attack sliced through the god clean in half. Xyaxon dropped his shield and sword as his body began drifting away. "I-I'm beaten. Do you think you two can hold my mantle, mortals? Mortals...? Gods...? Your futures escape me. This world is yours. Farewell." Ragnarok shattered like glass with his final breath, and Xyaxon's body faded out of existence in a plume of smoke.

CHAPTER 27: THE GOLDEN CROWN

Following Xyaxon's defeat, Selena and Thor were imbued in a flash of light, and the pair were teleported before the lonely glass castle in Niflheim. Azrael—in his human form and Doragon as a Sunbeam Shieldtail dragon beside him—and Ulrich appeared before the pair. "You two did it—you defeated Xyaxon," Azrael cheered, and he and Ulrich bowed before them.

Focusing on channeling her Aether, Selena resumed her elven form. She was relieved to see the return of her Aether hand, still wearing Silver's promise that Thor immediately began eyeing with interest. The dazzling moissanite stones reflected rainbow flecks, matching the colorful smoldering ember ropes clinging to his horns.

Contrarily, Thor maintained his current guise, and she assumed that this was a Divinity Dragon's proper form. After extinguishing the orb burning above his head and the flames writhing around his horns, and his wings reverting to their parchment-textured membranes, Ulrich snaked his head around to examine Thor's new physiology and confirmed their suspicions. "Much like how you reverted the Well's mistakes, Young One, Thor cleansed the Lich's corruption that wrought havoc upon his form and mind. Now, you two are pure once more, though this is the first time I've seen a fully realized Divinity Dragon. All the others before you two never unleashed their full power."

Thor tore his gaze away from her wedding ring, stood tall, and unfurled his spectral wings; wisps plumed from his edges, and Selena knew he was proud. Chittering in delight, Doragon—his head now only reaching Thor's chest—inquisitively observed his former rival's brilliant hide and spectral wings. The golden dragon's smooth, metallic scales couldn't compare to Thor's dazzling diamonds, and he bowed in acknowledgment.

Azrael bit his lip and crossed his arms over his chest, tilting his head in curiosity at their new appearance. "Who taught you this?" Selena's answer, "I learned how to control my Aether," was enough to make him smirk.

Thor snaked his head back down again and nudged his nose against the meteorite diamond, and Selena had to explain its purpose. **I want him to use my saved gold bullions and craft me some jewelry. You must tell me of your feats during our separation, but I'm happy for you and Silver.**

I'm sure he would oblige and thank you for the sentiments, but I wished you were there.

Azrael eyed the ring and clicked his tongue against his teeth. "For you two, that vow will be eternal. I wish you luck, but I can barely stand the bastard after five minutes."

They shared a hearty laugh, but their smiles faded when Ulrich explained how she and Thor ended Xyaxon's cycle of rebirth and destruction, and his attack vanished from their world. The Divine Emerald Dragon lowered his head in shame and despair. "Xyaxon believed that this allowed life to continue and flourish, where everything was balanced. Until now, we followed without choice. We loved our brother, but he lost his way."

A terrible pain throbbed in Selena's chest; Xyaxon was doing what he thought was best, but in the end, it destroyed him. "Life can continue and thrive; we change and grow."

Xyaxon could have seen that for himself, but it may have been too late.

Azrael reached over and patted Doragon's neck. "Despite what we went through with Xyaxon, it hurts us more than you two can imagine that it had to end this way. We thank you two for lifting Ulrich's curse and my banishment, but we lost a friend and a brother."

Our condolences for your loss.

"Thank you, but he died long ago when he lost his way," Azrael sighed, "There was no bringing him back."

But he did mention something interesting in his final moments. Thor repeated Xyaxon's last words to the two remaining Divines. When he finished, Azrael and Ulrich exchanged confused glances. **What did he mean?**

A furrow creased Azrael's brow; Ulrich hung his head as if he needed the moment to ponder. "Perhaps he meant for you to take his place. I don't know what the future holds, but that will be entirely up to you."

Selena declined. "We only want to live life as it comes."

I don't think we could be gods.

Azrael shrugged and bit his bottom lip. "Who knows? Maybe you'll grow to your positions. Maybe you won't, but that's all up to you two."

A pit grew in her stomach when she asked about Aydin's fate, yet Azrael's expression remained faithful to his indifferent disposition. However, like how he reassured her that Tiamat rested easy, he eventually gave her a small smile that soothed her conscience but suddenly grew tight-lipped as he pointed at her directly. "There is something else I do need to tell you. Do you remember when you went through the initiation by drinking demon's blood to join the Force?"

The vile memory almost made her want to vomit, but she nodded. "How could I not?"

"That was supposed to kill you because of your Divine nature, but it didn't. You somehow fought it off. When Doragon and I ran into you afterwards, we were afraid and intimidated by you because we both knew that you could do anything. I challenged you to that duel to test your abilities, and I don't scare easily, but to say I was terrified of your prowess was an understatement." The chittering Doragon dipped his head, clicking his nails against the icy stone platform.

"I see," was all she could say. "Did that truly make you stronger against demons, or was that a false belief with no basis?"

Azrael rolled his eyes. "You should know by now that it was all rubbish. It's poison; it's meant to kill you. We sacrificed a good number of soldiers for the Council."

Selena regaled the Divines with Xyaxon's dark intention to eradicate her existence and prevent her involvement from disrupting his cycle until realizing her usefulness when she met her end in Snowhaven.

Meanwhile, Azrael's eye twitched. "That's why your lifespan continued resetting, and there were no repercussions against my actions." Doragon groaned and rubbed his nose against his back to correct his mistake. "Well, aside from running into Venexus and almost bringing about the world's end." His hollow laugh nearly failed his witticism, but Selena couldn't help but smirk.

But Xyaxon didn't account for the power of our friends. All of our hopes and dreams were his ultimate downfall.

He thought he knew everything, but he had no idea what his creations wanted. He never lived among mortals to know what was best.

"But we have." Ulrich stepped forward and bowed his head, tail thumping from side to side in anticipation. "We will do whatever it takes to protect life as it flourishes and finds its way."

Death's grin was surprisingly bright; Doragon lowered his head and nudged his arm, chittering and chirping. "We will all grieve on our own time for Xyaxon, but now, we should celebrate. Our friends are waiting for us back in Alfheim."

Thor lowered his head and laid it on Selena's shoulder. **One of the only places we've ever truly called home. We'll be hard at work rebuilding the city.**

Selena reached up and patted his nose. *And the Empire.*

With Azrael's, Doragon's, and Ulrich's magic, the Divines joined Selena and Thor as they returned to Alfheim's covert. Yet, Selena and Thor were struck dumb as they gandered at the world: the Fire Kingdom capital had been rebuilt as if the war had never happened. She expected an unsightly welcome of debris and piles of rotting corpses, but Alfheim reveled in ivory glory—even the Pyre was back. She never thought she would be so happy to see the giant, grim clock tower again.

Thor spun around and saw that the dragons' new quarters—now an open garden with marked paved grey stones weaving in a winding path—had not stables but pavilions built of similar design to his own from Heaven's Tear for dragons of all shapes and sizes. Upon seeing the royal accommodations that dragons rightly deserved, his eyes sparkled in delight, chittering in glee.

Though Alfheim was rebuilt, the Hinterlands still suffered from the Nidhoggr's smoldering downpour, flames flickering among the blackened, scarred ground stretching for leagues over the horizon. Yet, the extramural damage avoided the dragon gardens and the city, but the once lush ancient grove was now trapped in an infinitely-burning prison.

"How is this even possible?" Ulrich asked.

"I think you should ask them." Azrael pointed over at Silver and Kain, racing each other down the stone pathway to greet them; all Selena could see was their trail of dust clouds. Ulrich held his head high and stretched out his wings as he chirped in amusement. "Ah, the demigod."

As Kain and Silver reached them, they immediately bowed. Silver's grin stretched across his face. "How do you like the new city?"

Kain scratched the back of his head. "The admiral and I worked alongside the Dreygur and Nidhoggr all night to rebuild everything while you two were fighting the Lich. When you killed him, they immediately stopped fighting us and were dazed and confused, unable to remember anything that happened."

As Silver beckoned them to walk with him through the new open garden, he couldn't contain his excitement as he explained all the modifications made to the repaired elven city. Alfheim's massive fort had been restored and remodeled for more comfortable accommodations for new and returning soldiers: refurbished beds and recreational room, a better meal plan, the courtyard thrice its original size for dragons of any weight to land comfortably. Because of how cold it usually was, he built a hidden heated spring underneath the ground that pulled water from the North Sea, allowing steam to vent to the surface that the pavilions captured for the dragons' comfort—similarly designed from Thor's gazebo at Heaven's Tear.

The only reason for the fire's safe distance away was thanks to Silver's enchantment, but he had been unsuccessful in dousing the dark flames. "Every time I believed I extinguished the fire, the smoldering embers would flicker to life again moments later. I'm not sure what else I can do, but for now, the blazes aren't a threat to us at present."

Aside from the new pavilions and alterations to the dragons' quarters, the streets were now wide enough for dragons and Nidhoggr to walk through undeterred among the populace. Silver wanted to establish citizenship for all of dragonkind by allowing business, trade, and the ability to purchase and work for goods. "It's a start in making amends for past ill-treatment," he said during their stroll, "and we need to remind ourselves that dragons are reincarnations of the Divines themselves and should be treated better than kings, as they serve none."

Pleased with Silver's compliment and the restitutions, Thor leaned back on his haunches and released a torrent of his Divine rainbow fire towards the heavens. Silver's eyes sparkled in admiration, matching the grin lighting every corner of his face. "I never imagined seeing a Divinity Dragon in full grandeur. All I've observed from the others before you were normal dragons who never fully realized their power. You astound me, Thor. It's good to see you again."

Thor lowered his muzzle, meeting Silver's open palm. **It's lovely to see you again, Silver.**

Selena was about to reiterate his words, but judging from Silver's growing smile, she knew Thor had just openly shared a mental link with him. Disregarding her original notion that dragons only spoke with their handlers, she realized it was their choice to communicate with whomever they deemed worthy; seeing Thor accepting Silver made her heart soar.

I also wish to offer my congratulations on your marriage, he added, **If only I could have been there.**

"Hmm...." Silver fished through his pocket, pulled out the black timepiece he used before to see Aydin's memory, and explained its use as Thor inched closer in great curiosity, his tail flickering with eagerness. "When we have time, my Divine friend, I will be more than happy to show you."

Yes, please. I would appreciate that very much. Thor whipped around and poked his nose at Selena's ring. **And, after you share those memories with me, I would like to ask for some jewelry, but I have something particular in mind.**

"Of course. Dragonstone Estate remained safe during the Red Rains of Alfheim, and your treasure hoard is still secure within my house vault. I would be more than happy to oblige." Silver immediately pulled out a folded parchment from his inside pocket and began writing down Thor's commission order. Thor spoke so fast that Selena couldn't keep up, and he intentionally blocked her thoughts, preventing her from hearing his gift ideas for her.

After Silver finished writing Thor's list, sharing in their happiness, Kain changed the subject, wishing to know more about their fight against the necromancer. "We thought the world was going to end for a moment."

Gratifying his curiosity, Selena did her best to share the tale—even as she recalled their story, the events began slipping away like a dream. Occasionally, Thor gave his side to Silver whenever she stumbled on a few details, hesitant at revisiting their darkest hour. Kain's and Silver's jaws dropped when the pair finished, but the two were trapped in a few moments of silence as their words failed them. "So, Xyaxon was the one truly behind this," Silver finally said, his face gleaming in awe and wonder, "Your people will be telling your story for eons to come."

Selena felt her throat squeeze. "But we're not gods."

"You two may as well be now. I suspect that the dwarves and elves will be painting and crafting murals that will forever share your tale, marking your new Empire's age." Silver grabbed and adjusted the hem of his jacket collar. "I'll see that the Fire Temple will be properly decorated to celebrate your victory. We shall call it, 'The Dance of Dragons.'"

Doragon lowered his head close to the ground to respect Thor's new status and might; Thor uncurled his neck, twittering in delight as plumes of rainbow Aether wisps writhed around his maw. Selena wished to object, but he swung his neck and nudged her shoulder with his snout in assurance. She was surprised by his cool touch; she ran her fingers across his hide and found that his scales were cut to absolute perfection—not even the best jeweler in the world could match their craft to Thor's diamonds.

Shadows flew across the ground, and Selena saw Aracania and Ysyra leading the Nidhoggr flight, including Lord Godfrey and Obsidian—the vampire lord donned in his protective cloak to keep him out of direct sunlight as much as possible. Trailing behind were Vulcan and Skyfyre with their handlers peering below, waving as they passed while General Araneus and Colonel Cyres saluted.

The formation landed at their assigned pavilions. The dragons and Nidhoggr curled up like mounds of treasure gleaming between the gold-streaked marble columns while their handlers removed their harnesses and began maintenance care by cleaning and oiling their scales. Obsidian couldn't help but chitter in delight from the royal treatment, and puffs of smoke plumed from his nostrils as Godfrey wiped him down.

Meanwhile, when Skyfyre landed and immediately fell asleep before Volt could dismount, Gromm continued muttering as Vulcan lazily laid down in the pavilion beside the Wraithclaw's and roared, refusing to move for Gromm to clean him properly; Beck stood to the side and laughed. After having her scales polished, Ysyra wrapped Cyres within her coils, and he tearfully returned her affections. The pain of losing Onyxria was still fresh, but the colonel slowly opened up to and accepted his companion.

With all of Silver's and Kain's accomplishments achieved on such short notice, they completed their repairs once the evening ended. Selena had no concept of time during her absence, but Azrael explained, "Time moves differently in Niflheim—a few minutes in the spirit realm could be hours here." Her first meeting with Xyaxon after succumbing to unconsciousness in the dwarven ruin cost almost half the day in the mortal world, so she understood completely.

Silver bit his bottom lip. "We may have rebuilt the city, but the pain still lingers. It's going to take some time to grieve over the dead."

"And we will never forget them. I, too, need to rebuild my city," Ulrich declared as he stretched out his wings. "Rhumbek will be free. It's time to see what my dwarves can do with their gift from me."

"We look forward to seeing their inventions shape the Empire, but what of the dragon eggs? Please, tell me they're safe," Selena pleaded.

Silver chuckled and patted down the back of his head. "Not to worry, my dear. Your father and I found the eggs hidden in Vidar's old office, and we brought them to the new Fire Temple to protect them. Upon careful examination, it looks like the whelplings are well, and they should be hatching soon. By my calculations from their already hardened shells, that could be days from now."

Thor snorted and flickered his tail. **They're very impatient, and I would be surprised if they go another week.**

I'm grateful they've lasted this long after what had happened.

Silver and the group strolled around the gardens and past the gold-streaked pavilions. Upon Selena's inquiry about the others' whereabouts, Fafnir and Noctis appeared from the city's confines and circled overhead; Niamh and Rahim waved from Fafnir's back, but Prince Damien astride Noctis bowed in respect, followed by a toothy grin showcasing his fangs. The Prince of Shadows, like his father, donned a thick cloak to keep the sunlight off his skin, but he still fidgeted uncomfortably within the harness; Noctis remained aloft as he and Damien approached their group, hovering in place. "It's good to see you alive and well, Your Majesty."

She returned his gesture, and Noctis landed near Thor before immediately bowing to the recognized Divine aura radiating like the new sun. Fafnir was grounded but kept his distance from the feral leader when Noctis growled and unfolded his bladed wings; Selena feared he would attack Fafnir, but Damien soothed his companion with gentle words, and Noctis turned away.

As Niamh and Rahim dismounted, Selena noticed that Rahim's behavior was odd, for they were celebrating their victory. She gave Azrael a questioning glare when she considered the worst possibility, but he offered no inclination other than his head hanging low; he and Doragon hid within Ulrich's shadow.

Their new arrivals paused amidst Thor's new glory and bent the knee to the fully realized Divinity Dragon.

Silver offered his explanation in Selena's place—including her recent transformation, as Niamh and Thor were the last of her friends to see. Thor snaked his head around to examine her new appearance during Silver's tale and hummed in approval. **It suits you, my dear one. You embody the beauty of an elf and dragon, which is only perfect for the Queen of Dragons.**

"Your hair is lovely." Niamh reached out to touch her snow-white turquoise gradient hair but withdrew her hand almost immediately and blushed. Selena couldn't help but wonder if Niamh still considered herself foolish for developing feelings for her while hiding under the old alias Andric, but the two shared a laugh.

When Silver finished, the sky suddenly screamed, and Kayda flew to a nearby smaller pavilion designated to her with all her passengers accounted for; the younglings circled above her head, with Sethak and Rhasydra squabbling. Volterion was the one who intervened on Kayda's behalf, scolding through snarls and growls, and the twins zipped towards the gazebo. A pair of gleaming gold bracelets and a ruby chain dangled from Kayda's claws that Thor eyed possessively. Selena couldn't help but smile when she saw Chaliss dismount Kayda and rush over; Rahim turned around, and his face lit up like a new star. "Mum!"

"*Matu!*"

Chaliss rushed from behind Silver and Kain, hurrying over to hug Rahim and Selena. "When the eclipse ended, and the sky cleared, Her Former Imperial Majesty assured us it was safe to return. I'm so happy to see all of you alive and well. I couldn't be more proud of either of you two." She then rummaged through a pocket and pulled out Thor's obsidian dragon totem left behind with his treasures. "Your mother told me to give this to you."

She accepted it when Thor snaked his head around. **Could you tie that around my talon, like how Doragon wears his?** He looked at the golden dragon looking down at his charm still fastened around his claw, and Selena fulfilled his request.

Kayda's other passengers, Selena's mother included, remained seated within the harness. Yet, before Selena could signal the others to join the group, Aryl gestured to Rune Citadel, and Kayda dropped off Thor's jewelry, leaving as quickly as she came as the hatchlings remained to rest. Within a blink, Kayda was already at the ivory mountain castle. Selena understood how this smaller weighted feral arrived promptly from Heaven's Tear; due to her daintier and more agile build, Kayda must have been the fastest flier among Noctis' flight.

Thor at once flew over to her pavilion and snatched his trinkets in fear that the ferals would steal them, but they didn't pay any mind; the wearied younglings fell asleep upon landing. **Thank you for saving them for me, my dear one. I want Silver to alter these, too.**

Of course, I would save them, but why? Your bracelets now match your scales.

Thor lowered his head, and Selena fastened his gold and ruby chain around his neck. **You will see.**

However, the group's happy reunion became dreary as—after Niamh and Fafnir pleaded—Rahim addressed the reason for his melancholy behavior. Upon recounting the difficult decision to end Arawn struck Selena across the face; her legs almost gave out from grief's weight, but she shuffled over to his side, commending him for accomplishing what Rahim feared to be inevitable. Thor and Doragon reared their heads back and let out a roar, their mournful cries echoing across the heavens.

"I had no other choice," Rahim continued; Arawn had no recollection of being human, and he would have struck them down with no remorse. Selena couldn't even begin to imagine how this made him feel; each word from his mouth made it seem like an eternity had passed. The world spiraled through the void, no longer the same.

"Our condolences for your loss, Young One." Ulrich touched his snout against Rahim's head, and Azrael and Doragon bowed in respect.

Silver stepped forward, biting his bottom lip as he offered Rahim a gentle pat, to which he gratefully accepted. "I'm so sorry, my friend. I pray not to add fuel to the fire, but the Dreygur don't remember anything before turning. Even if… if we were able to save your father, he wouldn't know who you or Chaliss were, and quite frankly, I'm not sure which would be worse." As Rahim and Chaliss dealt with their freshly opened wounds, Silver crossed his arms over his chest, and he bit down hard on his cheeks as he contemplated what to do with the rest of the Lich's old forces. "It will be hard to integrate the others back into society if they don't remember their past humanity, but we must have a plan."

Kain crossed his arms. "Then what in Oblivion are we going to do?"

"If I could make a suggestion," Silver examined the looks upon their faces before continuing, "Azrael should send the demons back to Oblivion. However, I'm unsure what to do with the Dreygur, as they don't have a home and were raised from their graves—it's not like we can reverse that."

Azrael rolled his eyes and looked up at Doragon. "I beg to differ."

Selena was appalled by his apathy, and her reaction made him take a step back. "I will not treat them with injustice when there is a chance they can live among us in peace."

His nostrils flared in anger, but he kept his temper in check. "They're unnatural abominations with no memory from when they were among the living."

"You were willing to condemn the Nidhoggr without giving them a chance, and those freed from the Lich's servitude joined and defended us. We won't turn our backs on them, nor will we do that to the Dreygur." Azrael turned away and paced around Doragon, caught within his rage; his dragon, however, was more concerned with subduing his partner's wrath.

Silver and Kain remained conflicted, and she immediately decided to allocate time for properly discussing these critical matters. "I wish for everyone's involvement. To rebuild Armageddon, we must be on the same side." She ended her affirmations, and for the moment, they were satisfied with a chance at a future debate.

The group held their breath when Fafnir slowly approached Noctis; Prince Damien kept his hand on his partner's neck, but Noctis growled through closed fangs and dug his claws into the grass, pulling clumps with every stride. Yet, Fafnir made amends with Noctis by offering his apology, "I'm sorry for everything," and "can you forgive me?"

Low snarls vibrated from Noctis' throat as his fangs remained clamped, but the feral leader began purring, to everyone's relief. "I... f-forgive." Fafnir lowered his head in respect, tail swishing happily like a playful cat.

Niamh's grin brightened her face, and regardless of Selena's reassurances, she began apologizing profusely for her past mistakes. "Fafnir and I still wanted to remain partners. As—"

"I understand." Selena smiled. "You have no reason to apologize; I was never angry with you or Fafnir." Rahim grumbled a "speak for yourself" but withdrew his remark when she struck him with a sharp glare. "We are so relieved that you're all right, and you and Fafnir eventually found each other. Through the madness, you two chose each other as partners. They're dragons too."

Fafnir and Noctis fluttered in place. "We're… d-dragons too." Despite the low jealous rumbles vibrating from Thor's throat, Noctis nudged Selena's arm with his nose, wanting her affections. She returned his fondness but gently reassured Thor that Noctis already has a handler. **I hope so because I will not see you riding another dragon.**

After Noctis pulled away to face his flight with Fafnir, Thor put out a possessive claw to bring her closer and gave a low warning snarl at the feral leader, which Noctis ignored. Once she was plastered against the royal blue sapphire from his harness, Selena begged him to release her from his talon prison. With pupiled-slits still fixated on Noctis as if he were prey, it took much coercion on Selena's and Silver's part before Thor finally obliged.

You accepted Silver, but why do you now see Noctis as a threat?

He's no threat. I'm a Divine, and Noctis cannot hope to compare himself to me. Still, Thor's eyes kept flitting between her and the feral leader, and no amount of convincing would make her dragon see otherwise. However, upon seeing Noctis and Prince Damien working together, she knew they had made an excellent pair deserving each other's companionship, and Thor relaxed his shoulders.

Selena caught Rahim looking at the newly formed pair with a glistening gaze, and she squinted at him with a crease in her brow. Disregarding her judging stare, he spun around to avoid all eyes and whispered a small prayer for Eshara's gift of protecting him. Upon hearing him, Azrael strutted over and silently clamped a hand over his shoulder, nodding in acknowledgment when Rahim met his gaze.

The party paused and looked at Selena for further guidance and direction, as she had yet to accept the throne formally. In between their fired questions regarding if she still wanted to be queen, Thor's tail swept across the ground through contented chittering. **The people of Armageddon will expect their Queen of Dragons to take the throne, but only if you want it, my dear. Nobody will force you to accept the responsibility.**

Yet, they will expect it.

It is your birthright, but is it what you want?

Her crowd awaiting a proper declaration, she held her head high and marched to the city. Her friends followed, fluttering with great anticipation as she silently agreed to begin her Divine reign. Thor extended his ethereal wings, unleashed a thundering roar, and exhaled a torrent of rainbow flames at the heavens. Noctis and his flight—Fafnir included—stood upon their haunches and showed their support in the same manner, their black Aether fire hailing the Dragon Queen as she swept by, her long white and azure gradient hair flowing behind with each graceful step she took. Trapped in awe and adoration of their new queen, her group unquestionably followed in collectively shared cheers over their victory.

After rushing to join her side, Rahim wore a huge grin and swung an arm over Selena's shoulder. "I prefer the sound of Queen of Dragons, One of Divine Birth, better." He laughed but flinched when he expected her to slug him like before. To his surprise, she smiled, and he added, "It's better than 'Empress' in my opinion, anyway. It sounded too plain for someone like you." Selena gave up on arguing with Rahim, as she knew he would find every opportunity to remind her. "Hmm. Maybe we should add 'God-Slayer' to your list of titles."

"Don't overdo it, Rahim."

Kain yawned as if the entire conversation bore him and nodded to Prince Damien. "Now, if you lot don't mind, and before I decide to blow my bloody brains out because of this fucking death glare, I need shade and a nap." After sharing a few laughs, he excused himself and trudged back to join Maria at the cemetery, muttering and swearing how much he hated the sun and wished he could douse its blaze.

Niamh wrapped her arms around Fafnir's neck before leaving with Rahim, and Fafnir dashed for the sky to pick out an empty pavilion to call his own. Selena bade her remaining company farewell before Chaliss followed Rahim and Niamh, who walked hand in hand; she couldn't help but think of the possibility they could have saved Arawn, but Rahim and Chaliss accepted his death.

After Prince Damien dismounted from Noctis and removed his harness, the feral leader made his way to an empty tower beside Obsidian's and fell into a deep slumber. After Godfrey finished Obsidian's care, he joined his son's company, and Obsidian became ensconced within his coils. The vampire nobles made their way inside the city gates to meet with Selena's parents for one final discussion about the succession of power as she accepted the throne, leaving Selena, Thor, and Silver behind.

Thor, however, remained protective over Selena as more ferals flew over him towards their new pavilions to rest while she and Silver busied themselves in removing his harness. His tail occasionally wrapped itself around the two in a protective coil, shielding them from view. **It was nice to see you make new allies while I was away. I hope you and Noctis hadn't bonded too much.**

You know me better than that. Besides, I think he and Damien formed their union.

Good. I was hoping that I didn't have to start a fight.

You wouldn't.

I would. The two laughed, breaking the tense and distressing atmosphere. **I'll ensure that the Nidhoggr make themselves at home.**

Thank you, and they will greatly appreciate that.

Free of the saddle, Selena clasped his diamond bracelets over his wrists after adjusting them to the correct sizes. Chittering with absolute glee, Thor nuzzled his snout against her head before snatching the leather straps, carrying the harness to his gilt-painted pavilion, his dazzling diamond scales and gems casting flecks of rainbow flair across the ground.

Ulrich, silently watching the others disperse, tilted his head at the city gates when howls echoed in the air like a harmonic melody; to Selena's delight, the Aynu finally joined their party, although relatively late. Kiba, in her wolf form, was the first to arrive. However, Selena's copper-tanned hue became almost pearlescent white when Kiba abruptly halted, digging dirt between her claws as she skidded, snarling at the Emerald Dragon. When Selena ordered her to stand down, all she got in response was, *I will kill him.* She growled and dashed head-on at Ulrich; the indifferent Divine stood like solid stone, completely unmovable.

He swished his tail as Kiba pounced and struck her down hard into the ground through a sharp gleam in his eye. Not a moment later, Maru and the rest of the Aynu pack flooded out of the city to meet with the She-Wolf, but the terrible scene made them pause. Before Maru could organize the group to circle Ulrich for striking his mate, the Emerald Dragon roared, swirling clouds of green fire mixed with ropes of lightning building in the back of his throat. The whimpering wolves recoiled, rethinking their tactical approach. Maru, however, cautiously inched to his mate's side with one eye fixed on Ulrich, snarling through clamped fangs. The She-Wolf jumped back to all fours, but Ulrich's wavering thick tail held her at bay.

Before Selena could address their hostilities, Ulrich's growls shattered the oppressive atmosphere: "I rightly deserve your anger, Followers of Artio, and since I'm no longer afflicted with my curse of madness, I will right my wrongs by you and my sister." He promptly explained the Divines' relationship with Artio when he noticed their confused stares and offered to find their treasure left behind from the Dreygur attack to extinguish the black flames and regrow the forest. Amidst Ulrich's proposition, Silver made several confusing gestures through his silenced mouthed questions—as not to offend the Aynu—but Selena quietly reassured him of the golden egg's power to repair what seemed an impossible feat.

After considering and deliberating Ulrich's suggested restitutions, Kiba gave him a firm, jerky nod in approval, but her pack snorted and snarled before turning their backs to the Divine. "We want the artifact back once you finish, *dragon*."

"As you wish." Disregarding Kiba's sneering comment, Ulrich spun, wings wholly unfurled, and launched himself skyward with his tail slithering off the ground behind him. His glimmering emerald hide scaled down to a dot's size before diving through the sea of infinitely-burning trees.

It was Selena's turn to uphold her promise when Maru confronted her in his human form and firmly added, "We still want our land back."

"As promised, Alfheim will welcome the Aynu, and we will live together in peace," her expression grew somber, "but murder is prohibited, as that's frowned upon in civilized society." Although Silver laughed at her witty sarcasm, she still felt it needed to be addressed; unamused, Kiba and Maru agreed. "You will have to swear it. The Aynu have been living among Artio's good graces for many years, and you've had to do what you could to survive."

"We swear it."

Silver held his chin while looking at the alphas but kept his distance, remembering when Kiba lashed out at him at the Templar keep. "If you and your pack wish, I can look into seeing about developing housing to accommodate your needs." Kiba declined and expressed their desires to be treated as ordinary citizens, to which Silver replied with, "Fair enough." Following the declaration, Kiba took off in her wolf form with Maru and their pack towards Rune Citadel for the first time as Alfheim's citizens; the She-Wolf turned and snarled upon seeing Ulrich twirl above the burning Hinterlands before withdrawing to the city.

The trek back to the ivory walls seemed like a dream, and Silver couldn't contain himself any longer as he spouted out, "I wish I could have seen your fight against Xyaxon. You were amazing in your battle with the Lich, but killing a god—magnificent."

She nodded to his pocket that hid the memory timepiece. "You could always see the fight yourself."

"Aye, that's true, but I would rather experience it with you, and you two were the ones who brought him the battle and defeated him. I can only imagine your epic fight. Before viewing the memory, I want you to tell me all about it in detail."

"I promise I will share this tale with you later tonight."

"Very good." He chuckled, and his eyes drifted over his shoulder and at Thor's pavilion. "I didn't want to ruin it for him, but Ebony also helped us rebuild the city." He sighed, but he gave her a faint smile. "You were right, my dear. She answered your letter, and she helped us fight. I'm surprised she came through."

Selena said, "They can use the time. Thor deserves to be happy, and it's been a while since the two were together."

"I've missed you." The two leaned in for a kiss, but he sternly remarked when they broke away. "Don't ever leave me again before an important battle." She gave him a half-crooked grin before falling into his embrace once more.

The pair peered at the Hinterlands when they pulled away. Selena's eyes shimmered when Ulrich fulfilled his promise to the Aynu; the black Aether flames died, and the guardian trees suddenly grew with the new opulent lushness fresh from a forest fire. The emerald sward swept away the charred ground, and as Ulrich dashed south over the dead scar, the Hinterlands awoke its sparkling green ballad of life.

"Well, I'll be damned," Silver grinned, "the magic of the Divines never ceases to amaze me."

Upon their return to the city, Selena couldn't help but be awestruck as Alfheim stood as a testament to Silver's work for accommodating the dragons. The cobblestone streets were wide enough for two dragons of Thor's size to walk alongside, with separate pathways built for civilian use. Yet, the Aynu dashed across the roads in glee, examining every nook and cranny.

Rune Citadel welcomed them in full grandeur upon its mountain home, spires of gold-streaked ivory stone reaching for the heavens. The Former Imperial Majesties stood with Lord Godfrey and Prince Damien on the marble steps, greatly anticipating their arrival, and bowed when Selena approached. Aryl and Vulduin ran over and coddled their daughter without a single word, and for once, she welcomed the affections.

Yet, making herself at home and walking through Rune Citadel's pearly-white walls was like a memory of a dream. While awake and alert, Silver barraged her with questions about the battle as she recouped, and Selena did her best to retell hers and Thor's victory story over the Fallen Divine. He was as excited as a child receiving a toy to hear how it all happened, but her mind still had yet to process their feat of killing a Divine.

Silver took his leave after the two shared an intimate evening and freshened up to make her usual drink of choice; Selena worked on some notes she wanted to discuss with her friends. After her coronation tomorrow, she wanted to meet with everyone to explain her first steps to restore the Empire. Yet, she was worried about what the others would think of her ideas but knew that eventually, her friends would understand and support her decisions.

When finished, she found Loki and asked him to bring her notes to the meeting room in the Fire Temple, where she could promptly begin. Satisfied with his delivery, Selena then poked at Thor's consciousness. *Do you think they sound okay?*

It took him a moment to reply. **I believe so, and if I think of anything else, I'll add it to your list.**

I'm not interrupting you and Ebony, am I?

Never. She's sleeping right now, anyways. Selena rolled her eyes, but she couldn't blame him for wanting their privacy; she was not in a position to criticize. **Did you miss me?**

Of course, I did. You wouldn't believe all that happened while you were away.

Please, enlighten me. Yes, I overheard bits and pieces, and Silver promised to show me, but I want to know everything directly from you. As she recalled her tale, she couldn't help but miss Thor again. From mastering her dragon state to her and Silver getting married, Selena wanted him there for every moment. Now, Venexus could never drive a wedge between them again. **I've missed you so much, and I'm sorry I couldn't have been there for you when you needed me most.**

In return, Thor recounted his painful adventure in fighting off the Dark Master's control, and Selena's heart shattered when she realized that he was there all along, but she missed him or couldn't sense his presence from the pirate fleet or Blackheart. Unable to find the right words to express her sentiments about his agonizing tale, Thor added: **I want you and Silver to come outside and join us.**

We will be in a short while.

When Silver returned with their beverages, the two discussed her drafted notes. He made a few minor suggestions, but he loved her ideas, except for the fate of the Dreygur. Yet, Silver finally agreed with her opinions after debating the plans to help both parties.

The two shared their tea before joining Thor within his pavilion, his eyes sparkling in pleasure to see the two in their dragon forms flying overhead. The sleeping Ebony curled beside his stomach, their tails wrapped around within their protective coils; the two gleaming like piled treasure from a distance.

After morphing back to their usual guises, Thor extended out a sheltering wing, herding the two as Silver and Selena collapsed on top of his foreleg. Making good on his promise, Silver pulled out the black pocket watch again and wound the dials to the exact moment after Thor conceded to the Dark Master's calling.

The painful memories replayed Selena's journey, from the pirates capturing her, to joining forces with the Nidhoggr, to the fight against the Lich, and for Silver's sake, the final battle against Xyaxon. During their viewing, Ebony yawned and opened one eye to see their feats in full detail, and she snuggled closer to Thor.

Silver couldn't help but praise the pair for their glorious victory and held Selena close. However, she and Thor grew weary and did their best to stay awake and answer any questions he had. **Thank you, Silver. I'm glad you were able to share those memories with me.** He nuzzled Selena's back and purred. **My dearest one, I will never part from you again.**

Wrapping his protective arms around and pulling the two near his chest, Thor and Selena fell into a deep slumber while Silver busied himself by sketching out Thor's jewelry ideas. For the first time in so long, Selena slept soundly that evening.

The early mornings of Moonstar would usually be draped in darkness during the winter, but the new day was so bright that the sunlight glistened like gemstones. Selena returned to her room as the sun rose to prepare for the upcoming celebrations, while Silver helped with the outside events and fulfilled Thor's commission orders for jewelry.

After setting down her wolf necklace on her bedside table, she stared from her wide window to see the Dreygur, Nidhoggr, and the Aynu beginning to live in peace and harmony within the newly built city; the demons had already returned to Oblivion, courtesy of Azrael. The Dreygur, to her relief, no longer acted like the mindless abominations that once attacked her allies. Even their forms slightly differed where they now looked alive— their flesh no longer rotted off the bone, but a slight discoloration upon their skin gave away their nature. From afar, they looked like ordinary citizens, preparing for Selena's coronation that was to happen when the new Pyre struck seven. Which reminded her—

She was already dressed for the occasion: a long white gown with gold trimmings, augmenting her sun-kissed copper-toned cheeks, matching her white heels embroidered with gold and mother-of-pearl. Selena fastened the front with a sapphire gem button while standing in front of a full-body mirror, tying her long ombre hair back in a neat, loose bun decorated with pearls catching the snow and azure hues. All she needed to complete her ensemble were her ivory silk gloves; she stared down at her Aether hand before slipping them on.

As confident as she was in her abilities to mend a new one of flesh and blood, Selena smirked at the ghostly and wispy look; she embraced the idea of being different. After losing the mark that defined her for so long, Selena now had a new characteristic that she wanted to carry proudly since the destruction of her mechanical hand. However, she never wanted to forget what she went through and would always be grateful for Silver's ingenuity for her to strive for normalcy as much as possible.

She slipped her gloves on one by one before wearing her ring and strapping Dragonheart to her dress belt. After maneuvering around Rune Citadel, Selena eventually found herself in the throne room where her parents ruled. The last time she strolled through the keep was her hearing, but she stood in awe before the royal diamond seat donned in soft furs. The throne served as a reminder that she and Thor would always protect their people and the world.

Mounted above was a dragon skull twice the size of Thor's massive head, where the diameter of one eye socket was the length of two fully grown adult humans.

Two colossal bony wings—one the size of Thor head-to-tail alone—unfolded from behind the throne, held by invisible twine threaded from unicorn hair: stronger than a diamond, like their horns.

Her parents stood before the enormous front doors, catching her looking in admiration, and Vulduin gestured to the dragon skull. "This was Yggdrasil. She was the one who helped us make peace with the dragons many years ago and the Divinity Dragon who birthed you and Thor." She recalled the stories of Epoch—the first Divinity Dragon—when she and Thor journeyed to Snowhaven; Yggdrasil was a behemoth Crimson Deathwing. "Yggdrasil lived longer than any dragon in recorded history. After passing her blessing to you and Thor, she left to die in peace. Months later, Silver found her remains in Shadowgreen Grove, where he claims Yggdrasil first hatched, as dragons always return to the place of their birth before passing away. We brought her back here and mounted her skull above the throne to testament her gifts." He paused and smiled as his eyes landed upon Dragonheart. "I used some of her bones to meld with steel for your sword."

Stricken with awe that she carried Yggdrasil's essence, her hand instinctively reached down, and her fingers traced along with the jeweled pommel. "You truly are a master blacksmith. It has served me well, and Dragonheart is a fine sword. The blade never dulls, no matter how many times I've used it, and it cuts through anything."

"Always keep it with you. It suits the new Dragon Queen."

Her mother smiled. "You look very becoming."

Selena bowed, but Vulduin stopped her. "You will never have to do that again. We will all bend the knee to you." Before she could object, both her parents bowed before her.

Aryl's voice was cracking as if she would break. "After all you've done and gone through, you deserve so much more. The last time we were all here in Rune Citadel together was when it all began for us."

Vulduin still looked stricken with grief. "We could never make amends for what we put you through. You've struggled and suffered from our mistakes, and all we want is for you to be happy."

Selena held her head high. "And now, everything is finally over. It's all so different." Her eyes glossed over like a frozen lake in winter as she found the courage to say, "I forgive you."

The two Former Imperial Majesties relished their reconciliation, but the three were interrupted when the Pyre began chiming. This time, however, the clock's rings sounded different, as before, they used to be so grim, but now—

"They sound beautiful." Selena's words echoed from her breath.

"It's time." Vulduin opened the door to the coronation platform above the massive castle courtyard. Selena walked out first, followed by Aryl, then Vulduin himself.

A large crowd waited for them: a mixture of locals and undead stood in front of the Nidhoggr—among them Noctis, Obsidian, Vyrilion, Fafnir, Ysyra, and Kayda— lined themselves in the very back, decorated in golden chains set with different colored gemstones that magnified the hue of their slick, black hides.

Zipping overhead were Sethak, Rhasydra, and Volterion among their tiny flutter of metallic-looking wings, dressed in small, gold chains holding glistening pearls displayed on their chests. Vyrilion snorted at the younglings in place of Kayda, and the three settled in between their mother's paws.

The Aynu pack lined up beside Lord Godfrey, Prince Damien, Lord Vanguard, Lady Maria, and the Shadow Templars—concealed in cloaks—with She-Wolf Kiba and Alpha Male Maru amongst the facade. A golden oval-shaped trinket gleamed from Kiba's arms as she cradled their treasure like a newborn child: Ulrich made good on his promise to restore the Hinterlands and return their paragon. Standing right beneath the platform were what remained of the denizens from Alfheim and the other kingdoms before the Lich's onslaught, including Chaliss, Rahim, and Niamh.

Like a statue to the platform's right, Thor donned a solid gold torque set with deep royal blue mixed with light green sapphires around the base of his neck and gold talon-sheaths tipped with the identical unique sapphires on his foreleg nails—yet, his totem remained wrapped around his left bare thumb claw. Thor explained that he displayed the gold and ruby chain gifted from Aracania upon a dragon-shaped mannequin in his trophy room Silver had granted him within his estate.

I swear he spoils you to remain on agreeable terms with me, Selena teased, but she was happy to see Thor lavishing in his treasures. His elegant jewelry glistened against his diamond scales. His newly altered golden bracelets forged from the old shop, Dragonfire and Steel, faceted the identical gemstones to complete his dazzling set—courtesy of Silver.

When Thor commissioned Silver for the new treasures and the possibility of a differently colored stone to better match the tint of Selena's scales, Silver produced a unique deep blue-green-hued sapphire that had never been discovered. Thor remained adamant that this new gem of choice would commemorate Selena's scale colors.

To his left were General Araneus and Aracania, dressed in their best attire for this momentous occasion. Aracania wore a golden torque set with deep royal topazes awarded by her rider for her bravery, loyalty, and skill from the Battle of Armageddon, glittering against her slick black scales. Matching his companion, General Araneus displayed his new heroic golden badge set against his black suit with gilded trimmings, donning his best breeches and polished hessian boots. Cyres stood proudly beside him, adorned with similarly rewarded trinkets, including his newly promoted title: Admiral Theron Cyres. He and Silver now shared the same rank directly below Araneus.

Newly promoted Captains Gromm and Beck Steelmane stood beside them, dressed in formal attire, heads high in pride as they were presented as war heroes to the cheering public. Lastly, from the lineup, Volt White, now Lieutenant, remained beside Skyfyre, displaying a platinum chain with a mother-of-pearl pendant sparking upon his chest.

Vulcan's large shadow dashed overhead as he landed as gracefully as he could with one hind leg extended, and the crowd backed away to give him space to sit back on his haunches. The red dragon puffed out his chest to also showcase his new treasure, a gold chain set with a large yellow diamond that he anxiously polished every so often.

Ebony circled overhead before landing upon the stone gate protecting the perimeter, decorated in a platinum torque set with sapphires around her neck, matching her talon-sheathes tipped with the deep blue gems—an addition to Thor's commission order.

Doragon, with Azrael astride his back, perched on top of a castle tower nearby as Ulrich spiraled above. The Emerald Dragon eventually settled not far from the two on the side of the mountain castle, as there was no more room to accommodate his size. The two Divines were the only dragons not dressed in expensive treasures, as they had no desire to relish in adorning mortal trinkets.

Silver—donned in the same attire he wore for their wedding, including the gold chain set with a dragon head pin—waited with his hands clasped behind his back while the Oracles, Neith, and Loki stood behind him, sharing huge smiles. As soon as Selena walked out, they bowed in respect, and the crowd began to cheer. She and Thor found each other among the adoring gathering, and their eyes sparkled upon contact.

May our mother Yggdrasil watch over us.

She would be so happy and proud.

When the noise settled and the Pyre rang its last chime, Selena cleared her throat and spoke. "Today, this war is officially over, marking the beginning of the Second Empire and the Age of Dragons. The Lich may be gone, but the path to restoration will be challenging. I promise we will all walk together hand in hand towards a better and brighter future as we rebuild the world better than it was before."

As Selena knelt, Neith made her way with the golden crown designed by Thor: a solid gold spiked halo headdress tipped with the unique blue-green sapphires. An intricate piece connecting to the diadem held a flawless oval white diamond—for Thor's new scale color— surrounded by pearls decorated Selena's forehead as Neith placed the royal headpiece. "All hail your Dragon Queen, Selena Liongod."

The crowd cheered once more as Selena stood, and the Oracles grinned. "May your Divine fire forever reign." Thor thundered and released a long torrent of rainbow fire, shooting like a fallen star across the sky. Noctis joined in his roar of victory as he, his flight, and the surviving dragons stood on their haunches—including the younglings—and spewed their combined fire skyward, wings unfurled. Selena walked closer to the edge with Silver by her side to see the new Dragon Empire screaming their love and devotion for their new queen.

CHAPTER 28: THE OLD COUNCIL AND THE NEW

Promptly following the ceremony, the rest of the crowd dispersed, and the Nidhoggr scattered back to their pavilions like a murder of crows; Selena met with her allies and the leaders with the request to have an official meeting at the newly rebuilt Fire Temple. Her parents agreed to sit in on the assembly, and although they wouldn't be in charge, she wanted them there for their support.

Everyone who passed by congratulated her for being crowned the new queen. Kiba and Maru, with their golden paragon, came in next to Lord Godfrey and Prince Damien; behind them were Kain and Maria; when the two locked gazes, Maria gave her a smile and a curtsy while Kain gave her a nod and a salute. After bending before her assembly, Gromm, Beck, and Volt excused themselves to tend to Vulcan's and Skyfyre's needs; General Araneus ordered their prompt arrival for the celebration later that evening—the five were required to attend, to which they happily agreed.

To Selena's dismay, the two Divines took their leave, but Azrael promised to return for the celebration dinner. "The demons have returned to Oblivion, but I suppose we can stay for a bit longer. Doragon and I wouldn't miss it." He winked, and he and Doragon departed. Selena thought they would have wanted to stay and talk for a while, and she feared their swift return to Oblivion—she dreaded that coming day.

Ulrich apologized, however, as there would be no guarantee that he could attend; Selena understood he had his repairs to make, starting with Rhumbek. Instead, the Divine bowed with his promise to remain for as long as he could and launched heavenward, unfolding his wings midair as the dust billowed from every flap he made.

Thor snaked his head around Selena and nudged his snout against her arm, fixating his twinkling eyes upon her royal headdress, admiring the gems and gold in extreme delight. Silver, meanwhile, examined the dragon in complete gratification with his alchemy work that produced the royal jewelry. "Are you satisfied with your order, Thor?"

Yes, indeed. My new gemstones will serve as my shimmering testament for the world to see my bond with the Dragon Queen.

Silver smiled and bowed. "It is a lovely tribute, and I'm glad to have been of service."

Before excusing himself to join Ebony in the sky, Thor addressed Selena directly, **I will be listening in on your meeting if you need me, my dear one,** and the two climbed the heavens and circled before flying away.

However, Silver's eyes scanned through the crowd. Selena was confused but understood why when she saw Loki running across everyone's feet. He made haste to be by her side, and when the fox met up with her, he bowed like everyone else. "It's so great to address you as Your Majesty. As you know, I've served Her Imperial Majesty for many years, and now, I serve you."

"Thank you, Loki."

When the fox looked up to see Silver, his orange fur turned pale, and he growled. Silver was about to snatch Loki off the ground, but Selena got in the way and intervened. "Leave him alone."

"But I want to eat him."

Loki hissed, and his fur stood up on end. Selena thought that the two resolved their differences from Godfrey's fortress, but she had been wrong before. "That's enough. We're stopping this feud since Loki now serves me."

Silver bit his lip but agreed and winked. "As you wish, Your Majesty." Still wholly unsatisfied, Loki snorted before dashing ahead and up the stairs. Although Selena helped diffuse the situation, the fox still didn't trust him. She couldn't blame Loki, but for the time being, it was enough.

Right before they made it inside the temple, the group was interrupted by Rahim, who parted his way through the crowd with Niamh following close. "Pardon us, everyone: best friend and brother coming through, thank you. Everyone can gawk at the Queen of Dragons from over here, but as for Niamh and I, we get to stand right there. Thank you very much. I think we've earned that right." The others laughed at him. "But seriously, how does it feel to be Armageddon's new queen?"

"I haven't fully realized it yet."

"While sitting on that diamond throne, don't forget about us." Rahim smiled and winked.

"Don't be daft, as we couldn't have done any of this without you. Your ideas and plans helped us win this war—you're the real hero." Rahim's face gleamed at her recognizing his accomplishments.

The general made his way as Aracania slithered around the crowd, her nails clicking against the pavement: she may be daintier than Thor, but she was still large enough to fill the temple as she squeezed through like a snake. Selena was about to salute, but Araneus knelt before her as he did back at Dark Blood Hold. Admiral Cyres approached from the pell-mell crowd and followed the general's example.

"Your Grace, it is an honor to serve you. Aracania and I pledge our allegiance to you and the Empire until our dying breath," said Araneus.

"Sir, you and Aracania don't need to address me so formally. I'm still Liongod."

"We serve the imperial family. You and Thor command us, Your Majesty." Chittering, Aracania approached Selena and knelt in turn.

The temple was almost how Selena remembered it, but now a tapestry hung from the back wall, showing Selena and Thor as dragons, with Azrael on one side and Ulrich on the other. The different murals cascading on the right side told a new story: instead of showing all three of the Divines ruling in peace, they were of Selena's and Thor's fight against Xyaxon battling in the eternal cosmos. The canvases narrated the tale of how the two killed a god in a beautiful tableau.

They have already finished the paintings celebrating our feat.

Thor hummed in delight. **They were quick, even working through the evening.**

Silver caught up to her and placed a hand on her shoulder. "Thor is right, my dear. No, My Dragon Queen." She bit her tongue when he laughed at his mistake, but she still smiled. "Our great artists worked all night to have this gift ready for your coronation. We call your greatest feat 'The Dance of Dragons.'"

Selena allowed the words to roll over her tongue; although honored that everyone would remember her and Thor forever for saving their world, she cringed that she and Thor were already being worshiped as gods. "Can you hear Thor freely now?"

Silver grinned. "Yes, but only whenever he includes me in your conversation."

A massive war room large enough for a dragon of Thor's size waited for them behind the drapes, and the group took their seats around a large, rectangular oak table. Aryl and Vulduin were already present, but instead of sitting down, they stood behind Selena's seat in the corner of the room.

Lord Godfrey and Prince Damien took their spots at the very end with two Templar guards standing post behind the nobles. Kiba and Maru sat beside them, with their artifact nestled between them. Silver ensured his seat next to his wife while Rahim took her other side; although Silver's seating arrangement was expected, Rahim couldn't help but make faces at him, but he quickly stopped when Selena glared at him.

Aracania sat outside the room while she kept her head in the doorway, as she couldn't fit her body through the entrance; her tail flickered side to side as she watched the party settle, ready for deliberations. Araneus took a seat closest to her, and Admiral Cyres settled on his right. Loki was already within, laying down Selena's scribbled parchments: on top was a map of Armageddon and her notes for the upcoming discussion.

Pedestals stood behind them with the Mythic Flight dragon eggs caressed in their velvet cases. As everyone situated themselves, they looked over at the eggs and made eye contact with Selena, half-expecting the treasured trove as part of today's debate. Their new queen smiled and gave a firm nod in confirmation; the eggs would need new riders soon, by Silver's calculations. Their hatching moment would be her chance at re-establishing the Mythic Flight.

"Thank you, all, for meeting me here right after my coronation," Selena began, "as I've said before, the road to fix Armageddon is long and harsh, but I know that we will get the Empire back on the right path and bring everyone together. The future is for all of us to decide.

"First and foremost, I want to establish giving citizenship to the Aynu, the Dreygur, and the Nidhoggr." She made eye contact with Kain, as he was still indecisive on the matter; Silver made his sentiments known the night before and, after much discussion and persuasion on Selena's part, eventually agreed that it was the right decision. "As much as the demons want peace, Azrael mentioned that they had already returned to Oblivion, where they belong. The Dreygur, from what I've seen this morning alone, can function and contribute to civilized society. Yet, they fail to remember being among the living, but they're willing to try."

Only Kain remained slightly reluctant while everyone else agreed. "I won't turn a blind eye to see their integration, but I'm worried about this change being an act or suddenly reverting to their old ways. Is this a risk you're willing to take?"

"I'm not considering it a risk, as Silver and I thought of a plan to prevent the worst from coming to pass."

Silver stood up when it was his turn to speak and pulled out a long schematic of a building, explaining that he was currently constructing a new temple that would provide housing and the resources necessary to help the Dreygur learn how to function in society. "I should have the House of the Undead finished before the celebration this evening." He finished with a smug grin, as he had a knack for building a full-sized structure within minutes.

Kain stood up and looked over Silver's drawn diagrams with interest, but he asked, "And what if they don't want to participate in this rehabilitation? You can't force them to do this if they don't want to, and if force is involved, then—"

"Then that will create an issue of racism, and it could lead to rebellion," Selena grimly interrupted, "that's why it won't be required, but it will be their choice. Those who don't want to participate don't have to, but if they break our laws, they will be punished accordingly, just like everyone else." When Kain remained slightly on the fence, Selena pointed out their change in appearance. "Surely you've seen their transformation from this morning alone. I'm beginning to wonder if they are slowly reverting their altered state."

"Aye, I have seen them, but I doubt that. Once you're among the walking dead, there's no reversing it. Believe me, I know." Kain made unblinking direct eye contact with her. "Just because they look alive doesn't mean they'll function as the living."

"Why are you so severe on your own kind?"

"Dammit, the Dreygur are not my kind." Kain eased his tone through deep breaths to keep himself from getting worked up. "With all due respect, Your Grace, I'm not as forgiving as you are. You should be holding these grudges out of everyone here, not me."

"I don't condemn those not responsible for their actions," Selena sternly retorted, "the Dreygur were controlled and used, just like the Nidhoggr, like Vyrilion." Kain hung his head. "Would you condemn Vyrilion?"

The room fell eerily quiet while Selena waited for an answer, and everyone jumped when Kain finally broke the silence. "Your Grace, you will have to make sure they are clear on these conditions because I don't want to bust in any heads if I don't have to."

"Fair enough, Lord Vanguard."

"Will the Nidhoggr have to go through the same as the Dreygur?" Kain still couldn't bring himself to look up as he remained deep in thought about his and Maria's dear companion, heavily considering Selena's argument.

"That will be our next topic, but for now, do we all agree on these conditions for the Dreygur?" Everyone released a sigh of relief as the tension between Selena and Kain made the party fidget in their seats, and one by one, they agreed with the plan.

Once everyone settled, Kiba and Maru nodded before placing their unique treasure on the table. "We want to gift your new temple with Artio's artifact as a sign of rebirth."

The room suddenly grew quiet; all eyes focused on the solid gold oval-shaped trinket, as everyone had witnessed its power over the Hinterlands' miraculous regrowth. Selena's hands shook as she held herself up over the table. "That is extremely generous of you, but are you sure?"

"Of course. We won't be needing it anymore, now that you've allowed us to return," and, when Kiba finished, Maru added, "Consider this as our token of gratitude."

"We are honored for your contribution to the House of the Undead, and we greatly thank you for it." Both parties satisfied, Selena leaned a little over the table and whispered to Kain, "I promise we will make it work."

"I can't trust on promises alone, Your Majesty."

"Like Death, I keep my promises."

Kain couldn't help but give her a half-crooked smirk at her boldness and sat back down, looking at Silver and pointing to her. "She's a pistol, my friend. I hope you can handle her."

Silver laughed; as a demigod, he feared no one but Selena knew that she was, perhaps, the one who frightened him the most. "That leads to my next focus: I want to rebuild the Imperial Air Force." Aracania clicked her tongue and snaked her head around to face her handler. The general, however, held his tongue as his face turned pale, possibly still blaming himself for their initial downfall. "Much like the rehabilitation plan for the Dreygur, the Nidhoggr may join and serve the Empire if they wish; otherwise, they will share the same rights and liberties as dragons, which should be above our own. It would be foolish to turn them away when they stood by our side and helped us achieve victory. Silver already began making modifications to Alfheim, such as expanding the streets and building pavilions for housing instead of stables. They've already bonded with new riders, like Noctis," Selena faced Damien and Godfrey, "and Obsidian."

"Eshara," Rahim whispered.

"Eshara, Fafnir, Ysyra, Vyrilion," Selena looked back at Kain, who slowly nodded. "After working with them at Dark Blood Hold, they still want to help, and they will be valuable assets to the new Air Force should they desire to serve."

A smile creased the general's face. "I see. Yes, you're right, My Queen. They will be valuable indeed. Very well, I shall have those who wish to join start training immediately." Aracania made chirping noises in agreement.

"Thank you, sir. On that note, I want to reverse how women are treated in this Empire built by men and, therefore, will have the same rights as men. That will include the privilege of serving in the Force and becoming a handler. On the same merit, every dragon will have the freedom of choice, not be forced like before. I don't grovel to anyone, and I refuse to see the others coerced as if bound by chains. Unless by choice, dragons and Nidhoggr serve neither man nor king and should live and die by their own will. Vidar and the old Council tried controlling dragons and using them as tools of war, but we will not make their mistakes. I want us to make amends for our betrayal, abuse, and defilement." Everyone within the war room agreed without hesitation; Thor hummed in delight upon hearing her heartfelt speech.

When it grew quiet, Selena continued: "However, any new riders and handlers must be trained to care for their companions properly if the dragon doesn't teach them first." The room filled with laughter at her witticism. "I have one other condition if we are to re-establish the Force: we will no longer host the initiation, as the tradition is barbaric and rubbish and has cost us many soldiers for, what I could imagine, the Council's amusement. Sir, do you and Aracania agree?"

The general's head spun around to the sound of Aracania's chirps and nail clicks. Admiral Cyres hung his head in defeat and said, "I always suspected the initiation was part of the Council's propaganda, and for what reason they imposed it upon us, I will never know."

"Perhaps some cruel, sick joke on their part." Araneus slapped his hand against the table. "Of course, we will abolish that practice right away, Your Majesty."

"Excellent." She looked over at Niamh, who was glowing in her spot; when she asked if her and Fafnir were interested in becoming recruits, Selena smiled. "Of course. If you two desire, you will report to General Araneus and Aracania as soon as they are ready. Your Highness," Selena nodded to Damien, "what about you and Noctis? Would you two like to join? You two fought spectacularly in the battle, and it would be an honor."

"Your Grace, I am honored, and I know Noctis will agree. Let me speak with my companion first, but I'm personally interested." Damien directed his gaze at General Araneus and Admiral Cyres. "Sir, Noctis and I will give you our final decision by today's end. Is this agreeable to you?"

The general looked to Niamh, who at first gave him a thumbs up, but he laughed when she corrected herself and gave him a salute instead. When Aracania dipped her head in approval, he and Cyres gave the prince a firm nod and grinned. "We can't very well say no to either of you two, now can we? Aracania and I will be anxiously waiting for your final answer, Your Highness."

Admiral Cyres' smile brightened his swollen, aged face. "And you will still have your officers, General. Ysyra and I will serve you." He and Silver exchanged lightened glances, and Silver confirmed his current status, to which Araneus wholeheartedly accepted.

Thor interrupted her thoughts. **I want to help, too.**

Are you sure?

Yes. I can assist Aracania and Ysyra train those who wish to join. See if General Araneus and Aracania will accept it.

There should be no reason for them to refuse you, my dear.

When she reiterated Thor's offer, Araneus and Cyres almost choked; Aracania chittered in delight. "Y-yes, of course. It could work—no, that will work. Aracania can work with him and Ysyra and share her wisdom." Everyone clapped to the good news, and her eyes scanned over her notes, but she looked up when the general called for her attention. "Your Majesty, if I may." Selena inclined her head forward, permitting General Araneus to continue. "I also want your brother, Rahim Branwen, to join."

Rahim's eyes widened at the offer. "What? Me? I'm not that good, and I'm not a handler."

"Of course, I mean you. Oh, take care, my boy, and maybe one day, a dragon will choose you as their handler, but you are a genius. Because of you, we won this war. Without your plan, we would have lost and been destroyed. The Force needs someone like you. I want you to be my battle strategist as a General Officer, where you will work directly under me with my officers, and I will not accept no for an answer."

Rahim's face lit up bright like the sun from the general's compliment of his abilities, and he shot up from his seat without wasting another second and gave Araneus a firm salute. "Sir, I accept."

"Very good. When we get everything situated and ready, we will discuss your job requirements and salary."

The table burst into applause. Selena shared a massive smile with Rahim before he took his seat. However, she knew that the next item on her list would be a considerable debate, but it needed to be addressed. She almost choked on her saliva as she spoke. "My next topic may sound a little unorthodox. Ironically, I want to maintain having a Council." She stopped when she heard gasps and protests around the room.

"That's a big load," Kiba shouted.

Kain snorted. "Oh, to Oblivion, we won't. Those damned rats caused enough damage, and you'll set us up for failure."

Damien placed an open palm on the table. "Your Grace, if I may. The Council has been nothing but trouble. We can't afford to see another political struggle."

Niamh shook her fists. "I object too. They used Fafnir and me to destroy Alfheim."

Maria chimed in for the first time during the entire discussion: "Think of what Vidar did to the Empire and my family." Selena didn't need reminding of the misfortunes that had tormented the Gundisalvus line, yet her face drained of all color when she recalled the horrors they endured. She nodded over at the general, who kept opening his mouth to speak but couldn't find the words. Aracania snaked over to him and rubbed her snout against his leg.

Rahim locked gazes with Selena, and his eyes looked like glass. "How do you still want to keep the Council alive, even after all Vidar put you and your family through? My family? Not to mention the rest of the Empire."

Selena's friends spoke against the idea, cluttering the room with their disapproving words. She felt her stomach tear open from the discussion, as this growing debacle was the last possible outcome that she wanted to happen. Then again, she couldn't expect everyone just suddenly to agree. However, her parents remained silent during the ordeal; they kept their opinions to themselves, but Vulduin's smoldering eyes glared at each of their reddened faces, and Selena assumed he was ready to jump up and strike them down.

Silver's lips trembled as he stood up and banged his fists against the table to gather the room's attention. "Hold your tongues, or I will. Listen to my wife: she has her reasons, and it would be best to hear what she has to say."

The room immediately turned quiet from his outburst. Selena believed they were more appalled by his extreme and sudden rudeness, but no one argued with him. "Thank you, Silver. Please, hear what I have to say first before further objections, as I wish to explain my reasoning and how I want to accomplish this.

"Vidar and the rest of the ex-Council members are gone and have fled Alfheim, and I doubt we will ever deal with them again. I like the original idea to help keep the peace and represent the public, but I want to make some changes: to have a new Council of solid and trustworthy leaders. Instead of appointing someone else to be in charge, I will be the head of the government to prevent another unjust political system like before." Her allies' whispers and murmurs resonated across the table. "I also want anyone here who is willing to serve to join my new Council, so we can unite and work together for what's best."

"Wait, why should you be head of the Council? Why not one of us?" Kiba asked.

"As I've said before, this will keep everything just and fair. We can't have another political struggle. As much as I trust each of you, I don't want a repeat of what happened before."

Kain's eyes darted all around the room to look at everyone's expressions, and Selena knew they were still not convinced. "My Queen, I think I speak for everyone here. We understand that you're doing what you think is right, but I want to know this: how can we be sure you won't turn out like Vidar? What can we do if it ever comes to that?"

"I will never turn into that foul, loathsome, vile creature that isn't worthy to lick the dirt off my shoes. Like we're doing now, I will host a meeting once a week here to debate the Empire's affairs and decide upon the best route to handle future issues. I will give each of you the power to have your voice heard by granting a voting system to prevent any injustice. This way, you will all have a say in what goes. I will depend on all of you to make this work."

Niamh held her chin. "So, does that mean if you want to enforce a new law, your new Council will have to discuss it and vote?"

"Yes, any decisions, laws, anything regarding the Empire, all of you who join will be involved and will have a say so. Vidar made all the decisions within the old

Council, regardless of the other members' opinions. They didn't have a choice, but you will. I can't run Armageddon alone. That's why I want to include all of you in this process."

The table fell into a deep discussion, whispering and sighing as everyone worked at coming to an agreeable conclusion. Selena kept her hands firmly on the table, knowing she had to make this work, but that wouldn't happen if her friends didn't concur.

Kain cleared his throat, breaking the silence, and scratched his neck. "How many did you want to be part of the new Council?"

"I'm not sure yet, as it will depend on who wants to step up."

"I may consider, but who do you have in mind?" Godfrey asked.

Selena smiled. "For one, I was thinking of you, my Lord. You can represent the Shadow Templars and keep their best interests in mind." Lord Godfrey didn't argue with that; instead, he and his son grinned. "Kain, after what you've done to help the Empire and me, I believe you deserve a seat in the Council. The offer is extended to Maria, too." The two vampire nobles looked at each other before nodding in agreement. "Kiba and Maru, since you two and the Aynu are now citizens of Alfheim, I was also hoping you two would join so that the Aynu are involved and have representation."

The paired alphas looked at each other. Maru gave a gruff, and Kiba agreed. "We accept, but if that power ever goes to your head, I will take you down myself."

"I have no doubts that you will if it ever came to that." Although Selena was strong enough to kill a Divine, she still feared Kiba. "Admiral Altessa, I know that your duties are to help rebuild the new Force, but I was also considering you to join."

Before Silver could answer, Rahim interrupted. "But wait, he will have so much to do. He has the Force, the Council, and the Divines know what else. Wouldn't he be the new king since you two are married?"

Everyone's gazes immediately set on Silver, who squirmed in his spot. "Er... no. I will not be the king." Upon further questioning for declining the royal position, Silver continued: "I've been at this for a long time—too long, in fact. I've witnessed the rise and fall of civilizations. I'm the one who invented magic after learning from the dragons; I've discovered every dragon species known to man, dwarf, and elf kind. I've found the cures and vaccines to many of the deadly diseases that have since died out," he nodded at Selena, "I'm the only one who has ever found a way to bring back the dead that's not necromancy. But I can't be a king—I'm not one to lead. I don't care for it, and I don't want it." He bit his bottom lip. "This is all yours, my dear. I will be here to support and help you with anything you need, but I will not be a king. The right to rule is yours, and yours alone."

She was sure as Oblivion to not argue with him on that. "Very well, and yes, I will still need your help. Will you at least consider the position as part of the new Council? I only ask this of you because you know how to do this better than anyone."

"Of course, I accept. I will help in any way I can."

Rahim stood up and pointed at himself. "Hey, what about me? Can I join as well?"

"Yes. I can't do this without you. You too, Niamh." Selena put her index finger on the table. "This will be our new Council. Everyone here. We've all been through so much together, and we know what is best for Armageddon." Her eyes immediately turned towards the dragon eggs when she thought she heard a sound, but they remained undisturbed within the shell.

Rahim swiveled in his seat when he noticed Selena's sudden attention change and scoped the room. "What's going to happen to the eggs?"

The chamber filled with murmurs and whispers about their fate, but everyone lowered their voices when Selena cleared her throat. "They are close to hatching, and we must find new handlers. Many of you know of the original dragon riders from the Mythic Flight, correct?" Selena gathered the consensus as yes. "Good. If no one knew of their importance, these eggs were laid by those from the Mythic Flight and are to be the next guardian specific to their element. Besides Divinity Dragons, these new guardians will be the most powerful creatures ever to walk this earth, which is why we must begin immediately at introducing potential riders to their eggs."

Niamh raised her hand halfway like a child asking permission to speak and asked, when Selena called out her name, "Did you have anyone specific in mind lined up as possible riders?"

Selena recalled when Thor chose her as his partner and gave the best answer she could to reinforce the importance of choice. "Ultimately, it's up to the hatchling on choosing their handler. All Armageddon's citizens may line up, and the new dragons could deny every one of them. We must be patient and—"

The group was interrupted when the eggs behind them began violently shaking.

CHAPTER 29: DAWN OF A NEW WORLD

Selena's heart raced as she and her group shot up and surrounded the quivering pedestals. With Silver's, Cyres', and the general's assistance, she picked up a corner of the velvet pillow, and the three laid it down on the ground as the four dragon eggs forcefully wobbled in place.

They're hatching.

Thor hummed in delight. **How exciting! They were highly impatient.**

Cracks spiderwebbed across their shells, and altogether without warning, the pieces flung apart, and all four slimy dragon hatchlings took their first, gentle steps out into the new world.

The fire whelpling was slightly larger than the others; its underbelly like hardened lava, a smoldering fire blazing beneath the crust and the tip of its tail while its eyes burned like the tiny embers blasting from its nostrils after a sneeze. The two horns on its head were shaped like Thor's, a red orb of energy suspended above its triangular-shaped head—each new hatchling had a matching sphere corresponding with their element: the water had blue, the earth had green, and the air had yellow. Its ruby scales looked like gem-encrusted jewelry, surrounding an emblazoned golden imperial topaz upon its chest, sparkling like the sun while unfurling its flaming wings.

Contrarily, the water hatchling pushed away from the pieces of its shell while walking towards the group, sniffing the air as it unfolded its wings like a lady's fan; its ice-blue eyes were like massive jewels plucked from a pendant. The dragonet was slippery and smooth, its turquoise hide and parchment-textured wing membranes gleaming with the colors like the ocean's surface. Its mermaid-like tail trailed behind as it walked in a zigzag motion; jagged spikes covered its chest, and spiked fins lined in dazzling deep royal blue sapphires trailed down its spine and tail.

The dragon of earth looked to be made of stone, and as small as it was, the baby must weigh as much as a giant boulder. Its calm, amber eyes darted between its siblings as it flickered its thick tail strong enough to bend metal—the tip resembled Kain's morning star, and it appeared just as deadly. Glowing underneath its crusty hide were perfectly cut deep green emeralds jutting as spikes along its chest. Moss, plants, flowers, and other vegetation grew in between its rock scales and the membrane of its wings, and when they extended, bits of dust and rock crumbled from expanding its muscles.

Last but not least, the strikingly white air dragon slithered its neck like a snake as it unfurled its feathered wings—inside tips decorated with rich, intense yellow diamonds—stretching at least three times its lean body length. Its five ivory claws on each foot clicked against the stone floor with every step it took. Two long tendrils appended to each side of its snout flowed and graced the floor, the small ruff along its jawline flaring and trembling slightly. Lightning pulsated around its pupiled-slits and shimmering emerald eyes and mouth, sparking like flames as it writhed around its smooth and glossy hide, bouncing between its electrical conductor spikes.

Selena looked over to Silver, and the two smiled, but they needed to start finding others who wouldn't mind the possibility of becoming a handler. She wasn't sure how this would work or how the whelplings would choose their riders; it was different for her and Thor, as they were already linked in more ways than one.

Before she could propose the plan to gather everyone back in the courtyard, the fire dragonet made its way to Rahim without a second thought. As he was unsure what to do, Rahim looked to his friends and backed away while holding his hands up, but the whelpling chirped at him and ran. Yet, he stopped when Selena asked him to; as the hatchling finally reached him, it bobbed its head up and down and rubbed up against his leg like a cat. "Good dragon," he said, though it sounded like a question.

Selena couldn't stop herself from grinning, and Silver clapped his hands together as he stepped forward to examine the hatchling's behavior. "It looks like we'll have to start training you to be a dragon rider immediately."

Rahim's eyes widened as much as his mouth did; he exercised great caution as he bent down to pet the new dragon as it forced its head into his palm. "Am I? D-did it…?"

"It chose you." Selena finished for him, her smile brightening up the room.

The fire dragon looked up at him and nuzzled its head into Rahim's hand. He couldn't stop beaming as he scooped up the hatchling in his arms, the blazing embers from its chest and wings only tickling against his skin. "I-I can't believe it—a dragon chose me."

General Araneus plopped a hand on his shoulder, watching with enthusiasm as the whelpling squirmed and chittered within Rahim's arms. "Now, you have your very own dragon. There are no more excuses for why you can't join the Force as my General Officer." Aracania bobbed her head up and down and gave a series of clicks and chirps in approval.

Everyone laughed but stopped when the water dragonet made its way towards Kain and Maria, its curved talons clicking against the stone floor. The group waited in anticipation as it smelled Kain, and then the baby stood on its haunches, thumping its tail against the floor with its large eyes fixated on the vampire lord. Kain stepped back; the dragon followed his movements and mimicked him when he tilted his head before chirping and climbing up his leg and chest to be held.

Unsure of the hatchling's decision, Kain stretched his arm, allowing the whelpling to attach itself, scrambling to his shoulder before establishing eye contact. "Oh, for fuck's sake. I don't believe I'm the best choice." It stared at him with its chilling eyes without blinking. At that moment, Kain closed his and nodded before bursting out laughing. "I can't believe this. Me? A dragon rider, and for the Mythic Flight, no doubt. You know what?" His eyes snapped open, and he lowered his face down to meet the hatchling's as it inched its nose closer. "Why in Oblivion not?" The dragon ruffled in place as it completely unfurled its wings, chattering and purring. Selena was pleasantly surprised to see how much Kain could smile, and his bliss was contagious; Maria shared his joy, and the two came for an embrace with the whelpling trapped in the middle. "I don't know what Vyrilion will think."

"I'll take care of Vyrilion. I'm sure he would understand." Maria laughed, reaching out to stroke the new hatchling as it twittered from her touch.

However, the group was interrupted when they heard Kiba's sudden growls and snarls—even Maru was surprised. The She-Wolf had her eyes fixed upon the earth dragon that approached and sniffed her with no introduction. Apparently, Kiba took it offensively, yet, the hatchling remained unfazed by her hostility but rather curious about her nature. The whelpling sat down upon satisfying its curiosity, flickering its weapon tail and scraping it across the floor.

Selena was unsure if Kiba fully understood the situation and her new position; the She-Wolf crossed her arms over her chest and tilted her head as she squinted at the gleeful creature. "It's a curious little dragon, isn't it?" She bit her lip, bent over, and placed a hand on the hatchling's head as it perked up and sniffed her fingers; it pushed its muzzle further into her palm and extended its six-spined wings, billowing dust and pebbles from every motion made. "I like you. An earth dragon? I've never seen one like you before, but I'll show you a thing or two about the earth." The whelpling ignored Maru—silent as usual while stepping forward to sniff the creature—and rushed over to head-butt Kiba in the leg. Despite its massive weight, the She-Wolf stood her ground, bellowing with laughter as she took the blow. "I think we're going to be best friends."

While the group was distracted, the air dragon vanished in a bolt of lightning, followed by a burning smell that always followed an extinguished candle. Among their frantic search for the hatchling, when Silver spun on his toes, the whelpling reappeared on his right shoulder, wings completely unfolded as it balanced itself by latching its talons to his jacket, wisps of lightning sparks tickling his skin. "Very interesting. Never in my years have I imagined…." He reached up to pet the dragon as it chirped and rubbed its head against his cheek. "I've never sought out a dragon's companionship, as I could change into one whenever I desired."

Selena couldn't hold back her joy as her broad grin stretched across her face. "But it's different when chosen to serve one. It's not just about needing each other, but rather the lifelong bond and friendship."

"You're right, my dear."

Kain snickered and held up his dragon next to Silver's. "It looks like we're both riders now. I can never get away from you, you old bastard."

As the remaining audience burst into a cheer for this glorious occasion, Selena, General Araneus, and Admiral Cyres stood beside Aracania's head, asking the new handlers to line up with the fresh hatchlings. Rahim couldn't help but admire while stroking the smoldering dragon, firing off many questions at once regarding its care, when training would begin, and so on; Silver and Kain only interrupted their attention to laugh at Rahim's absurdity. Oblivious to the three, Kiba was deep in conversation with her hatchling about how she originally dueled Selena to test her tenacity. To Selena's amusement, Kiba showed the dragon how a handshake worked; similar to the alpha's initial reaction, the whelpling bounced in its spot, chittering in delight.

"As your queen, I am thrilled to announce you four as the next generation of riders for the Mythic Flight. You will follow General Araneus' and Aracania's training, and the dragons will guide you. Trust in your companions, but you do not rule them, for they serve *no one*. They are incarnations of power and magic itself and live by their will alone. *You* are theirs to command."

The general, grinning ear to ear and unable to contain his excitement, stepped forward with his hands clasped behind his back. Aracania snaked her head across the floor, joyfully chirping as her tongue slithered forth from her clamped fangs. "We will begin training in three days. You five," he nodded to Niamh, "will report to

Admirals Cyres and Altessa for duty by the gardens. Aracania, Thor, and Ysyra will work with the dragons. In the meantime, the new hatchlings must be brought over to our recently built hatchling care unit so our scholars can examine them to ensure they're healthy. There, they can suitably feed and rest to promote proper growth." General Araneus raised his right closed fist above his head. "Long live the Empire!"

Niamh and the four new handlers of the Mythic Flight copied his gesture and returned with, "Long live the Empire!"

After Selena adjourned their meeting and the group followed General Araneus and Aracania towards the dragon grounds, Vulduin and Aryl reconvened to express their satisfaction at handling the Empire's affairs. "Being the queen suits you, and we trust that Armageddon will prosper under your rule." Vulduin's stoic face brightened the world with his smile, taking both Selena and Aryl by surprise. She was proud to receive her parents' approval of her competence as she grew to her station.

Aracania ordered the new handlers to carry their hatchlings over to the recently built dragon care unit—courtesy of Silver and Kain after reconstructing Alfheim. It was a single stone tower as tall and wide as Silver's library at the far end of the garden next to a fenced area filled with livestock, mixed with cows, pigs, and sheep, set apart explicitly for the hatchlings. The next few weeks would be crucial for the whelplings, as the caretakers needed to ensure they ate enough to oblige their early rapid growth. Silver explained they ought to prepare for the Mythic hatchlings to reach a more suitable and formidable size by three months.

Rahim was hesitant to leave his dragon behind, even for a day, but Selena reassured him it was for their proper care, and he could visit the hatchling later. "I can't wait to show mum—she'll be so proud."

The others showed reluctance in parting with their companions; Kain didn't care if they saw his tender side, as he was very endearing to the whelpling during his farewells. Kiba and her dragon shared a cute headbutt while Silver talked to his hatchling as if speaking with another intellectual. Yet, just as the butchers slaughtered the first cow, the whelps flapped their wings—only strong enough to glide from their handlers' arms to the ground—rushed over and immediately dug right into their meat feast.

The ravenous carnivores didn't take long, as they devoured the cow right down to the hooves within minutes, bones and all. The hatchlings wobbled inside the tower and fell asleep within their coils after finishing; the dragons lay sprawled over each other like a gleaming pile of treasure. Selena swore the newborns already looked bigger than when they first emerged from the shell, and at this rate, she was confident they would be Thor's size within a year, maybe less.

Thor and Ebony circled above and landed gracefully near the nursery, watching the slumbering hatchlings with delight. The rainbow flames writhing around his horns illuminated the hallow entrance, and the whelplings' gems glimmered from his light. **They were growing anxious when you mentioned how it could take a long time to find suitable handlers, as they already knew who they wanted.**

I didn't mean to bore them, but I wanted to emphasize the importance of choice.

They understood, but you should understand that we know better for ourselves, and we will do as we please.

How could I ever forget?

Selena smiled and stood in admiration of the two dragons, but she froze upon observing how Ebony's eyes sparkled as she rubbed her head against Thor's neck. She had this odd feeling that there was a certain glow about her, and her midsection looked swollen. That was when she realized—

Are you and Ebony…?

Chirping and chuckling in amusement, Thor whipped his head around to meet her dumbfounded expression, and Selena grinned ear to ear. **I can't hide anything from you, now can I?**

Congratulations! I'm happy for you two, but when did this happen?

She realized it before we started training with Ulrich a few weeks ago.

When will she lay her clutch?

Her time is coming soon, perhaps in a week or two.

Selena wanted to jump for joy, as she couldn't help but be ecstatic—Thor would be a father. Though dragons would lay their clutch within weeks after the act, hatchlings could remain in the shell for months or years, as they could sustain themselves indefinitely by drawing in the surrounding Aether; it was ultimately up to the dragon when the time was right to hatch.

Divinity Dragons could only produce one egg at a time, thus allowing them to pass on the Divine's blessing to their hatchling. However, she felt a stone drop in her stomach as the dreadful thought took root. *Will you pass on the Divine's gift to your new hatchling?*

His ethereal golden wings unfurled, Thor stepped closer and snaked his head around, fixating his amber pupil-slited eyes upon her. The snow-white mist gracing his triangular face felt like a misty fog kissing her cheek.

I'm not going anywhere. I promised I would never leave you.

Relief washed over her like the soothing ocean waves. She couldn't bear to lose Thor again, not then. As crucial as it would be to bring about the next generation of Divinity Dragons, Selena wasn't ready to say goodbye. Yet, she wondered how it would affect her if Thor did pass on his blessing—would she be the one to say goodbye, or would she join him in the next life? If Xyaxon meant for the pair to take his place as the next Divine, perhaps she and Thor could change that.

He lifted his massive jewel-tipped talons to wrap and pull her into an embrace, and she looped her arms around the base of his neck, touching the cold golden torque emblazoned upon his chest. Thor's thumping heartbeat was like sweet music to her ears, and she never wanted to be parted from him again. **I love you, my dear one.**

I love you, too.

After she finally released him, Thor stepped back and bound skyward in one leap, with Ebony following. Rahim, Kain, and Maria waved to the dragons' faint drifting silhouettes before leaving the gardens, but Silver remained behind, his stymied gaze not daring to pry away from the hatchlings; Selena feared for his unusual silence and probable melancholy character. "How does it feel to be a dragon rider?"

It took him a moment to turn around and give her a smile that melted her worries away. "Strange, but I'm also intrigued and honored to help rebuild the Mythic Flight." After assuring the hatchlings were well, the two walked down the winding grey stone pathway towards the city. Silver's grin grew as he looked over the horizon to see the glorious mid-afternoon sun. "Of course, I don't want you to think that this would interfere with our marriage, my dear. I love you and always will."

Her face sparkled, and she relaxed. "I love you, too, and there's no doubt in my mind. I've already asked so much of you today, and I wanted to ensure you weren't overwhelmed."

"Not at all! My dear, I'm like a one-person army. Besides, as an admiral, I can now set a good example to recruits to be seen with a dragon."

Selena shared his enthusiasm and wondered if he could understand hers and Thor's connection; he was never bothered by their bond, but she believed this would be good for him. He finally had companionship for the first time in over sixteen thousand years, aside from hers.

Silver kept his promise and guaranteed the new House of the Undead was fully operational before the celebration began upon returning to the city. He immediately went to work on constructing the temple; when they heard the announcement for receiving assistance, the Dreygur were more than willing to accept help and take advantage of the resources that would readily be available. Because of the recent development to widen the streets, the city's center—the length of five giant weighted dragons standing head to tail—was the perfect spot as it provided enough space to support its structure.

Upon hearing its completion, Thor made his hasty return for a walk-through with Selena. Silver's new sanctuary immediately introduced the trio to a lovely marble fountain with crystal-clear water surrounding the base of a pedestal holding the sacred golden egg Kiba herself placed. The sunlight gleamed upon its smooth surface through the atrium. Ensconced sections to the right were barracks, providing sleeping arrangements for the Dreygur in need. In contrast, the cellar below was stocked with food, clothing, and other necessary supplies to support rehabilitation.

Thor examined every nook and cranny of the magnificent temple and gave his final approval directly to Silver. **It's a beautiful step forward in the right direction, and we will continuously improve the plans to better their quality of life.**

Silver's face gleamed in delight while Selena approached the golden egg, admiring its gilded gleam sparkling across the azure water-filled marble dish. "This is lovely, Silver. Thank you." Awestruck by his construction skills, Selena pitched the idea of utilizing his abilities to help rebuild Helshire Village, but with a better layout. "Perhaps we can make it more like a fortress, with castle towers and a line of shop buildings instead of stalls."

He agreed without hesitation. "We can do the same for the Grand Exchange and Blackheart. My dear, I will begin work in no later than a week."

Selena caught a glimpse of her unrecognizable reflection as she did when the pair first served in the Force; she still couldn't grasp the recent changes and their effects on their world. Unsure of what urged her to do so, she knelt before the egg to pray, offering a blessing upon the new temple. Tail swishing side to side, Thor joined her as he bowed, nose touching the marble.

However, as the two finished, a sudden gale rushed from the opened ceiling and writhed around the golden paragon like the rainbow fire burning around Thor's horns, and the ground began to quiver; the egg trembled, and much to their shock and dismay, its solid shell cracked open. Bemused and confused, a sapling sprouted from the cracks and exponentially grew to the size of a fully-grown white ash tree within seconds.

The porcelain trunk and branches began stretching beyond the confines of the temple; Thor dashed outside faster than a bolt of lightning, and Selena snatched the hem of Silver's robes, dragging him out while he was in mid-protest of the tree's rapid growth rendering to destroy the new House of the Undead.

It outgrew Silver's new building, leaving a pile of stone rubble amidst a massive ash tree, its snow-white branches and leaves reaching for the clouds, almost touching the heavens. Its trunk jutting from the enlarged marble pool alone was the width of two dragons the size of Thor. Yet, the tree destroyed only the temple from its sudden, massive growth, and the only sign of the tree's roots skidded near its base before sinking and stretching deep underground. Much to Thor's and Selena's relief, the tree neither harmed denizens nor other structures, but that didn't stop the civilians from panicking. After realizing the earthquake had stopped, the entire city rushed over to the new tree, including the Shadow Templars and Aynu.

After Silver finished his rant over losing his building, he, at last, stopped to admire the glistening ivory ash tree with a colossal fountain serving its new size; Kain and Maria arrived moments later and joined him in his awe. Selena's parents parted through the crowd to find her and Thor to ask what had happened, to which they denied their involvement, for they were at a loss, but the tree whispered from the wind rustling through its white sward.

Kiba rushed over, sodden and breathless, eyes as large in wonder as theirs. "W-what is this?" Silver's throat constricted as he mouthed his speculation that Artio had gifted the Aynu with a magical tree seed. She, however, settled apathetically to the possibility, and both she and Maru stood in awe of the extraordinary phenomenon.

As the leaves fell, they sparkled like stars; the Dreygur walking towards the massive tree paused to look up, and when the glittering petals touched their skin, they grew imbued by a soft blue light like the twinkling diamonds adorning the cosmos. The glimmer dimmed away, along with the melting discoloration from their new and revitalized skin—now full of life and color—and Death's glaze vanished from their eyes.

The crowd held its breath in fear of interrupting the miracle. While the reborn praised the tree for their transformation, Aryl stepped forth, regardless of Vulduin's apprehension and warnings; she reached out with opened hands as a glistening petal descended upon her. Vulduin watched as she was kissed by blue starlight, and she fell to her knees when it faded; her sickly-looking face now blossomed with color, and she laughed through tears while holding her sides. Vulduin rushed and pulled her to her feet, and her arms immediately locked around his neck as she buried her face into his shoulder.

Before Selena could ask about her wellbeing, Aryl spun around and greeted her with a tight hold. "H-how did you two…?" She pulled back and smiled through her shimmering eyes, and Selena was left to wonder at what had befallen her mother. "You two healed me. I've been sick for so long, and not even Silver…." Aryl's voice vanished from her trembling lips, and she embraced her daughter again. "Thank you." Still dazed and confused, Selena met her father's same perplexed expression, and he sprinted over to join his family, reveling in jubilation.

The three pulled away when Thor stood on his haunches as he raised his celestial wings and extended his neck to inspect the ash tree he and Selena were responsible for; one leaf drifted and graced the tip of his nose, and a glimmer ran across his scales. **I wonder.**

Wonder what?

He arched his neck around while remaining on his hind legs. **I believe this tree is infused with our power to cure diseases and lift curses.**

Suddenly before Selena could ask what he meant, an idea came to him: her parents stood back as Thor scooped her with his jeweled claws and swept himself off the ground, tail snaking behind him, his ethereal wings shimmering like his adorned treasures in the sunlight.

She watched the world pass by like a blur between his talons, the only protective barrier between her and the earth. Though she could have quickly joined him in the sky herself, it never stopped her from enjoying their flight; Thor hummed and chittered in deep content to share this skyborne moment, even for the brief distance to the dragon gardens.

The tree's branches stretched beyond Alfheim's limits and reached the pavilions, the wind carrying its leaves and drifting towards the curious Nidhoggr. Noctis was the first to step forth down the steps of his gazebo, drawn to the familiar Divine energy that drove him forward, and a fleeting, sparkling leaf slowly made its descent. Selena held her breath as Thor coasted closer, and as soon as the petal kissed Noctis' snout, a blue light shining like a newborn star consumed him whole; as the gleam began to fade, standing in Noctis' place was a brilliant black and red dragon: a Blackland Steelwing.

Thor descended gracefully but floated above the pavilion by beating his wings forward and backward. Selena anxiously peered through his claws to see Noctis' jagged shiny onyx scales—like perfectly cut volcanic glass contrasting the brilliant gold chain holding a blood diamond pendant draped around his thick neck. His crimson wings with edges dabbed in minor cuts and nicks unfolded beyond the length of his large pavilion, and he took his first steps among the living, his tail slithering behind him like a venomous black snake. Yet, he still retained the bone mask covering his face, but instead of the smoldering glow, his eyes were now like Thor's: narrow slits against the fiery colors burning within.

When he looked up at the pair, Noctis released a roar—not in anger or intimidation, but in celebrating and praising his new transformation—and he flapped his new wings and joined Thor in the air as a living dragon. His mouth twisted, and his lips curled through snarls and grunts, but his speech was more intelligible than before. His voice no longer sounded like the guttural series of shrieks but rather a low husky tone more gentle on the ears. "Thank... you. Your Divine b-beacon... c-chased... away... the darkness t-that... consumed me."

Selena reached out to pet his obsidian snout through Thor's talon cage, and Noctis purred as he nudged her palm. The sparkling leaves continued their gentle dance downward, and upon seeing Noctis' transformation, the rest of the Nidhoggr hurriedly made their way out in the open. One by one, a simple touch of the miracle petal triggered their transformation, welcoming the flight back among the living through a new flutter of dazzling colorful scales.

Selena's heart soared higher than the sun and beyond; Vyrilion—the Regal Flamescale—a red and orange dragon with specs of emerald green speckled across his hide and the edges of his topaz wings, spun around in absolute ecstasy, chittering and chirping as he stomped the ground.

Obsidian, a Royal Tidalwalker with ocean blue scales and massive frilled wings matching those from his tail like fins from a fish, joined in his happy dance. Nearly dwarfing the other dragons, his flat face was decorated in a crown of spikes, with numerous more covering his back and tail. Obsidian's brilliant, smooth azure hide caught the light like a sword's glimmer, casting blue and purple specks across the ground.

Among their new rainbow, a Malachite Diamondwing, Fafnir's jade-colored hide speckled with orange, yellow, and red along his spine and tail contrasted the emerald green hue of his diamond-shaped wings. His narrow snout and smooth jawline were devoid of any adornments except the two horns curving from his head top.

It didn't take long for Kayda, an Imperial Pearlscale, to join, and her ghostly white scales gleamed as she zipped overhead. Her beautiful albino hide lacked all color—wings and underbelly alike—but her pink eyes radiated joy as her new pupiled-slits spun around to catch her flight in celebration. Despite the absence of hue, Kayda's five-spined wings sparkled like a fairy's crystal-cut pair, casting rainbow flecks like Selena's wedding ring and headdress as she descended. Spikes neatly decorated her jawline, increasing size as they reached her crown.

Sethak and Rhasydra chased the glittering petals but paused once their snouts caught the leaves, and the twins became imbued by the miraculous blue light. The brother suddenly dashed forth from his heavenly orb, emerging as a Regal Flamescale hatchling, his emerald eyes sparkling in glee. Green and yellow flecks speckled down his spine and trailed the edges of his five-spined citrine wings.

Rhasydra, now matching her mother's strikingly white hue, flashed her sapphire eyes; she and her brother had a similar horn and wing design to their mother's, an undeniable resemblance. Volterion—a reborn Regal Flamescale like his father—circled the twins. The three younglings raced back to Kayda, landing among the blissful, colorful party.

Ysyra, a resurrected Crimson Deathwing, soared happily under the sun, her blood-red scales catching the sun's blazing rays. Her obsidian six-spined wings' bottom edges were dappled with oval markings in purple and grey. She joined Obsidian, Vyrilion, and Fafnir, galloping around Kayda as her long, slender tail flickered across the ground, wafting billows of dust from every sweep. The hatchlings joined the cheerful assembly while Kayda hid behind her unimpressed disguise; Noctis gave her a series of deep-throated growls and clicks, and she finally gave in to her excitement like the others.

Selena couldn't help but shed happy tears to see them soar in circles, enjoying the fresh air filling their new lungs. The rest of the reborn dragons dashed across the gardens, stretching their strong fleshy legs and wings again; among them were Skyfyre and Vulcan as they contributed to their merriment while Volt, Gromm, and Beck watched beside their pavilions.

Thor spun in mid-hover as he saw an emerald blur dash from the tree's massive canopy to meet them; Ulrich only paused his hasty venture to witness the dragons' rebirth. Zipping overhead was Ebony as she launched herself towards the ivory branches, wings tucked into her sides as she fired off like a bullet. She perched on one of the bottom branches with her wings half-furled to her sides, observing the group with eager curiosity; her tail twitched like she was ready to pounce. Thor met her slitted gaze and responded with a few low groans and clicks in what Selena assumed was his way of reassuring Ebony of the situation. The black dragon remained an iridescent flicker, her sparkling platinum jewelry set contrasting the porcelain white ash tree.

The leaves fell like twinkling stars, even when the curse lifted from every last Nidhoggr and Dreygur. The Emerald Divine landed after Noctis and Thor descended gracefully, and at last, Selena was released from Thor's protective hold. The newly awakened dragons immediately dashed over to the group and reveled in Noctis' new form;

the leader stood on his haunches and released a roar and a long stream of fire blazing in red, orange, and yellow. His flight replied with their elemental breaths: ice, lightning, fire, wind, poison, a rainbow display of their restored magical abilities conjoined with flair.

The impressed Ulrich said, "Only when I believe you two could accomplish no more, I'm proven wrong again. You and Thor never cease to amaze me." He stretched out his neck to further assess the dancing petals. "I had a hunch that my sister gave the Aynu the Great Seed to bring about the World Tree as a gift for mortals when I used it to restore the Hinterlands. You temporarily imbued this World Tree with your powers, and, as I suspected, all the inflicted have returned to their previous altered state. However, I trust that the tree's abilities will fade by nightfall."

Her chest tightened when Selena saw Rahim and Niamh dashing across the garden hills with their allies. It wasn't fair to save the Dreygur and Nidhoggr when it was too late for his father; yet, she recalled the Divinity Dragon's resurrection ability, and the weight from her heart briefly lifted when she considered the possibility of rectifying this injustice. "Could we bring someone back from the dead?"

I believe we can do that with or without the tree, my dear.

Yes, but after seeing the reborn Dreygur and Nidhoggr, it wouldn't be fair for Rahim to suffer. I forgot we could do this.

"You are correct, Divine Thor. The gift of resurrection can be for yourself only moments before or after death or on someone else regardless of the time frame of their passing, but you can only use this gift once. Choose wisely."

"Even if two Divinity Dragons exist at present?"

Ulrich's eyes flickered to a brief shade of grey. "You two are connected, and therefore your abilities come as one, including this offering."

I wonder why Yggdrasil didn't use her gift to help me. Realizing that sounded selfish, Selena profusely apologized.

No need for apologies, my dear. Our mother may have already used her one blessing.

"Thor is right. Your Dragon Mother Yggdrasil saved her mate's life many years before laying your eggs, Divine Ones, but she still helped in any way she could to preserve you." Ulrich's gigantic emerald eye fixated upon Selena. "She loved you as if you were from her clutch, and she was willing to save you, no matter the cost."

Touched by the saving grace of a mother's love, she wiped her tears away, but Thor nudged her back before bowing in agreement to the exciting possibility of what would be the greatest gift of all. *Are you sure about this?*

Of course. It would be the right thing to do, and I know he will never forget it.

After confirming from Ulrich that only praying was needed, Selena reached out her Aether hand to gently catch the fallen star leaf sparkling within her wispy palm. Thor joined her side as soon as Rahim and the others arrived, sodden and breathless. Before he or Silver could make their inquiry, Ulrich immediately silenced them by snapping his large fangs shut, urging the group to wait and watch.

Lord Godfrey and Prince Damien stood behind Rahim with the Shadow Templar horde, anxiously waiting to see what their new queen would do next after marveling at Obsidian's and Noctis' transformation. Kain and Maria joined Vyrilion's side upon witnessing the World Tree's miracle, looking at the pair in awe and admiration. They were slightly fearful that, like Death, Selena always kept her promises.

Fafnir inched his way closer under Ulrich's heated and guarding gaze as he crawled towards Niamh so she could silently marvel at his rebirth, and she collapsed against his chest while waiting to see the final act. Aracania zipped overhead with Araneus but paused to hover as Admiral Cyres slowly approached the chittering Ysyra; the blissful pair united after celebrating Ysyra's resurrection, for she reminded him of Onyxria.

Selena peered over her shoulder and still saw the vampirism in the Templars' eyes, but she realized the World Tree only lifted the Lich's curse upon the Dreygur and Nidhoggr; the vampires didn't carry the evil darkness that shrouded the others. Ignoring the growing crowd watching in anticipation, Selena spun around to face Thor with the leaf exposed. The two bowed their heads in prayer, whispering over the shimmering petal. Unsure of how to word the plea, the pair kept it simple:

"Please, bring Arawn back—"

The man he was before the Lich took him.

Their whispers beckoned the crowd forward, but Ulrich warned them by flicking his tail; Noctis and his flight took a step back when they realized what Selena and Thor had attempted to achieve, and the dragons impatiently lingered for the next miracle.

Immediately following their blessing, the leaf flared to a glittering ball of blue light and shot upwards to the glowing twilight sky, and the heavens wept twinkling stardust barely grazing the earth. A strong gale picked up and carried a collection of leaves swirling and twirling overhead before breaking ground, forming a vortex with their Divine wind. The leaf bearing Selena's and Thor's wish dropped from the heavens and struck the middle of the tiny gale storm, and within a snapping flash lasting only seconds, a man appeared.

Chaliss was one of the last to arrive, only to witness Rahim, unable to keep his face from shimmering, stepping forward; he looked like he had been struck by lightning while shuffling his feet to the man he once remembered from an old photograph. Almost like walking through a dream, Chaliss had to be escorted by Silver, and when the restored Arawn looked between her and Rahim, his eyes widened as he finally made the distinction.

There was no mistaking his and Rahim's relation: the matching shaggy sandy-brown hair with freckles dotting the nose and face gave it away. Dazed and confused, and before he could brace himself, Arawn was nearly tackled down by Rahim. All he could say was, "Dad…."

Arawn lifted a trembling hand to Rahim's head before seeking confirmation from Chaliss' tearful gaze. Arawn lost his speech to a series of confusing grunts as he tried to find the right questions to ask but instead lifted a free hand for her to take, and the three fell into a deep embrace. The once lost man finally sputtered, "I-I thought we lost each other for a moment." He looked down at Rahim with amazement. "A-are you really…? H-how long was I asleep?"

Rahim forced out a chuckle in between sobs. "About sixteen years, dad."

Arawn's pale face drained of any remaining color as he looked over at Chaliss' sparkling wet face as she forced out a laugh. "The last thing I remember was deciding what to name our son."

Her lips trembled over Rahim's name. "It was the one you chose, remember?"

"Rahim." Arawn allowed the syllables to slip over his tongue before bringing his wife and son into another tight huddle.

Selena smiled at their happy reunion, but as she was about to turn away, Rahim dashed over, grabbed her arm, and urged her to follow him. Meanwhile, Arawn looked around in wonder at the city and the dragons but flinched when he saw the vast crowd watching in astonishment. Few from the group voiced praises as their queen walked by, and everyone dropped to their knees while whispering, "Glory to the Dragon Queen" and "World Tree Giver."

Arawn paused as Rahim brought her over and quickly fell to his knees upon seeing her unmatched beauty and the halo crown that gave away her status. "Dad, this is my sister." When Arawn almost fell over in shock, Rahim had to rapidly explain their relationship wasn't by blood and proceeded to regale his father of who she was and of their adventures. Selena laughed when he exaggerated some parts or the added titles he kept tacking beside her name.

Thor couldn't help but join in on the teasing. **Selena Liongod, Queen of Dragons, One of Divine Birth, God-Slayer, World Tree Giver.**

Are you finished? He only stuck out his tongue, and she sighed. *Why can't I just be Liongod? It was much shorter and easier to remember.*

I would be proud of those earned titles.

After Rahim finished his story, Arawn suddenly grew weary and dizzy. "I-I need some time to ponder all this, my son." His face suddenly lit up with a huge grin. "My son."

The cheering crowd cleared when Chaliss helped Arawn walk back into Alfheim, but Rahim stayed behind. His eyes glossy like glass, he hugged Selena tightly as he was close to breaking. Rahim's mouth kept opening and closing while stammering, "I-I can't... I could... could never—"

"I promised we would find a way to help him, didn't I? A queen is always true to her word."

Rahim laughed, but he squeezed until she almost couldn't breathe. He only released his grip when Thor gave him a slight nudge, and he latched on to Thor's muzzle. "Thank you... thank you! You are the Almighty Thor, King of Dragons—"

"Perhaps that's enough titles." She gave him a half-crooked smile through the furrow of her brow as her eyes nervously darted among the wide-eyed faces that inched closer to hear every word of Rahim's sincere devotion. Thor, however, was amused and glowed from the praise; Selena could swear she saw his diamond scales shimmer rainbows from delight. **It's all right; allow him to continue.**

Rahim resumed offering heartfelt praise through his glistening gaze while dashing away to join his mother and father. Before the crowd could push their way to her, Ulrich stepped forward and deterred the others away through intimidating roars and snarls. Eventually, when they realized Selena and Thor wouldn't grant them an audience, the horde slowly faded out while still fixated on the World Tree and praising its miracles.

When Silver marched over, Kain shoved him out the way to confront Selena about her recent actions, but instead of words, he reached out and gave her a firm handshake, followed by Maria drifting over and offering a hug. Selena felt guilty for not extending the gift to her mother, who passed away before Snowhaven's botched mission, but Maria showed no malice or scorn for her decision. "You did the right thing, and we both know Rahim will never forget this." More than what she expected, Kain and Maria were relieved at the new solution for the Lich's undead, and the rest of Alfheim would have an easier time welcoming their new citizens.

After Ulrich permitted them to come forward, Noctis and his flight surrounded her as they twittered and chirped, but Vyrilion stopped and rushed over to the vampire lord and lady to flaunt his new appearance. Godfrey and Damien were next to reunite with their companions; Noctis and Obsidian wrapped the two nobles within their coils and fell into deep content over the affection from their handlers and the World Tree's gift. Upon seeing how the dragons expressed their love and adoration for their riders, Fafnir extended a protective claw around Niamh and herded her close.

Godfrey patted Obsidian's thick arm while muttering, "You great oaf, you're nothing but a softy." The happy dragon blew out a slight chilling breeze from his nostrils before squeezing Godfrey closer.

Through a flurry of new wings, Sethak and Rhasydra circled Selena and Thor with cheerful chittering, and the twins took turns in rubbing their snouts against their faces. **Rhasydra and Volterion helped me escape the _Blood Diamond_. I'm glad for the chance to thank them.** Thor returned their affections and dipped his head, showing gratitude to the now purring Rhasydra.

With caution, Kayda took a few steps and snaked her pearly-white muzzle over Selena's head, calling her hatchlings through clicks and chirps before paying her respects to the Divine dragons. Volterion trailed behind but grew distracted by his flared ruff coating the end of his tail, and he began chasing it like a playful puppy. Soon, the other dragons joined and coddled together as one heap of differently colored jewels after releasing their handlers.

Silver reunited with Selena and Thor at long last, fully embracing his wife; Ebony dashed overhead at record speed. Sharing a heart-warming farewell, Thor parted from Selena and joined his mate in the sky with his promise to unite at the celebrations later.

When satisfied with the events, Ulrich excused himself before snapping another glance at the great ash tree. True to his assumption, the starfall glitter vanished as the sun crossed the line where the earth met the sky and the last of the dancing leaves drifted to the ground.

"Your gift is a beacon of hope for the dawn of this new world. As long as the World Tree stands, darkness will never again consume Armageddon. Farewell, Divine Ones. Until we meet again." Ulrich bowed before the two as he unfurled his colossal wings; Silver and Selena watched the Divine make one massive leap skyward, heading towards Rhumbek's ruins to fulfill his promise of rebuilding the fallen dwarven city.

She watched the glittering Emerald Dragon vanish beyond the horizon, his dazzling scales melding with the diamond stars adorning the evening curtain, suspecting this being their final meeting. But Selena caught a glimmer of a figure hiding beyond the pavilions; Azrael observed the entire affair, and she wondered if he took any issue of their deed.

However, he only shrugged and smirked after Silver accused him of eavesdropping and strutted forward with his hands thrust into his pockets. "How am I supposed to keep my promise if you won't attend your celebration? I think your adoring crowd is working at Divine speed in putting it together."

Unsure on whether to be amused or annoyed, Selena bit her tongue. "Do you have nothing else to say, such as the foolishness of the tree existing or for breaking the unspoken laws over life and death?"

"Am I supposed to?" Azrael raised a brow in genuine confusion. "Your gift to Rahim doesn't concern me. Before my banishment, I seem to recall that *I* decided to grant Divinity Dragons the ability under the condition that you can only use it once. That was my blessing after Ulrich and Xyaxon created Divinity Dragons." He peered up at the christened tree. "As my brother said, the World Tree's temporary powers have faded as soon as daylight ended, so I'm not worried about you two disrupting the balance of life and death. This new beginning is a chance to give everyone a fresh start after our supposed doomsday." He laughed, but his face turned serious, and his smirk disappeared. "Consider your act as a way of saying you owe me a soul."

Flaring in anger, Silver quickly called him out on his bluff, but Selena already knew Azrael's sense of humor by now and laughed. His grin once again stretching across his face, Death vanished within the shadows in a plume of smoke.

As the two made the trek back to Alfheim, Selena said, "I'm sorry about destroying your new temple, Silver."

He shrugged, but he looked more impressed than annoyed, judging by him continuously looking back at the World Tree with a sunny grin. "This turned out better than I could have hoped, my dear. You dragons never cease to amaze me."

Selena paused, gaze frozen upon the great blessing. She and Thor still possessed their abilities to cure diseases, and her face brightened when an idea came to her. "The tree's magic may have waned, but what if Thor and I assisted with your work?" As she proposed using their powers to help Silver's alchemy, creating potions and vaccines to cure and eradicate deadly diseases, Silver couldn't help but exclaim that "this would be a massive and advancing step in developing modern medicine."

Upon returning to the city limits after deciding to begin this feat in the morning, Silver and Selena were ecstatic that the reborn Dreygur slowly regained their lost memories. However, like Arawn, no one recalled falling under the Lich's curse. As Kain and Maria predicted, Alfheim welcomed the former undead back among the living.

Selena made it a point to help the formerly inflicted with housing and employment resources; they lost their livelihood before the Battle of Armageddon, but the old residents retained their skills and talents. After their celebration, Selena planned to assign them jobs they were best suited for or return to previous surviving employers, depending on their choice. In the meantime, a reasonable sum of gold would be divided among them for a fresh start.

As Silver and Kain already took it upon themselves to build multi-floor duplexes during the city's reconstruction to provide housing for the homeless, Selena ensured the former Dreygur that all would be provided for until they received employment and permanent living accommodations. However, she made it conditional that the resources would only be available for a time frame of no more than three weeks to help deter those who would take advantage of the system. As all the shops and suppliers were in high demand of laborers, finding work would be no issue.

"Is there a plan for those who can't find a job or another place to live?"

Selena bit her bottom lip to Silver's question as she thought more of it. "If it comes to it, we can sit down with those unsuccessful and figure out why, but I can't have them living on free handouts forever." The two walked by the newly refurbished duplex within the Sky District, ready to be used now. Already, the former undead moved inside and made themselves at home, eager to begin their new lives. "Three weeks from tomorrow, we can renovate the building to be an inn or perhaps a massive blacksmith shop, opening new employment opportunities offering fair wages. If the worst happens, I could assign them a job they would be best suited for based on their current skill level. I will not have them groveling on the streets like beggars after freeing them from the Lich."

Much to her delight, some reborn immediately found proper employment as cooks to help prepare for the evening's event. Others honed their skills in crafting jewelry, using the gemstones Silver created to sell to the populace. General Araneus and Aracania wasted no time granting opportunities for the new residents to join the Force as soldiers; those who accepted the offer would transfer to their different living quarters in the morning.

Silver suggested establishing a construction crew to rebuild Helshire, the Grand Exchange, and Blackheart, and Selena couldn't agree more. Many formerly inflicted happily consented to join and begin work that same week. Selena was pleased to see that more than half of the new citizens found employment within hours, and she was confident the others would follow suit before the three-week time frame.

True to Azrael's word, the city was busy preparing the celebratory feast and ball in Selena's honor. Special pigs and boars were butchered and cooked by the finest chefs around the Empire, spending hours arranging gourmet dishes fit for the Queen of Dragons herself. Many elaborate decorations and tables adorned in the finest cutlery and silk dinner cloth were set up around the city's center near the base of the World Tree.

Brightly lit jeweled lanterns sat within gemstone platters, serving as centerpieces at each table as more lamps strung along the edges of the buildings circling the tree. Different stalls carried various foods and tiny treasures, such as toy windmills and masks for children. Lights threaded around its lower branches through large jeweled chains. The World Tree illuminated from the rainbow flair of fairies that began making themselves at home; their tiny extravagant houses made of wood and woven leaf and limb hung like ornaments. Specks of magic dust fluttered from their rapidly beating wings and kissed all they touched.

The musicians took their place before the fountain and the great tree and began gracing the bustling city with twinkling light tunes. The decorated General Araneus saddled upon Aracania donned in her treasures and led their long parade with Ysyra and the embellished Admiral Cyres. Behind them were Skyfyre and Volt, clad in his best dress suited for his promotion, and Vulcan with the two regally dressed brothers astride his back.

The remaining flight marched through the streets; wings unfurled and displayed. Behind them were Noctis and Fafnir. Vyrilion, Kayda, Volterion, the twins, and Obsidian followed their pageant, all dragons flashing their polished gems and chains. They had no issues walking through the improved streets amidst the blitz, and, even without the sidewalks, the citizens had more than enough room to carry on in normalcy without disturbance. They stopped and stared in awe and wonder, shouting praises at the newborn dragons strutting by.

Next, Thor and Ebony landed gracefully behind them, and the city bowed to their grandeur splendor. The two royally adorned dragons flaunted their jewels, gold, and draconic beauty; Thor appreciated the vastly different treatment than before the Lich's defeat. Yet, to his and Ebony's surprise, a few audience members fell to their knees in prayer.

As if to save their glorious tableaux for last, Silver and Selena descended and followed the parade in dragon forms—after Silver adjusted his size to match hers—

donned in matching illustrious treasures, save for the queen wearing her august headdress. The two wore heavy golden torques set with deep blue-green sapphires, jeweled chains dangling from the pieces and loosely wrapping around their necks. Solid gold talon-sheathes tipped with the unique sapphires over their foreclaws clicked against the cobblestone pavement. Golden tail bands faceted with the sapphires and with hanging strings of jewels lightly decorated the base of their tails. As the royal couple marched by, the citizens lined the streets and shouted out in adoration, "World Tree Giver," "Dragon Queen," "God-Slayer," along with their many praises.

Before the events unfolded, as Selena wanted to make her grand entrance with flair, Silver suggested wearing similar jewelry as Thor and Ebony and quickly crafted new pieces for himself and her. As beautiful as the trinkets were, Selena believed the display was too much, but he disagreed. "Dragons love treasure, as you well know. The new flight deserved their rewards, but the Queen of Dragons is supposed to flaunt magnificent jewels, and no other should ever come close to her beauty."

The dragons lined up around the Fire Temple, where their allies watched and waited: Aryl and Vulduin stood among Loki, the Oracles, Neith, Lord Godfrey, Prince Damien, and the Shadow Templars, with Kiba, Maru, and the Aynu pack; the dragons exercised caution when stepping around the wolves, as some were still young pups learning how to behave and sit still. Much to Selena's delight, Azrael and Doragon kept their promise; the two stood within the shadows, observing the formal event unfold, and they smiled and bowed as they made eye contact.

The Former Imperial Majesties bent the knee when Selena took her spot beside them. "You and Thor gave us our lives back, and the Empire will finally know peace." Aryl stood up, and Selena's muzzle met her open palm. "We pray that your Divine fire never extinguishes as it chases away the darkness." Likewise, Vulduin offered his praise to Thor during their communion.

The flight fidgeted in place, impatient to begin their feast: whole roasted seasoned spitted cows and pigs strung like a delicacy chain of jewels waited just for them, while the rest portioned out on the tables for the civilians. If it weren't for Thor, Ebony, and Aracania watching the ferals, they would have run amok. Skyfyre and Vulcan were of no help, yet, after fighting off his impulses, Noctis assisted in maintaining order.

Even as Selena altered her form as the elven Dragon Queen, the crafted jewelry modified to her transformation; the smaller pieces decorated her neck, wrist, and fingers but never lost their luster. Only upon her word did the gala officially begin, and the party poured across the streets; the dragons immediately dove after their meals, tearing and ripping meat and bone through chittering pleasure while the civilians indulged in celebration, resplendent with dance, song, food, and wine.

The dragons only paused mid-bite when the Mythic Flight hatchlings fluttered overhead, drawn in from the appetizing series of smells wafting across Alfheim. The ferals snarled when the dragonets inched over for a taste. The air hatchling vanished and reappeared to steal a mouthful of Fafnir's meal and disappeared in a plume of smoke before Fafnir could swat it away; he wrapped a protective arm around his pig. Thor and Ebony, however, were more generous and openly shared their banquet with the hungry whelplings. Seeing their more sophisticated example, Noctis growled but ruefully moved his claws away, allowing the new fire guardian to swoop in for a few bites.

Silver's grin brightened his face from the spectacle, and the air dragonet raced over and perched on his shoulder. Its frills flared when Selena extended her Aether hand, and it chirped as it shoved its head into her open palm. Silver said, "Etherius likes you. He was drawn to your aura and kept asking me questions about the Divine Dragon Queen."

"It's wonderful to meet you, Etherius."

The whelpling locked his large emerald eyes with hers and bowed. **Divine One.**

His gentle voice resonated similarly to Silver's; Etherius fluttered and vanished and joined his squabbling siblings playing tug-of-war with Sethak and Rhasydra over scraps. Yet, Silver draped an arm over her shoulder and pulled her close. "He has your eyes," he said, smiling, and she laughed.

Soon, Rahim, his parents, and Niamh rushed over when they saw the baby dragons swarming over another spitted cow like flies drawn to honey. As the little fire guardian looked up, it rushed over and nearly tackled Rahim in sheer excitement. Niamh laughed before taking her spot upon Fafnir's foreleg as he tore through his third stuffed pig, purring and twittering when his handler arrived.

Arawn, no longer dazed, smiled upon seeing his son's recent accomplishments. Rahim held up his hatchling for him and Chaliss to see, the hatchling's ruby scales gleaming like Vulcan's under the jeweled lamps; the massive grin on Rahim's face made Selena's heart soar. "Mum and dad, meet Cyndrexia."

The little fire guardian hovered over his hands and chirped as if introducing itself. Face beaming, Chaliss asked, "Cyndrexia is lovely. Did you come up with that name, or did it… he…?"

"She," Rahim corrected, "and no, I didn't. Cyndrexia told me she picked out the name herself while waiting to hatch." His parents watched the dragonet zip out of Rahim's hands and circle the three as they burst out laughing; Selena grinned, assuming Cyndrexia's siblings were equally impatient, and decided to name themselves as Thor did upon hatching.

Meanwhile, Kain and Maria joined Vyrilion, and the water hatchling rushed over between them. Kain extended his arm for the dragonet to perch, and it rubbed its body against his face like a cat showing affection. "I hope you're staying out of trouble, Nytheria." The whelpling flickered her fish-like tail and purred. When Kain approached, Vyrilion lowered his snout to the hatchling's and sniffed as Nytheria loomed in, tiny wings rapidly beating to keep her aloft from Kain's shoulder, and their noses touched. When satisfied to meet the dragonet's acquaintance, Vyrilion offered to share some of his meal, and Nytheria ravenously accepted his token of friendship.

Kiba's voice boomed over the fast music, and she, with Maru and a few from her pack, strutted from the crowd, tearing through a giant turkey leg with the earth dragonet hovering above; it swooped in to steal a bite but ended up robbing the entire drumstick. Realizing the size of its prize, the dragon dashed away to enjoy it in private as Kiba pursued a chase. "Hey! Get back here with my food, Exidrion."

Exidrion rushed by Silver and Selena, fangs sunk deep into the meat and eventually vanished into the dark shadows as a faint emerald glimmer from his chest spikes and glowing orb. Kiba transformed into a wolf and gained speed after the disappearing whelpling, but Selena swore she heard Exidrion snicker in the back of her mind.

She couldn't help but laugh, but Thor snaked his head over and nudged her arm. **I don't quite recall behaving that way when I hatched.**

Only when it came to your insatiable hunger.

Bah. Thor finished gulping down the last of his cow and licked his chops.

Her friends and family urged her and Silver to join them for the feast inside the Fire Temple while the dragons gorged themselves on the remaining outside dishes. The banquet tables were lined with delectable delicacies that made her mouth water: cheese wheels served with loaves of bread, whole roasted deer and pigs displayed on golden platters, decorated with different herb garnishes and smoked vegetables, strung down the tables as crown jewels of the feast, glazed in a butter sauce—courtesy to the Shadow Templars, no one used garlic. Large platters of stuffed game hens with various spices and herbs were presented with fruits and nuts. Decorating the center of the enormous table was a perfectly cooked boar laying on its back on top of a golden platter, all drizzled in a special honey sauce.

The temple echoed with stories of their previous epic adventures. As Loki dashed between their feet, looking for a plate the cooks set aside for him, Lord Godfrey regaled everyone on the tale of how Emperor Enyalius Xyrrion bested him in combat. Maru shared how Selena and her friends allied with the Aynu by saving Kiba and their treasured Great Seed. Per Aryl's and Vulduin's request, Captains Gromm and Beck offered their story of how they infiltrated Mount Blackrock to rescue her and Thor and their first meeting with the Shadow Emperor himself.

General Araneus and Admiral Cyres were especially interested in their heroic feats, as they most likely hadn't received all the details because of the old

Council. In the meantime, as Volt sat between his commanding officers, his face burned, but he turned away when Selena caught his stare; he mumbled what she could assume, but Silver's icy glare was enough to make Volt flinch.

Selena enjoyed their peaceful time and only spoke when the others asked her questions, but soon she wasn't given a choice when everyone asked her to tell the tale of the battle against Xyaxon. As she enlightened everyone of the details, Ulrich's words twinkled across her mind: *As long as the World Tree stands, darkness will never again consume Armageddon.*

After the punch settled in, everyone took the pleasure of dancing in front of the great ash tree—including Azrael. Selena was happy to see him return for the evening gala and enjoy the festivities. The flickering jeweled lamps shimmered across Doragon's golden metal-plated scales; yet, he wasn't amused to see his companion concede to his drunken stupor. He extended an arm to herd him close as the music ended, only to begin again for the next group of dancers.

Silver asked her to join him as the others lined up; like the affair before the venture to Snowhaven, a few bystanders giggled and gawked at the two, but it wasn't just the women ogling over him this time. Selena did her best to ignore the onlooking men and ladies failing at their beguiling attempts to woo and seduce her; instead, she was bemused and charmed by both parties. "Don't worry about them; it's just you and me right now." Silver grinned and winked, twirling her around and kissing her in mid-dip; their audience clapped and cheered.

The dragons watching the merriment roared to the skies and clicked their nails against the pavement in approval. All of the dragon hatchlings—Volterion included—swirled overhead and chittered, but Exidrion was still busy avoiding Kiba; he finished eating her turkey leg, but he zipped over to Thor as the She-Wolf rounded the corner. Thor lowered his head and snorted as the hatchling almost collided with him and immediately recoiled back, giving Kiba a chance for capture. "Gotcha! You big oaf, you owe me another drumstick." Exidrion floated above her head after escaping and belched loudly, and everyone laughed.

However, Selena's heart dropped faster than a boulder sinking to the ocean floor when she saw Azrael escape from the distraction. Doragon followed his example by launching himself skyward; after the two were far enough away from the party, Doragon snatched Azrael in his talons and made haste towards the garden pavilions undetected by the others.

After explaining Azrael's sudden departure, she excused herself from Thor's and Silver's company as she transformed in mid-leap and flew after them in pursuit; the moonlight caught her newly emblazoned diamond gleaming rainbow streaks from her chest. Upon spotting the two landing within the dragon gardens, she made her descent.

Doragon nudged Azrael to turn around, but he sighed as he knew it was her who followed. "Why aren't you enjoying the party?" She glared at him and flickered her tail, waiting for a better explanation, though she knew what would happen. He sighed when she wouldn't back down. "I didn't want to make a big fuss about leaving."

Despite her growing anticipation and preparation, the news still struck a blow; she morphed back to her usual guise and crossed her arms, staring at the two in disbelief. "Oblivion awaits, I suppose."

Azrael gestured between himself and Doragon. "We have to. The demons have already returned, and now it's time for us." He looked to the World Tree and smirked. "It had been many years since we held Oblivion's throne, and we're looking forward to that moment."

"Don't you wish to say goodbye to everyone?"

Azrael shook his head, but he turned away. "I hate goodbyes, and I've already done enough damage to this realm. Besides, I won't be gone forever." Before he could brace himself, Selena hugged him; he was not one to accept affection, but to her surprise, he squeezed her back and laughed. "I can't believe I used to hate you, but now —"

"But now, we're friends."

The two pulled away, and Azrael's grin brightened the evening. "Friends."

Doragon looked up as two shadows coasted across the ground; Thor and Ebony landed on their haunches near the three, wings still unfurled, the moonlight twinkling upon their exquisite jewelry. Thor's tail swept across the ground in agitation for being left behind, brushing dust clouds with every pass. **Do we not deserve the same courtesy of saying goodbye?**

Chittering, Ebony nodded; she gave Doragon a series of chirps and clicks, and he responded likewise. Thor took his turn by giving the two a bow in respect.

Azrael clapped his hands when they finished their final exchange, and Doragon flapped his wings, hovering aloft. "Now, if you'll excuse us, we have a realm to reclaim."

"Will you return soon?"

"I'm Death. You may see me again soon, or you may not. You know I can't tell you that."

Selena scoffed but smiled. "The Divines have a sense of humor. Take care of yourselves."

Thor and Ebony roared in unison as Azrael stepped back, and Doragon swooped overhead, scooping him with his claws; the trio watched as the Divines soared, flying directly into a black hole swirling against the night sky. Dark hands radiating with purple and red magic thrashed forth from the gateway and reached for the pair, but Azrael waved at Silver's slithering dragon form approaching the gardens. The shadows pulled Azrael and Doragon through the portal, returning to Oblivion's realm.

Selena sucked in her cheeks before meeting Thor's disappointed gaze. *I'm sorry, my dear, but I thought you two would follow me.*

Of course, we would, but you still should have mentioned it.

Thor snaked his head around to see Silver strutting towards them with his hands deep in his formal jacket pockets. Ebony flapped her wings in preparation for take-off, but she bowed first before launching herself for the stars at incredible speed. Silver gave his sister a jerky nod as he approached and reached out to rub Thor's muzzle, and Thor pulled him close. "I wish you two many happy years together. Take care of her—"

And never let her go, Selena heard the two of them say simultaneously, finishing each other's sentences. Before joining his mate, Thor drew her into a hug as well.

We'll always be together.

Now and forever.

She kissed his nose, and Thor made one massive leap with one wing beat, his ethereal wings melting into the starry night's velvet curtain, and the two dragons swirled together overhead in an eternal dance.

Silver turned around to look at the great World Tree, a standing testament to their new beginning. "There's no telling what the future holds—there are endless possibilities."

"The best part is, we'll figure that out together." As the two spun around and faced each other, he drew her into a tight embrace before kissing her, and Selena deepened it.

Thor and Ebony hovered above them with the blue ore moon glistening upon the world; the dragons stared at each other lovingly before flying away into the night.

SOAR THROUGH
THE ARMAGEDDON TRILOGY
By C.D. MULLER

Don't miss out on these exciting adventures!

ABOUT THE AUTHOR

C.D. Muller (also under the pen name Crystal Summers for romance) was born on December 9th, 1990. From her love of *Harry Potter*, she wrote the first installment in the Armageddon Trilogy when she was fourteen.

She graduated from Patagonia Union High School in 2009 and attended college to study Computer Science and programming. She participated in community events, such as writing plays for the Tin Shed Theatre and preparing presentations for elementary classes.

Her husband's death heavily affected Muller's writing and art. She almost gave up on both but ended up using her talents to help her cope with depression and anxiety.

She currently lives in Tucson, AZ, with her new husband, newborn son, and three cats. For more information, go to https://crystaldsummers.com for updates and her social media.